Home from Away

Eric Van Meter

Published by Eric Van Meter, 2024.

This is a work of fiction. Similarities to real people, places, or events are entirely coincidental.

HOME FROM AWAY

First edition. September 30, 2024.

Copyright © 2024 Eric Van Meter.

ISBN: 979-8227915658

Written by Eric Van Meter.

Figure 1: Author's note

---

1. http://www.mondayspenny.com/junius-intro

CHAPTER 1

Junius Whitman could not see the mercy seat, but he knew well enough not to trust it. His vision was blurry, as it always was in those days, and twenty-odd grownups blocked his view. But he had heard the distinct sound of splintering wood when Mr. Stuckey plopped onto the stool moments before—heard it over the cacophony of ecstatic prayer and the shouts of amen and the musical offering of Hilda Rhea Pillwitch, who banged out "I Surrender All" on the piano as though her song were the only thing holding back the very demons of hell. While the adults at Claremore Assembly Church praised Jesus in holy revelry, Little Whit knew the score. The whole spectacle rested on busted legs.

Sure enough, a few seconds later the biomass of prayer lilted to the right, and the stool gave way. The impact of Mr. Stuckey on the chancel sent shockwaves through the new CDX subfloor the men's group had installed after a leak around the baptismal font last summer. The lectern wobbled dangerously, teetering out over the edge of the first step before falling back into place as though righted by very hand of Jesus. Shouts of "Praise the Lord!" and "Hallelujah!" mingled with orders like "Look here!" and "Watch out!" Some of the elders knelt beside Mr. Stuckey and continued to pray. Two of them picked up the mercy seat and tried to shove the fractured leg back in place. Whit squinted to gauge their success, but a heavy hand landed on his shoulder like the judgment of God.

"It's time, boy," Bro. Reinbeck intoned.

He hooked one of his fleshy hands beneath the child's left armpit. Before Whit could protest, his father did the same with his right. The two men hoisted him up out of the pew and half led, half dragged him up front, through the opening between the altar rails, up onto the chancel and toward the mercy seat.

"It won't hold me!" he cried.

But Brother Reinbeck was taken by the Spirit, and Cole Allen Whitman was on a mission. His eldest child had always been afraid of storms, but this spring those kid fears had swollen into full-blown panic attacks, which threatened to land Whit in therapy and thus embarrass the family name, such as it was. His kindergarten teacher had recommended as much when Cole Allen picked the boy up from school, saying that advances in child psychology could do wonders for a smart but emotionally mixed-up kid like Junius. That same afternoon, he'd gone straight to Bro. Reinbeck to ask what to do.

"Therapy?" Reinbeck said, working his front teeth up and down as though trying to dislodge a raspberry seed between incisors.

Cole Allen spit on the ground. "I know it."

"That's just the way of the world," the older man answered. "They think they can fix everything by asking you how you feel about it. My Lord."

"You think it's—" he glanced warily at Whit—"some sort of demon, causing him to fear?"

"I don't know that we can pin down a cause," Bro. Reinbeck said. "But I do believe that, whatever the problem, prayer is the solution. And you couldn't have better timing."

Whit fought the urge to roll his eyes. He'd known from the start what his father was up to, going to see the pastor just a few hours before CAC's healing service. He'd wanted to get Whit on the unofficial docket, to make sure he wouldn't get passed over in favor of cancer patients or alcoholics or old Mrs. Warner, who always needed prayed over for this malady or that. They'd arrived at church early so that they could get a seat in the third pew, close enough to be a visual reminder to Bro. Reinbeck to give this troubled child a turn in the mercy seat, where sinners and sufferers were brought nearer to the throne of God by the elders.

And now his time had come. Six feet from the stool, Whit could finally make a diagnosis of the mercy seat's injuries. The leg had not been shattered by Mr. Stuckey's weight, as he'd assumed. Rather, it was cracked lengthwise on one side, right through the hole where the cross support had been. Mr. Stuckey must have somehow gotten a foot onto that poor support piece, judging by the splintered shards that now lay beneath the stool. As long as he could keep his weight pressing down vertically, Whit thought, it might hold. But if any little force pushed him to one side or the other, the stool would collapse. He made a contingency plan to throw his weight to the left if that happened, so as not to land on Mr. Stuckey or the praying elders. When the men spun him around, he could barely make out two parallel tracks in the new carpet, left by the toes of his shoes as his father and the pastor hauled him forward.

He tried one last plea. "I can stand! Just let me stand!"

His cries were to no avail. The men dropped him onto the stool, and for a moment he feared disaster. It held his weight, though, long enough for a few of the elders to crowd in and place their hands on his head and shoulders and back. He could more or less make out who was in front of him, picking them out based on their most obvious characteristics—Mrs. Gleason with her thick glasses, Mr. Koontz and his enormous wristwatch. He could smell old lady perfume and so knew that Mrs. Spietz was somewhere in his neighborhood, and he could hear Brother Reinbeck behind him, binding Satan and casting out Whit's childish fears and asking the Lord to sweep out the house of his little mind so that it might be a dwelling fit for the Holy Spirit, amen and amen.

Whit didn't move, though. He'd heard some of his Baptist playmates say blessings over their lunches, and so he knew that for some people *amen* signaled a conclusion to prayer. Not so with his church. *Amen* might be the end, surely, but it was more often an all-purpose word—an amplifier, a placeholder, an onramp to the next line of supplication, a question awaiting a response from the brothers and sisters engaged together as warriors in the unseen battle for eternal souls.

Reinbeck went on, praying not only for Whit but for Cole Allen and Bethany Whitman, and for sweet little Libby, not yet six months old. Some of the words had extra syllables spliced into them, and the space between sentences usually contained snippets of prayer language—*Humbahlah! Kahkahkah!*—that were unintelligible to all but God and so gave Reinbeck's prayers a special, holy feel.

"Amen, Lord! Amen!" he cried, and Whit could tell this was another gateway *amen*, the one that would lead into a prayer made entirely out of those nonsense syllables.

It was at this point—and not for the first time—that Whit felt convicted of his unbelief. Earlier in the service, ninety minutes back at least, Bro. Reinbeck had read aloud a story out of the Gospel of Mark to remind them of the connection between faith and healing. A desperate father begged the Lord to heal his son despite his own shortcomings. "I do believe, Lord! Help my unbelief!" the father had cried, a petition which might as well have been the caption for little Whit's first six years. If there was some belief mechanism necessary for curing his faulty vision or receiving mysterious checks for just the right amount, Whit didn't have it. He knew Brother Reinbeck's prayers wouldn't rid him of his panic attacks because he didn't—couldn't—believe that they would. First, he would have to get real faith into his heart, and that would take a confession he wasn't ready to make, not that anyone was listening at the moment.

"Jesus Lord Christ!" Mrs. Koontz squealed from where she knelt beside fat Mr. Stuckey.

The others continued carrying on with their singing and shouting and praying and tongues, accustomed as they were to outbursts of the Lord's name in CAC's healing services. Something in Mrs. Koontz's voice sounded wrong to Whit, though. He tried to turn his head, but Reinbeck's hands were placed firmly on each side of his skull as though ready to squish that demon out like the center of a pimple.

"God Almighty!" Mrs. Koontz shrieked. And then, "John Robert!"

The sound of Brother Reinbeck's given name pulled the emergency brake on the congregation's ecstasy. Hilda Rhea Pillwitch, who had modulated into "Just as I Am" several minutes earlier, stopped cold in the middle of a chorus. Without the piano, the whole scene devolved into a silence more jarring than anything Whit would experience until his first love affair, still more than a decade off but already set in motion.

Brother Reinbeck released Whit's head too quickly for the boy to adjust his weight distribution. A half second later, he crumpled to the floor along with the ruined stool. But that was of no consequence to any of the adults. Every eye in the sanctuary was trained on Mrs. Koontz, who was now standing with her back pressed firmly into the corner of the choir loft. She pointed toward Mr. Stuckey with a trembling finger.

"The Lord called him home," she said. "He's gone."

Rogers County Coroner Don Ray Spietz confirmed Mrs. Koontz' diagnosis, adding that the poor man appeared to have been dead for half an hour before anyone in the congregation realized it. Don Ray enlisted four men to roll the body into the thick black bag for transport and two more after that to lift it onto the long-suffering gurney that would bear Mr. Stuckey along the Glory Land Way. The men rolled him down the center aisle to a chorus of sighs and sobs, tears flowing from the eyes of every church member as thunder from a late evening storm rumbled in the distance. Whit shifted his weight from one foot to the other.

"We should pray," Bro. Reinbeck said once the doors to the hearse had closed. "Gather up, y'all."

The forty-odd souls that comprised the faithful remnant dutifully circled up around the altar. Whit joined them, hoping no one picked up on his reluctance. It was one thing for prayer to fail a doubting soul like his. But for faithful Mr. Stuckey to drop dead on the altar, right there in the middle of all the hand-laying and Satan-binding? If such was the Lord's plan, Whit couldn't see how it was supposed to help his unbelief.

Pink lightning flashed through the windows. A few seconds later, peals of thunder shook the walls. Whit's stomach churned.

Thankfully, Bro. Reinbeck tapped Alton Jennings for the closing prayer, and the old man sensed that the moment called for an economy of words. Two minutes later, Whit was climbing into his father's pickup. He buckled his seatbelt—a habit he'd picked up from a television ad campaign—and waited while his father stood by the tailgate listening to Brother Reinbeck. Cole Allen nodded. Kept nodding while the preacher laid a beatific hand on his shoulder. Lightning flashed through the windshield. Whit counted—*one one thousand, two one thousand, three one thousand.* At *four*, a loud crack of thunder caused the men to jump. Whit felt sweat on the back of his neck. The bolt originated less than a mile away, if the counting method he'd learned from his teacher was correct. He rapped his knuckles against the rear windshield of the pickup. Cole Allen grinned and shuffled toward the driver's side door. As he pulled back on the handle, he told Brother Reinbeck that he got off work at 4:00 tomorrow and to bring him—he didn't clarify to whom he was referring—by the house about 4:30. Cole Allen started the engine but left the transmission in park. He drummed his fingers on the wheel. His eyes danced with adrenaline.

"Did you feel it?" he asked.

"When Mr. Stuckey hit the floor?"

"No, son! The Spirit."

"Yeah," he said. "I felt it. Can we go?"

"Don't lie to me, now. Did you receive a healing? Or a blessing?"
"I don't know. Maybe."
"Don't lie to me, son."
"I'm not lying. I just want to go home."
"Do you feel any different?"
"No."

For at least the millionth time in his young life, Whit wished to be free of the particular chain with which he was most tightly bound. Although he as yet lacked the words to express it, Little Whit knew in his heart that he was a slave to the truth. No matter what narratives his teachers or parents or anyone else offered—no matter the friction he caused by his quiet yet resolute dissent to those narratives—he could not help but think and speak of the world as it truly was, at least in his understanding of it. Such a trait created all manner of difficulty for Whit, both within his still developing psyche and out among the adults in his life—parents and teachers and church people, mostly. If Whit had a choice in the matter, he would have no doubt determined that bald-faced honesty was not worth the price he paid. But he was wired for no other disposition. And so he soldiered on. Held his tongue while his father considered the situation.

"Maybe you just don't feel it yet," his father said. "Could be that your kind of healing takes a while to go into full effect."

Meanwhile the storm drew nearer. They drove northward out of town toward the farm they rented from Mr. Jennings, trailed by billowing clouds illuminated by flashes of lightning.

Big drops of rain assaulted the windshield. Whit squeezed his eyes shut. Hail would be next, and then the roar of nature's perfect killer. He could already imagine what people would say to his poor mother when the twister wrapped Cole Allen's pickup around the tree. It was the Lord's will. Little Whit has joined the angel choir. At least you and the baby were safe.

His father, on the other hand, might as well have been driving on rays of heavenly sunlight. He cracked his window and lit a cigarette and even hummed to himself. He was happy, Whit realized, which only heaped frustration on top of the boy's misery. If he had any sense of his only son's distress—even more so, of the tragedy of Mr. Stuckey's sudden demise—Cole Allen didn't show it. He eased the pickup into its place in the driveway as though the world was all honeysuckle and butterflies.

Nickel-sized pellets of hail stung Whit's skin as he ran from the pickup to the porch. He bounded up the steps, past his mother and into the laundry room. Reached down for the metal ring on the trap door and pulled it open, revealing a short wooden ladder that led to the crawl space. He settled into the hideout he'd constructed out of old pallets and layers of blankets, arranged with the help of his mother and only just tolerated by his father. As he eased the door closed, he could hear Cole Allen bragging that soon, thanks to his prayerful intervention, their son would be able to face the weather like a man.

Here in his hideout, though, little Whit had no interest in facing up to anything. He let the safety of his very own space envelop him, the smell of cinder blocks and crackle of Visqueen as much a comfort as the psalmist's rod and staff. The block walls around him and sub flooring above muffled the sounds of the thunder and hail and left him to ponder his old plastic toolbox and the assortment of fragile things he'd placed therein. A half-chewed baby blue pencil with "Houston Oilers" printed in pink. A plastic ruler with tiny portraits of all the U. S. presidents, Washington through Clinton. A yellow sperm whale eraser that was smooth to the touch. These were of no account to the world, and so it fell to Whit to protect them. He settled them into the box with his flashlight and snacks, and he promised them they'd be safe here with him, below the tumult, where flying debris couldn't pierce them and downed trees couldn't crush them.

On the main level of the house, the world was not so serene. He could hear his parents moving across the floor, pacing from one room to the next the way they did in the early phase of an argument. He traced their footsteps with his flashlight until they settled into their bedroom. He slid over to the edge of the pallets and lifted his ear up to the hole in the floor through which the TV cable ran.

"I never seen anything like it," Cole Allen was saying.

"You see something like it every time you go to church," Bethany Whitman replied. The floor beneath her creaked gently as she bounced the baby. "Anytime Johnny Reinbeck gets to praying it's a goddamn circus."

"A man *died* tonight."

"I know. And I'm sorry, truly I am. I didn't have nothing against Mr. Stuckey. But you kept our boy, who has enough problems of his own—"

"Which he was healed of tonight."

"—and you kept him there with a dead man just so you can feel important."

"It's not like that. The Spirit—"

"And Whit's in the fucking crawlspace. He ain't healed."

A pause, and then his father's voice. "Give me the baby."

"Why?"

"Because I don't want her first words to be some sort of cussing she learned from you."

"Jesus Christ."

"That'd be better—just not the way you say it. Now hand me the baby."

"No."

Whit held his breath. The storm should have passed over by now, which should have sent his mother stomping across the floor and yelling for him to come get ready for bed. The fact that she did not told him the tension between his parents might snap into open warfare at any moment. He adjusted his position and listened, growing surer by the second that he knew exactly what lay at the center of the conflict. His father's next words confirmed his fears.

"It's our Christian duty to care for the prisoner," Cole Allen said.

"They can find another Christian then."

"I've got a gift for this sort of thing. It's an offense to the Lord if I don't do it."

"Johnny's just flattering you. You ain't nothing."

"I'm more than you ever been."

Whit squeezed his eyes shut. Tried to pray away the argument. At least twice in his memory, someone from Brother Reinbeck's prison ministry had come to live with the Whitmans after finishing up his sentence with nowhere to go. The first one Cole Allen brought home, a balding man about fifty years old who went by "Scooter," was nice enough. He stayed three months before hopping a Greyhound to California to live with the only one of his wife's four children that he claimed as his own. Whit couldn't remember the name of the second man, only that he'd gotten drunk and pinched his mother on the behind, and that she'd clocked him with a frozen dinner so hard that his glass eye fell out onto the table.

"We'll move the crib into our room," Cole Allen said. "It'll just be for a little while."

"We ain't got money for a little while, even."

"Don't matter. The Bible says what it says, and it says to care for the prisoners. That's from Jesus."

"Jesus never paid a damned penny for rent."

"Maybe it was Paul that said it."

"God, I'm tired," Bethany moaned. "We can't keep doing this, not with another baby around. You call Johnny back and tell him no."

"I can't do that."

"I'm so tired, Cole Allen."

"That ain't my fault."

And that lit the fuse. Even down in the crawlspace, Whit could hear his mother's breaths getting shallow, her heels tapping on the floor as she fidgeted. If she held onto Libby, things might die down before the worst could happen. But Whit could already hear her footsteps, stomping across the hall and into the kids' room, where she would stow the baby in the crib while the parents fought.

He lay down on his side and curled his body around his collection of fragile things. Hoped joy would come in the morning.

CHAPTER 2

Joy did not come, not in Claremore. And so they left.
The morning after the healing service dawned clear and cool, with bright sunshine and blue skies spread over the carnage left by the storm. The farm the Whitmans rented escaped with a few downed limbs and some hail damage, but an E-3 tornado leveled the little town of Pryor to the east of them—a disaster which almost certainly mobilized every screw gun and chainsaw at Claremore Assembly. When Whit ventured out of the crawlspace and into the kitchen, however, he found his father still at home, seated at the table and dabbing a wet cloth against bloody scratch marks across his face with his swollen left hand. Whit took his place in the chair next to him, unsure whether to seek comfort or offer it. They sat in silence until Cole Allen asked his son if he knew what a crazy bitch his mother was.

"No, sir," Whit said, and braced for a slap. When none came, he opened his eyes and studied his father's distant gaze.

"She's gone," Cole Allen said. "Packed her things last night and took off."

"To where?"

"Can't say for sure. Probably back to her people in Kentucky."

Whit's heart raced, but he knew better than to cry in his father's presence, even now. He waited until he was sure his voice would be steady. "When will she be back?"

"I don't know. She may not." He pulled away the cloth. Turned it to press a clean patch against his bloody knuckles. "I don't aim to wait around for her though."

So it was that Whit found out they were moving away from the only home he'd ever had. Before he could even feel the sting, however, Libby's sweet little cry sounded from their bedroom.

"She's hungry," he said.

"Then I guess you better feed her," Cole Allen answered. "Change that diaper while you're at it. I got to call a man about a job."

They rolled out of town a week later with all their earthly possessions crammed into a fourteen-foot U-Haul truck. The job in question turned out to be in the mechanic shop of the Gray Butte Mining Company in Gillette, Wyoming—a thousand miles to the northeast of Claremore. Little Whit couldn't take in such distance, nor could he imagine what awaited him at the end of the move. All he could do was stare out the window as the miles ticked by, wondering if the pieces of his life fit together anymore.

Two hours west of Salina, Kansas, the final blow in that season of loss landed on little Whit. Between packing and mourning his mother's departure and learning to care for his little sister—changing a diaper was much easier than feeding or burping or entertaining, as it turned out—he had barely even thought about the move until the day they left. But a billboard styled like a Colorado license plate reminded him of a magnet he had in the shape of Ohio in his toolbox of castaway things. The realization that he'd left them all in the crawlspace back in their Claremore house struck him with the force of a lightning blast, right in the middle of I-70.

"Daddy!" he cried. "Daddy, we have to go back."

"We ain't going back."

"It's not too late," Whit pleaded. "I forgot something."

"If it's forgot, it's lost. Now quit your bellyaching."

Whit turned to the window. Tender shoots of green sprouted in the fields to the north, little signs of hope and renewal. "Maybe someone would mail my stuff to our new house."

"Who you gonna get to do that?"

"I don't know. Mrs. Spietz?"

"Mrs. Spietz," his father mumbled. Ever since the night of the big storm, he'd become a great mumbler on all manner of subjects. Anytime he started that, the conversation was over.

Whit looked down into the car seat that sat on the bench between him and his father. He tried not to cry, and when that didn't work tried to hide the fact that he was crying by thrusting his head further down toward his sister. But he could feel his nose starting to run, and thus faced the impossible choice of sniffing audibly or letting a glob of snot roll out of his nose and onto Libby's smooth forehead. The thought of a squalling baby in this tiny truck cab was enough to make his decision, though. He opened his mouth. Tried to sniff quietly.

"Are you crying?" Cole Allen said.

"That was Libby."

"No it wasn't. You're crying, aren't you. You think when you start school up north, those other kids are going to cry like sissies? Over a bunch of trash?"

"It wasn't trash to me."

"Well it was trash, too. Hell, just because you think a thing one way doesn't make that thing so. Your mother—." He caught himself. Chewed on his bottom lip for a moment. "Anyway, I threw that stuff out. You don't need it."

Whit clenched his fists, wishing he could scream without waking the baby. Big raindrops pinged on the metal roof above them. The sky was growing dark. The air smelled of rain. His tears turned to sobs.

"Dry it up," Cole Allen ordered. "You can't undo none of it."

For all the lessons from his father that would not stick, that particular nugget—you can't undo none of it—took root in little Whit. Long before he took a physics class that taught him that time moved like an arrow, he meditated on the unchangeability of the past. He looked back on the short span of his life and could already see the events of his history piled like cow shit in a pasture, endless patties fossilizing where they dropped. They couldn't be scraped away. You just had to wait until time and earth absorbed them.

He ruminated over the truth in the manure metaphor as he waited the principal's office at G. A. Custer Elementary School on his fifth day of first grade. It was his third trip already, which was fine by him. Dr. VerHagen's office smelled pleasantly of old wood, and he preferred the quiet of adult workspaces to the chaos of his first-grade classroom. Still, he'd picked up the vibe that such visits were not the norm among students and were, in fact, a sign of something wrong—so wrong, in fact, that Dr. VerHagen's secretary had called his father to attend this particular session. And so, despite the pleasant surroundings, Whit waited restlessly while the grown-ups sorted things out.

Thankfully, his teacher had also been summoned to the office for this visit. When Cole Allen marched in ready to tan little Whit's hide, Miss Corelli had intercepted him at the edge of the secretary's desk. She was younger than his father—Whit couldn't tell by how much—and not quite as pretty as his mother. Still, she was short and thin, with an expressive face and tender eyes. She reminded him of the Mary statue in their old church's nativity set, except that Mary had been a blonde, while Miss Corelli's dark brown hair flowed down over her shoulders. She wore a simple cross pendant, which prompted Cole Allen to comment that he'd recently rededicated his life and started taking the kids to church again. Miss Corelli touched his arm and told him how important she thought faith was to a child's sense of well-being. Cole Allen let her talk, not once interrupting to correct her on spiritual matters. It unnerved Whit to see his father so completely subdued by another person. By the time they reached VerHagen's office, she had not only tamed the lion. She'd gotten him to purr.

"Dr. VerHagen got called away," she told Cole Allen. "He'll join us in a second. Whit, why don't you wait in the chair by Mrs. Welkie's desk until he gets back."

The boy wandered out into the secretary's office, even though it was the one grown-up space he'd just as soon avoid. Mrs. Welkie was the opposite of Miss Corelli in every way, wrinkled and irritable and smelling of camphor, with a flat face and lined neck that made her head look for all the world like a turtle emerging from her gray sweater. She glared over the top of her glasses at Whit.

"Did Miss Corelli tell you to sit?"

"Yes."

"Then you better sit."

He sat. Tried to listen in on his father and Miss Corelli without looking like he was eavesdropping. He picked up one of the children's books tucked into a sleeve that hung from Mrs. Welkie's chair and opened it, adjusting it back and forth until it came into focus. From behind the principal's door, he could pick out a few of the words Miss Corelli was using—anxiety, therapy, medication—but had a hard time making sense of his father's responses. He would have sworn the subject had changed once again to church when Dr. VerHagen returned from whatever errand had kept him away.

"They in there?" he asked Mrs. Welkie on his way past.

"Yeah but hang on," the old woman said. She motioned for him to bend down so she could speak softly. Whit trained his ears back on his father and Miss Corelli. Before he could get any traction, though, VerHagen pulled the book from Whit's hand and replaced it with a glossy magazine.

"Can you read anything on this page, son?" he asked.

Whit held the magazine out, then pulled it closer, then out again until the print finally came into view. He didn't know all the words, but he could make out enough to know that it was an issue of Newsweek with a cover story about Saddam Hussein and the escalating conflict with Iraq. He told the principal as much, but had to shift the page again to see the smaller print. He was trying to decipher the subtitle when Dr. VerHagen plucked it from his hand and proclaimed, "That'll do."

He squatted down next to Whit and stared at him. "Your daddy teach you how to read?" he asked. The boy shook his head. "Your mom, then?"

"Some," Whit answered. "And my kindergarten teacher. And I had to figure some out on my own too."

"Is that so." VerHagen shifted positions, as though to get a better look. "Miss Corelli tells me you get scared pretty easily."

"Not really. Just storms."

"Storms?"

"Yes, sir."

"And what about storms is so scary?"

Whit explained to him what he knew about tornados, which he felt was a considerable amount for a boy his age. He explained all the things he'd read about or seen on television—air temperature and humidity, wall clouds and the deafening roar of an approaching twister. The Fujita scale for measuring the damage caused by winds of certain velocities. Dr. VerHagen eyed him doubtfully.

"Not many tornadoes popping up here in Wyoming, son."

"I can hear them, though. Sometimes even when there aren't any clouds. It's like *whoosh!*" Whit tried to imitate the sound without coming off as merely cute. He wanted VerHagen to understand that he wasn't crazy, nor was he making anything up. The principal conferred with Mrs. Welkie, turned back to Whit and mulled things over for a long moment.

"You say you came from down south. Think you could show me on a map?" Whit nodded, and VerHagen pulled a travel atlas from a shelf behind Mrs. Welkie's desk. He opened it up to Oklahoma.

The print was too small for Whit to make out the town names, but he saw an orange blob that he figured to be Tulsa. He put his finger there, then slid it an inch or so to the right, to the general area where he knew Claremore was situated. "Well then," VerHagen said. "That's not too far from Ft. Chaffee."

"About eighty miles," Whit said proudly. Several of the men in their church had been in the National Guard, which put them on the prayer list and made them a subject of honor on every patriotic holiday.

"They fly planes out of Ft. Chaffee? Jet fighters, I mean."

"Yes."

"And you know that we're close to Ellsworth Air Force Base here, right? Over in Rapid City?"

Whit nodded as though everyone knew that, although it was new information to him. He wished Miss Corelli would open that door and save him from this interrogation. He wasn't sure where VerHagen was going, but he could tell the wheels were turning in a way that would upset Whit's life in some manner. He offered a feeble, "I could be wrong about the jets."

But Dr. VerHagen had moved beyond listening. He took Whit by the elbow and gently led him into his office, where Miss Corelli and his father were standing closer than strictly necessary. She stepped back and smoothed her skirt, and even though her facial features weren't clear to him from this distance, he could see she was flustered. Cole Allen shifted a few inches away and stood at parade rest, hands folded in front, the way he had when they'd wheeled Mr. Stuckey out of the sanctuary in Claremore. VerHagen dropped into his worn leather desk chair and rubbed his chin.

"Mr. Whitman," he said slowly. "Have you ever had Junius' eyes examined?"

"His mom did, I think. Back in Oklahoma."

"I'm doubtful that she did."

"Well, I'm sure of it."

VerHagen raised a weary hand. "I'm not accusing you of anything, Mr. Whitman. But I think you should have them checked—again, that is. Junius shows some remarkable aptitude, but when I asked him to read something he'd never seen before, it was like he was playing trombone with it." He moved his arm back and forth to show how Little Whit had adjusted the magazine. The boy slipped further down in his chair.

"If he reads okay, then I'd say there's not a problem," Cole Allen said.

"There will be if he doesn't get those eyes fixed," VerHagen said with authority. "And this whole tornado phobia he's developed—I'm not ready to call in the psychologists yet."

He explained to Cole Allen his theory that Whit couldn't see the military jets flying over on training exercises, and so was attributing the roaring noise he heard according to what categories were available to him—lightning and thunder, the roar of wind. The constant fears of imagined tornados set him on edge, so much so that a real thunderstorm sent him spiraling out of control.

"You don't think there's anything wrong with him then?" Cole Allen said, his voice laced with triumph.

"I don't think we can make assumptions until you get his vision corrected."

Cole Allen thanked them and motioned to Whit that it was time to go. He shook hands with Dr. VerHagen and with Miss Corelli, holding onto hers a half second longer than Whit would have liked. He had never witnessed affection like that between his father and mother. Even when they were passing Libby back and forth, Bethany and Cole Allen tended to approach one another as though circling a bobcat. Maybe if they'd been nicer to each other, Whit thought, his mother might not have moved back to Kentucky. His father might not have dragged them away to Wyoming, and he would even now be in the crawlspace with the treasures that he still mourned the loss of.

He meant to say as much to his father once they climbed into the pickup—meant to lob these new insights into Cole Allen's lap and see how they landed. But his father was in no mood to listen. Instead he mumbled through his usual targets—his faithless ex-wife, the burden of two young children, the godless schools, the liberals, the government. This time he added know-it-all principals and optometrists to the list of the accursed. When he came to Miss Corelli, though, he stopped.

"You like your teacher?" he asked.

"Not as much as I like Mom."

The words had barely left his mouth before Cole Allen reached across and popped him in the lips—not hard, but enough to sting. "Your mom's the one taught you to backtalk. No more of that. Answer my question."

"I like her all right."

"You think she's pretty."

"Not as pretty as—." Out of the corner of his eye, Whit saw his father's hand twitch. The next blow would land a little harder. "Sure. She's pretty."

"You like her?"

"I guess."

"You guess?"

"I like her."

"Good." He gripped the steering wheel. Finally, he said, "We ain't going back to Oklahoma. Your mom ain't coming up to Wyoming. Understood?"

"Yeah."

"Try that again."

"Yes, sir."

Cole Allen nodded and grinned. He even reached across and tousled little Whit's hair.

Within the week, the boy had new pair of glasses, the lenses thick enough to burn sage grass with a sunbeam. And Miss Corelli began accompanying them to Wednesday evening services at Light of Azusa Holy Spirit Tabernacle.

Figure 2: Craft Talk—Supporting Characters

CHAPTER 3

By the time he began his fifth-grade year, Whit had mostly outgrown the "little" moniker. He'd hit his growth spurt early, shooting past the five-foot mark while some of his classmates still needed a stool to reach the water fountain. His cornsilk hair had darkened, and he had the perpetual tan of a boy who spent the summer riding his bike and weeding their small garden and learning to play guitar outside, since his father couldn't stand the racket in the house.

But he'd matured in more than mere physical appearance. Whit had come to understand things about the world that he never suspected as a first grader. For instance, he had more or less figured out the lay of the land at Custer Elementary, where any extreme—being tallest, or smartest, or wearing the thickest glasses—was in invitation to ridicule. He couldn't change his height or his eyesight, but he learned not to volunteer the right answer in class or correct other kids' grammar, and he found ways to mitigate his other failings. His height made him an early choice in pick-up basketball games. And even though he wasn't very good—his heavy glasses bounced around too much on his face for him to ever get a sustained look at the rim—he snagged the occasional rebound and high-fived his teammates and pretended to care. Towns like Gillette respected two kinds of people—miners and athletes—and Whit already knew he wasn't cut out for mining.

In September of that year, another realization struck Whit like a thunderbolt to the skull. VerHagen had assigned him to the classroom of old Mrs. Schulte, the elder sister of his crabby secretary. She was shorter than Mrs. Welkie but of significantly greater circumference and much more devout. An uncomfortably detailed crucifix hung on the wall behind her desk, along with photos of two sour-faced grandchildren and Pope John Paul II. When the class misbehaved or did poorly on an assignment, she could be seen gazing at the little shrine, lips moving in private lament, before inflicting the next subject upon her pupils.

Whether tipped off by her sister or informed by her own observations, she could tell from the start that Whit was holding back academically, and she didn't like it. In fact, she didn't really like him—not the way Miss Corelli had, before she'd broken up with his father, or that Miss Jamison had in third grade, again before her brief relationship with Cole Allen flamed out. Schulte didn't put an understanding hand on his shoulder when she passed by, didn't write gentle notes when he intentionally gave the wrong answers on tests. If anything, she was even less kind to Whit than to the other students, and less still to his father. She'd waited in the circle drive in front of the school on the first day of class, just so she could point a fat finger in Cole Allen's face.

"I don't want to see your boots hit the ground on school property," she told him. "You want to meet women, go to a honky tonk."

It took Whit a few days of pondering before he could put all of this together. His eureka moment finally came during a droning lecture over long division. He'd been gazing out the window at a blanket of stratocumulus clouds, which always promised rain but never brought it, wishing he was in Miss Reyes' fifth-grade class next door, when he understood that Dr. VerHagen had sent Mrs. Schulte to do his dirty work, and while his tactics might have been cowardly, his motives were justified. Three times in five years, Whit's father and teacher had paired off romantically, only to have the relationship blow up in the spring. Such volatility wasn't exactly new for Whit, but it occurred to him as he watched the placid drift of the clouds that he was living a life outside the norm. He was perhaps the only kid at Custer Elementary who routinely woke to find his teacher sneaking out the back door of his house to her car just before dawn.

There was no danger of such a scandal with Mrs. Schulte. She was older than Grandma Helene—Cole Allen's mother—and still married, even though her husband had been stashed away in St. Elizabeth of Hungary Senior Care Center since the Berlin Wall fell. Worst of all, she was unapologetically Catholic, which in Cole Allen's book was about as far from Christian as any American could get. VerHagen surely knew that the Whitman patriarch would not be making advances at such a woman, and he was damned sure that she would never return affections in the unlikely event that Cole Allen offered any. Such was her disdain for that womanizing Protestant outsider that she insisted on calling Whit by his given first name—Junius—no matter how much he hated it. To pronounce even half of the Whitman family name was something Mrs. Schulte could not abide. And so Whit would be mired in the old woman's class for nine long months, being called the wrong thing while the adults in his life took turns hating each other.

This was the realization that nearly caused Whit to fall from his chair as the clouds rolled on and old Mrs. Schulte tried to explain remainders. He was not now—and he might never be—taken as his own person. He was the son of a divorced mechanic whose holy roller beliefs didn't necessarily translate into righteous observation. The father's faults were the son's faults, in the eyes of others. He was an outsider, the kid who still spoke with a trace of Oklahoma despite years living in Gillette. He was the smart kid, the half-blind kid, the tall kid, the Whitman kid, defined by lineage and circumstance before people got to anything else. And while that didn't seem fair, it was nonetheless the clearest truth the had learned of the world thus far.

Cut off from dating his son's teachers, Cole Allen focused his energies back on church. At a tent revival over Labor Day weekend, he'd testified—much to Whit's embarrassment—that he'd wandered away from the Lord and into the wilderness, pinned there by alcohol and desires of the flesh. But no more. Cole Allen Whitman was not a slave to the darkness, but a child of the gospel and captive of the Spirit. The good people at Light of Azusa had shown nothing but love to him and his beautiful little children, and it was high time he paid the Lord back for the bounty that had been heaped on his undeserving soul. He promised to preach the Word and pray for the sick, which was all well and good. But he also vowed to welcome the outcast and the prisoner, which he'd neglected since those years in Oklahoma.

Whit thought he knew what that meant, and something inside him bowed up against it. In his head, the protests rang out in his mother's voice.

Sure enough, on the same weekend that the Gillette football team suffered a 63-2 defeat at the hands of Thunder Basin, Cole Allen drove to Rawlins to pick up an ex-con named Zane Braun, whom Brother Dahl at Light of Azusa had trained as an evangelist during his monthly revival meetings at the state pen. Whit's father didn't say much to him about their new boarder, except that he needed to double the amount he'd been making for meals, since Mr. Zane had been subsisting on prison food all these many years. For nine days, Braun ate them out of house and home, even as he piled up laundry presumably acquired through the church clothing pantry. Whit barely managed to keep up, and the effort left him exhausted to the point of falling asleep in class. Mrs. Schulte woke him with a sharp rap of her ruler against his desk, then shuffled back toward the front, mumbling to JP II and Jesus about this thorn in the flesh she'd been given.

On the first day of October, Braun absconded with the neighbor's bicycle and $40 Whit had stashed in the silverware drawer for weeks that grocery money ran short. Whit discovered the treachery after walking Libby home from kindergarten, and he spent the next ninety minutes waiting for his father to get home, wondering how he was going to explain everything without inviting a raging fit. But when Cole Allen heard the news, he brushed it aside like a mosquito and told Whit to have a seat.

"You know how I've been doing more at the church lately" he said, eyes wobbling with excitement. "Well, Brother Dahl had a conflict with a revival meeting he's supposed to preach over in Sundance, and he asked me to fill in as evangelist. How about that?"

"Good I guess."

"You guess?" Cole Allen wrinkled his nose. "You guess? Son, this is an opportunity to be a vessel for the Lord."

"I thought that's what we were doing for Mr. Zane."

"What did I tell you about talking back?"

"Sorry."

Cole Allen leaned forward, elbows on knees, and looked into his son's face. "I want you to come with me," he said. "I want you to be a part of this."

Whit nodded somberly, the way he'd learned to do these past few months. Somewhere along the way, Cole Allen had decided that his son was ready to be a man, and so began pausing at random intervals to impart some bit of fatherly wisdom. Usually, these mini lectures involved the importance of routine vehicle maintenance or the mystery of the female species. This time was different, though. It was more than just advice for making everyone's life easier. This was an emotional invitation. Tears welled up in Cole Allen's eyes, and even though none actually fell, Whit felt a compassion toward his old man that he'd never suspected was possible.

"I want you to be a part of it," Cole Allen repeated. "And Libby too, of course." He leaned in closer. "Son, this is where all the trials have been leading—your mother abandoning us, the move up north, all the trouble we've had with your school—all that has been for this moment, so the Lord could lift me up and the weak along with me."

He stood from the couch then, riffing on being an unworthy vessel tasked with the most precious of messages—that God loves sinners, and it's time to beat down the devil and leave behind wicked ways and turn to the Lord in repentance, *Humbahlah! Kahkahkah!* Whit thought it better not to point out that he'd borrowed his Spirit language from Brother Reinbeck back in Oklahoma.

"Amen!" Libby called from where she sat on the couch, squeezing a silver bag hard enough to make juice shoot up through the straw. Her father reached across and swept her up in his thick arms. She giggled and squeezed harder, sending red liquid spraying in every direction. "Amen!" she called again, and Cole Allen called "Amen!" too. He laughed and twirled the little girl as though he'd just discovered the most wonderful thing. If anyone had asked, Whit would have admitted to being jealous of his little sister hijacking the moment. But he was dabbling in the art of rationalization by this time, and while he would eventually reject that practice altogether, for the moment he told himself that silence was not falsehood. He'd never seen their father like this, so caught up in rapture, so willing to share the moment with his children. Maybe there was something spiritual in his dreams of evangelizing, after all. And if not—if it was just a random oasis in a sea of family struggle—then Whit was willing to suspend his doubt so that he could be a part of it.

"Amen!" he yelled, and giggled along with the others, and wondered at the scene in their living room. He had not been much of a pray-er, not since that night in the busted mercy seat. But now he found his heart in fervent conversation with the Spirit—not in gratitude, but in supplication.

God, let us stay happy like this.

CHAPTER 4

The ecstatic sermon that played so well on the Whitman children did not make the same impression on the frozen chosen at the Sundance Ecumenical Revival, who proved to be as spiritually expressive as bowling pins. Cole Allen slogged on through forty minutes of sermon material, all for only a single rededication, and that from the local Pentecostal preacher. On the way back to Gillette, he railed against formal education, the Devil's tool for making philosophers out of preachers. He bounced between audiences, sometimes speaking to Whit and sometimes to the Lord. Libby fell asleep between them, or at least pretended so.

Brother Dahl put a different spin on matters. He reminded Cole Allen that dark spiritual forces were at work all over the world, and being rejected by them put him in company with Jeremiah and Hosea and even Jesus himself. God often humbled his servants to test their resolve, but the call to preach remained. The thing to do was look for the next opportunity and get right back on that horse, so to speak.

And so Cole Allen agreed to a monthly slot in the preaching rotation at the state penitentiary in Rawlins. Brother Dahl went with him the first few times as spiritual support, but by the time the calendar turned on a new year, his protégée had hit his stride. Male inmates, it seemed, were far more receptive to his turn-or-burn style of preaching than the godless mainliners in Sundance. They converted and re-converted, were baptized and re-baptized in such numbers as to validate Cole Allen's suspicion that he'd been touched by the Lord in ways those who judged him failed to see.

"Look at the fruits," he told Whit. "That tells you a man's value clearer than anything."

Whit muttered an amen, his father's preferred sign of assent. He had yet to accompany Cole Allen to the state pen due to age restrictions on non-family visitors, but he had become fully engaged in his father's research and development process. Anytime a new speaker came to Light of Azusa Holy Spirit Tabernacle's youth group, Whit took notes. Was he effective? What made him so? What kind of examples did he use? How much time did he speak in tongues? What was the ratio of condemnation to forgiveness? Whit paid close attention, careful to observe anything that might find a place in his father's toolbox in service of the Lord.

"You need something to repeat," he would tell Cole Allen. "Some sort of phrase that ties everything together."

"You mean like, 'Praise the Lord'?"

"More specific. Like"—he stopped to consult his notes—"'The main thing is to keep the main thing the main thing.' Or here's another one: 'The Devil don't relent until you repent.' Something catchy. You know, with rhyme or alliteration."

"A little what? Talk like a real person."

He'd harvested that bit of wisdom—talk like a real person—from Brother Dahl, who was spending more and more time at the house and, at Cole Allen's request, providing one-on-one training to both children in spiritual warfare. The preacher expressed some concern that Whit, now a teenager, had still not yet been baptized by the Holy Spirit—meaning he'd not yet spoken in tongues. He counseled Whit, prayed over him, encouraged him. In the end, however, all he could credibly preach was patience, knowing God well enough to say that he would someday remember and bless Whit. Both Brother Dahl and Cole Allen cited their newest star pupil as reason for hope.

"Maybe it's just not your time yet," they said. "Maybe you're just like Bonner."

According to local legend, Bonner Hanson was the best athlete ever to don a jersey for the Gillette Muleriders. He'd lettered in four sports and been all-state in three. He was on his way to play fullback for Nebraska before a cheap shot in the state championship tore every ligament in his left knee. Most people quietly viewed the injury as a blessing in disguise, though, since Bonner was now clear to earn an honest living in the mines rather than fight indoctrination by liberal university professors.

Unfortunately, his reputation as a marvel of physical prowess put a target on his back for every young buck wanting to make a name for himself. Almost every time Bonner went to a bar, someone tried to pick a fight with him. At Hell on Wheels Saloon on a hot July night, a man came at him with a knife. Bonner calmly smashed the end off his beer bottle and proceeded to slash the guy's forearm deep enough to sever a tendon and render the hand permanently useless. Even though the locals backed up his claim of self-defense, Bonner ended up doing time in Rawlins for assault with a deadly weapon.

In the eyes of Cole Allen, however, Bonner's incarceration was nothing short of the Lord's perfect plan. He was a late convert to the faith, only joining in with the prison revivals a few months before his release. Yet he became Cole Allen's most effective volunteer evangelist, and he agreed to come to Gillette upon his release to continue the work. He was discharged on Whit's seventeenth birthday and moved into the spare bedroom at the Whitman house that night. A week later, he had his old job back at the mine. A month after that, he became a volunteer youth counselor at Light of Azusa. By spring, he was chaperoning the kids to Firestorm, held the week after Easter in Cheyenne.

For the youth at Light of Azusa, the Firestorm Youth Experience was the reward for all those Wednesday nights spent memorizing Bible verses and tracing Paul's missionary journeys. For three days, youth from all over the Mountain West rocked out to electric guitars and drums, praising the Lord and taunting the Devil. Some of the most renowned preachers in the country gave the evening sermons, and luminaries like Jerry Falwell and Pat Robertson greeted them via video message. Firestorm's altar calls produced waves of repentance that would be unheard of outside of youth events and prison revivals. Worship began with baptisms and testimonies at 6:00, and by the 10:00 altar call kids were shoving past one another to get to the prayer rail to lay down their vices—cigarettes, bong pipes, tiny plastic bottles of whiskey, even a few porno magazines smuggled right into the sanctuary. The condoms laid across the altar made Whit most uncomfortable of all, but he tried not to judge. Whatever presaged such a gesture was between that person and the Lord, and while it was maybe too strong to say that Whit didn't want to know the story, he could safely say that he didn't *want* to want to know it.

He thought of these things as his youth group stood in a circle in Light of Azuza's parking lot for the pre-trip prayer. Brother Dahl, who apparently knew plenty about the sins of his youth group members, prayed for God to call them to repentance and guard their hearts from evil and rain down his purifying fire upon them all—especially those who had not yet received their Holy Spirit baptism.

"Yes," Cole Allen muttered from where he stood next to the pastor. "Yes, Lord Christ, *yes!*"

Whit glanced up, certain that everyone was looking his way, either judging or pitying him for his defective faith. But every head was bowed and every eye closed, except for his 12-year-old kid sister Libby, who smirked at him.

Although technically too young to attend Firestorm, Libby had gotten special permission from Brother Dahl, thanks to some maneuvering on Cole Allen's part. Whit didn't like the thought of babysitting on such a big weekend, not with all the note-taking his father expected him to do. But he saw no way around it. Libby had demonstrated time and again that she couldn't be trusted to behave in religiously appropriate ways. Even in the most passionate of worship experiences, her sharp little eyes pierced to the heart of the spectacle, darting back and forth between the stage and the congregants and making connections that Whit could only guess at. She didn't raise her hands or sing or shout herself hoarse like her teenaged peers. But he could tell her mind was roving, picking up details everyone else missed and boiling them down to their stark-naked essence. Each week, Whit grew a little more terrified that his kid sister would one day solidify his own doubts about God and church through sheer power of perception.

Dahl plowed onward with his praises and beseeches. Whit motioned for Libby to bow her head like the others. She raised her middle finger toward him, only assuming a more appropriate posture once she sensed the landing gear coming down on the prayer.

As the other men made a final check of tire pressures and fluid levels in the van, Cole Allen pulled Whit aside. "You know you've got a charge to keep," he said.

"I know. I'll watch her."

"Her?" Cole Allen paused a moment to connect the dots. "Oh no. I'm not talking about your sister. I mean Bonner."

"Bonner?"

"He's older than you, but he needs help finding his way. You got to make him feel welcome on the path. You hear me?"

"Yes sir," Whit answered.

"And Brother Dahl says that it's possible your own Spirit baptism might come easier if you quit worrying about yourself and started trying to help others."

"I do try."

"Well quit trying and actually do it then."

Whit didn't answer. Pointing out the myriad ways that he put others before himself would just be counted as backtalk, and it wasn't worth getting the weekend off to a bad start. Instead he met his father's gaze and waited until Cole Allen was satisfied that his meaning had sunk in. He reached out to shake Whit's hand—a habit he'd begun the day his son came home with his driver's license—and slapped him on the shoulder. "Lord bless you."

Of all the weekend festivities, the Saturday night service at Firestorm held both the most promise and the most danger, in Whit's estimation. After a weekend of Bible studies and training in spiritual warfare, the 1500 kids and chaperones were primed for a movement of the Spirit, which he ought to have considered a good thing. But what if his blessing still didn't come? And what if Libby acted out?

Whit mulled the problem over through the music and baptisms and testimonials, on through more songs and 55 minutes—far too long to be effective, he scribbled in his notebook—of the evangelist's sermon. He was still thinking it over when the altar call began and Bonner Hanson received his baptism of fire.

The evangelist had closed with a flourish, tearfully acknowledging that the Spirit had revealed to him that someone in their midst had lost their salvation and was falling into the arms of the Devil. He begged his hearers not to be the one, but to come down to the altar and fall on their knees before God. As he finished, the band leader sat down at the piano and began to softly play "I Surrender All." Whit tried to gin up some holy feeling that would draw him forward down the aisle. Or maybe his father was right. Perhaps he first had to tend to another's soul. He leaned down to whisper into his sister's ear. She swatted him on the nose like he was a cat.

"Hey!" he protested.

"Zip!" Libby ordered. She pointed to the row in front of them, where Bonner held a hand on the back of Tamara Riker, a girl in Whit's class at GHS. She covered her face with her hands, swayed and sobbed, leaned in toward her comforter. Bonner sidled in closer until he noticed Libby's gaze boring down on him. He didn't exactly acknowledge her, but his face did change ever so slightly. A half second later, his eyes widened and his hands shot up toward the rafters. His breathing appeared to stop, leading Whit to wonder if he were having a stroke. After a few seconds, however, a sound like train whistle blew out from his throat, followed by the choppy stream of nonsense syllables that everyone around him recognized.

"Bonner's got the Spirit!" one of the youth called.

"I believe the Spirit has Bonner," yelled another.

The entire section watched as Bonner turned slow circles, arms raised, eyes bugging out. He stepped to the right as though going for the aisle, then whirled and caught Tamara by the wrist. The two of them wove their way through the pressing throng until they disappeared from sight near the altar rail. Libby stood on her seat to get a better look.

"Hey! Get down!" Whit ordered.

Libby waved him away, but then changed her mind and waved him up to join her. "No," he said.

"Come on! You have to see this."

"See what?"

"You won't believe me if I tell you."

Whit turned toward the altar and stood on his tiptoes. Tamara was balanced, arms spread to heaven, on the kneeling rail that had been erected below the stage. Bonner stood below, his big hands on her hips to keep her steady. One of the evangelists' attendants politely motioned for her to get down, and so Bonner lifted her from the rail and set her gently in front of him. She knelt at the rail. He dropped his palms onto her bare shoulders and held them there.

"Young lady!" an usher yelled at Libby from the aisle nearest them. "Young lady, you are in the presence of the Lord! Please do not stand on the seats."

Libby glared at him, and Whit braced for a scene. Instead she hopped down, a chastened smile on her face. She waited until the old man shuffled away before stepping back up onto her perch. But the sea of worshipers had roiled again, swallowing Tamara and Bonner.

"Can you still see them?" Libby asked.

"No."

"You think Tam is okay?"

He shrugged. "Why wouldn't she be?"

Libby glared at him with the intensity of a thousand suns, but turned away from him to watch the throng once more. Her message was clear enough, though. If her brother was too stupid to pick up on how things were, she wasn't going to waste her time explaining.

On the drive home, while his Light of Azusa companions slept in the contorted positions required by travel in a church van, Whit stared through the windshield and picked at unknowable things. What was going through Libby's young head as she watched the spectacle of repentance? What had caused such emotional responses from Tamara and Bonner? The Spirit, maybe, but Whit had his doubts. The loud music, the crowded room, the violence of the preaching—all of it was carefully designed to produce a reaction from anxious and guilt-ridden teenagers. And for what gain? The kids that laid their cigarettes down on the altar bought new packs on the way back to Gillette. Even though he couldn't verify it, he suspected a similar thing was true for alcohol and condoms and pornos. If none of the change lasted beyond a night, where did all that praying leave them?

"You're thinking awful loud," Bonner called to him over the whine of tires.

"Sorry," Whit said, and stretched. He'd been given the front seat of the 15-passenger van because of his long legs, and because everyone else wanted to sleep. He knew it was his job to keep the driver awake, but he hadn't spoken in sixty miles at least.

Bonner dropped a used pouch of smokeless tobacco into his Styrofoam spit cup and tucked another into his cheek. "You have a good time this weekend?"

"I guess."

"You guess?"

"Yeah. I did."

"Then what's eating at you?"

"Nothing."

"Don't look like nothing."

"I just didn't like the way it ended." Whit turned to make sure no one behind him was awake and listening to their conversation. None of them wanted to admit how anticlimactic Firestorm's closing worship had been that morning. Neither cajoling by the band nor harangues from the preacher could wake the weary youth from their slumber. Despite a few "amens" from the positive thinkers, the service fell flat. "Maybe we were all just tired," he finally said.

Bonner considered this for a second before giving a quick shake of his head. "We weren't ready for the Spirit." He turned his head to look straight at Whit, held the stare far too long for someone behind the wheel of a van going 90mph. "*You* weren't ready."

Whit winced. "I tried to be."

"*Try* don't matter, not with sin in your heart. I seen the way you were looking at Tamara."

"Tam?" he said. His mouth went suddenly dry.

"She was wearing that spaghetti-strap top, which was her fault," Bonner said. "But I seen the way you looked at her."

"I wasn't—how was I looking at her?"

"Like you'd fuck her right at Jesus' feet if she let you."

Whit felt his face go hot with shame. He liked Tamara well enough. She was a little wild, maybe, but big-hearted. Girls were still a mystery to him, and what thoughts he had of them were not worth the guilt they produced. Now that Bonner had put the image in his head, though, he felt that familiar swelling in his groin. Tried to push it down without Bonner noticing.

"It's not like that," he protested.

Bonner spit a brown stream into his cup. "The Spirit won't come near you until you confess. It can't stand your kind of sin."

"I wasn't sinning."

"It's sad to hear you talking like this."

"I wasn't, though. I think—"

"And that's it," Bonner said, jabbing a thick finger into the air between them. "You keep trying to think things out. I know. I watch you. You think you're pretty smart, always trying to figure out this from that. Well, some things can't be figured out—especially when your heart's full of lust. You ever *think* about that?"

Whit looked in vain for a way to argue with Bonner, but he had to admit he had never contemplated how the state of his soul might derail his efforts at understanding the world. In truth, he'd considered his metaphorical heart to be in pretty good shape until now. What if Bonner was right, though? What if something inside him was plugging his ears to the voice of God? As much as he hated to admit the possibility, it all made sense.

"I'm not trying to tear you down," Bonner said softly. "I just want to warn you. Drugs and booze, they may be dangerous to your body. But sex goes after your soul. You watch yourself around girls, hear me? Tamara most of all."

Whit nodded somberly and said thank you and leaned forward in what he hoped looked like a contemplative position. He wasn't praying, and he knew it was a lie to trying to make Bonner think he was. But that pressure between his legs was not going away any time soon. How much worse would things be for him if anyone saw that? Better to risk the fires of hell than give Bonner one more round of ammunition.

And so he hunched over and waited, trying not to think about his unruly teenage body nor his poor faithless soul. Instead, he let his thoughts wander south, back to Claremore, back to that mercy seat. He'd known all along it could never hold.

CHAPTER 5

If Whit returned from Firestorm with a crisis of faith, his sister took on every other crisis available to a 12-year-old. She refused to go back to youth group, citing the appalling level of hypocrisy she witnessed in Cheyenne. Despite Cole Allen's insistence that she talk like a normal person, Libby employed a vocabulary intended to both confuse and provoke, accusing her brother of duplicity and their father of obdurate religiosity. Still, such verbal dexterity didn't translate into scholarly success. She let her grades slip into territory that scandalized even a proudly uneducated man like Cole Allen.

It was her temper, however, that finally led their father to make good on the years' long threat to ship her off to live with their grandmother. The victim was poor Gabriella Fortuna, who made the mistake of taunting Libby about her holy-roller brother in the lunchroom while Mrs. Lenderman—née Corelli—was on duty. According to Mrs. Lenderman's report, Libby had stood up from her seat as calmly as could be, then unloaded a punch right into the middle of Gabriella's face. Almost before the blood had dried, Libby was suspended for the remainder of the semester.

"You just wait until I drop you off at your Grandma's house," Cole Allen said. "We'll see what stunts you pull once she gets ahold of you."

"No we won't," Libby snapped.

"Don't backtalk me."

"All you are is talk."

Thus challenged, Cole Allen felt forced to act on the threat that, in Whit's estimation, he had no prior intention of enforcing. Whit had been in fourth grade the last time they'd visited Grandma Helene in Libby, Montana, the picturesque mining town for which his sister had been named. Whit could recall the dollar-store Christmas tree, the greasy chicken and stuffing, the singed smell of Grandpa Ernest, who had moved up to work in the vermiculite mines thirty years ago and was now dying of lung cancer. Not long after they'd opened presents, an argument broke out over Helene's sale of four tires that her son had left in the shed two winters ago. Cole Allen carted his kids back to Gillette that very afternoon and had not returned to his parents' home since. But Libby had thrown down the gauntlet, and it was enough to overcome his boycott.

"You'll see what I am," Cole Allen said. "Pack your bag, little girl."

They delivered Libby the girl to Libby the town just after daybreak on Saturday. In Whit's memory, Grandma Helene had been old and withered during their last visit, seven years before. Now she had dried up completely, prompting Libby to call her an anthropomorphized slab of desiccated jerky. The old woman had not moved while they unloaded the girl or her luggage, electing instead to remain planted on the front porch under a stack of blankets that might very well have outweighed her, the oxygen tube draped down around her neck so as not to get in the way of her cigarette.

"If you come for them tires, I still don't have 'em," she said in lieu of greeting.

Cole Allen nodded as though he'd expected as much. But for all his compassion for repentant criminals, he could not forgive slights from his kin. Every challenge to him amounted to outright rejection—especially from his mother. Without so much as cup of coffee, he'd ordered Whit back into the truck and backed out onto the street. Two hours later, when he barely made it out of the median after falling asleep at the wheel, he grudgingly allowed Whit to drive.

Left alone with his thoughts, Whit fared little better at keeping the pickup between the lines. His issue wasn't fatigue—he'd slept nearly the entire way to Montana—but wonder. When they'd come north the night before, he'd been vaguely aware of mountains and trees and water somewhere in the darkness. With the Clark Fork

River and the Cabinet Mountains now illuminated by sunlight, Whit could hardly take his eyes off the ever-changing shimmers and shadows. He spotted mountain goats and bison herds and glimpsed mule deer, which bolted away when he swerved into the drunk bumps along the shoulder. Thankfully, his father was a heavy if infrequent sleeper, giving Whit four solitary hours to revel in the beauty of the natural world. More than once he had to chase away the thought that the earth might actually be more interesting than heaven, and certainly was worth more than fleeting glances through stained glass windows.

His epiphany dissipated in Livingston, and not just because they were leaving the majesty of the mountains for the grassland doldrums. Cole Allen awoke with renewed energy both to scheme and to communicate. He and Bonner had cancelled their Sunday night trip to Rawlins, since Cole Allen had expected to spend two nights at his mother's house. But she had obviously not opened her heart to the Lord, given that she'd thrown those tires up in his face before she'd even said hello. He felt released from any obligation. She could die however she chose, and if her choice was to burn the bridge with her only son, it was something he could live with just fine.

"What about Libby?" Whit asked.

"Those two deserve each other."

By leaving his mother's house almost as soon as he'd arrived, Cole Allen had opened up the possibility of returning to Gillette in time to make it to the prison for Sunday evening services. He used the payphone in Livingston to call Bonner at the house, but whoever picked up on the other end merely listened for a moment and hung up again. Cole Allen chalked it up to dialing the wrong number but had no patience for trying again. He got behind the wheel and peeled out of the station, driving 95mph as he bounced from one topic to another, planning the things they could do now that they didn't have a stubborn adolescent girl to hold them back. Whit could put in some extra hours at the gym with the hope of sliding into a starting role by the time the basketball team started conference play. Cole Allen would focus more on the prison ministry, maybe even work on getting a new revival started. He'd have to fight off the Devil, of course, and probably the liberals and the government. But the Word of the Lord never returned empty. A huge harvest of souls was waiting.

He was still going strong when they crossed into Wyoming and had barely slowed when at last they pulled onto their street, twenty-five hours after embarking. But the sight of an unfamiliar car parked beside Bonner's beat-up GTO stopped Cole Allen in mid-diatribe. He mumbled something to himself. Whit searched for a response, some insight or change in subject that would ward off whatever trouble was coming. But when he looked down through the pickup window at the two-toned Ford with the cracked windshield, he abandoned hope.

"You stay here," his father said.

Whit waited until his father disappeared through the front door before he climbed out of the truck and sat on the front bumper. His father's shouts sliced through the late afternoon cold, punctuated by the squeals and protests of the girl inside. Moments later, Tamara Riker stumbled out on to the porch, shoved out by a thick male hand. An unfastened belt swayed from the waist of her blue jeans, and she clutched a hoodie to her chest with her bare arms. When she turned to the house, Whit could see mottled red and pink splotches on the skin of her back, pimpling from the cold. She bent forward to hurl her rage.

"Give me my fucking boots, you fucking dick!" she screamed. "I'm not leaving without my goddamn boots! Fucking hypocrite!"

A moment later the window to Bonner's second-floor bedroom opened and a pair of boots fell onto the dirt, tossed out as casually as a beer bottle on a Friday night. She whirled around to get them and noticed, to her terror, Whit watching the whole scene. Big tears welled up in her eyes. She tip-toed toward him, picking up speed as she went, and he braced himself for whatever blows she would deliver. Instead she leaned forward, her head on his shoulder, and sobbed. He draped his arms around her, tried not to think about her bare skin beneath his hands.

"We were just watching movies," she began, but only cried harder. He held her as steadily as he could, despite the cold that numbed his hands and the shivers that wracked her body. When she finally caught her breath again, she said, "Your father is an asshole."

Whit didn't argue. He still wasn't 100% confident in his understanding of human emotion, but he knew enough to keep quiet when someone cried like this. Besides, after the way things had gone sour with Libby in such a short span, he didn't entirely disagree with Tamara's assessment.

Through the window of the storm door, he could see that Cole Allen had met Bonner at the bottom of the stairs. They stood toe to toe, arms folded, locked in tense conversation. It could come to blows at any minute. Whit had seen them do it before over some gaskets Bonner had charged to Cole Allen's account at the parts store. This one had the potential to be worse, though—maybe even worse than the knock-down, drag-out matches he still remembered between his parents in Oklahoma.

"You can stand between the cars and get dressed," he told Tamara softly. "I won't look."

"Promise?"

"Promise."

He dropped his hands and she moved around the fender. He stole a glance at her back as she passed, could see the white outline where his hands had been and something else—an angry red scrape that rippled over her right lat muscle. Impulses flooded his mind—protect, comfort, avenge, speak, love, ignore. He blushed at the thoughts, berated himself for the less pure among them. But as she got ready to sift through her clothes, he turned his back just as he'd promised and tried to stand in the line of sight between her and the men inside.

"Okay," she said a few seconds later. Whit turned around to find her looking like the same Tamara he was used to seeing at youth group—pretty but disheveled, hands pulled up into the sleeves of her oversized Cowboys hoodie. He stepped forward, not exactly sure what he should do, but she backed away. Held up her hands. "You just—hand me my boots, okay?"

Whit looked down at her feet, glowing bright red and probably frost-bitten. He quickly retrieved the boots, holding them by the toes as he extended them to her. She winced as she pulled them on.

He glanced again through the open door. The fight between Bonner and Cole Allen had never materialized. In fact, he could see the two men embracing, his father's hand resting tenderly on the back of Bonner's head as the younger man wept. Bile rose in the back of Whit's throat. He sidestepped again, this time hoping to keep Tamara from witnessing the reconciliation happening inside. He turned to her and spoke.

"I won't say anything. Not to anyone."

The girl emitted something that might have been a grunt or a laugh, but he could not parse it. She climbed in behind the wheel of her GTO. Stared into the house through the open front door, now that Whit couldn't block her view. Without so much as a glance in Whit's direction, she started the car and threw it in gear and backed away.

CHAPTER 6

When the foreman at Gray Butte, shotgun in hand, announced on a Friday afternoon that the mine would close by August, the blindsided townspeople of Gillette turned to their most tried-and-true sources of comfort—alcohol and religion. That night, every bar in town set a record for sales, only to have that record broken again on Saturday. By sundown the only bottles on liquor store shelves were ginger-ale and high-end whiskeys that even the most desperate miner could not afford. The sheriff's department reported a twelve-fold increase in alcohol-related violations, most of which involved vandalism or public urination on Gray Butte property.

On Sunday morning, though, the hung-over masses showed up for church, packing the pews in almost every sanctuary in town. At Light of Azusa, Brother Dahl reminded the throng that hardships really weren't surprising at all. God often tested his most loyal servants by beating the shit out of them to determine their mettle. He worked through a dizzying array of biblical passages that included three prophets and six epistles, never explicitly condoning retribution on Gray Butte, but neither strictly forbidding it. After all, he said, had Ehud not assassinated King Eglon and crawled out through the sewers? A thunderous *amen* rose from the congregation, the ensuing applause sustained even by those whose heads throbbed at the noise.

When he thought back on the sermon later that afternoon, Whit was almost certain that the preacher hadn't really used the word "shit," but it was hard to say, given everyone's state of mind. He doubted that Brother Dahl had used many of the words he intended, and doubted even further than his hearers had received the message with clear heads and pure hearts.

Whatever the preacher's intent, Cole Allen and Bonner interpreted the sermon as a call to arms, or at least to a clandestine revenge campaign they were uniquely suited to mount. As mechanics, they knew which bolts to loosen or hoses to slit to render equipment useless without putting miners at risk. By Tuesday morning, the skid steers only worked in reverse, and the glow plugs had stopped warming the diesel engines. Gus Mankampf, the mechanic shop foreman, chewed his guys up one side and down the other, but they all swore the failures were mere coincidence, perhaps the result of bad luck called down by Grey Butte's heartless owners.

Buoyed by the fruits of their sabotage, the two men decided to up the ante on Wednesday after church. When Whit emerged from youth group, the men had already left adult Bible study and were scheming in the narthex. Cole Allen handed Whit the keys to the pickup before he'd even asked for them.

"Go on home and get yourself ready for school tomorrow," he said. "Me and Bonner have some business to take care of at the mine."

"You going to booby trap the boss's locker?"

"Shut your mouth," his father snapped.

"Nothing like that," Bonner said. He grinned. Flicked Whit's arm with the back of his knuckles. "Best if you don't ask questions. It's man business."

"I'm as much a man—"

"Go do what I told you," Cole Allen ordered. "You remember what to say if anyone comes by looking to cause trouble?"

Whit sighed. "Yes, sir."

"Go on then."

And so Whit went on home and set to work on the domestic tasks that occupied much of his home life. He cleaned up supper dishes and threw in a load of laundry and set about doing his and Libby's chores. He supposed all of them were technically his, now that she had moved to Montana with Grandma Helene. But thinking that way made his sister seem dead rather than exiled, and he was working to keep hope alive. He'd posed as his father on Monday to switch their long-distance plan to include free calls after 8:00pm, but he hadn't yet mustered the courage to telephone his sister. He could imagine his grandmother's rusty-hinge voice on the other end of the line, telling him that Libby had run away or been mauled by a bear or moved to Anchorage with some transient oil rig worker. None of these things were likely, perhaps, but neither were they inconceivable.

The men still weren't home at 10:00pm when Whit heard an unfamiliar engine approaching. He put down his dust rag and listened as tires ground to a halt on the gravel. Headlights shone through the front curtains, casting the man who ascended the steps in silhouette. Enough time passed for Whit to contemplate at least a dozen horror movie scenarios, all of which ended in his gruesome demise. But when the knock came, he knew what this plot required of him. He picked up the cordless telephone receiver and gripped it tight. Stepped to the door. Opened it.

The man on the porch was not the hulking menace of slasher films, but a short, wiry mine worker whose ragged breaths told of high emotion and damaged lungs. His voice quivered with pent-up rage. "I need to speak with your dad."

"He's not here," Whit said, and silently begged the Lord to either usher the man away or strike one of them dead with lightning. He didn't much care which.

The man raised a bony finger toward the drive. "That's your daddy's truck."

"He's not here. I drove his truck home. He's at church. Or he was, last I saw him. He had to go take care of some things."

"Things?"

"He didn't say what."

"Well how about Bonner, then. He around?"

Whit shifted his weight, hating the whole thing. His father had given him a script for this scenario, and it made him want to vomit.

"Bonner? No. He doesn't live here. Not anymore."

Mr. Riker narrowed his eyes. "Tam said she saw him with Cole Allen at church tonight."

"Yeah, but Bonner's been drinking bad since the mine closed. Dad told him he needed to pack up and find somewhere else to go."

Whit squinted against the headlights. He could see another figure in the car. Rivers of sweat formed on his back and in his armpits. "Want me to tell them you stopped by?"

"Them?"

"Him."

The man coughed. Spit on the floorboards of the porch. "Do you know who I am?"

"You're Mr. Riker," Whit said.

"And do you know what that means?"

"It means you're Tamara's dad."

Riker stared at Whit's face, the corners of his eyes quivering with rage. "So you understand why I goddamn well want to talk to your daddy and his friend, before the mine closes and they skip town."

"They aren't—I mean, Bonner isn't—"

"Don't you say it, Whit. Don't you do that to my daughter."

Whit tried not to look down. Looked down anyway. Cole Allen would have found a convincing lie for the moment and doubled down on it. Probably he would have been able to sell it. Lying might be a sin, but surely the Lord understood that some things just had to be done for the greater good. Whit, however, did not possess his father's capacity for falsehood, and he was already discovering the toll rationalization could exact on a person. Moisture ran across the creases of his palms.

"I think maybe Bonner has to get a few things here still," he said at last.

"I might just wait for him then."

Riker folded his arms. Whit told himself not to flinch, and yet he flinched. He pondered the fact that the effort to not do something seemed to always result in the thing you were trying to avoid.

"I don't know if he's coming back tonight," he said weakly. "Or at all, to tell the truth."

"Well."

The lie swirled inside Whit's skull before finally settling in a place just behind his eyebrows. He hoped Riker didn't notice the pulsing bulge of falsehood, writ large across his face. More than that, he hoped to God that his father and Bonner stayed gone until Riker cleared out.

"Dad?" Tamara called from somewhere behind the headlights. "It's not Whit's fault. Let's go."

"Hush," Riker snapped. He squared up to Whit. Folded one hand over the other in front of his belt buckle and stood eerily still. "I ain't going nowhere."

Tears welled up in Whit's eyes at the sound of Tamara's voice, and he had to work hard to keep them from falling. Late on the night they'd returned from Montana, Cole Allen had come into his room to explain that Bonner had fallen into temptation, but that he had also repented. The two men had made amends, and already he could see that the whole thing happened for a reason.

He had not mentioned Tamara. Not even once.

The electronic ring of the telephone in Whit's hands didn't faze Riker, but it nearly sent Whit into orbit. His heart leapt with such force that he feared it might blow out right through his sternum. The receiver flopped out of his grasp like a walleye before he managed to catch it with both hands. He pressed the TALK button with his thumbs.

"Whit you hear me?" the tinny voice on the other end of the line said. It belonged to his father, but it sounded far off and wrong in a way Whit couldn't define. "Boy, are you listening?"

"Yeah, I'm here."

"Get yourself dressed and come down to the police station. Bring my checkbook."

Whit looked up at Riker and knew at once that the man had overheard. He stepped to the side so that Whit could see his face in the glow of the headlights. He smiled. Tipped his hat and backed away.

Whit turned back into the house and spoke softly into the receiver. "I'll be down there quick as I can."

"Hurry," his father answered. "I got to think about where we're going to go."

"Go?"

"We're leaving, soon as I get this cleared up. Ain't nothing left for us in this town."

Figure 3: Craft Talk—From a Distant Memory

CHAPTER 7

What was left for Cole Allen Whitman in Gillette turned out to be a plea agreement. Gray Butte reluctantly agreed to drop felony trespassing charges against him and Bonner, providing that the two men remove the gremlins they'd planted in Gray Butte's machinery and get the hell out of Gillette.

And so Cole Allen begrudgingly set right what he had sabotaged, thus setting Whit on the path that would lead him finally to his freshman year at Covenant University.

His first impression of his dorm room was not so different than his memory of the Campbell County Detention Center, where he'd retrieved his father and Bonner Hanson on the night of the mine incident. The rooms in Finney Hall were constructed with the same cinder blocks as the holding cells at the county pen, and the same yellowed tile covered the floor, chipped here and there to reveal the black asbestos glue used to set them in the 1950s. Whit glanced over to see if his father made the same connections. Cole Allen was beaming.

"*Whooiieee!*" the elder Whitman called out when the Resident Assistant unlocked the door and handed Whit his key. He clapped a thick hand down on his son's shoulder. "You're moving up, college boy!"

His voice rebounded off the cinderblocks in Finney's hallway, barren except for a water fountain and two enormous plastic trash bins. Whit searched the echo for some hint of irony or sarcasm. A thousand times a day since they left Gillette, he'd heard Cole Allen inveigh against so-called higher education. So fierce was his hatred of anything to do with college that Whit had to convince his high school counselors to keep the two dual credit courses he'd taken—algebra during a brief return to Claremore and biology during the subsequent sojourn in Dardanelle, Arkansas—off the grade report mailed home to his father. When he scored in the ninety-sixth percentile on his SAT—"blew the goddamn top out of it, is what," as Mr. Golden in Dardanelle put it—he didn't even call Libby, who had gone to live with their mother in Chattanooga after lung cancer finally sent Grandma Helene to her eternal home.

"No alcohol or cigarettes," Stephen, the RA, said. "Visitors only during appointed hours. Bed checks at 10:00pm on weekdays and 11:00 on weekends. No girls on the floor—ever."

"That won't be a problem for my boy," Cole Allen said, again shaking him by the shoulder. "He's here for the glory of the Lord, right son?"

"Amen," Whit said. It came out less as he intended to say it and more as he actually meant it—an ironic, irritated response to his father's deepening fanaticism. If anyone noticed Whit's tone, no one responded to it.

Cole Allen's conversion to higher education came thanks to Brother Earnest Arneson, the chief evangelist at the Montgomery-Ward Blessing, so named for the defunct department store once housed in the 6000-square-foot building where revival meetings were held. Cole Allen had diagnosed a bad starter in the preacher's car one night after services, then tapped it with a ball-peen hammer until the engine fired. Arneson was so impressed with Cole Allen's ingenuity that he made him his personal mechanic on the spot. A few weeks later, with the Blessing growing daily in both adherents and offerings, Arneson bought a new SUV and hired Cole Allen as his full-time driver.

Whit was, the best anyone could tell, nearly graduated from high school by this time. He'd attended five different schools in four different states since they'd left Gillette, and the task of cobbling together transcripts was the very definition of Frankensteinian. Most of the college admissions officers he secretly contacted threw up their hands in less than a week. And so, despite his test scores, Whit's only real option was his father's choice—Covenant University, where Earnest Arneson sat on the board of trustees. He declared his major as evangelism and missiology, and he signed up to play drums for marching band in exchange for $750 per semester.

Stephen let Cole Allen explain his connection to Brother Arneson until he finished, then turned toward Whit. "Dinner is at 5:00 and new resident orientation is at 6:00. Don't be late for either or you'll be fined. Any questions?"

"No sir," Cole Allen said smartly, as though he and not his son was the new Christian soldier in the Covenant barracks.

"All right then," Stephen said. "Blessings, y'all."

"Hang on," Whit said as the young man turned to go. "Do I have a roommate?"

"Probably so. If you don't, then you may want to find one. They'll charge you for a private room if you try to stay here by yourself."

"How much is that?"

Stephen shrugged. "Jerry would know, but he's in Cambodia until school starts."

"Cambodia?" Cole Allen said wistfully. In these ultra-religious days, the very prospect of unsaved souls in some exotic place turned him on.

"Who's Jerry?" Whit asked.

"Your RA for the fall. I'm just filling in until he gets back. You could also inquire about the roommate with housing, but they don't much like to be bothered."

"Why not?"

Cole Allen stepped in before the RA could answer. "Really nice to have met you, Stephen."

The interim RA nodded at father and son, wished them blessings again, then turned and walked down the hall, leaving the Whitman men alone in the cinder block room. Cole Allen shook his head in wonder.

"All those years in Wyoming—the wilderness wandering we've gone through since—all to get here," he said. He moved to the window and looked out over the manicured blue-green lawn. "This is the Lord's doing, and it is wonderful to see."

Whit's first thirty-six hours in Finney Hall confirmed anew that his definition of the Lord's doing did not line up with that of his father. The cafeteria food was good enough—better than any of the high schools he'd attended—and the new resident orientation was at least recognizable from all those Firestorm revivals of his youth. The housing director mixed up a stew of promises and threats and praise and invectives, heating it all up with religious fire in a sermon that boiled for ninety minutes. Once they were finally dismissed, Whit carried his guitar out onto the lawn and sat down in the soft grass to play. He'd only been there ten minutes when a security officer gave him a verbal lashing and a $20 fine—whether for disturbing the peace or trampling the grass, Whit could not tell.

He stayed behind his locked door the rest of that night and all day on Saturday, subsisting on the Green Lightning soda and donuts his father had left as a parting gift. On Sunday morning he was reaping what he had sown, doubled over by a raging stomachache. But he feared skipping church might incur more wrath and possibly further financial penalties. He walked across the street to Covenant Harvest Church and stayed through the first few minutes of the altar call before deciding he could sneak out without being seen. Back in his room at Finney Hall, the deadbolt snapping into place sounded for all the world like a judge's gavel, hammering home his sentence. He sat down on the bare tile and pulled his phone toward him to dial his mother's number. On the second ring he heard the line click.

"Hello?"

The sound of Libby's voice made his eyes tear up. He shook his head.

"Hey Lib."

"Whit, hi! Jesus Christ, I didn't think they'd let you have a phone."

"I get one call per week, if my behavior is good."

"Please tell me you're joking."

"Yeah," he said, although now that he'd spoken it aloud, he wondered if he'd missed some such rule.

"Are you in the shower? It's all echoey."

"It's my new room," Whit said. He didn't want to describe it though. Didn't even want to think about it. He closed his eyes.

"How's school?"

"Boring as shit."

"You better not let Mom hear you talk like that."

"She's worse than I am," Libby said, giggling. "Besides, she's at the hospital. Weekend shift."

"Ah."

The line went silent for a long time. Whit could hear his sister shuffling through papers—homework, maybe, but probably some magazine or trashy paperback. He asked her about it, but he didn't care about the answer. He only wanted to hear her talk, to know that someone in this world might be able to absorb for him the loneliness that ricocheted off these empty walls.

No one thing made him decide to quit college on that first day—not the empty room nor the conversation with Libby, not even the fine for, as it turned out, showing too much thigh when he sat in the grass playing his guitar. It was all of these things, but also a growing lack of faith that conditions would improve. Training camp for the marching band started at 7:00am Monday morning, and it would be nice to be around people again, but what kind of people would they be? All he'd witnessed in his brief walks to and from the cafeteria were the judgmental gazes of the security guards and the lockstep piety of the handful of band members and fall sport athletes already on campus. And even though Whit was still plenty pious himself—compared to Libby or their mother, anyway—the whole police state atmosphere rubbed him the wrong way. He decided he would drive home in the morning, hunker down while Cole Allen fumed for a day or two, and find a job at a mechanic shop somewhere back home.

A Sunday night visit to the Finney Hall showers—his first since before they'd loaded the car on Saturday morning—was like a sign from heaven confirming his decision. The community bathroom was clean and dazzlingly bright and smelled of highly concentrated chlorine bleach. A plastic sign on the door of each stall asked that users kindly call to those in the shower before flushing so that its occupants did not get scalded when the cool water was diverted from the showers to the toilets. One-inch olive green tiles covered the shower room floor to ceiling, the perfect rows interrupted only by three silver towel hooks opposite three water spigots, each with about seven feet between them. Whit hung his towel on the furthest hook and turned on the water, willing it to warm quickly and get him the heck out of there.

But, as Whit had learned in his days of childhood meteorology, fears had a way of conjuring their very object. He was still trying to home in on a passable water temperature when he heard someone enter the room, singing a song Whit didn't recognize in a manner he would later learn is used in musical theater. The man kept singing, even as he peed loud enough for Whit to hear over the splatters of his shower.

"FLUUU-uuuusshhhh!" he sang loudly.

The stream from the shower head weakened so that the arc fell right on top of Whit's foot. It felt like someone had pressed an iron against his skin. He yowled in pain and hopped back into the corner.

"Got to be quicker, pale sir!"

A thin, muscular man with jet black skin had appeared at the shower entrance, hands poised on the towel he wore over his hips.

He wore a bluish shower cap and had a thick green cream smeared over his face. Around his neck he wore a simple gold chain, from which dangled a simple gold cross. He whipped the towel from his waist, hung it, and started the water. "Isaias Granderson, at your service. What's your name?"

"Whit."

"Whit what?"

"Whit Whitman."

"Freshman, clearly." He turned and shamelessly faced Whit. Wagged a long black finger toward his feet. "Well, Mr. Whit Whitman—my god what a name—you better get some shower shoes or you'll be growing mushrooms between those toes before fall break. Now get going and move along. The water pressure isn't nearly so good when two are in at one time."

Whit didn't have to be told twice. He lathered and rinsed in strokes that were quick but ineffective. He didn't realize until he dropped the towel over his head that he'd forgotten to wash his hair. Never mind, he decided. Twelve hours from now, he'd get a real, solitary shower in his own house. He gathered his things and speed walked back to his room.

He had barely finished getting dressed, however, when he heard the first knock on his door since he'd moved in. The person on the other side announced himself as Stephen, the RA. Whit froze, sifting through his recent actions for anything that might have broken university policy.

Keys scraped against the lock. Whit leapt across the room and undid the bolt, lest obstruction of a residence hall investigation be somehow added to the rap sheet he was accumulating. The figure that greeted him at the doorway was not Stephen, but the dark-skinned man he'd showered with—Isaias, who entered the room with small, choppy steps like a wind-up toy. He held up the keys—Whit's own set, not the RA's—and sat down on the unmade bed. Reached out his hand to offer something wrapped in brown paper.

"If it's drugs I don't want it," Whit said.

"Drugs? Drugs!" Isaias clutched an open hand to his chest. "Sir, I am offended to the point of injury. *Drugs*."

Whit kept his eyes on Isaias as he took the package. Inside were two giant, homemade chocolate chip cookies that smelled like comfort itself.

"Courtesy of Mama Granderson," Isaias said, bubbly once again. "If your mama makes better, then I'm Rush Limbaugh." He surveyed the room. Wrinkled his nose. "You haven't unpacked a single thing. Why are there no sheets on your bed?"

"Sorry," Whit said, feeling as though he should offer a general apology but not quite sure why.

"Other people use those mattresses, you know. If you have a wet dream and no sheets—my lord. I can't even."

"It's okay. I'm leaving tomorrow."

Isaias wagged a long finger back and forth. "No, no, no. No, no. No. How can you and I be roommates if you skip out fifteen minutes after you arrive."

"It's been longer than that," Whit said weakly. He cocked his head and stared at Isaias. "I didn't think I had a roommate yet."

"You didn't until ten minutes ago." Isaias walked to the center of the room and spread his arms as though reaching for the walls on either side. "By some happy architectural accident, rooms at the end of the hall—such as this one—have an additional eighteen inches of length, which translates into fifteen extra square feet. Hence this is the perfect room for two men with simple needs and big aspirations."

Whit wrinkled his nose. "Hence?"

"Hence."

He knew his stomach didn't need any more sugar, but the smell of those cookies worked on him. He pulled one from the bag and bit into a side that looked particularly heavy on chocolate chips. The taste was nothing like the store-bought fare his father brought home or the hard-tack frisbees he'd gotten in the caf. Isaias was laying out his plans for the room, but Whit's sense of hearing was temporarily disabled, overwhelmed by the best culinary moment of his young life.

"YOO-hoo!" Isaias finally called. He snapped his fingers in front of Whit's face. "Come back to me, Mr. Big Man. You hearing anything I say?"

"Oh. Sorry. These were really good."

"I told you, didn't I? Now, if we're going to get everything set, we have to do it this week. Once Jerry gets back, it's toe the line." He gave a snappy salute, palm forward in the style of the British.

"Jerry? You mean the RA?"

"The man himself. Jerry Fosdick. He is a Covenant man through and through—the kind who likes rules, but who *loves* to enforce rules. You couldn't get a toothpick up his ass with a sledgehammer."

Whit let the metaphor settle in his mind. Tried in vain not to imagine it in the literal sense. "I have a long drive tomorrow."

"No you don't," Isaias said. He reached across and snatched Whit's car keys from the windowsill.

"Hey!"

"Relax, Mr. Big Man. I don't even know how to drive. I'm just going to hold onto these for safe keeping until I get everything moved in." He opened the door. Turned and waved over his shoulder. "There's something about you I like, Whit Whitman."

"You mean my quick showers, or the dimensions of my dorm room?"

Isaias broke into a big smile, which opened into an even bigger laugh. He jingled the keys as he walked away, and Whit—despite all the warnings in his head—smiled too.

CHAPTER 8

On the last Thursday of September, Whit returned from marching band practice soaked to the bone and buzzing with adrenaline, only to discover that Isaias had set up a mercy seat in their dorm room. The beds had been pushed together against the dresser, the cinderblock walls lined with heavy moving blankets. Gray and pink sheets hung in layers in one corner, their bottom edges cascading onto a thick gray throw rug. Wires of all types—microphone cables, power cords, lighting wires, video recording cables with strange input jacks—tied the spectacle together.

But the object of Whit's attention was the simplest and lowest-tech item in the room—a standard wooden stool carefully positioned in the center of the rug. He walked to it, ran his hand over the smooth finish of the seat, squatted down to inspect the legs. He wrapped his fingers around the edge of the seat and pulled gently, wiggled it back and forth. The only flaw he could see was one upper support that looked to have shifted about a quarter inch, which threw the whole thing just out of square. He stood again. Pressed hard downward. Water from his drenched shirt dripped onto the lacquer. He wiped it away. Backed up onto the tile and peeled off his wet clothes.

A late September heat wave had broken during marching band rehearsal, thanks to a line of fierce storms that came at them from the northwest. Everyone on the practice field could see the black and green clouds racing toward campus, billowing up behind Dr. Stone's director's tower like the very end of days. The director pressed on, even after a gust knocked a diminutive sousaphone player on her butt as they got set for the finale. It wasn't until a bolt of lightning blew up a tree on the other side of the parking lot that Dr. Stone considered the hazards of his elevated position and dismissed the band. Before he'd even descended his tower, the floods of Noah had broken open and sent the girls running, hands over breasts in hopes of avoiding any modesty code violations brought on by cooler temperatures and wet clothing.

Whit glanced through the window at the sheets of rain and flashes of lightning. He could feel the storm in his teeth, the way he used to when he was a kid. He did not look over at the mercy seat, or whatever it was. Instead, he crawled across his bed in his boxer shorts to try to wrest dry pants from his dresser drawers, which now opened only a few inches against the bed. He was still struggling when he heard the door open behind him, followed by hushed and hurried voices that stopped all at once when they noticed Whit. He thought about wrapping up in his sheets but decided maybe that would look more suspicious still. And so he backed off the bed and turned to the two bug-eyed faces staring at him, mouths agape.

"My god," Isaias whispered in awe. He raised a trembling finger. "Does rain make white people whiter?"

"Very funny."

"Look, though. My *god!* You could blind aircraft with that skin."

He laughed then. Whit crossed his arms and tried not to take it personally. During their six weeks as roommates, he'd gotten more or less used to Isaias' needling humor, enough so that he trusted the jokes to be good natured—even the ones about his whiteness, which he still didn't quite understand. This time, though, there was another person in the room to laugh along with Isaias. When Whit heard the voice, he froze.

"She's a girl," he said.

The other two fell into more laughter. "A woman, technically," Isaias said at last. "But yes, your observation is very near the mark. Kayla is, in fact, a young female human."

"I just mean we could get in trouble," Whit said. He looked over at the girl—the woman, Kayla. "We aren't supposed to have, ah, visitors of the opposite, er, gender. It's a pretty big fine. We could get kicked out of Finney."

"With great risk comes great reward," Isaias said. "I'll be happy to explain, once we get you clothed."

While Isaias tested connections and adjusted lights and checked the sound in the overhead mic—all things that Whit would learn to do as his roommate's apprentice over the next few weeks—Kayla helped Whit move the bunk beds so that he could get into the dresser. Rain rattled against the plate glass window, punctuated by the occasional snap of thunder. Isaias adjusted knobs on the mixer board and repositioned lights, unconcerned with the torrent outside.

As he tinkered with his set up, he filled Whit in on his new project. The equipment, he explained, was all legally checked out of Covenant's media lab, which was happy to arm young Christian filmmakers with the weapons they needed to counter the attacks of Satan so prevalent in mainstream entertainment. Isaias had sweet-talked the communications director into loaning him the lot until after midterms.

"He thinks I'm making a film about overcoming temptation," Isaias said. "I can assure you the truth is much more interesting."

Kayla stood by the window, watching some of the college men playing frisbee in the rain. Whit wondered if she was listening. He fidgeted on his bed. "Then why not just tell the truth?"

"That, Mr. Big Man, is exactly the point."
Whit frowned at him. "I don't like lying."

"Lies are one thing. Subversion is another. Hold this up." He handed Whit a blank piece of copy paper and motioned for him to sit on the stool.

"What's this for?"
"I need to check the white balance."
"No. I mean the, ah—." He patted the seat of the stool.

"It's for sitting down. Now sit." He closed one eye and peered into the viewfinder on the camera. "*Tales from Repression U.* How does that sound for a working title."

Whit glanced at Kayla. Shook his head. "I don't get it."

Isaias stood up straight. Folded his arms across his chest and considered his roommate. "You ever see those books of secrets?" he asked. "The ones where people send in things they've said or done and never told anybody?"

"I guess not."

Isaias nodded as though he expected as much. "It's fascinating stuff. People have all of these things they keep inside—things they're dying to speak to the universe. But no one ever asks for those stories, and so they stay buried."

Kayla had turned toward them now, head cocked to one side and listening.

"So you're going to film people's secrets?" Whit asked.

"I'm going to film the stories they want to tell—real stories about pain, about love. And yes, maybe secrets." He looked over to Kayla. "You ready, hon?" he asked, and motioned for her to take her seat. Once she'd settled in and fussed with her hair for a bit, Isaias lifted his finger to the RECORD button.

"Wait," Kayla said. Doubt clouded her face. "What do I say again?"

"Whatever you want," Isaias said. He offered a reassuring smile. "You had something in mind when you agreed to do this, right?"

"I did." She glanced at Whit. "I'm just not so sure now."

"Don't worry about him," Isaias said. "Nobody judging nobody in this room."

"And you're going to play this back for people? Like a movie?"

Isaias shook his head. "I might. I don't know yet. We'll see what emerges. Right now, I just want to hear your story."

"Can it be funny?"

"It can be anything." He opened his hand toward her. "Whenever you're ready."

A minute later, she had settled into her narrative, a winding confession about some petty vandalism when she was in high school. As Whit understood it, she and a friend had spray painted the outline of male genitalia in blue on the sidewalk in front of the girls' basketball coach's house. More than once, Isaias covered his mouth to stifle his laughter.

If Whit didn't entirely get the point of the story—or, in truth, the point of drawing penises and testicles on sidewalks to begin with—it was not because of the strangeness of her tale. Rather, it was the familiarity. Nearly three years ago, when he was helping Cole Allen ferry Libby up to live with Grandma Helene, his sister had folded a page from her notebook into a paper football and flicked it at him. Cole Allen snapped at her for distracting him while he was driving, and so Whit tucked it into his pocket rather than throw it back at her. He rediscovered it two hours later while he was in a men's room stall at a rest stop outside of Bozeman. He opened it to find a cartoon version of a grown man's privates, beneath which was the caption, *ALL FOR ONE AND ONE FOR ALL*. Having no idea how to interpret such a thing, he'd torn it into tiny pieces and threw it into the toilet. As the flecks swirled down the bowl, he wondered how he should address this with Libby. When he got back to the truck, though, she looked so pleased to see him flustered by her artwork that he resolved not to satisfy her with any form of acknowledgement—now or ever. He kept to his promise, and before long the incident was buried beneath the Gray Butte saga.

He shook off the memory. Tried to focus on the scene in his dorm room. When he looked up, he saw the others staring at him again.

"What?" he asked.

"You were doing this thing," Isaias said. "Like grinding your teeth or something."

"I was?"

"It was loud," Kayla said.

They sat together in silence for a moment, eyes focused on the same corner of the gray rug. At last Isaias turned to Kayla. He spoke with a softness that surprised Whit. "We can try again if you want."

"I don't know," she said.

"Me either," Isaias said. He took in a deep breath. Let it out slowly. "I don't think that was the story you wanted to tell."

Color drained from Kayla's face. "What do you mean?"

"It wasn't bad—don't think that. I just had the feeling that you had a thing you wanted to say, and you said something else instead."

Tears welled up in Kayla's eyes. Whit could feel a tickle starting in his own. He pretended to yawn.

"You're right," Kayla said softly.

Isaias walked to her and squatted down in front of the stool. He laid a hand on her knee. "We don't have to do this now. You can think about it and come back."

"I can?"

"Sure, anytime." He stood up. Smiled at her, then at Whit. "The Big Man and I are just getting started."

Thus, despite the lack of any formal agreement, Whit became Isaias' key accomplice in *The Story Project*, as they'd decided to call it. Isaias taught him how to adjust lights and set microphone levels and run the camera. More important, he showed Whit how to sit still and keep his mouth shut while their peers revealed themselves. The interviewees told funny stories about ruined family vacations, tragic ones of divorce and death and loss, frank ones about love and sex. Isaias had a way of drawing the deeply personal out of his subjects, at times laughing or crying right along with them. He also had a knack for knowing when a story cut too close or had the potential for unintended damage. When he sensed the interview going that direction, he pretended to adjust the lens and discreetly ended the recording. Whit tried to figure out how Isaias could get people to be so honest in front of a camera. It wasn't simply a matter of technique. That would have been easy enough to copy. Rather, it was something about Isaias himself—something at once brash and vulnerable that made people feel safe and courageous. After three weeks and dozens of recording hours, Whit thought he understood the source of his friend's power.

He cared.

Just before midterms, a gunman opened fire in the fellowship hall of a Nazarene church a few blocks from campus, killing nine adults and six children before an associate pastor retrieved his handgun from the office and killed the shooter. The incident rocked the evangelical world, but it demolished whatever sense of security existed at Covenant University. Every slammed door and dropped lunch tray sent students either ducking for cover or drawing their firearms. One sophomore man was expelled for popping a roll of bubble wrap in the mail room, which resulted in a trip to the heart hospital for the elderly mail clerk.

Covenant's response to the attack was to impose something very near to martial law. In a time of chaos, President Timothy Crutcheson told the campus in one chapel sermon, people needed order, and Covenant was ready to give students what they needed. Low tolerance for rule-breakers became zero tolerance. When a late fall heat wave brought temperatures into the 90s for three days, women still wore turtleneck sweaters rather than risk being called out for immodesty. Mandatory chapel attendance went from one day per week to three. Anyone caught with alcohol in the dorms was expelled without a hearing, and sexual misconduct was not only punished, but often made public. Dr. Crutcheson authorized conceal and carry on university grounds, so long as those so armed completed the "Army of God" instructional course taught by a local police officer. For a month solid, Crutcheson himself addressed the student body at every chapel, each time warning them that those who failed to get in line risked not just expulsion, but the very fires of hell.

On the bright side, the tension on campus resulted in a windfall of volunteers for *The Story Project*. People desperate for emotional release practically lined up to talk to Isaias' camera, so many that the men of Finney Hall created a smuggling system to get visitors of all genders into and out of the studio—it was more studio than dorm room by this point, after all—without being seen by Jerry or the other residence hall staff. Whit kept a log of participants. In only a few exhausting days, they recorded dozens of hours of stories from well over a hundred different students. As Halloween approached, Isaias decided they had enough raw footage.

"Okay then," Whit said. "Start tearing down?"

"Not just yet," his friend answered. "One more to go."

They fell into their usual evening routine—Whit plucking at his guitar, Isaias taking notes on his films with headphones clamped tight over his ears—until the sound of finger pads tapping on their door caught Whit's attention. He thumped the outside of Isaias' headphones and opened the door. Without a word, a woman in one of the baggy jackets they used as disguises slipped inside and pulled off the hood.

"Kayla!" Isaias said warmly. He crossed the room and took her hand. "One more try, hon?"

"Yeah. I guess."

"Are you sure, though? That you want me to record this?"

"I'm sure."

"Well all right then."

Isaias adjusted the lighting while Whit worked to position the overhead mic. Within seconds, they were ready.

Whit recognized the familiar elements of her tale—parental strife, invisibility, abandonment, the internal processing of the American young adult. But she bore down hard on the details, staring without blinking as though she and not the camera held the lens into her story. The longer she spoke, the surer Whit became that she was saying more than her words could convey. He closed his eyes. Thought of his sister.

At last Kayla finished. Isaias killed the lights and helped her gather her things and checked the hallway to make sure Jerry would not see her leave. When they were alone again, he squared up to Whit and folded his arms and tapped a fingernail against his incisors.

"What was that?" he asked. "That thing with your teeth."

"My teeth?"

"You were doing it again. That grinding thing."

"Oh, sorry. I didn't realize—was it loud again?"

Isaias eyed him for a long moment. "There's something about Kayla, isn't there?"

"What? No," Whit said. He could feel sweat beading up on his scalp. "I barely even know her."

"But something she said got to you. Come on, Mr. Big Man. Out with it!"

Whit thought hard. Shook his head. "I don't know. I think she just reminds me of my sister."

"Your sister!" Isaias said, clutching a hand to his chest. "You have a sister?"

"I told you that."

"You most certainly never told me that. A sister! Half or full? Older or younger? Tall or short? A sister—and you never even told me."

"I must have," Whit protested, but he could tell it was no use. "Okay then. Full sister, five years younger. She went to live with our grandmother when she was eleven, so we lived apart since then."

"So this sister lives with your grandmother in...?"

"No, Grandma Helene died a year and a half ago, so she's with our mom now."

"With your mom in Wyoming? Or Oklahoma or Arkansas—wherever the hell you're from."

"Tennessee. I mean, that's where they are. Chattanooga." Isaias' eyes widened. Whit raised a hand to fend off the next inquiry, wishing he could start this whole story over but knowing it was no use. Unless he was behind a camera, Isaias couldn't help but interrupt with questions. He sat up straight. "Why don't I sit down and you can record me talking about my sister?"

Isaias shook his head, appalled. "It would be unseemly for the gods to appear in the universe they create. Besides, you haven't finished answering me yet."

"It might be easier."

"Not happening. Please continue."

Whit rolled his eyes and rubbed his long hands over his knees. "She used to be short. I guess I haven't seen her in a while."

"How long is 'a while'?"

"I don't know. Months? Maybe a year?"

"A year!"

"We talk on the phone sometimes."

Isaias brought his fingers again to his mouth, this time pinching his lip the way he did when some new idea occurred to him. At last he snapped his heels together and gave a loud clap. "Time to pack." But when Whit began unplugging cables and winding them up, Isaias balked.

"Leave it!" he commanded. "What I meant to say, good sir, is pack your overnight things. We are going to visit your sister."

CHAPTER 9

They drove through the night.

Whit could not remember exactly where his mother lived, only that it was near one of the three Walmart Supercenters located in Chattanooga. And so, while Isaias slept in the passenger seat, Whit looked for the telltale signs of American retail—the sodium lights, the gas stations, the fast-food restaurants—and hoped for a street that looked familiar. Nothing matched the images in his head, however, and the needle on his fuel indicator seemed to drop by the mile. At last he pulled off into a shaded neighborhood for a quick nap. He had barely fallen asleep before he felt Isaias shaking him.

"Brother Big Man," Isaias whispered. "Where have you taken us?"

Whit rubbed his forehead and looked around with more critical eyes than he'd used coming in. Around them were mansions the size of Dr. Crutcheson's presidential residence—four-story brick affairs that occupied half a block. He opened his door to stretch his legs, but the movement set off some sensor in the house nearest to them. Yellow light instantly flooded the yard and the edge of the street.

Isaias sank in his seat. "Do you know how many Black people live in this neighborhood?" he asked.

"No. How would I know that?"

"Zero!" Isaias was nearly shouting. "The exact same number as Whitmans who live here. Now let's go before the cops come."

"Cops?"

"Just drive the damn car."

"Where to? We're lost."

"Anywhere but here."

Whit started the pickup again and pulled away, careful not to gun the engine too loudly. A few turns later, they were back on

Dodson Avenue, heading south. Isaias pointed to a sign for Mercy Medical Center. "You said your mom is a nurse?"

"Right. In the emergency room."

"What are the chances she's at work?"

Whit did not answer. Nevertheless, he followed the signs to the ER. They entered through the automatic sliding doors. Without so much as a word, Isaias veered off to an empty place in the waiting room and curled up catlike on one of the vinyl sofas. Whit managed to get a bored desk worker to check if Bethany Whitman was at work.

"You mean Bethany Farris?" she asked.

"I don't think so."

"Well that's the only Bethany on tonight. Maybe that's who you mean. Hang on and I'll find her. What is your name again?"

The woman punched in a code into the box above the handle to a door behind her desk. Once she'd disappeared, Whit began to wonder if she were really checking on his mother, or if she were going to fetch security. A few seconds later, however, the door opened again, and his mother strode through into the waiting room.

"Whit!" she snapped. "Oh what the hell! Are you okay?"

"I'm fine."

"Then what are you doing here?"

"I came to see you and Lib."

"For God's sake, though." She ran her hands over her face. Laced them together on top of her head and took stock of her son. "How long's it been since I saw you?"

"About a year. Maybe."

"Well, you should have called. Honey, I've got to get back to work."

"I can't remember, though. How to get to your house. I have a friend with me too."

Whit motioned toward Isaias, curled up on his chair and snoring. Bethany winced.

"He's—," she began, but stopped. "Never mind. Y'all just sit tight. I get off work at 5:00. You can follow me home."

Home was not how Whit would have described his mother's house. He'd been there only twice, once for Christmas and once for a birthday—he couldn't remember whose. When they arrived, Isaias fell onto the couch and was asleep before he hit the cushions. Bethany motioned for Whit to be quiet as he followed her into the kitchen. She made coffee with the quick efficiency of the Waffle House waitress she'd been during nursing school. From there she veered into the laundry room, stripping off the top of her scrubs as she went. She'd gained a bit of weight since he'd last seen her, but she had tight muscles across her shoulders and back, with pale, smooth skin that reminded him that she was still a young woman. Whit looked away, embarrassed.

But it wasn't Bethany's reaction to his Black friend or the sight of her in a bra that most bothered Whit. It was the golden band she'd picked up from a bowl below the light switch and placed on her left ring finger. He slid the name badge she'd left on the table across and looked at it while she pulled on a clean T-shirt. "Bethany Farris, LPN." Farris. When had that happened? He felt he should know, and so didn't ask.

"Morning sweetie," she said to someone behind Whit. He turned to see his sister glide into the room on bare feet.

"Hey," Libby said in reply, and then looked squarely at Whit. "What's up, dumbass?"

She went to the sink and laid her head on their mother's shoulder. Bethany kissed the crown of her head. "I'm going to go take a shower," she said. "Why don't you two catch up?"

Libby poured two mugs of coffee and sat down across from Whit. "That your girlfriend on the couch?"

"Just a friend."

She shoveled three scoops of sugar into her mug. Slid the dish across to Whit. "How's college life?"

"Different."

"I thought you'd be right at home with all the Jesus freaks."

"Don't start." He lifted the mug and smelled the coffee inside. Glanced over the rim at his sister. She was what, fourteen? Fifteen? But she had filled out in womanly ways. If she'd showed up at Covenant, she would have blended in with the freshmen girls. A ray of orange-yellow light shone through the window, and another thought occurred to him. "Why are you up so early."

"Light sleeper," she said, but it sounded like *sleep-uh,* more Tennessee than Wyoming. "Did mom tell you she got married?"

"I saw the ring. Why didn't anybody tell me?"

Libby lowered her chin and looked at him over the lip of her coffee mug. "I'll let you work that one out for yourself."

Whit sipped his coffee. His brain was running on fumes. "How's school?"

"Fine, I guess. I got expelled." She studied his face. Seemed disappointed with his reaction. "It was a big misunderstanding, really. This girl was bullying one of my friends, and so I had a talk with her.

"A...talk?"

She shrugged. "After I smashed her over the head with a metal lunch tray." She smiled at the memory in a way Whit didn't like.

"You tell Dad?" he asked.

"No. And you won't either."

"I think he'd want to know if you were in trouble."

"Since when does our father want to know anything about me, trouble or otherwise?"

Whit looked down at the rainbow-colored film on top of his coffee, thinking that those who said they liked the taste were probably lying. He took a drink anyway. "I worry about you."

Libby cackled. "You might as well be a goddamned therapist, talking like that." She leaned forward on her elbows. Stared hard at her brother. "You can shove your worry up your ass. I'm fine."

"No you're not."

"Then I'm a lost cause."

Whit rubbed his eyes, trying to remember what had possessed him to drive all night to get here. "Just tell me what happened—the whole thing, I mean."

Libby wrapped her hands around her mug and tilted her head, looking—to Whit's relief—like a child once more. "It's a long story."

"I have time."

"You assume I want to tell it."

Above them, the pipes shuddered as their mother turned off the shower. They looked up together, following the creaks of her footsteps across the floor.

"What about Mom?" Whit asked.

"She's starting to show, huh?"

The sip of coffee in his mouth seemed to congeal into one solid lump and held its shape all the way down. "Show?"

"Come on, bro. Even you aren't that clueless. She's due around Christmas. Know what they're going to name the kid?"

"No..."

"Zebadiah," she whispered. "You believe that?"

Whit shook his head, tried to focus. "So this means—he'll be our brother?"

"Half-brother, if you want to be more precise. Half mom, half her dickhead husband."

"Husband," he repeated.

"Yeah. Byron." Libby smiled. Stretched her arms over her head and yawned. "Don't worry—you get used to the idea. Go on and lay down. You look like shit."

Two hours later, Whit's eyes popped open, the lids pried apart by the sudden, terrifying realization that it was Sunday morning.

According to Covenant policy, students who did not attend services on campus had to present a signed bulletin from the church they attended to a member of the residence life staff when they returned to the dorm. Most RAs looked the other way, preferring to spend their relational capital on matters of more consequence to communal living. Not so with Jerry Fosdick, the RA on Isaias' and Whit's floor, who demanded that every jot and tittle of the law be performed. Unfortunately for Whit, Isaias did not share his aversion to white lies—"luxury of being a non-white, Brother Big Man"—and left Whit to face Sunday morning on his own. Bethany and Byron were both asleep, and Libby offered no pretense about her feelings.

"Have fun," she told Whit. "I'm sure church is good for people like you."

Whit agreed, though not as enthusiastically as he would have liked. In truth, he believed in God more by rote than by intuition, and he supposed that had always been the case. Thankfully, the storefront church near his mother's house let out in only ninety minutes, and the pastor was more than happy to autograph a bulletin for him. He stole a second one for Isaias and presented it to him back at the house. He and Libby had become fast friends—everyone did with Isaias, it seemed—and had spent the morning drinking coffee and swapping stories. On the way back to Covenant, Whit asked his friend if he'd learned anything worthwhile from the conversation.

"What's that supposed to mean?" Isaias asked.

"Did she tell you anything important. Anything I'd need to know."

"Well now those are two different questions. A lot of what she said was important. Your sister is a fascinating girl—and sharp for her age, let me tell you. But things you need to know?" He laid his head back against the headrest. Drummed his fingers on his thighs. "Your mama—that's the one you need to talk to."

"She got married. I know." He held up his ring finger and wiggled it.

"That's one thing," Isaias said.

"And she's pregnant."

"You think? She's got a baby bump the size of a cantaloupe. Your sister said you didn't even notice."

"I noticed."

"Before Libby told you?"

Whit let that slide. "I noticed."

"You got to watch, Brother Big Man. You got to listen. Otherwise you'll end up lost. Or dead."

CHAPTER 10

When he opened the door to his room in Finney Hall later that night, Whit asked himself—and not for the last time—whether death might actually be preferable to the reality in front of him. The lights and cameras and microphones from their interview stage had been dismantled and stuffed into cases, all neatly stacked beside the door. On top of the stack was the laptop computer Isaias had been using to edit the video files. Three men in dark suits—Brother Arneson, Dr. Crutcheson, and Cole Allen Whitman—sat in folding chairs beside the window. The way they comported themselves, however, they might as well have been wearing black hoods and carrying scythes.

"Hello gentlemen," Dr. Crutcheson said. He put his hands on his knees and pushed himself up. "Mr. Granderson, if you'll follow me please."

Isaias crossed his arms tightly against his chest. Looked up at the ceiling while Crutcheson repeated his name. At last, Isaias turned to Whit, palms up, and smiled.

"To the gallows," he called cheerfully. "Trai-la-lee, trai-la-lai!"

Whit opened his mouth to speak, but had no idea what was going on, much less how he should respond to it. Still, he would have rather gone with Isaias and taken his chances with the executioner than to turn and face the two others who sat behind him.

"Son," Cole Allen said gravely. "You better sit down."

"I'm fine," Whit answered.

His father winced. Stole a glance across at Brother Arneson, who grunted with disapproval.

"Sit down, young man," Arneson boomed.

Whit sat. "What's he doing with Isaias?"

"We have reason to believe that your friend is guilty of academic fraud," Arneson said. "Mr. Granderson turned in work that was not his own. To put it plainly, he's been cheating. As have several of the people you interviewed."

"They have?" He thought about that. Wrinkled his nose. "That seems unlikely."

"I don't really care how it seems to you," Arneson said.

"Isaias doesn't usually turn in work, though," Whit said. "He says homework—."

"Don't back talk me!" Arneson snapped. He leaned forward, elbows on knees. "As I said, we have uncovered an epidemic of cheating among some of your friends. And as you failed to report any of this inappropriate activity, I consider you an accomplice. Such a shame, too—the mountains I moved to get you into Covenant, and on scholarship no less."

He shook his head sadly. Whit turned up his palms.

"The videos, son!" Cole Allen hissed. "The videos!"

All three men reflexively looked at the dark screen of the laptop. Arneson calmly walked over to it and ran a finger over the track pad. Almost instantly, Heather Frank appeared, smiling bashfully as Isaias finished adjusting lights. The volume was muted, but Whit didn't need to hear to remember the story she'd told about discovering that she was bisexual. It was one of the longer interviews they'd done, and it included more than one pause for tears. Isaias had intended to edit out the most vulnerable portions of the interview when they got back from Chattanooga. But if the men had accessed the computer, they'd seen the raw footage—for Heather and dozens of others.

"Oh God," Whit mumbled. A half second later, his father's cupped hand smacked into his left ear.

"You know better," Cole Allen snapped. "You're in enough trouble without taking the Lord's name in vain."

Whit didn't answer. He had listened in on interviews with maybe half a dozen gay men and women since the project started, and while he still didn't quite know how to square that with the preaching he'd heard all his life, he could see that a complicated humanity was at work. The thought of his father and Brother Arneson and Dr. Crutcheson sitting in judgment on the story when they weren't even in the room felt like a violation.

"It's because some of them are gay or bi or something else," Whit said. "That's why you're doing this."

"Son—"

"Call it for what it is. We didn't cheat on anything."

Brother Arneson held up a hand. Whit could see fine white hairs sticking out across his curled knuckles. "I'm afraid that's what all cheaters claim."

"Say what you mean," Whit said. "Go on."

"What I mean to say is that we have substantial proof of academic violations," Arneson said. "Now, as an institution of higher education whose students receive federal loans, we cannot discriminate on the basis of homosexuality. We don't condone it, but those are the rules forced on us by the government. Our decision is strictly academic."

"We didn't cheat," Whit repeated, but he knew already it was no use. He and Isaias and their friends who had interviewed had been convicted without regard to actual guilt, and nothing he could say would sway the jury. Still, the injustice of it pounded on his brain. Another thought rose in his mind. "How did you get in here? How did you even know about those interviews? Was it Jerry?"

"An anonymous source did his duty to God and institution," Arneson said.

"I want to see your proof."

Cole Allen's hand flew out once again toward Whit's ear. This time he was ready for it. He knocked it away.

"Boy, I didn't raise you to be disrespectful," his father said. "You listen up."

"Now let's just all calm down," Arneson said. "The real question is what happens now—to *you*." He jabbed a hairy finger toward Whit's chest.

Whit sat up straight. Even seated, he was a head taller than the other two men. But Brother Arneson was not one to be intimidated, what with the Lord on his side. He smiled. Folded his hands in his lap. Allowed time for Whit to run through his lousy options before finally speaking again.

"I believe we have a plan, your father and I, that Dr. Crutcheson will also agree to. You'd best consider our offer before you make your plea."

PART II

Figure 4: Part I Refresher

CHAPTER 11

Whit emerged from the Trujillo airport into a noisy and strangely lit Peruvian world. He'd embarked from Montgomery, AL, after agreeing to take an *Incomplete* grade in each of his courses for the fall. Once his plane crossed the equator, however, the seasons flipped. Summer was just around the corner, and the high angle of the sun cast shadows in unexpected places, making it hard for his brain to convert light signals into objects. He had to squint for several seconds before he finally realized that one of the taxi drivers was motioning toward him with a handwritten sign that read, "Wiht—EEUU." Whit walked carefully to the car. The driver threw his bag into the backseat of the Yaris while Whit folded himself into the front, only to discover that the seatbelt was jammed.

For the next half hour, Whit had a close-up view of city commuting, Peruvian style. The driver zoomed in and out of traffic, squeezing the little car into spaces that looked impossible, blasting his horn in varying rhythms according to some communication system Whit never would be able to parse. The trip felt like a midway ride at some small-time carnival, sheer speed and gravity, combined in nauseating proportions. All Whit could do was stare straight ahead, trying not to see, and go over for the thousandth time how it came to this.

Unlike Isaias, who had been expelled along with seventeen others for "academic fraud," Whit had been given a choice between finishing out the semester under probationary conditions—meaning with his balls in a vise cranked by Jerry Fosdick—or joining the university's international missions program, which had lost scores of participants to domestic political action groups since the last election. Whit was prepared to tell Reverend Crutcheson where to shove his offer, but Isaias talked him out of it, framing his participation in the program as an act of civil disobedience.

"You take their money," his friend said. "Maybe find a part of the world that isn't so irreparably back-assward as Covenant. And then you finish your degree somewhere else and never give them another cent. Sound good?"

"I don't know," Whit answered. "It doesn't feel right—after what they did to you, I mean."

"To me?" Isaias wrinkled his nose. "What they did, Brother Big Man, is release me. They have set me free. It's time to move, and move I shall."

And so Whit had decided to move too, partly because of Isaias' encouragement and partly because he had no idea what else to do. Given the choice by the mission organizers between a tourist town off the coast of Peru or a shepherd village in the Mongolian highlands, Whit decided to go where it was warm and he had a fighting chance of learning the language.

"*Treinta y cinco soles*," the cabbie said when he dropped a breathless Whit onto the street in front of a convenience store named Roger's. Whit was too rattled to check his Covenant-issued guidebook for translation, much less to pull up any of the Jesus-saves jargon that had been drilled into his head at missionary boot camp. He pulled out a $20 bill. The driver laughed, and Whit feared he may have short-changed the man. Before he could fish out another bill, however, the cabbie noticed someone coming from behind Whit. A half second later, he snatched the $20 and made for his car. Before he could get back into traffic, however, a stout woman of about sixty threw open the passenger door. She shouted in dizzying Spanish syllables, gestured back and forth between the man and Whit. At last the driver handed her several Peruvian bills and pulled away, reaching over to shut the passenger door as he merged. The woman sent him off with a dismissive wave, turned to Whit and looked him square in the face.

"Yoonius," she said slowly. "You are called Whit?"

"Yes."

"You're late." She stood on her tip toes and made a kissing sound toward each of Whit's cheeks, which remained a good foot and a half above her reach. "Come. We have work to do. Call me Pilar."

Operación Amor, the residential center that served as Whit's missionary placement, was half a mile or so from Roger's. Pilar led the way, walking slowly but determinedly, winding through a maze of narrow sidewalks, past honking cars and gawking pedestrians. He could feel their eyes on him, the white-skinned giant moving through their midst, greeted at every turn with a cry of *Dios mio!* One group of girls asked to get a picture with him. As he turned toward the camera, a thin older woman sidled up to him and put her arm around his waist.

"Smile!" she said. "You are in a wonderful place, don't you think?"

"Right," Whit answered. "I am. Wonderful. *Muy bonito.*"

The girls snapped photos with their smartphones and told him thank you and walked on, giggling.

"We've got to work on that accent," Pilar said.

"Call me Tía Luz," the other woman said. She studied his face. "You look hungry. I worry about you."

"I'm fine. Maybe tired."

"I don't think it is a maybe thing. Did you eat?"

"A little. On the plane."

"No, no," Tía Luz said, her face scrunched in disapproval. "That is not real food. It is—how do you say it?—crap. Come. We are almost there."

They made a right turn, then a left, then another right, past an enormous open field Whit guessed at a quarter mile on each side.

Trash was piled haphazardly across the dirt, pushed into mounds here and there by a man running an old skid-steer. A hundred or more people—many of them children—sifted through the piles. Whit did not let himself wonder for what.

Just past the dump, Tía Luz veered to the left, down a low hill and onto a poorly paved road. Gray sewage ran in the ditch to their right, on its way to irrigate patches of tomatoes and beans that grew in the fields behind the makeshift houses. They wound their way back to a two-story concrete building partially dug into the side of a hill. Pilar inserted a key that turned the heavy lock. She pushed the door open and walked inside, leaving Luz and Whit to face the dumbstruck children who had stopped their play to marvel at this giant with the white skin and enormous glasses.

"*Niños!*" Tía Luz called, and spread her arms.

That broke the spell. The younger kids all ran up to hug her, politely waiting their turn until she had greeted each child by name, placing a loving hand on their heads in blessing. Whit fought the urge to reach up and touch his own, remembering the way Brother Arneson and Reverend Crutcheson and Cole Allen had made him kneel right there in the airport so that they could place their hands on his head and pray the Spirit into him. So lengthy and fervent was their prayer that an apologetic security guard had to ask them to please keep it down. While the three men grumbled about what this country was coming to, that Christians couldn't even pray in public, Whit went to the bathroom to try to wash off the holy-roller handprints.

Tía Luz' touch was different, though. He could see that even from a distance. She was not imparting power, as the men had tried to do to him. No, she was simply telling the children that she loved them and moving them along so that they didn't cling to her. And when she'd finished with the little kids, she moved to the brick wall along the flower bed where a dozen older kids sat, playing it cool. They rolled their eyes but let her fuss over them until they couldn't help but smile. The whole thing took at least fifteen minutes—enough time for Whit to wonder if Tía Luz remembered him at all. Finally she turned and motioned toward him and made an introduction in Spanish. He caught maybe every tenth word—tall, friend, America, university, church. Her last sentence made the kids laugh. She turned around and translated it into English for him.

"I tell them get used to looking up at this big guy. He's going to be around for a while."

The next morning, Whit woke in a near panic. Not that he didn't know where he was, although the smell of saltwater and the sight of the baby blue walls were a momentary jolt to his senses. But that passed quickly enough, clearing his mind to ponder with devastating clarity that he was now a resident of a foreign land, and that he was going to miss church.

For all the hostility he'd developed toward religion since his and Isaias' sentencing, Whit had maintained the habit of weekly worship. It was, if nothing else, a pole by which to calibrate his compass. Even in those wilderness years between Wyoming and Alabama, when they were seldom in the same town for two holidays in a row, the Whitman boys had always managed to find a place to pray and sing hymns and listen to preaching. Going to church was built into the very fabric of Whit's identity. Missing it felt like chopping through the bungee cord while he was still dangling from the bridge.

Before the first tear had even hit his pillow, he heard human sounds on the concrete floor outside his room—little feet shuffling past, the door swinging open, a child sniffling. Whit froze. He wasn't about to turn over and let one of the kids he was supposed to be helping see him crying like a baby. Plus, he suddenly became aware of the morning stiffness in his crotch, and he knew without question that he'd rather cry a million tears than have his anatomy become the story the kids told. He lay still and hoped whoever was there would go away. Instead he felt a tap on his shoulder, and he heard a girl's voice.

"*Señor, cocinara usted la almuerza? Los niños tienen hambre. Señor?*"

Whit rolled onto his stomach, wiping his face on the pillow as he turned to face the girl. He remembered her from the thin scar above her left eyebrow, a line of white inlaid on her dark skin. She had been sitting on the wall with the older kids, even though she looked no more than twelve. He searched his memory for her name but came up empty.

"The kids," she said, and pointed to her mouth. "Hungry." He blinked away tears to get a better look at her face. Sweet though her voice might be, the girl wasn't playing around. She crossed her arms and stared at the edge of his pillow, just below his face. Spoke the English words with unmistakable clarity. "You cook."

He heard footsteps on the metal stairs at the end of the hall.

"Yesenia!" a woman called.

An instant later, a slim figure appeared in the doorway. She was about the same age as Whit, but the similarities stopped there. This was another creature entirely, beautiful and commanding and fierce as a mountain lion. She rattled off an admonition in Spanish that felt like verbal bullets whizzing past Whit's head. It wasn't until the girl slipped out of the room that he realized the woman was not yelling at the child, but at him.

"Sorry," he said once she paused for air.

The woman put her hands on her hips. "They said you spoke Spanish."

"I'm not very good. Yet."

"*Ay, Dios mio.*" She pinched the bridge of her nose between the thumb and forefinger of her strong hands. "This is not going to work."

"I'll get better. It's—I just got here. You can't say it's not working if I just got here."

"Okay. But we can't have a grown man sleeping on the same floor with a bunch of young girls. Who put you in here?"

"Tía Luz."

She threw up her hands. "Mama! Jesus Christ!"

Whit did a mental check to make sure nature had retreated enough that he could sit on the edge of the bed. He pulled himself upright and swung his legs around and looked closer at the woman. She did bear the image of Tía Luz, now that he thought of them together. Her daughter, then, but not as kind. She put one hand back on her hip and motioned with the other for him to get up.

"You've got to cook," she said. "I'll help you. This one time."

Whit held one foot against the base of the door as he got dressed, just in case Yesenia or some other kid tried to walk into his room again. When he came downstairs into the patio area a few minutes later, he was surprised to see that it was already full daylight. The older kids were playing soccer and hopscotch while the little ones ran after one another in no apparent pattern. He passed through them and into the open-air kitchen on the west side of the patio. The woman was standing at the sink, filling an enormous stainless steel pot with water.

"I'm Whit," he said.

"Fine. Start washing the carrots." He picked up the bowl and brought it to the sink compartment next to her. When he reached for the tap, she slapped his hand. "No! You can't use it from the tap unless you boil it first. Use that." She pointed to a large plastic jug of water mounted to a homemade spigot in the corner. "And wash your hands."

He did as he was told, first with the carrots, then with the rice, then with the chicken. By then the sun was glaring off the smooth concrete of the patio, sending rays of light and heat bouncing into the kitchen. Whit knew better than to complain. Instead he followed the lead of Luz' daughter until it was time to make the plates. She made a sample so he would know how to arrange and portion each item and left him to it while she got the children settled in the dining room. When they had finished serving the kids, she handed him a plate and made one for herself.

"Milagros," she said.

"Milagros," he answered. "Amen."

She laughed. "Milagros is my name. It means 'miracle.'"

"Oh. Right, well. *Mucho gusto.*" He wiped his hand on a nearby towel and extended it to her. She let it hang between them for a second before she took it.

"*Mucho gusto*," she said, her face as unreadable as a hieroglyph. "You really have no clue about anything, do you?"

Whit tried to think of a way to defend himself. A quick sorting of the facts produced only one logical response, however. "I don't. I'm trying. But no. No clue."

She pinched her nose again, but this time she smiled. "At least you're an honest guy."

"To a fault."

"I can work with that." She sat her plate on the counter. Clapped her hands onto her thighs. "My mother is not the best at thinking through details. She is the more trusting kind than I am. She should have given you better instructions. And she should not have let you stay in that room."

"It's okay," Whit said, but couldn't read Milagros' face. "I mean, I'm sorry."

"I just have to protect the kids, you know? Make sure you aren't a pervert."

"I'm not."

"Oh I believe you, but—." She let the words trail off. Held up her palms for a long second, and then dropped them onto her thighs and sighed. "Go pack up your things."

"Where can I go?"

"Just pack."

Mila—as he would learn to call her—drove with the same aggression as his taxi driver, weaving in and out of traffic and blowing through intersections as if she were in a video game. He acclimated more quickly this time, however, and soon was taking stock of the rows of shops and apartments in a higher rent district than the one where Operación Amor was located. Before long, the street opened up into a park to his right. A huge concrete monument depicted soldiers at war and peasants struggling for justice. A giant yellow church whose age Whit couldn't even guess at rose up on the left side of the street.

"*Plaza de Armas*," Mila explained. "Lots of history, if you're into that sort of thing."

She turned south, then west, then south again, finally stopping in what looked to Whit like a wide alley. She got out of the car and opened a heavy iron door and pulled the car in.

"My parents' house," she said. "Let me do the talking."

It was not exactly a house, at least according to his American definition. The structure shared its brick side walls with the dwellings next door, like the old downtown buildings in Claremore. Above him, a sheet-iron roof covered three quarters of the garage, leaving plenty of space for natural light and what little rain fell on this costal desert to filter in. While Mila closed the iron door behind him, Whit examined the structure of the home itself. Directly in front of him were two doors, with the kitchen on the left and a small dining room on the right. Two more concrete stories were built onto the first, and the columns on the top floor had rebar sticking out six feet above the concrete in case another became necessary. City living, Whit thought. Nowhere to go but up.

He followed Mila down a long hallway lined with entrances to other small rooms. A metal staircase ascended in a spiral in the center of the house, but Mila strode past it, out into a patio area. Laundry hung from two lines stretched from wall to wall, partially obscuring a small garden of flowering vines and lime trees. They passed through it all, finally stopping at a tool shed in back. A stout Peruvian man in a white t-shirt paused from cleaning an old carburetor and offered a courtesy smile toward Whit.

"*Quien es?*" he asked Mila.

As father and daughter conversed, Whit tried to pick up Spanish words or phrases that he recognized, holding each in his mind until he could translate it into English. *Casa* means house. *Habitación* means room. *No* means no, which was easy enough to translate, but also something both Mila and her father seemed to be saying a lot. After a while, Whit gave up, tired of identifying verbal trees when there seemed to be a lot more at stake in the conversational forest. Mila kept pointing to the door to the shed. She went over and opened it so that she could gesture inside, and he saw that it was actually a one-room apartment with a bed, a small dresser, a tiny table and two chairs. Two five-foot screens were set up in the corner, he assumed to hide the toilet and shower.

"*El es más alto del cielo,*" the man said.

"*Pero esto es mejor de vivir con las niñas. Puedes imaginar, papa!*"

The older man stopped to think. At last he looked up and said the first thing Whit had truly understood since they'd arrived at the house.

"Okay."

And with that, Whit was home.

Figure 5: Plaza de Armas

CHAPTER 12

As he became more familiar with the streets and landmarks, Whit began to understand that traffic in Trujillo wasn't defined so much by haste as space. The streets were too narrow for so many commuters. A person had to stick his nose out into the fray if he wanted to get anywhere. But doing so—especially on a bicycle, which was Whit's only means of transportation—took a kamikaze approach.

One morning on the way to the Plaza de Armas—the park where he'd seen the giant stone statues that first Sunday with Mila—he'd encountered a Chinese man thinking more about where he needed to be than where he actually was. Whit was in front of the yellow cathedral, waiting to cross so he could make his way to the currency exchange, when the man whizzed by on his bike. In his haste to get ahead of the flow, he neglected to check traffic at the intersection. He was still pedaling when he t-boned a taxi at near full-speed. The force of impact was enough to hurl him headfirst over the hood and into the side of a box truck. Even over the noise of engines and car horns, Whit could hear the collision. Like a cantaloupe against concrete, as he would write to Libby. The poor man was dead as soon as he hit the pavement. A young priest ran out from the Catedral de Santa Maria la Menor and began administering last rites. Two policemen who had been keeping tourists off the grass at the plaza chased him away and dragged the man's body out of the street. The priest stepped back to where Whit stood and spoke to him in English.

"Don't see that every day," he said cheerfully. "Maybe once a month, though. My, you are a big fellow. Do you enjoy coffee?"

As it turned out, Father Guillermo had come to Trujillo in much the same way as Whit—that is to say, because it was the least bad of the miserable options before him. He'd been born to wealthy parents in Argentina, but a romantic meltdown with the child of a

General presented him with a choice between becoming a *castrado* or entering the priesthood. Guillermo decided he would rather live intact and celibate than give up the family jewels, so to speak. His father arranged for him to study at Notre Dame, which led to a friendship with the archbishop of Peru, which landed him a position as curate at the *Catedral de Santa Maria la Menor* upon graduation two years ago.

"Like the kids say, you can't make this shit up," Father Guillermo said as they sipped coffee in a little shop two blocks from the Plaza. "Like your name."

"My...name?"

"*Junius*. It is Greek. You know this, right?"

"I guess. It's from the Bible."

"The book of Romans, yes. 'Greet Junia, prominent among the apostles.' She was a friend of the Apostle Paul."

"She?"

"Ah! You see the difficulty, but you do not know why." He leaned forward on his elbows. Raised his hands as he explained. "The King James Version that is popular in the States lists *Junius*, which would be a male name. But the Greek almost certainly refers to a female—*una mujer*—who was a prominent leader. Later on, the men running the church decided it would not do for a woman to have authority, and so they performed a verbal transitioning, you see?"

Whit nodded and sipped his coffee, which was his typical response to the Father's musings. Half the time he had no clue what his friend was saying, particularly when it referred to some minutia of doctrine or mood of some Greek verb. For Whit, faith had always been dynamic, immediate. The further he let himself delve into the underlying questions, however, the more he realized how little he had to undergird his beliefs. Father Guillermo seemed to find the complicated world of academic religion endlessly fascinating. Whit suspected few people seriously listened to him and so was glad to lend an ear.

"Your Spanish," the priest said all at once. "We've got to work on your Spanish."

"It's getting better."

"Ah yes, for certain. But your Spanish, it is all concrete—everyday nouns, everyday verbs. It is a child's version of language. You spend all day working with kids, no?"

"Not all day," Whit said, although he had to admit there was truth in the accusation. He cooked and cleaned around Operación Amor, gave guitar lessons to a few of the kids, did some shopping. He could follow conversations well enough and usually speak without one of the kids laughing at him.

"But you have no language for what you seek," Father insisted. "You cannot share your ideas. Your speech is—how should I put it?—transactional. How does one speak of love when one only has words for counting change?"

"Love?"

"*Bien.*" He leaned forward. Smiled broadly. "I know you want the girl. Mila."

Whit's face went hot, and he knew every dark-skinned Peruvian on the street could see him blushing. "I wouldn't say 'want.'"

"Ah but that is the word! I can see it in your eyes, my friend."

"You do?"

"Do you think I cannot see such things?" he said, turning up his palms in protest. "Do you think I don't know what it is to want?"

"No. I mean, I guess you do."

"Of course I do!" He leaned forward. Spoke in English. "Look, becoming a priest doesn't mean you lose your need for intimacy, okay? Neither does it mean you can't recognize desire when you see it. If you were Catholic, I would have much to say about marriage and children and the family. But you are a Protestant and so I have no responsibility for that. Go do your thing, as the kids say. It is clear you want Mila, perhaps according to multiple definitions of wanting. This is your story, though, and I am doing all the talking. Tell me about her."

"Well, she's—"

"In Spanish."

"*Si, claro*," he said, but immediately fell to stammering. Father Guillermo responded with a self-satisfied grin. He was gracious enough not to pursue the subject any further that day, but he'd laid bare thoughts that Whit had refused to let his conscious mind entertain. Three months after his arrival, Mila was still showing up on Sunday mornings to help him cook for the children. She claimed it was so that the kids got a break from his awful cooking, but she would spritz him with water from the newly washed vegetables, would sidle up to him at the sink and bump him to one side with her hips. When the kitchen grew hot during these summer days, she would bunch up her t-shirt and tie it in front, leaving her smooth brown midriff exposed. He tried not to think about touching her, about more than touching her.

"Who can understand the heart of a woman?" Father Guillermo said. "It is difficult enough on its own, but impossible without knowing the language by which she expresses herself. Next time we meet, speak only Spanish. I will help you."

As valuable as Father Guillermo's Spanish lessons were, it was participating in the daily life of the Paredes family that worked most deeply on Whit's soul. True, Carlos and Tia Luz fought almost every day, shouting in clipped Spanish that he now understood at about sixty percent. Every now and again, Carlos would move into his work room, adjacent to Whit's bedroom, and sleep until things quieted down. Whit noted their interactions, waiting for the blow up he knew from his own childhood must be coming. When no such explosion came, he watched in near wonder, trying without success to imagine Cole Allen Whitman behaving with any such restraint.

Over time, the family began to incorporate him more into their everyday tasks. Luz was the first to draw him out, asking him to help with her with her faltering patio garden. He would rise early to weed and hoe and water before leaving for his job at OA, then help prune the plants in the evening. Once Carlos found out that Whit was a mechanic, he began asking him to help with the small engine rebuilds that constituted most of his business.

"But what about the girl?" Guillermo—he'd asked Whit to drop the "Father" when they were speaking English—asked one day at the coffee shop. "She is your real interest, no?"

"Not really. I came here to help the kids. And I'm helping the Paredes to pay them back for the apartment. They're nice people."

"That's what you think of Mila? That she's nice?"

"Yeah," he said, but immediately reevaluated. "She can be nice sometimes."

"And that's all you think?"

Whit reached for a napkin to blow his nose, hoping to hide his blush. He'd gotten bolder in his fantasies of late, daring to imagine Mila lying unclothed in the patio garden, her dark body surrounded by the scents of mint and cilantro. The thought inevitably produced certain physical responses, which were muted by the echo of Bonner Hanson's warning that women were a greater danger to his soul than any chemical he might ingest. However true that may be, Whit saw no way to confess his desires even to himself, much less to a celibate priest.

"I think she's a nice girl," he said. "That's all."

Guillermo smiled broadly. "You are, as the kids say, full of shit."

"I—"

"No." He held up a hand. "Tell me more about her. What does she do? What things does she like? Where does she work?"

Mila's employment had been a mystery to Whit ever since he moved into the Paredes' spare apartment. Best he could tell, she worked some sort of accounting job for a collection of small businesses that included a laundry, a grocery, and a music store. If she had hobbies beyond volunteering at Operación Amor, Whit never saw them. At night, he could see her silhouette through the curtain to her room, which overlooked the patio on the second floor, but he could not make out any discernible activity, except for the rare occasions when she leaned out the windows to curse the noisy roosters their neighbor kept staked to a chair on his roof.

"Roosters?" Guillermo said with disgust. "Do not tell me she is into cockfighting."

"I think she just hates the noise."

"Then perhaps you should offer her a different something to listen to. You are a musician. You teach the guitar to children, no? You play well enough to woo the girl?"

"I've never tried."

"*Ay, Dios mio!* You have grown so tall and yet your brain is a child." He leaned in closer. "Here is the thing you do. Get out your guitar and play it beneath her window. Do you sing?"

"Not really."

"It's okay. Playing is enough. Choose something lively, but sweet. Perhaps haunting. Something that will make her forget about the chickens."

"Roosters."

Guillermo smacked his hand against the table. "See? You've made me forget just by talking about it."

Every time they met for the next two weeks, Guillermo asked if Whit had made his play for Mila. The priest cajoled and threatened and called him a chickenshit in three languages, warning him that she would soon grow tired of waiting and he would lose his opportunity. When Whit asked how he was so sure about all of this,

Guillermo wagged a finger and said, "Remember, I was a man before I was a priest."

CHAPTER 13

When the thought of one more harangue from his friend at last became less palatable than rejection from Mila, Whit decided to act. After work one night, he packed up the guitar he kept at OA to play with the children and brought it home. Later, once he and Carlos finished rebuilding the engine for a moped, Whit tuned up the instrument and took a seat on an ancient wooden bench beneath Mila's window. He wrapped his long fingers around the neck, settled his other hand over the strings, and realized he had no idea what to play. After several minutes, he decided to simply pick through a chord progression until something emerged. He'd barely made it a single measure before one of the roosters began to crow, screeching like prophets at the end of the world. A half second later, Mila thrust her head and shoulders out the window and cast a death glare at the dumb fowl. She drew in breath to curse them in Spanish, as Whit had heard her do a hundred times. But then she saw him sitting below, guitar in his lap.

"What the hell?" she said. "Are you serenading the roosters?"

"No."

She folded her hands beneath her chin and leaned forward on her elbows. "Then are you serenading me?"

"I'm just playing."

"Oh. Well, then play something interesting at least."

He nodded, but his mouth went dry as the Andean desert. He tried to remember if Guillermo had suggested anything in particular, but came back with only the word "haunting." He began to play the first thing that came to mind. A few seconds later, he heard Mila laughing.

"Is that 'Hotel California'?"

He nodded, mortified.

"You are ridiculous," she said. "Keep going, though."

She disappeared, leaving Whit with no good options. He wanted to slink back into his room in defeat, to die in his sleep rather than have to face her in the morning. But that was the unlikeliest of outcomes, and he didn't want to have to confess to Guillermo that he'd wilted so easily. He began to play again, this time an arrangement of some bluegrass song whose name he couldn't remember. To his surprise, Mila soon appeared on the patio with him, a glass of wine in each hand. She waited until he'd finished and extended one to him.

"Thanks," he said. "I really don't drink, though."

"Wine is not drinking," she said. "Pisco is for drinking. Wine is for—what do you think? For lovers?"

Whit tried to smile, hoping he didn't look as overloaded as he felt. In fact, his brain was a roiling stew of inner conflicts, his body a cluster of random electrical impulses. He accepted the glass, held it as she clinked hers against it. He copied the ways she swirled it lightly and raised the cup and sipped the wine. Tried not to cough when it hit the back of his throat. She laughed at him, but he didn't mind so much. He sipped the wine and talked with her, feeling himself becoming warmer and more detached by the moment. Mila leaned forward, halting barely an inch from his face.

"Is this what you want?" she whispered.

"Yes."

"Then you better do something about it."

A pulse of energy shot through his body, and even without time to form the words, he knew this was one of those moments in which trying to understand a thing would ruin it. And so he did not let himself think. He leaned in and met her lips. They kissed for a moment before her lips tightened and she began to laugh.

"Oh, sorry," Whit said. "Did I—?"

"Did you finally get around to something you should have done weeks ago?" she asked. "Yes. Yes, you did." She reached down and took his hands. "Come on. We don't want Papi to see."

She led him back to his apartment, pulling a fresh blanket from the clothesline as they passed. She spread it over his unmade bed. Sat down. Motioned for him to join her. She pressed his shoulders down and pulled herself on top of him. Took his wrists and guided his hands beneath her shirt and onto the skin of her back.

"*Solamente aca*," she said. "*Por el momento.*"

They kissed again, and Whit's heart raced—half from excitement and half from fear that he was doing it all wrong. He could feel a slight tremor taking hold in his hand. She giggled, her teeth clacking lightly against his. He paid attention to every sound she made, every movement of her wonderful body. She told him to relax, put her lips up to his ear. Spoke to him in Spanish what she wanted him to do—where to put his hands, his lips, his legs. And he had done everything she'd asked, thrilled not only at the sensation of contact, but at the prospect of making her happy.

"Okay," she said. "*Tratamos algo más.*"

She slid over to one side, so quiet that he barely heard her move. When she settled in against him again, he knew right away that she'd taken off the rest of her clothes. He could have died happy right there on the spot. She took his hand again, guided his fingers over her hips and around to her torso and down. For the briefest of seconds, he considered backing away, preserving the ideal of sexual purity that had been drilled into his head since his first wet dream. That impulse left as quickly as it arrived, however, replaced by a desire so consuming he would have signed over his soul right there on the spot just to stay with her, this woman whom he wanted more than heaven itself.

The next day, Whit related his evening with Mila to the plants at Operación Amor as he watered them, to the floors as he swept, to the garbage as he carried it out. Three glasses of wine and a slew of unfamiliar emotions had cast the previous night in a tangled ball—snippets of conversation here, a laugh there, a kiss—his first real kiss, although he didn't dare admit that, even to the inanimate objects that made up his morning duties. These and so much more, sensations of skin and emotions that defied words in any language.

What he told the plants was irrelevant, though. The real question was what, if anything, to say to Father Guillermo. Whit wasn't exactly sure what Catholics thought about such premarital intimacy, or whether someone who had pledged a life of celibacy would want to hear about it at all. But, knowing Guillermo, Whit figured he'd better have his story ready. His friend would likely pick up that something had happened with Mila without him even saying it, and he never hesitated to ask uncomfortable questions. How much could Whit say before he said too much, either about himself or about Mila?

As the time approached for the children to return from school, Whit rehearsed his story again, this time to the rabbits as he placed new fronds in their cages. They nibbled on, oblivious, as he tried out different versions, some more explicit than others. The rabbits, he decided, would have the same reaction if he had told them he'd had acrobatic sex with Mila in the middle of the Plaza de Armas, or if he'd stripped naked and danced in front of the cage here and now. A night that had felt so seismic to him was of no interest to the bunnies, who for that matter had no shame in copulating in broad daylight, right in front of giggling children.

"Señor?" a quiet voice said from beside him.

He froze. Turned his head slowly. "Hola, Yesenia."

The girl picked up a leaf that had fallen onto the concrete and slipped it through the mesh for the cage to a brown and white rabbit, which received it gladly with its teeth. Whit waited for his heartbeat to slow. Yesenia had a ninja-like knack for appearing or disappearing at will, noticed only if she allowed herself to be so. It was a skill honed for self-defense, a relic of life with her birth family. If no one could see her, no one could hurt her.

"Do you find the rabbits interesting?" she asked in near perfect English.

"I don't know," he answered slowly. When had she learned to speak like that? More importantly, had she been within earshot for anything he'd said to the rabbits about Mila? His heart pounded. "Do you?"

Yesenia shrugged. "Sometimes. I just wonder what they think about."

"Oh, well I suppose—what do you think they think about?"

The girl shrugged. "Maybe food. Maybe other rabbits. Maybe sunshine."

"Well, those sound like happy thoughts."

"I think you should bring me to the United States to live with you."

Whit felt himself stumble, even though he hadn't been moving. "Come again," he said.

The girl looked away, concentrating on the foreign words to make sure she had them right. When she turned back toward him, her confidence had doubled. "I think I should live in the United States, and you should be the person to take care of me."

"That's—ah, well. That's an idea."

"You don't want to?"

"No," he said quickly. "I do. I mean, that would be terrific. I'm just not sure it would work."

"Why not? You are good with children. I am a child."

"I'm only twenty."

She considered this. Spoke numbers softly. "In six years, we could be married."

Whit froze. Waited. She looked like she might say more, but a pack of boys arrived on the patio, throwing down their books and running in all directions the way they did when they got home from school. One of them whizzed by the rabbit cages and pulled Yesenia's pig tails as he passed. Whit opened his mouth to scold the boy, but Yesenia held up her hand.

"I can take care of myself. Watch."

In a flash, she was in hot pursuit. She caught up to the offending boy in less than ten strides, reached up and tweaked his ear. The boy yelped and swung his hand, but Yesenia dashed away, weaving in and out of the pin-balling children until the boy lost interest in the pursuit. She veered toward the entryway and wrapped her arms around Mila's waist. Whit felt a strange jolt through his legs and back. Wondered why he hadn't noticed her arrival. Mila put one arm around the girl and talked to her for a long time. About what was anybody's guess, and Whit knew he should be concerned. But Mila had a way of filling up his vision to the point that, if a grenade was incoming, he would never see it.

CHAPTER 14

A week later, Whit sat on a bench facing the Catedral de Santa Maria la Menor, his thoughts flipping back and forth between images of hell and memories of Mila. He'd talked it through with the rabbits a few more times, and while they offered no answers, their little faces seemed to ask if he was sure about this whole thing. Was he really ready to reject a lifetime of Bible teaching for the pleasures of the flesh—and the fact that they were pleasurable was not up for debate, but still. Perhaps his lack of guilt was an indicator of a heart seared by sin. He promised the bunnies he'd do better. Recommitted himself to the spiritual battle.

But each time Mila came into his room with an unbuttoned shirt and a bottle of wine, he knew right away that biology was going to overpower theology. And so it did.

He was whispering these things to the birds around his bench when the squeal of tires on pavement caused them to scatter. He looked up to see an old woman beating the hood of a car with the plastic bags she'd been carrying. The driver screamed back at her. All around, cabbies popped their heads in and out of their windows as if the scene were one big game of whack-a-mole. Father Guillermo emerged to take stock and, seeing that no one was in need of extreme unction, he crossed the street and joined Whit on his bench. He picked up the rest of Whit's uneaten sandwich and began feeding the birds as he quietly spoke to them in Latin.

"What are you doing?" Whit asked.

"I am offering the sacrament to the pigeons," he said. "They are all Catholic. Probably."

"I don't think they are anything."

Guillermo shrugged. "How do you know? How do they know? They live their lives without awareness or reflection." He stopped. Tore off a small piece of bread and ate it.

"What's wrong?" Whit asked.

"Nothing, really. Acedia, perhaps—the noonday demon."

"But it's nearly six."

"Which makes one wonder, doesn't it?" He tossed the rest of the bread to the birds and clapped his hands on his knees. "Well, it is all good, as the kids say. But what about you? I hope you have something to confess with Mila."

"It's more confusion than confession."

"Oh? Well, such is the human condition. Tell me about it."

Whit tried to relay the story to his friend, but he wasn't quite sure that he understood it himself. The conversation with Yesenia had unsettled him, and even though he drove it from his mind when Mila came into his room that night, the little ninja girl crept back into his thoughts while he and Mila shared a postcoital glass of wine. He asked her what he should do about it, which in hindsight was his first mistake. She bowed up at the idea of his adopting the girl, accused him of manipulating a child and insinuating that he might do worse. When he pushed back, she threw the wineglass at him. It had taken an hour to make sure he'd gotten all the shards out of his bed.

"So this lover's quarrel is something more than that," Guillermo said when he had finished. "She accuses you of terrible things."

"She knows it's not true," Whit answered. "She was just angry."

"But angry in a way that made her want to inflict pain. This is not a sign of health."

Whit stared across at the Catedral. The earlier commotion had dissipated, and traffic had returned to its normal frantic rhythm. People walked along the sidewalk, some merely passing by while others stopped to enter the Catedral doors. Guillermo followed his gaze.

"What do they do in there?" Whit asked. "When you're not having church—mass, I mean."

Guillermo rubbed his chin. "That is a more difficult question than you might think. The easiest answer is maybe to say they go to pray. But what is prayer?"

"I guess it's talking to God."

"Of course, of course. But that is only a part of it. You and I, we do not communicate if I am the only one talking. So people go in to pray. They weep before the Virgin or prostrate themselves at the foot of the crucifix. They bring in photographs and keys and locks of hair along with petitions for blessing or cursing. This is all talking to God."

Whit shook his head doubtfully. "It sounds like superstition to me."

"So how do you discern, then, the superstitious from the faithful? It is not so easy. Everyone—even people who don't believe in God—want something from God."

Whit thought about that for a long moment. His father used to rail against Catholics for their idolatry—statues and priestly wardrobe and veneration of Mary. In his mind, all their chanting and congregational responses amounted to something worse than witchcraft—an attempt to tame the Holy Spirit that rendered Christian faith as dull as a foam wafer. But now that Whit was out of the evangelical stew, he couldn't say that the Catholics in Trujillo were all that different in their approach to God than the faithful at Light of Azusa.

"So the point of prayer is to get God to do what you want?" Whit mused.

"Ah!" Guillermo said. He clamped his fingers together in the air in front of him as if to catch Whit's suggestion as it flew past. "There is your answer, perhaps. Superstition is trying to get God to do what you want. Prayer, though, is offering your heart and waiting for an answer—whatever answer may come. Do you see?"

"I guess."

The priest laughed. "Don't worry. No one really understands shit." He tossed the last of the sandwich to the birds and dusted crumbs from his hands.

In the silence that followed, Whit tried once more to pray. He started with Mila, but he wasn't quite sure how to address the Almighty when it came to urgent sexual desires. Besides, he'd seen enough quarrels between Cole Allen and the women in his life—Bethany, Miss Corelli, and so forth—to know that such relationships were bound to dissolve eventually. And while it pained him to think that he might never again share such intimate moments with Mila, he discovered that the answer he most wanted from God involved someone else entirely.

"What will happen to Yesenia?" he asked aloud.

"The girl, yes, of course." Guillermo brought the tips of his index fingers together and tapped them on his chin. "I'm going to sound like a priest when I say this, but that is in God's hands."

"I guess. But what are her chances?"

Guillermo took in a deep breath and let it out slowly, which more or less told Whit what he already knew. In a few years she would age out of OA, and then? Tía Pilar was forever working on transitional programs for children when it was time for them to leave, but there were no guarantees. Yesenia might move on to the hard life of an urban peasant, perhaps working retail or housekeeping. She might find herself weighing the potential income of the sex trade against its inevitable risks. Tía Luz and Sonia and Mila would do everything they could to help her toward a better life. It was a coin flip as to whether all that effort would matter in the end.

"I couldn't do it, could I?" Whit said.

"Take her to America? Not unless you want to be arrested in the airport. And I'll just let you imagine what it would be like for a skinny white guy in a Peruvian prison. Anyhow, I thought this was about Mila?"

Whit's mood sank even lower, and his body along with it. He was nearly flat against the bench when Guillermo tapped his leg and pointed toward the side door of the Catedral. Three men were struggling to get a giant plastic camel through the small opening.

"The camel through the eye of a needle," the priest said. "This is one of my favorite things to watch at Christmas."

"Christmas?"

"Only a week away now, yes? They will set up the nativity set in the plaza and that is cool, as the kids say. But the camel is my favorite. Are you okay, my friend?"

Whit nodded, but something gnawed at him—something he was missing or had forgotten. It wasn't until the camel had fully emerged that he realized what. Invisible hands squeezed every drop of blood out of his heart.

"A week?" he asked softly.

"From today, yes."

"So that makes this..."

"The seventeenth."

Whit stood up, hands on his head. For weeks now, Tía Luz had been reminding him of the American mission team from Covenant University that was set to arrive a week before Christmas. He had a list of shopping and cleaning and other prep to be done before the team arrived at 17:00 on 17 December.

He checked his watch. 16:23.

"Oh god," he moaned.

"What is the matter?" the priest asked.

Whit shook his head. The late afternoon sun was just touching the tops of buildings on the west side of the Plaza de Armas. In less than an hour the Covenant team would be landing, and Whit's world would suddenly be consumed by hosting, scrubbing, translating, organizing projects, and otherwise catering to the nine students and two faculty members who had signed up to come. Mila had railed against the presumptuous Americans, who expected to be coddled and thanked and fawned over in exchange for a few days' work that Whit would likely have to redo the moment they left. But they were paying good money, which infused Operación Amor with much needed cash.

"I have to go," Whit said.

"You don't look so good," Guillermo answered.

"We have a mission team flying in tonight. I've got to go shopping."

The priest winced as though he'd smashed one of his delicate fingers. He composed himself. Nodded somberly. "That is terrible news," he said. "Godspeed."

CHAPTER 15

Mila arrived at the Paredes house with the Covenant University team before Whit finished the shopping. The travel-weary missionaries descended on him before he even made it through the door, grabbing rolls of bread and fresh bananas from the sacks as though they'd just emerged from a Russian gulag. He searched the faces for anyone he knew, or for some sign that any might know him. He came away with only two—Dr. Lawson, the fanatical New Testament teacher who managed in each class period to work in his conviction that Oral Roberts was the very instrument of God, and a football player named Trey Calhoun who had lived on second floor in Finney Hall.

"Whitson!" Trey called through a mouth full of food. "How are you, boy?"

Whit smiled, but he braced himself. Trey was an inch shorter than Whit but at least a hundred pounds heavier, with arms like high-line poles and the gut of a Santa in training. He strode past the girls and thrust the heel of his hand into Whit's chest. "Check!" he cried, showering Whit with little globs of bread as he laughed. Whit brushed himself off and slipped out into the garage. Trey followed.

"So this is where you've been living?" Trey said. "I gotta say, I thought it would have a lot more jungle—you know, vines and monkeys and stuff."

"That's further inland. Once you get over the Andes."

"This town, though—it's like the desert."

"It is the desert."

"Like Afghanistan or something. My brother is somewhere in the Middle East now, kicking ass." He looked over his shoulder to make sure he hadn't been heard. "Don't tell Dr. Lawson I said that. He's got a thing against cussing."

"Sure. No problem."

A sudden look of recognition spread across Trey's face. "Hey didn't you used to run with that Black guy that got suspended for being queer?"

"Isaias, yeah," Whit said. "But he shouldn't have been suspended. And he was—."

"He was what?"

Whit thought for a moment. "It's complicated," he said at last. "Dr. Lawson thinks that queers caused 9/11, back in the day. Everybody's afraid to say it, but that don't mean it ain't true."

Whit squatted down to pick at some imaginary stain on the floor. His father had been mailing him a package of clippings every week, convinced that Peruvian news stations were run by socialists and thus only slightly better than the liberal mainstream media that was ruining America, what with its support for abortionists and homosexuals and feminists. Whit had to admit that it was all perfectly logical, when you approached current events through the same lens as Cole Allen and his pastoral idols. But the further he got from that world, the more ludicrous its principles seemed. He decided to switch the focus to local.

"How are things in Finney Hall?" he asked.

"Ballin'," Trey said. "Hey dude, you got any more of that bread?"

When it came to doing the projects for Operación Amor, Trey turned out to be a useful if limited workhorse. He could haul 40-kilo bags of concrete two at a time up the front ramp, and no one was faster at mixing it with water and sand so that the team could set bricks in the retaining wall. When the weight of the sand caused the axle of the wheelbarrow to snap, Trey simply picked up the wheelbarrow and carried it where it needed to go.

This ability to serve as a human forklift could not help him in the interpersonal realm, however. His insistence on showing off left little room for others to do meaningful work. His American peers rolled their eyes and wandered off to find other things to do. The

OA children assigned to his project ran up and down the ramp, trampling the succulents Whit had been cultivating as ground cover. One of them, a four-year-old named Josue, climbed onto Trey's back and held onto his neck.

"He shouldn't be doing that," a girl whispered in Spanish. Whit looked down to see Yesenia standing next to him, her little arms crossed in judgment.

"I know."

"Then why don't you stop him?"

Whit winced. Operación Amor's rules for physical contact with kids were usually tightly enforced by Pilar. No one—not even Mila—was allowed to cling to a child for too long, much less to leave him swinging from his neck while lugging concrete. But the rules were more relaxed for American teams, whose return year after year were vital for OA's economic survival. He glanced up to the second-floor window where Pilar was holding a cup of coffee against her forehead, pretending not to see.

Yesenia waited on an answer that Whit didn't have, but he knew from experience that he couldn't outlast her. He drew in breath to offer whatever stumbling explanation he could, but she lifted a little hand to stop him. Motioned for him to come with her.

"There's another problem," she said.

She led him back through the front door, across the patio where Covenant college girls were playing circle games with the younger children, and up the stairs to the girls' side of the *dormitorio*. The room that Whit had stayed in his first night in Peru had been converted to house four sisters, all of them under the age of five, who had been sent to OA a month earlier. The Americans had painted a circus scene on the north wall, with cartoonish animals and a two-dimensional merry-go-round and a badly proportioned circus tent, too tall and too thin, and with disproportionately large balloons floating at its base. It reminded him of the drawing Libby had thrown at him on that trip to Montana.

"You see?" Yesenia said.

He saw. Could not unsee it.

Making matters worse yet was the figure in the foreground—a hunchbacked clown, scowling down with uneven green eyes at the bunks where the children would sleep. Its thick red lips peeled back to show blocky white teeth that seemed to be grinding together in anticipation of some evil. Taken in isolation, the circus was perhaps clumsy, but not particularly threatening. But that tent and that clown cast everything in the dim light of a nightmare. Whit shuddered.

"This scares the children," Yesenia said. "They won't sleep here."

He stepped to one of the bunks and sat down, cocked his head to one side to try to find an angle from which to judge the clown more generously. "Maybe they won't notice."

"They will."

On cue, sniffling sounds emanated from the doorway. The four girls stared without moving, somberly eyeing the macabre clown and its ghoulish entourage. The smallest one chewed on her fingers. Another cried softly.

"You see?" Yesenia said. "This will not work."

One of the college students, a sophomore named Jessica, slipped past the girls and into the room, carrying a plastic bucket of paint and a wide brush. She stopped short when she saw Whit and Yesenia, moved her eyes back and forth between the mural and her hosts. Tears fell onto her cheeks.

"I'll take the children," Yesenia said, and ushered the little girls down the hallway to the stairs.

Whit motioned for Jessica to get on with her errand. He slipped away to the tool closet and returned a few minutes later with a brush of his own. The young woman had slapped a frantic coat of paint over the clown and was now busy trying to cover up the balloons. He dipped his brush in the bucket and put a second coat on the clown. When he and Jessica stepped back to admire their work, she broke into tears again. The paint had begun to dry, but to no avail. The scene beneath was muted, but still plainly visible. Exactly how many coats of the cheap Peruvian paint they would need was a mystery Whit could not fathom.

"I tried so hard," Jessica said, wiping snot from her nose. She dropped the brush onto the concrete floor—another mess he'd have to scrape up later—and nestled her face into Whit's chest. He lifted his arms around her, noticing how small and fragile she felt compared with Mila. His hands spanned nearly the width of her back, and he had to squat slightly to get her head onto his sternum instead of his rib cage.

"We can fix it," Whit said. "It's just going to take some doing."

She hooked one hand around his back as she sobbed. Laid the other hand flat on his chest. He held her in his arms because she gave him no real choice, even though he felt himself getting antsy. Working at OA had implanted a timer in his head when it came to physical contact. If she were a child, he would have already backed away. Were the rules different when it came to adults—even adults who barely knew one another? He wasn't sure, and so he held on. Settled into the pose. Rested his chin on top of her head.

"It's okay," he said softly. "I know."

And it was true, at least in part. She'd tried her hardest, and yet things hadn't turned out, and that was a condition with which he could empathize. He was beginning to suspect that adult life might be defined by scenarios such as this.

He placed a big hand on the back of her head, the way he did with the smaller children when they were upset. As he did, the sound of a shoe brushing over the concrete caught his attention. He looked up, expecting to see one of the sisters, back to check on her room.

Instead, Mila's stern frame filled the doorway, feet set and arms crossed.

"Hi," he said.

Jessica pulled back, confused because she thought the greeting was aimed at her. When she saw Mila, however, she jerked away and began smoothing things—hair, t-shirt, shorts.

"Sorry," Jessica said. "Whit was helping me. A couple of things didn't quite turn out—"

Mila stuck out her bottom lip the way she did with the little children when she was trying to show empathy for a skinned knee or broken toy. She held out her arms, and Jessica spun into them. Mila pulled her close and whispered reassurances while she cried. But the look she fired at Whit over the girl's shoulder was nothing but daggers, and Whit knew that, no matter how truly innocent the scene she'd just walked in on, he was going to pay for it.

"There, there," Mila said again. "Don't cry. It's Christmas Eve."

As he applied the seventh coat of white paint over the clown from hell, Whit wondered how the calendar had gotten away from him so. True, Peruvian time was different than any other temporal construct he'd ever lived in, and he had learned to set aside most of his American definitions of punctuality. But to miss Christmas Eve—by his reckoning it shouldn't be for another three days—troubled him. Perhaps it was the weather, the summer heat that inverted his mental images of the holiday. South of the equator, it made no sense to dream of a white Christmas, which made it hard for Whit to dream of Christmas at all.

What bothered him most of all, however, was a pang of homesickness he hadn't felt since the second Sunday he and Mila had cooked for the children, when his new life had begun to feel more natural than novel. He imagined his father spending Christmas, as per usual, working at the church, troubleshooting lighting failures or filling paper sacks with treats for children or running interference for

Brother Arneson, who was far too busy with the work of the Lord to be bothered by the needs of individuals. It shamed Whit to think how few Christmas Eves he had spent with family, and shamed him even more to be missing the first Christmas with his new brother, Baby Zeb, born just after Thanksgiving.

"Yo, bro," a booming voice called from the hallway. Whit turned around just as Trey strode into the room. He touched an index finger to his brow in salute. A plastic bag full of something heavy dangled from his other hand. When he saw the phallic tent, he broke into a laugh. "Jessica told me it was bad, but dude! It's a candy-striped dick."

"I'm working on it."

He sat the bag down. "You need help?"

"I think I'm okay."

"I don't know, captain. You got a situation here, looks like to me."

"It's better than it was."

"Better still isn't good." He sidled up to Whit and dumped the contents of the bag onto the floor. Small bottles of acrylic paint and a few tattered brushes spilled out in every direction. He waved a hand at the mural as though casting an artistic vision. "So my idea is to turn these bad boys into something new. Use what's already there and add onto it, I mean. We could turn it into a soccer mural, I bet."

Whit shook his head. "I don't know about that."

"Mila loves the idea," Trey said. "She said she underestimated my creativity when I first got here."

"Oh. Well."

"You know how you can just tell when a chick is into you? I get that vibe from Mila—and I mean a heavy vibe. Like alarm bells going off. But I don't know what to do, man."

"Why is that?" Whit asked, managing with some effort not to grit his teeth.

"Well, it's never going to be a long-term thing, right? But even in the short term, I've never had a married chick come onto me before."

A sickening warmth flooded Whit's body, and he knew that every vessel in his face and neck was glowing red. He couldn't diagnose exactly which part of all of this he was reacting to, but he knew he'd better keep his answer short, lest his voice quiver. "She's not married," he managed to say.

"For sure she is, bro. She said it's not really a thing because they've been separated for like a year, but that they don't have an official divorce yet. So he's out of the picture. Still, you know? Feels kind of like I'm weaseling my way into someone else's property."

"She's not—" Whit answered, but lost his line of thought. She's not property? She's not married? Thirty seconds ago he wouldn't have questioned either of those statements, but that was before his emotional firmament dissolved into soup.

"I'll let you know how it works out," Trey said, breaking into an enormous, self-satisfied grin. "Never saw this coming, did you?"

"No."

"Hey, you okay, dude? Those paint fumes getting to you? Here." He took the brush from Whit's hand and set it to the side. Cracked his knuckles and squared up to the wall as though it were a defensive end. "Let me have a go at this bad boy."

And so Whit left him to it, knowing even through his hazy, shell-shocked consciousness that it would create more work for him once the Covenant Team had left. He wandered out onto the patio, but Operación Amor was alight with Christmas decorating, which offered zero quiet in which to compose himself. At every turn, someone was asking him to hang this strand or translate that bit of conversation. He finally ducked into the office, hoping for a bit of respite. But the women on staff at OA were gathered around the long folding table, wrapping presents the Americans had brought for the children—video games and exercise gadgets and superhero action figures—all of which would be discarded in favor of soccer balls and circle games before the new year began. When Mila saw him enter the room, she made a beeline past him and out the door.

"What's with her?" Pilar asked.

The other women shrugged and kept working. One of them slid a box across the table for Whit to finish wrapping.

"These toys," Pilar said, and turned up her nose. The other women shook their heads sadly, careful not to glance at Whit lest they make him feel even more gangly and ill-suited for their company. Lest they unwittingly bring to the surface the myriad ways in which, even after twenty years of walking the earth, he was still lost.

CHAPTER 16

All his life, Whit had been conditioned to face difficulty with prayer. Even though he suspected God was not inclined to listen after all his fornicating with Mila, he decided it couldn't hurt to try. And so, as the Christmas party with the Covenant team dragged into its third torturous hour, Whit slipped up to the rooftop to have a little talk with Jesus, only to discover that he had no idea what to say. Instead he looked down upon the party and wished for a meteor to wipe out the whole scene.

Three stories below, his former classmates were cycling through phases of grief and self-congratulation. Most of them had never missed a Christmas with their families, but any tearful sadness was met with elevated talk of the sacrifices they'd made to do the Lord's work here in Peru. There were blessings to be had for their faithfulness, and they had brought so much joy to those children, hadn't they? They re-told stories of how the kids' faces lit up when they opened their presents, how their work had brought so much relief to such an underprivileged group. They truly believed that ten days with American visitors would somehow transform the fortunes of these poor orphaned children.

The whole thing turned his stomach with its falseness. Three months at Operación Amor had cured him of the notion that he was anybody's savior. He'd seen kids pulled away from OA in tears because the courts ordered them back with their no-account families. Others arrived at the facility with black eyes and welts on their backs, as angry and confused as any tiny human could be. All of them had stories, and not one of them involved his great white gringo self as more than a janitor or guitar teacher.

He'd hoped things might be different with Mila, although as he stared down at her, seated on their bench with Trey the football jock, he realized that he had no idea what *different* might entail. She was deep into her flirtations with Trey, and her motivation was evident even from Whit's high perch. She wanted to show how quickly she could get a man to admire her, how easy it was to slip a knife into Whit for putting his arms around another woman. Seen from that angle, it wasn't a leap to think that she'd used him just like she was using Trey right now. She might actually be married, for God's sake.

But—and he knew the truth behind it, of course, but—whatever mechanism connected that which he knew to that which he felt completely malfunctioned when it came to Mila. Gospel admonition to pray for his enemies notwithstanding, Whit's supplications went straight to plague-level judgment. He wished boils to rise on Trey's face, for flies to infest his every orifice, for his skin to break out in leprosy so repulsive as to send Mila into fits of vomiting.

Those outcomes were, of course, out of his hands. And so Whit's mind turned to things he could control, actions he could take. One in particular kept surfacing in his brain, and even though he knew what a terrible idea it was from the start, he also knew from the moment of inception that he would follow through. He made sure Mila saw him watching so that she'd be encouraged to keep up the performance with Trey. Once he was certain she had, he slipped away, down the spiral stairs to the second floor, and pushed open the door to her room.

The light through her open window wasn't much, and he had to wait a few seconds while his eyes adjusted to the darkness. He'd only been in there twice, both times while Mila was grabbing something on their way out, and never for more than thirty seconds. She had a small nightstand with a clock and a lamp, a full-sized bed with a yellow comforter over it. Over the bed were two high shelves containing books with titles he couldn't make out. Opposite that stood a small chest of drawers, on top of which sat a large mirror with photographs tucked in between the glass and the wood frame.

He crept closer, trying to stay out of the rectangle of light cast through the window, and leaned forward to inspect the photos. Mila was in almost all of them, usually cheek to cheek with one of the children from OA. He recognized younger versions of Miguel and Ronni and Yesenia, but found nothing to suggest a significant other, much less a spouse. But before he could breathe a sigh of relief, he noticed a 5 x 7" frame that lay face down on the dresser next to a cup full of pens. Best to walk away, of course. But deciding not to know a knowable thing was no better than lying to yourself. And so, against his better judgment, he turned it over to see.

Later, speeding through the streets of Trujillo on his way to the airport—and, more to the point, away from Mila's father and husband—Whit would reflect on the futility of foresight. He had known damn well that he was inviting trouble just by sneaking into Mila's room, and infinitely more so by actively snooping among her things. And so, while the subsequent events were no surprise to him, he did regret both his actions and their inevitable outcome, beginning the second Mila appeared in the doorway and flipped on the light switch.

"What the holy actual *fuck?!*" she screamed. She reached across to snatch the photo out of his hand, but it was already seared into his memory. In it, a younger version of Mila looked into the camera with a giddy expression, her face bracketed on three sides by overly styled hair and on the fourth by the high white collar of a wedding dress. She held up her right hand next to that of the man in the photograph, each of them showing off their golden bands.

"Sorry," Whit managed, but a sharp smack across his right cheek cut him off before he could say more. He wobbled slightly. Ran his tongue over the inside of his cheek. "I guess I deserved that."

"You dick. I should tell Trey to kick your ass."

"Don't."

"Or I should kick your ass myself." She stepped to the side. Pointed through the open door. "Out."

"Why didn't you tell me you were married?"

"Now you know."

"Now is too late, isn't it? After everything?"

"Everything?" she spat. "You mean after nothing. *Nothing*."

She went on, cursing him alternately in English and Spanish, driving knife after knife into his heart until he regretted how much of the local language he'd picked up. After a time, though, she began to tire, and Whit became aware of an awkward silence that held sway over the party on the patio. For a long and unsettling moment, he thought everyone had stopped to listen through the open window as Mila dressed him down. But when she paused for breath, they both heard Luz shouting on the patio, angry Spanish syllables pouring out of her at a rate that Whit couldn't keep up with. Mila's face went ashen.

"*Dios mio*," she whispered, and bolted from the room.

She bounded down the spiral stairs twice as fast as Whit's long frame would allow. By the time he reached the patio, Mila was already on the far side, grasping her mother by the shoulder, quietly pleading with her to calm down. Luz was in no state to be soothed, however, and Whit correctly surmised that rage of this magnitude must be directed at her husband. Carlos sat on a chair outside the door to his workshop, casually smoking while his wife melted down. Luz pointed one minute at Carlos and the next at Jessica, the failed mural artist, who stood behind two of her friends with her arms crossed, glaring at the patriarch.

"*Mami! Mami!*" Mila cooed. "*Ahora no, por favor.*"

The college students gaped, wide-eyed and frozen, caught in the headlights of the moment but powerless to get off that emotional freeway. All except Trey, who sidled up to Whit and said, "Shit got real, bro."

Whit peeled his eyes away so that he could look at the football player—perhaps the only person in Trujillo who could stand flat-footed and look him in the eye. "What?"

"Mila, dude. Is there anything hotter than an angry woman?" He shook his head, made a kind of *woof*-ing sound. "Shame we got interrupted. Did you see how into me she was just now?"

Whit ignored him. Instead, he tried to work the problem as it developed before his eyes. He thought he was starting to piece things together, and he sensed danger in every detail.

"Jessica," he said quietly. "What's she been up to this afternoon."

"Helping the old man, I think."

"Helping?"

"Yeah. She was still all upset about her sucky mural when we got back, so Señor Carlos was teaching her how to do some sort of mechanical thing. I don't know what set the old lady off. Unless..." Whit watched Trey's face as the thought—the same one Whit had been rolling around for several seconds now—dawned on the young man. "Bro, you don't think, do you? She and the old man?" He clapped a hand on Whit's shoulder. "Got to admire his boldness."

"I don't think there's much to admire," he replied.

But Trey was no longer listening. He and the other team members had been summoned by Dr. Lawson, who sent them back into the house with the assurance that he'd work things out. The professor walked to where the girls stood, palms spread in front of him. He spoke too softly for Whit to make out every word, but the gist of it was that they were guests and that Carlos didn't mean anything by it—whatever "it" was. The two friends nodded as though they understood, but Jessica wasn't having any of it. When they turned to comfort her, she shook them off, hugging her elbows against her chest and fighting back sobs. She might as well be Tamara Riker, Whit thought, the girl whose boots Bonner Hanson had thrown out the window those years ago in Wyoming.

Lawson gave a final instruction to the friends, who nodded and turned to plead his case with Jessica. The professor stepped away, more or less satisfied with the result of his errand, and moved over to where Whit stood.

"Can you tell what our hosts are saying?" he asked softly.

"Yes."

Lawson frowned. Rephrased the question. "What are they saying, Junius?"

Whit shook his head. The amount of dirty laundry being aired between Luz and Carlos staggered him and clearly embarrassed Mila—insults and affairs, promises broken, lies on top of lies. Even if he wanted to explain, it was hard to know where to begin.

"It's family business," Whit finally said. "I wouldn't worry with it."

"Not when it involves one of our students," Lawson said. "If she's broken any of the codes of conduct the students agreed to on this trip, I need to know."

"Nothing like that."

"Oh, I think it might be, sad as it is to think." He leaned in close. "One of our other students saw her run out of his tool shed, still trying to fasten her bra. Now I don't know what that looks like to you, but it's pretty clear to me."

"It wasn't her fault," Whit said.

"She has to bear some responsibility. That is, unless you know something I don't."

Whit folded his hands on top of his head. The information stream had more or less ceased, now that Mila had managed to get her mother back into the kitchen. But the things Whit heard had been enough.

"You should make sure she talks to someone when she gets back," Whit said. "A counselor maybe."

Lawson winced at the suggestion but didn't spit on it the way Cole Allen would have. "I'll pray on that," he said.

Voices inside began to sing, and the two men turned to look at the open doorway. Someone from the team had picked up Whit's guitar and started the others in on a three-part version of a carol. "Snow had fallen, snow on snow," they sang. "In the bleak midwinter, long ago." Whit had to hand it to them. Those Covenant kids knew how to sing. Even when things went sideways, they knew how to sing.

· · · ·

FIGURE 6: HELP FOR *Victims of Sexual Violence*

CHAPTER 17

The Covenant team rallied after the Christmas Eve debacle, thanks in no small part to Mila's redoubling of her hospitality efforts. She'd spent most of Christmas morning making her signature *tres leches* cake, and when the college students raved about it, she made another that evening and a third the next day. She was manic with attentiveness, feeding them and organizing games and praising them for their good work with the children. Whit suspected she was also drinking a bit, but she never let him close enough to tell for sure. And so Whit spent the final days of the calendar year trying to be helpful and invisible at the same time.

The morning before their flight back to Lima, the team stopped at Huaca de la Luna, an ancient Temple set out in the desert south of town. Dr. Lawson insisted that he didn't need to hire the on-site tour guide, which was a failure in etiquette that Mila had to blunt with a handsome tip to the jilted park worker. However he might have frozen during the crisis situation on the patio, Lawson had a field marshal's confidence among the ruins. He pointed out—correctly, as best Whit remembered from a tour he and Mila had taken in November—that seven different temples had been built, each one circumscribing the last. The inner walls were lined with astonishingly well-preserved images of *Ai apaec*, the decapitator god, whose expressions ranged from angry to murderous. Lawson explained in gory and semi-accurate detail the cult of human sacrifice that, not surprisingly, grew up around the worship of such a deity.

Despite a few wild inaccuracies—he insisted the temple was Incan, even though the Moche had built it seven hundred years before the Incas had moved into the neighborhood—Lawson proved to be a compelling tour guide. The students were transfixed by the authority with which he spoke, and by the moral lessons he drew from the demise of this pagan empire—namely, how any society that didn't submit to the power of the cross would inevitably fall into ruin.

Somewhere along the way, Mila disappeared entirely. Whit knew better than to look for her. Instead he lagged behind the group, thinking he might enjoy a little quiet among the ruins. But his religious upbringing, which saw pagan temptation and cautionary tales around every corner, had been rekindled by recent events. Ever since helping Isaias with his interview project, Whit had struggled to define sin as those preachers at the Firestorm youth rally did. For them, holiness was a matter of abstinence from smoking and drinking and sex. But reality was different. People did what they did, and sometimes they thought about it, sometimes not. Maybe the Moche were just doing the best they could with the information they had. Maybe doing your best was all anyone could do.

Still, there had to be boundaries, and Whit had toppled over one. As much as he might rationalize all kinds of behavior his father's religion would frown on, he had to admit that the prohibition against adultery was about as rock-solid as they come. He'd fooled around with Mila, and maybe that was okay and maybe it wasn't, when he thought she was single. But a married woman? Even Guillermo, who liked Whit in part because he didn't feel any pressure to make him a good Catholic, bowed up at that. It was a good thing that Mila and Whit had fallen away, he posited. The safest bet was never to stand up to temptation, but to remove it entirely.

That advice wasn't news to Whit or, he suspected, to any human over the age of two. Knowledge of a boundary didn't always equate to observation of it, and sometimes quite the opposite. Sometimes what passed for moral willpower was nothing more than the absence of opportunity. Besides, if he'd gleaned anything at all from Bonner Hanson it was that sins of the flesh not only presented a barrier to true religion, but also a quick path to a cubic crap-ton of trouble.

Now that opportunity with Mila had seemingly waned, his soul and his flesh were both on more stable ground.

Still. If the devil had appeared right then and there, offering to trade his eternal soul for another night with Mila, he wasn't sure what his answer would be.

Whit was at the pinnacle of the temple, considering the devil in hypothetical, when he realized that the Covenant team was gone. He scampered outside, over the chalky path and down the ramp that led to the final stop on the tour, a wide area at the base of the temple that offered a view of the most spectacular of the outer murals. A handful of other tourists milled about, reading the information signs or listening to official tour guides. Dr. Lawson had taken a prime position next to a character actor dressed in ancient priestly garb.

"As you can see, the Inca were polytheistic," the professor said. He lifted a hand toward the murals. "They feared their gods, and with good reason."

He paused for a moment so that his students could reflect on the terrible deities inscribed on the wall—spiders and dragons, angry faces, misshapen heads—and how tragic it was that such lost souls were burning in hell along with the false gods they served. But Whit was more interested in the priest. He was shifting from one foot to the other, working his lips as though holding back vomit. Before long, his gaze landed on Whit, who wished for all the world that *Ai apaec* had just eaten his head and gotten it over with. Instead, he quietly made his way toward the priestly actor while Lawson continued his sermon.

"*Hola*, Miguel," he whispered.

"*Señor*," the fake priest mumbled. "These friends of yours?"

"It's complicated."

Miguel raised his eyebrows in agreement, as if those two words contained the sum total of mortal existence.

Whit had met him a few weeks ago, when he brought the motorcycle he used for his delivery business to the Paredes house for repair. While Carlos fussed over the engine, Miguel had been eager to engage Whit in conversation so he could practice his English. He'd mentioned having another job, but never in a million years would Whit have guessed it was as a Moche priest. And yet here he stood, in full ceremonial garb, understanding every blessed word that Lawson spoke about heathens and idolaters.

"This clown talks like we still sacrifice humans here," Miguel said in Spanish, although not as quietly as Whit would have liked. "Like it's any crazier than their Catholic shit."

"They aren't Catholic," Whit answered.

"Whatever they are." He adjusted his breastplate. Cleared his throat. "What are they, then?"

"It's complicated."

Lawson appeared to be gaining steam—getting his preach on, as Brother Arneson would say. His voice rose, drawing bewildered stares from the groups from Argentina and Brazil and China. He ranted against false gods and sin and—Whit had trouble following the logic here—the dangers of premarital intercourse. Beside Whit, Miguel ground his teeth and occasionally grunted his disapproval. Unfortunately Lawson misread that signal, taking it instead as a kind of "amen" encouragement, and lifted his hand toward the actor/delivery guy and, with revivalist gusto, declared that the spirit of the Incas still threatened the godly to this very day.

"Moche!"

Every eye turned from the preacher to look at Whit, confirming his fear that the voice everyone had heard was in fact his own. He took a deep breath. No point running from it now.

"The Huacas were built by the Moche. Almost a thousand years before the Inca." He shifted his feet, willed himself not to look away. "No disrespect."

HOME FROM AWAY

Those whose primary language was Spanish or Chinese looked on in confusion, but Whit had neither time nor inclination to explain, preferring instead to let the handful of bilingual tourists translate for those around them.

"Even so!" Lawson shouted.

But the crowd had moved on, passing by a set of ornate double doors preserved from the most recent Temple construction and then out through the gift shop and to their buses beyond. Lawson must have made some joke heard only by his students, because a polite if nervous laugh rippled among them. Whit reached into his pocket for the money Luz had sent with him in case the group got into trouble. He dropped a 100-soles bill into Miguel's rough palm before shuffling off at the back of the American group.

As he passed by the ancient doors, he looked up at the ruins and saw Mila, feet planted as though she were the high priestess herself, ready to receive the blood of the sacrifices in a golden cup.

Figure 7: Huacas del Moche

CHAPTER 18

Obnoxious though Dr. Lawson's sermon was, it had laid out in plain view the distance between Whit and the God he'd known all his life. He lay awake much of the night, pondering the state of his soul. He was no longer quick to repent when the gospel was preached, and in fact was more inclined to question both the preacher and the preaching. And even though it often made logical sense to do so, such skepticism held neither warmth nor security.

And so when the sun rose on the next day, the third of the new year, Whit rededicated himself to practicing the presence of God. He sang hymns as he whitewashed the circus mural, even though it took eight additional coats to finally bury the nightmare clown, now dressed in a clumsy soccer jersey thanks to Trey. He silently blessed everyone and everything he encountered—children, Pilar, tables and chairs, cleaning supplies, the rabbits and their food. And if he encountered Mila somewhere in the day? He decided he would bless her too, since that was what a good and spiritually mature person was bound to do.

All this goodness was exhausting, however. By mid-afternoon, he was spent. He helped get the children settled in from school and put water on to boil for that evening's rice. As the steam rose up and fogged his glasses, he felt a different sort of moisture collecting in his eyes. He could not remember the last time his tears had fallen. The Whitman men didn't cry, his father was wont to remind him, and he had no good reason to do so now. But there they were, sure as the world—tears pooling between his lenses and his cheeks. He turned down the water and made a beeline for the tiny library across from the kitchen. Closed the door and tried to pull himself together.

When he thought about it later, he couldn't decide if Yesenia had been in the room when he'd arrived or had snuck in without his hearing, little ninja that she was. But when he dried his eyes and looked up, he saw her sitting across from him in one of the little chairs. She waited to speak until he acknowledged her.

"You are very sad," she said in English. "What's wrong?"

"Nothing."

"When nothing is wrong, people are usually happy. Aren't they?"

"I don't know. Maybe."

They sat in silence for a long while. Whit considered the connection between what people felt and how they expressed it. He'd been raised to think of emotions as more of a woman thing, and it alarmed him to be overcome by them. The present situation made it no better. He was at once grateful for and horrified by how easily this little girl comforted him.

"What's for supper?" she asked.

Whit laughed, blowing a long snot rope out onto the table. He reached for a tissue to clean it up.

She laughed too and got up and left the room. Whit lifted his head to watch her go and saw another figure, leaning against the doorframe, arms crossed.

"Mila," he groaned, and he knew what was coming. According to OA policy, staff were not to be alone with a child out of sight from at least one other person. "I can explain."

"Sure," she said, raising her eyebrows in such a way that Whit knew he was toast. He braced himself for impact.

"She was just checking on me."

"Because it's a twelve-year-old girl's job to check on a grown man."

"It's not like that."

"It's not?"

"You know it isn't." He stood up, and she flinched. So he stepped back. Slowed his movements.

"You were upset," she said evenly. "Pilar saw you crying."

"I wasn't crying, really. Much."

"So what has you upset?"

He felt the tears again. Willed them away and said nothing. He'd hoped practicing God's presence would quell his growing sense of the loss of God. But for all his effort, he felt both hollowed-out and tingling at the same time. However aware he was of the Almighty's absence, he was equally cognizant of Mila's very real presence. He wanted nothing more than to feel her body against his, even now. She uncrossed her arms. Rubbed her hands against her hips.

"That thing you did at Huaca de la Luna, correcting your professor like that. Why?"

He waited until he thought his voice wouldn't crack. "I don't know."

"Yes you do. Why?"

"Because it bothered the guy playing the Moche priest. I was just being nice."

"Bullshit. Why?"

Whit squeezed his eyes shut. "Because it wasn't true."

"And you can't stand things that aren't true."

"No. I can't."

She pulled her arms in tighter. Ran her tongue over the back of her lips. "Here's something true for you. My father is living in his shed again. He likes girls, you know."

"So I gathered."

"Do you think he touched that Jessica girl? At the Christmas party?"

He shifted his weight, considering how cleverly she'd boxed him into a response he didn't want to give. "I suppose that's what your mom thinks," he said.

"Answer the question."

"Well, if he's got a history—yes. I think he probably did."

He glanced up at her face, expecting to see her gathering wrath to inflict upon him. Instead she stared blankly at the floor. Dug her hands deeper into her folded arms.

"Me too," she said.

Whit thought about his encounter with Mila all day, as he'd done the first time they'd made love together. He was careful, though, not to speak aloud, even to the rabbits. After work, he stepped back into the sunlight and rode his bicycle to the Plaza de Armas. He settled onto a concrete bench and opened his Bible to read—the Sermon on the Mount, complete with its admonition that looking at a woman in lust amounted to adultery in and of itself. He prayed for forgiveness and for strength to go in a different direction, and for a while that felt like progress.

But, as tended to be the case, doors that opened to the spiritual overlapped with ones into the sexual. Memories of Mila's body rose unbidden in his mind—the smell of her neck, the warmth of her skin, the wonder of her breath. She was firm in some places and soft in others, but now that he thought about it he had trouble remembering any individual part. It was the whole of her—how it all went together—that enchanted him. The smooth fold of skin at the front of her armpit was of a piece with the hard muscles in her thighs, and though he lacked the breadth of experience to say for certain, he was wholly confident that she was a unique cocktail, a potent and unmatched blend of tenderness and ferocity that had chosen to let him drink for a time.

He crossed his legs and dropped his Bible into his lap to hide the outer workings of his feelings. Wondered if confession worked for Protestants.

"Take and read," a voice said. When Whit turned to look, Guillermo was seated on the bench next to him.

"How long have you been there?" he asked.

"*Tolle lege*," the priest said. "'Take and read.' Saint Augustine heard the command in a child's voice. When he read the Scriptures, he came to faith in Christ. Not that you lacked faith, my friend. Or that you are Augustine."

He laughed at his own joke—apparently it was a joke, Whit couldn't tell. The laugh was too fast and high-pitched. He wasn't wearing his collar, which was not unusual in the cafe but didn't seem right here in the Plaza, so close to his workplace. Instead, he had unbuttoned the top two buttons on his black shirt, and he fidgeted with the little plastic collar in his trembling fingers.

"What's wrong?" Whit asked.

"Nothing. I am fine. And you?"

"Fine. Really, though—"

"Ah! You are fine. But this is a strange thing for English. What is 'fine'? It means many different things, and sometime meanings are opposite of the word itself. You see?"

"Are you sure you're all right?"

"Fine, fine," the priest repeated. "I am glad. And your girlfriend. She is good?"

"I don't have—"

"Milagros? I think that is her name."

"She's fine."

"Ha! Fine, yes of course. You are fortunate to have someone like that. It is not good for a man to be alone, as the Holy Book teaches. I hope you will get married."

"But she's married already. We talked about that a few days ago."

Guillermo drew in breath but pulled up short of speech. He furrowed his brow as if trying to make sense of what he'd just heard. Whit wondered if the priest might be having some sort of breakdown, or episode at the very least. Before he could bring it up, however, Guillermo clapped a hand on his shoulder. "I can tell you are sad."

"I'm fine."

"It's hard ending a relationship. You worry. I will pray for you."

"Thanks."

He half expected the priest to bow his head and break into prayer right on the spot, which is what every single pastor of his youth would have done. But Guillermo's eyes were now fixed on the sidewalk in front of the Catedral. Whit followed his gaze and saw another priest, slightly younger than Guillermo, standing beside the open side door and obviously in a state. He wrung his hands out in front of his midsection as he scanned the plaza. When he spotted Guillermo on the bench, hand on Whit's shoulder, he dropped his head and covered his eyes as though weeping.

"No," Guillermo whispered. "*Dios mio.*"

The younger priest extended his arm as though pleading, and Whit suddenly understood what he was looking at. This was a lover's quarrel, maybe not all that different from his own with Mila. The scene would have repulsed Whit's father, who would have cited it as confirmation for all of his prejudices against gays and Catholics—not specifically gay Catholics, but that was probably because he just hadn't thought of the category yet. Regardless, Whit could see that Guillermo's heart was tied in knots over this, whatever *this* might be, and it made him sad for every forlorn lover of every stripe and creed across the globe.

But his friend wasn't sad. He was panicked. He shot up from the bench and began walking toward the Catedral, arms raised toward the man on the sidewalk. The young priest reached down to take hold of a crucifix around his neck. He lifted it to his lips. Stepped onto the street.

Even from his perch on the Plaza bench, Whit could hear the impact of fender on flesh, a sound that was at once both sharp and squishy. The priest's legs snapped beneath him at seemingly the same instant that his body ricocheted off the windshield and into the air. Whit tracked the arc of his flight until the man landed on the pavement twenty feet away. He looked to Guillermo, but the priest was already sprinting straight across the grass despite the police whistles directed at him. Whit didn't try to catch up. He didn't need be near the scene to know that his friend's lover was gone, and that fact as unchangeable as the rock on which the city rested. What was left was not really a person, not anymore. It was merely a body that, like all other bodies, could only take so much.

CHAPTER 19

Whit watched Father Yairo's funeral from the topmost seat in the northernmost corner of the Catedral's balcony. It was hot in the way that old churches get when filled with people on their best behavior, too polite to refuse to cram one more person into an already full pew. Given the Peruvians' lack of concern for time, Whit had no idea when the service might start, which gave him an eternity to think about being miserable. But things would happen when they happened, and nothing was imminent until the priests arrived. He wiped sweat from his face and tried to distract himself with the brightly colored paintings on the ceiling, but his eyes kept falling back to the casket in which the dead priest lay, mostly reassembled after the collision.

"Except for his legs," Guillermo had said. "The coffin hides the legs. For all we know, he isn't even wearing pants."

For a man who had just watched his ex-lover's gruesome demise, Guillermo had rebounded surprisingly well. Part of it, he claimed, was due to the simple fact that his and Father Yairo's relationship had fizzled weeks earlier. But of no doubt equal impact was the vexing difficulty of organizing the funeral, which kept all the living priests hopping from one crisis to the next. Father Yairo had been a popular man and a deft fundraiser, Whit gathered, which meant that several local dignitaries needed their egos massaged in advance of the funeral in expectation of a memorial gift. Surprisingly, the affair between the late priest and Guillermo didn't seem to be a hang-up. If anyone knew—and Guillermo suspected that lots of people knew—no one wanted anywhere near the acknowledgement of it. The apparent suicide was more problematic, given Church teaching on the subject, but in the end the Monsignor advised a strategy of ignorance. Best not to know. Best not to say.

Still, there had been moments when Guillermo let his sorrow show to Whit. Throughout their friendship, the two men often sat together for long stretches without conversation, each lost in his own memories or observations or musings. In the days leading up to the funeral, however, those silences often ended with Guillermo's heavy sighs or even sniffles. He murmured in Spanish and shook his head and occasionally wiped his eyes. Whit couldn't exactly relate, having no idea what it might be like to be in love with another man and no inclination to find out. But he was learning the weight of intimate loss, what with his first real love exiting his life nearly as soon as she'd entered it.

All at once, the people in the main level stood, followed closely by the mourners in the balcony. Whit rose as well and, with the benefit of height, could look over the congregation to see the bishop and the priests filing down the center aisle. Guillermo had warned him about the funeral mass, both its high-church content and its temporal length. He took a deep breath of the hot air and settled in.

Except for a few Spanish cognates, the Latin mass made no sense to Whit. He wasn't alone though. Everyone around him seemed more or less checked out of the service, except for the sporadic responses and sit-stand-kneel calisthenics. Their religion was free from the desperation of Light of Azusa, but it also lacked the energy, the immediacy. Whit didn't think he could ever be a Catholic, no matter how passionately Guillermo explained the finer points of dogma. Then again, with his efforts at restoring his faith stalled out, he wasn't sure if he was or even could be any religion.

The people stood again—Whit had no idea why—and he let his eyes roam over the disinterested congregation. Instantly he regretted it. To his left, on the front row of the balcony, stood Milagros, fingers just brushing the railing. He studied what he could see—her hair, her shoulders, one ear—and longed to be near her. Before he could give in to any impure thoughts, however, she turned her head around and looked straight at him. Smiled politely. Nodded a greeting.

And that was the end of it, in terms of honoring the departed Father Yairo or even supporting poor bereaved Guillermo. Thoughts of Mila detonated inside Whit's frontal cortex. He fought off memories of those few precious nights, replacing them with visions of a grand wedding here in the Catedral. But thoughts of a wedding led to thoughts of a honeymoon, and once again he was mentally romping in bed with her, this time in a hotel suite overlooking the beach at Huan Chaco.

On he went, alternately fighting and indulging his fantasies. She was married, he reminded himself, and tried to come to grips with the fact that their intimacies were over. He wondered if things ever felt normal between two people who'd had sex together, but who probably weren't going to have sex with each other ever again.

So consuming were his thoughts that he was slow to sit down at the end of some liturgy, leaving him with an even clearer view of the place where Mila sat and, more to the point, whom she was with. A short man with the broadest shoulders he'd yet seen in this country—coal miner shoulders, Bonner Hanson and Cole Allen Whitman shoulders—occupied the pew seat next to her. He leaned over and said something to her that she appeared to find funny. She reached back to smooth her hair, and there it was—a wedding band on the ring finger of her right hand, as per Peruvian custom.

Whit turned toward the front pews, hoping against hope that he might catch Guillermo's eye. Between his racing thoughts and the veritable sea of black shirts in the pews where the priests sat, it took what felt like a long time for him to even find his friend. Even from this distance he could see that, whatever poise Guillermo had displayed in the days before the funeral, he was now a wreck. His shoulders shook. Tears poured down his cheeks so quickly that they made a river wide enough to be visible from the balcony. Whit blinked rapidly, both to chase away the moisture in his own eyes and to give himself something to do. For the first time in a long time, his father's voice resounded in his thoughts.

Dry it up, boy. You can't undo none of it.

Whit waited after the funeral mass for a chance to talk to Guillermo, hoping to offer a consolation that his priestly brethren might be bound by creed to forego. It turned out to be for nothing, however. The gaggle of priests filed out together before the rest of the congregation, disappearing into some inner chamber of the Catedral. Three hours later, they still had not emerged. A man in a uniform—a security guard, possibly, but more likely the janitor—politely asked him to leave the church. Normally, in such a situation, Whit would have walked across to the Plaza de Armas to sit on his bench and wait for the priests to start exiting through the side door. But it didn't feel right to just go back to normal, not when he'd watched from that very spot when Father Yairo stepped in front of the taxi a few days earlier. Instead he hopped on his bike and rode back to the Paredes house, more aware with every honk and swerve of a passing car just how precarious his existence in this body was.

The house was uncharacteristically quiet as he closed the steel door behind him and lifted his bike onto the hooks in the garage. He walked through the kitchen and down the long hallway, past the spiral staircase that led to Mila's room on the second floor. He thought about going up there just to peek in, to see what kind of luggage her broad-shouldered husband had carried from wherever on the globe he'd been. But getting caught like that had caused one major blow up already, and he feared another might ruin whatever slim chances this had of turning out okay. Instead he emerged into the laundry area of the patio and walked past it into the garden. As he approached his apartment door, he noticed Mila's husband, still in the dress clothes he'd worn to the funeral, stripping wires with a pocketknife.

"Hey there Whitman!" he said in perfect English. He grasped Whit's hand, shook it hard enough to rattle his teeth. "Diego Santos de Montoya."

"*Mucho gusto.*"

"Ah, *gusto también*. Senor Paredes tells me you're quite the mechanic. Mind chipping in here?" He pointed with his knife to another tangle of wires and parts on the table. Best Whit could tell, Diego was trying to repair the solenoid on a riding lawnmower engine. Whit stared for a long moment, confused not so much by the task at hand as by the need for it in the first place. Here in the city on the desert coast, where the few people who had something like a lawn rarely had any grass in it, a riding mower seemed more than a luxury item. It felt like an alien relic. Nevertheless Whit sorted through the tools and went to work, despite his unease over whether he should be engaging in such collegial activities with his first love's spouse.

"I saw you at the funeral today," Diego said. He gestured up and down Whit's long frame with his knife. "You're hard to miss."

"I guess so."

"You're a big guy—tall and pale as you are, it's no wonder that people react the way they do to you."

Whit felt his throat tighten. He laid the solenoid down on the table and placed his hands around it to keep them from shaking. "I guess so," he said again.

"Eh, I'm not sure you get what I'm saying," Diego said. His tone was still calm and friendly, but his fingers worked that knife like a Japanese prep cook, shaving and snipping with terrifying precision. "A lot of people really like having a big *gringo* like you around. You're interesting, is what I'm saying—different, at least. My Mila, she likes you. You know that, right?"

Whit pressed his chin against his chest, stared down hard and hoped Diego would not look over to see the bright red that he felt overtaking his face and neck. "She's nice."

Diego laughed. "Of all the words to describe Mila, 'nice' is not one I would use. But she can be friendly to get her way. She's twenty-one years old, but she's still a little girl. She knows how to get what she wants, but she's always changing what she wants. Somebody puts a thought in her head, and she chases that thing for long enough to do a lot of damage. Then she throws it away. You know what I'm saying, right?"

"I—maybe."

"I think it's more than maybe."

"Maybe," Whit said, and let a brief silence hang between them. He didn't think Diego would try to cut him, not as long as they were in the Paredes' house. But he was a long way from certain. He took a half step away from Diego, just in case. "So the two of you are still married, right?"

Diego's hands kept moving, as though the question were no more to him than a comment about the weather. "She gets these thoughts. They make her hard to live with sometimes, you know? A man has business to attend to, and that takes a while, and she gets impatient like he's never coming back. But I'm right here, my friend. Right here beside you."

"All right," Whit said. "Good. I'm glad you were able to work it out."

Diego laughed, and it sounded genuine enough. Whit tried to laugh too, hoping to show that, even if he didn't really mean what he said, he at least knew that he ought to mean it.

"I like you," Diego said. But he had stopped laughing. Whit could feel him staring hard in his direction now, and he turned so that they were face to face, or would have been if Diego had a height to match the breadth of his weightlifter's build. As things stood, however, Whit had the odd sensation of looking at a man at least ten inches shorter than he was, yet feeling as small as the child he'd been back in Claremore, waiting on the mercy seat to collapse.

"But...?" he said.

"But I don't think it's good for Mila for you to be here. You should leave."

Whit's face grew hot again, this time from anger. "If she doesn't want me here, I'll move back to Operación Amor."

Diego waved that idea away with his knife blade. "You misunderstand. If you are anywhere in Trujillo—anywhere in Peru, for that matter—I think it's not good for Mila. So I want you to take your scrawny white ass back to the States and park it there for the rest of your life."

Whit fought the urge to step back, but he shifted his weight to be ready if he needed to move quickly, and he made sure the hand with the knife stayed in his peripheral vision. The blade wasn't long, but the expertise with which Diego wielded it left him sweaty and cotton-mouthed. He tried to slow his heart rate so that his voice wouldn't tremble. After a moment he said, "I'll think about it."

"I wouldn't take too long if I were you."

The shorter man looked up, and Whit knew he was being scanned for fear, or at least for doubt. Much to his dismay, Diego must have found what he was looking for. He relaxed his shoulders and went back to his repairs, humming to himself as though Whit were a mosquito, a buzzing yet easily dispatched irritant.

It was enough of an insult to make Whit's mind up for him.

"All right," he said. "I believe I'll stay."

"Good!" Diego said, smiling broadly. "That's really good. Hand me those pliers, man."

CHAPTER 20

The next day, as he repaired one of the rabbit cages shattered by a wayward soccer ball, Whit tried to emulate Diego's manner with his knife. His efforts cost him several minutes' time, most of which was lost as he tended to a deep gash he'd inflicted on the webbing of his thumb. That complicated the repair efforts, and it would make the upcoming guitar lesson with Yesenia painful, if he could play at all. But he figured nothing worth learning came all that easily, and so he bound up his wounds and went back to it, albeit more cautiously than before.

He was just setting the cage back upright when he sensed another person on the patio. He turned, expecting to find Pilar coming over to inspect his work or add to his to-do list. Instead he saw Mila standing just inside the doorway. For an instant, her face was tender again, maybe even worried. He held up his bandaged thumb.

"Only a flesh wound," he said in a terrible British accent.

But she did not laugh, nor did she reply. Instead her face hardened and her eyes bore down upon him.

"Mila?"

She spoke to him in English through clenched teeth. "Of all the dumb-fucks in this godforsaken city...." She trailed off, but before his apology was halfway through the air to her she spoke over him again. "Were you so stupid as to think that you were anything more than a way to kill time?"

He held up his palms to protest, but another figure appeared in the doorway, shorter and broader, but of a kind with Mila.

"*Dígale, Mama*," she said, and stormed through the door. As she stomped away, Whit noticed his suitcase and backpack, both stuffed full and waiting ominously behind Luz. All at once, every pore on his body opened, expelling a cold, sticky sweat.

"Tell me what?" he asked.

Tía Luz refused to answer questions at OA. Rather, she insisted that he say his goodbyes to Pilar and the rest of the staff, and that he make it quick. His flight, she said, departed in two hours. For everyone's sake, he could not miss it.

"I don't want to go," he protested. "Where am I going?"

"Home," was all she would offer.

"But the kids will be here any minute. Can't I at least tell them goodbye?"

Tears welled up in Luz's brown eyes, but she shook her head. Her expression left him no room to argue. He did as he was told, then looked around for Mila. Luz took him by the wrist and gently led him to her car, which she'd left running in front of Operación Amor.

"Please tell me what's happening," he said as he stuffed his luggage into the back seat and folded himself into the passenger side.

Luz looked at him with something like contempt, further shattering his already broken heart. "If you think about it, you will know," she said.

He did think, and was shocked to realize how clearly the answers came. As he replayed the stories of his time in Trujillo, every little detail led him to something he should have seen before, something that was right there like a turd on the sidewalk that he'd still somehow managed to step in. Diego worked for an international firm based in Peru? The only such syndicates he knew of traded in cacao products in the shadowy lanes of human commerce. And risk management? Whit didn't like the sound of that at all. It meant that Diego had probably—well, it was no wonder he knew how to filet anything in reach of that knife. And all the friendly chitchat over the busted solenoid? He'd gotten Whit to offer up names and cities of residence for almost every important person in his life. All of that added up to leverage. If Whit was foolish enough to throw his own life away—and now that he thought about it, he didn't really want to follow through with doing so, but even if he had—Diego also had enough information to locate his entire family. All he needed was Google and a plane ticket.

"Do you think Diego would actually have done anything?" he asked Luz. "To me, I mean."

Luz clucked her tongue. "*Idioto.*"

She drove on like a bat out of hell, just as he'd seen her do countless times these past few months. But her person remained a fixture of tranquility, unbothered by the chaos around them even as she plowed ahead according to the customs of the road.

"Mila," he said.

"Don't ask me this."

"I know she is your daughter."

"Yoonius—"

"I just want to know if I mattered at all to her. If she—somewhere deep down, I mean—"

"If she loved you?"

"Yes. That."

She shook her head again. Muttered something that might have been a prayer. By now they were at the airport, though, and time was short. She parked the car and scooped up his backpack and carried it ahead of him to the terminal. They stood there for a long moment while the attendant at the airline counter punched at the keys of a boxy computer. When at last she looked up to greet them and ask for his flight number, Whit found that he had no access to any of the language files in his brain. English, Spanish, the handful of Latin words he'd picked up from Father Guillermo—delirium had cranked down the valve to all of them, and he couldn't manage so much as a *grácias* in response. Luz stepped forward and helped him check in. Marched him down the ramp to the terminal, her eyes scanning the crowd for Diego or his ilk—anyone who might want to do him harm. She made him hold his suitcase and stand by the gate for a picture, probably to prove to Diego that he really was leaving. Then she settled him into a chair beside the desk and gave some worried instructions to the attendant.

At last, she knelt in front of him and took his hands. "Yoonius, I love you. And that God you believe in, I think he probably would love you too. As for Mila?" She smiled. Shook her head. "If a thing cannot be, then why waste yourself on it?"

Whit nodded as though he understood, even though he didn't. But he somehow knew to stand up again and take Luz into his arms. She was older than his own mother by decades, but she gripped him as tightly as he'd ever been hugged in his life. He could feel her starting to shake and wanted to protest, but the connection between his brain and his mouth was still offline. So he held her and let himself be held. Let Luz cry as though he were her very own child.

"*Señor*," the desk attendant said softly. "*Ándale, por favor.*"

Luz released him with one hand. With the other, she turned him around and gave him a tiny shove. He looked down for his luggage, unable to remember if they'd already put it on the plane or not. Then again, what did it matter?

He walked out onto the tarmac, past the security guards in their camouflage uniforms and bulletproof vests, assault rifles clutched in front of them. He followed the orange cones to the stairway that had been rolled up to the jet. He counted the steps as he ascended.

One. Two. Three. Four.

Uno. Dos. Tres. Quatro.

Four more, and four again, like he was counting out time for Yesenia as she played her guitar.

INTERLUDE
CHAPTER 21

He awoke in an empty airport terminal in front of giant plate glass window which opened to a vast white plain. A pickup with an orange light on the roof and a wide yellow blade attached to the front was clearing snow off the concrete. But it wasn't until he saw the giant mural of Prince on the wall to his right that he remembered where he was and how he'd gotten there.

For as good as her spoken English was, Luz had a terrible time reading the language. He supposed that explained how she ended up booking a ticket not for Montgomery, where his father lived, but for Minneapolis. Whit hadn't realized the mistake himself until the pilot announced that the temperature on the ground was -24° Fahrenheit. It was, after all, winter in the northern hemisphere. Whit hadn't known such cold or seen such sharply angled shadows since those visits to his grandmother's house in Montana. He'd looked down at his freckled knees, left bare by his cargo shorts, and wondered if he had anything long—sleeves or pants—in his luggage.

It turned out not to matter, as his suitcase had apparently taken a different flight that the airline could not trace. He made do with a thin blanket and a small pillow the flight attendant had gifted him with, wandering from terminal to terminal for two days and trying to make a plan. Airports, he decided, were fascinating places that made you look for ways to harm yourself.

He had folded up his blankets and was finishing off the last of the peanut butter sandwiches Luz had made for him when two security guards approached him from opposite sides of the aisle.

"Afternoon, sir," the fat one said. "How are you today?"

"Quite well, and you?" The two men stared at him, then at each other, then back at him. It was only then that he realized he'd answered in Spanish. He cleared his throat. Tried again. "Sorry. I'm fine. How about y'all?"

Another look passed between the guards. "We're fine," the fat one— he was the talker of the two—said. "You know, there've been a couple of reports about a guy matching your description wandering around. If I didn't know better I'd think you were living in the airport."

Whit tried to laugh, but it came off all wrong. "I'm just a little lost," he said.

"As in you don't know where you are, or don't know where you're going?"

"Kind of, yes."

"Well which is it?"

"I'm fine."

The other security guard, a blue-eyed Norwegian nearly as tall as Whit, stepped back with his right foot. That would make him hard to run over, Whit realized. Now that the thought was in his head, though, he had to force himself not to give it a try.

"You got any family around here?" the fat guard asked. "Anyone who might be able to give you a place to stay? Or maybe a ride somewhere?"

Whit sensed the need to act fast, if he was going to avoid some sort of institutional visit, whether to the police station or some psychiatrist's office for evaluation. He wasn't sure—never would be sure—where the idea came from, but in a flash of inspiration he asked if the airport had a chaplain.

"Chaplain," the fat one said, clearly exasperated. "Lonnie, who's the chaplain on duty this week?"

The Norwegian was already thumbing through papers he'd stuffed into a small black notebook. At last he tapped the line he was looking for. Snapped his book closed and looked unhappily at his partner. "Sarah Frisch."

"Jesus," his partner muttered. "All right, come on. We'll point you that way."

The security guards escorted him to the very edge of the terminal, down an escalator into the no man's land of connecting tunnels. Golf carts lined the wall, some of them plugged into chargers, others with their wiring exposed for repairs. A few of the food service workers stood smoking at the far end. When they saw the security uniforms, they dropped their cigarettes into their coffee mugs and hustled up the escalator. Halfway down the hall, the guards stopped.

"Got one here for you, Rabbi," the talkative one called. "You might want to meet with him in the hall. He's a little ripe."

Whit clamped his armpits down and folded his hands in front of him. He hadn't thought much about the way he might look or smell, but the astonished expression on the chaplain's face told him it was worse than the guard had suggested. She composed herself quickly, though, and smiled.

"Hello there," she said, looking him up and down. "Okay. First things first."

Rabbi Sarah started him out with a set of clean clothes and a fifteen-minute time slot in a shower in the employee dressing room. The hot water cleared his head some. When he emerged into the hallway, she greeted him with another smile, and he realized what an unfamiliar animal he was dealing with. He'd heard plenty of preachers—his father included—talk about the trouble with Jews, but to his knowledge he'd never met an actual Jewish person. And while he'd known that liberals—Episcopalians and Methodists and such—had women preachers, it had never occurred to him to think that Jews might have an analogous practice with their rabbis. He wanted to ask about it, but he still didn't trust his lingual synapses to fire when called upon. Instead he looked at her in what he hoped was a polite way.

"You look like you feel better," she said.

She was young, he now noticed—in her thirties, maybe—and would have passed for any of the professional travelers he'd observed in his two days in the airport. But what was she doing here? He wondered if she was the low-man at the church—low woman at the synagogue? He wasn't sure how to phrase any of this, and was fairly certain that Mila would have labeled at least some of his thoughts as sexist. But he pushed Mila out of his mind as quickly as he could, and questions about Rabbi Sarah Frisch along with her. He said he was fine and told her he needed to get going.

"Where to?" she asked. And before he could answer, said, "You have no idea, do you."

Whit smiled. Shook his head.

"Let's start in my office then. You can tell me how you got here."

Three hours later, the rabbi was still helping him unravel his story. They'd moved out of her office and to a table at the back of the main food court near the drink station. Whit threw down cup after cup of coffee until he at last felt his brain begin to function on a basic level. The more aware he became of the person across from him, the more interested he got.

Rabbi Sarah was nothing like Johnny Reinbeck or Brother Arneson or even Father Guillermo. She didn't praise the Lord with every third breath, didn't look for every opportunity to lecture on some finer point of dogma. She just talked, and not like Mila either, who was—he could see this, now that he had a little distance from her—using him from the start. Rabbi Sarah, on the other hand, was funny and smart and genuinely interested in what he had to say. It was clear that she didn't get a lot of visitors in this airport gig, stuffed down in the golf-cart morgue as she was. Still, he could tell she liked him, and that the longer things went, the less she thought of him as a kid.

"So you can't go back to—what did you say the name of that city is?"

"Trujillo."

"Okay, so you can't go back to Trujillo for obvious reasons. But what about your parents? Is it money? We can find you a bus ticket."

"That's all right."

"Not if you don't have a place here to sleep, it's not. Do you want me to help you call your family? I mean, if there are wounds that need to be healed, maybe it would help to just be honest with them."

He tried to consider this. She made a fair point, after all. What did he think he could do, trapped here in the great white north with nothing but $40 Luz had given him and a plastic tub of yogurt he'd saved from the in-flight meal? And really, how long could he expect to keep his father in the dark about what had happened? Once word of his departure and the circumstances surrounding it got back to Covenant, President Crutcheson would be on the phone to Cole Allen with his next breath.

Still, none of that had happened yet—not that he knew of. He had time to work things out. Maybe.

"I'll be all right," he said.

She wrapped her hands around her paper cup. Tapped its bottom rim against the laminate tabletop. It had been empty for a while now, which was how Whit realized, to his sorrow, that the conversation was ending.

"No you won't. Not in this cold."

"I'll figure something out."

She shook her head, her face registering annoyance. She reached into her pocket and pulled out a card for something called Shalom House.

"Let's go," she said. "I'll drive you there."

She was parked in the chaplain's space in the employee lot, which was only a hundred yards or so from the airport exit. But that small distance was the coldest, windiest, most miserable trek he'd ever taken. The only pants from the chaplain's supply closet that would fit him in the waist stopped six inches short of his bare ankles, and the airline blankets he was using for a coat might as well have been tissue paper. Why, he wondered, had anyone ever settled in this godforsaken part of the world in the first place?

He climbed inside the rabbi's Subaru, his shivers so powerful that they shook the car. She turned the key, but the engine didn't crank—no dash lights, no radio.

"Battery's dead," Whit offered.

"No kidding." She reached into her purse and retrieved a cell phone. "Earl?" she said after a moment. "Hi, Earl. It's Rabbi Sarah. Yeah. Battery's dead again. Okay. Thanks." She pressed a button on the phone and dropped it in her lap. "He says fifteen minutes."

"All right," Whit said.

"You want to wait back inside?"

"N—no. I'm good."

"Are you sure? This isn't the equator."

"I have learned to be c-content in all situations." He smiled, cuing her to appreciate the Biblical reference. The Apostle Paul had been in prison when he'd told the Philippians that he could be happy anywhere, under any circumstances. If he could say that in a Roman jail, surely Whit and the rabbi could handle a cold car for a few minutes. But her blank expression reminded Whit that the rabbi had no reason to know the New Testament, including nuances regarding the Apostle. "Sorry," he mumbled, and for reasons he didn't quite understand, added, "Sarah."

"Rabbi Sarah," she said, correcting him almost before the name had left his lips.

"Rabbi. Right, sorry. I didn't mean to offend."

"Who is offended? I'm not. But you need to know. I am a scholar and teacher of Torah. The appropriate way for you to address me includes the word 'rabbi.'"

"Okay."

Whit looked out his window at the frozen plain, ghostly still and devoid of hope. Guilt squeezed his heart like a vice, in part because he'd offended her—and regardless of how she'd played it off, clearly he had—but also because the way she bowed up reminded him of how Mila treated him at Operación Amor. Who would help cook breakfast for the kids now? Who would comfort Guillermo? Who would teach the boys at OA to clean a carburetor or Yesenia to play guitar?

The answer, of course, was someone else. That world would go on just fine without him. He was the one left rudderless, and it was his own damned fault.

Headlights flashed through the driver's side window. Whit had to lean forward to see around Sarah—Rabbi Sarah. He could see the smooth curve of her chin, the fine hair illuminated by the oncoming vehicle. Whit could hear powerful tires plowing through the slush. A second later, an enormous pickup turned into the lot and parked beside the Subaru. The driver—Earl, he presumed—hopped out. Rabbi Sarah popped the hood and waited. Whit opened his door.

"Where are you going?" she asked.

But Whit was already out of the vehicle. Cold or no cold, he wasn't about to sit inside that car while someone else did all the work. Earl lifted the hood on his pickup, turned and took stock of Whit. Without a word, he handed over one end of the jumper cables. Whit fastened them to the battery posts and waited. His ankles went from cold to itchy-hot to completely numb. He wondered how long before frostbite set in.

"You one of the Rabbi's projects?" Earl asked, motioning to Whit's bare calves.

Whit didn't bother asking what he meant. "I guess so."

"Are you the crazy kind? Or the unlucky kind? Hard to tell, way you're dressed."

"I just came from South America."

"Let me guess. It's complicated."

Earl leaned around the open hood and made a winding motion with his finger. Rabbi Sarah turned the key. The engine coughed but did not start. Earl held up his palm. "We'll give it another minute," he called, and turned back to Whit. "The Rabbi here is a brave soul—close to fearless, even. So she'd have a conniption fit if she heard me say this. Fact is, though. I don't much like the notion of her ferrying around a shabby young man twice her size. I'm sure you understand."

"It's fine," Whit said through the knot gathering in his throat. "We had coffee in the airport."

"Oh, coffee, well then." Earl sent a glob of fluid through the banked snow in front of the parking space. "You need a place to stay and some work to get you back on your feet, am I right?"

"Yes sir."

"Well between me and you, you aren't going to get that from the Rabbi here. She'll drop you off at whatever Jewish charity can look after you for the night, but you're not going to know what to do with them. In a day or two you'll be back in the cold with nothing but some airline blankets and your capri pants. So tell you what—come with me and I'll set you up in my garage apartment for the evening. Then in the morning we'll talk to Pastor Franklin about finding a job."

Whit looked down at the tiny hole left by the snot missile Earl had spat into the snow. "I'm not sure I'm in the best place as far as religion goes."

"Who said anything about religion? I'm talking about a paycheck, maybe a little self-respect. Pastor Franklin knows people who hire people like you. Now you want my help or not? Because I'm not letting you leave here with Rabbi Sarah."

He leaned back again and twirled his finger. This time the engine cranked, and so he began disconnecting the cables. Whit closed the hood and picked his way through the slush, all the way around the Subaru until he reached the passenger door of the pickup. The rabbi rolled down the window.

"Everything okay?" she asked.

"Yeah, it's fine. Earl said he'd take me to his place."

Rabbi Sarah frowned. "Did he give you a choice in this?"

"Not really."

She muttered something he didn't understand—Hebrew, maybe—then looked back up at him. "Well then, I'll give you a choice. If you want to go with Earl, that's up to you. I've told you I'm willing to set you up for the night."

He looked over at Earl, who was finishing winding the jumper cables, and he could tell that this wasn't a man who could handle a knife. This was the more garden-variety bully, one that Whit could bluff on most days. But this wasn't most days, and Whit was at least aware enough to know he wasn't quite himself.

"Maybe it's best if I go with Earl," he said. "I'm—."

He waited for the rest of the sentence to come to him, but the words were frozen somewhere in the space around his head.

"Goodbye, Mr. Whitman," the rabbi said. "Shalom."

"Shalom," he said back, hoping as he did that was an appropriate response. It seemed to be, judging from the smile on her lips as she rolled up the window and put the car in reverse. Whit watched her go, wondering what it would have been like to be close to her tonight—nothing sexual. Just close.

But when he'd settled into the warm cab of Earl's pickup, Whit decided he'd made the right choice after all. He pulled down the visor and checked himself in the little mirror—scruffy face, chapped skin, droopy eyes. The haggard face of a man who'd been dealt more than one hard blow. He'd seen that visage before, back in Wyoming after the closing of Grey Butte Mine. It stared back at him now, not as his father's, but as his own.

PART III

Figure 8: Part II Recap

CHAPTER 22

Halfway to work on his first day at Northern Lakes Community College, Professor Junius Whitman realized that he was about to show up to class unprepared. He'd left his clunky college-issued laptop on the kitchen counter, along with all the paper notes he'd scribbled to help him navigate the four Spanish classes he was scheduled to teach that day. And so he made a U-turn in the middle of the street and raced back home, weaving in and out of traffic with all the confidence of a Peruvian cab driver. In his vehicular zeal, however, he forgot about the fast-food coffee cup he'd tucked between his thighs on the way to the office. When he swerved to avoid a slow-moving tanker truck, he squeezed his legs together for balance with enough force to pop the plastic lid off into the floorboard. The cup crumpled, sloshing hot coffee everywhere. He snatched it up and lobbed it out the window, but not before a puddle of the scalding liquid landed in his lap. He cursed loudly and felt, as he did every time he cursed, both release and shame.

He burst into his apartment and stripped off his pants. An angry crimson burn ran across his thighs, looking in some places as though it was starting to blister. He cursed again.

"Wooieee!" Isaias called. "I didn't think you went to those kind of parties."

Whit growled, more for the loss of his dignity—not to mention his pants—than for Isaias' teasing. They'd shared an apartment—nearly triple the time they'd been roommates at Covenant, back in the day—and, after a few tentative weeks of getting to know the full adult versions of their erstwhile selves, had more or less settled back into the same type of easy friendship they had shared in Finney Hall.

"I spilled," Whit said, and didn't wait for a response. He grabbed a fresh pair of khakis from his closet but didn't put them on yet.

Instead he wrapped some ice in a dish towel and ran back down to the car, jumped in and sped away with the pack laid over the worst of the burn. He pulled into campus on two wheels and, as he slammed the gear selector into park, realized that he'd forgotten to retrieve his computer or his notes. A terrible warmth rose in Whit's body. Sweat beaded on his skull. He flung open the door and let the contents of his stomach loose on the pavement, right in front of a couple of college girls in hoodies and sweatpants. They stepped off the sidewalk and peered over his car door in concern. That is, until they saw he wasn't wearing pants. Then they looked at each other and giggled. One of them, he was pretty sure, invited him to a back-to-school party that night, but he was too busy wishing the earth would swallow him right then and there to know for sure.

"Whitman!" a booming voice called from the direction of the administration building. Whit raised his head to see Dr. Zevon, the provost, standing at the edge of the sidewalk.

"Yes, sir," Whit answered. "I'll be right there. Give me just a minute."

He waited until Zevon had gone back inside before he closed his car door and, defying laws of spatial relationships, maneuvered around the console and steering wheel and into his fresh khakis. He took a long stride over the foul puddle outside his door, smoothed his clothes the best he could, and marched into Zevon's office.

"Not off to a great start, are we, Mr. Whitman." Zevon pulled a roll of breath mints from his desk drawer and handed them to Whit. "You better keep these handy today. Nervous?"

"A little, maybe."

"Well don't be. Hell, every teacher in the world had a first day, and I bet half of them tossed their cookies at some point. You'll do fine."

Whit shifted his weight. Wondered if Zevon had been able to see his state of semi-undress from his vantage point on the sidewalk. "I left my laptop at home. And all my notes."

"Eh, don't worry about that. It's syllabus day. You give out a bunch of copies and threaten the plagues of Egypt on them if they get out of line. Ten minutes later, everybody goes to get coffee and wait for the next syllabus day class."

"Right," Whit said. He thought it best not to mention the vocabulary lesson—one that he was, in fact, rather proud of—he'd planned for his first session.

"Look," Zevon continued. "It's just the social contract with students, all right? These aren't your go-getting Ivy-League types. They want to get their credits and earn their certificate and get the hell out of here so they can start making money. Don't expect too much. And don't put so much damn pressure on yourself! I'll send maintenance out to scrub the puke."

Zevon's advice—don't expect too much—may have lacked inspiration, but it reflected the attitude of Western Minnesota with dispassionate precision. Perhaps it was the early-onset winter—the first snow came a mere five weeks after school started—or the unending prairie winds. Whatever the reason, Whit encountered a level of pessimism among his faculty peers that would have made the Buddha swell with pride. This may be the land of the Lutherans, but anyone with any sense at Northern Lakes Community College would have told you that life is suffering, and the best thing you could do for your psyche was to assume things would get worse.

"Realistic expectations," Zevon said again at the midterm faculty meeting. "That's the key to everything."

It was this settle-before-something-worse-comes-along mentality that landed Whit in Wilmer, Minnesota in the first place. Earl had been true to his promise when he'd brought Whit home from the airport. After a week in the tiny garage apartment, Whit was set up in an even tinier apartment above a Somali restaurant in Midtown with the deposit and first two-month's rent paid by Earl. But, Whit soon realized, his benefactor wasn't the model of Christian charity that Cole Allen had been for the jail birds back in Wyoming. Rather, he expected to be repaid for his investment, and with 30% interest. So motivated, Whit took a job bussing tables for the Somalis until he landed a better-paying gig at a daycare facility for mentally ill adults who were violent or sexually aggressive. By late summer he'd paid off his debt to Earl and enrolled in night school to study Spanish, which was, he decided, the path of least resistance toward a certified education.

The fact that the pinnacle of his academic study resulted in a mere associate degree failed to dissuade Dr. Zevon and NLCC from hiring him as a junior faculty member. Señor Weisenfels, their popular longtime Spanish instructor, had died a week before school started from injuries sustained at an amateur MMA tournament in Fargo. In Whit's phone interview, Zevon didn't come out at say the word "desperate," but he did volunteer to waive the policy requirement of a face-to-face interview and offered Whit the job on the spot.

"The world belongs to the adventurous," Isaias said when Whit relayed the conversation.

"I will pack my things, Brother Big Man, and accompany you on your latest sojourn. Small town America, here we come! We will have stories to tell."

In Whit's estimation, both Isaias and Dr. Zevon turned out to be right about Wilmer. Isaias rebooted The Story Project among the people in the little town. He sweet-talked his way into a part-time job at the library and spent everything he earned upgrading to digital video equipment. He used some of the quirkier local businesses—the combination pub and barber shop, the tattoo parlor in the back room of a funeral home—to unearth tiny little counter-cultures, right there in the middle of the Great White North. Whit helped lug in gear and drove Isaias around while he shot B-roll footage. Through Isaias' careful eye, Wilmer practically teemed with interesting characters.

Whit's own story, however, turned out to be exactly what one might expect from a first-year teacher—which is to say, outside of that first nauseating day, boring as hell. He nailed some lectures and bombed others, learned to hate grading the way some people hated the sight of snakes or the texture of canned beets. Outside of his occasional ride-alongside with Isaias, he had no life to speak of. He gave church a try and found he just couldn't do it anymore—the same songs, the same sermons, the same guilt. The faith of his youth now seemed anxious and a bit unhinged, but the Minnesota Catholics were too stodgy and the Lutherans too political. Once, when Isaias was in Chicago visiting one of his filmmaking buddies, he even tried driving back to the Cities to the synagogue where Rabbi Sarah worked. But his presence put her out of sorts—scared her, even—and he got the hint. When it came to making friends, the religious sector was just as bad as—maybe even worse than—than the bar scene.

In the end, he took a second job at KFC to help fill the time, reasoning that if he was going to be lonely and unfulfilled, he might as well get paid for it. He often wondered if any of the chicken pieces in the freezer—thighs, wings, legs, even livers—came from the same bird, or if the poor fowl was chopped up and dispatched to various locations according to its component parts. He found the second scenario more likely, if unsettling in philosophical terms. Was a bird aware of the grisly fate for which it had been hatched? Did it hope for anything else, or did it simply adjust its expectations toward the unavoidable? Plenty of people did that very thing, and Whit supposed Zevon was right about the value of his philosophy when it came to his night job. In terms of congruency between what Whit expected and what actually was, frying chicken had to be on the high side of the bell curve.

It was outside the Wilmer KFC on a bitter January night that, using a new cell phone he'd signed up for at an after-Christmas sale, he called Libby to wish her a happy eighteenth birthday. She gave him the obligatory family updates. Byron, her no-account stepfather, had already quit the job at the tractor dealership that had precipitated their recent move to northeast Arkansas. To make up for the loss of income, Bethany was picking up extra shifts on the transplant unit at Methodist Hospital in Memphis, a 90-minute drive but worth the extra money. Zeb—their half-brother, born to Bethany and Byron during Whit's sojourn in Trujillo—was four and terrorizing everything in his path.

"Oh, and I quit school," she said, the tone in her voice daring him to make an issue of the decision.

"Lib—."

"Don't start," she said.

"I'm not starting anything."

"Right."

"I just think—."

"I did a full semester at Arkansas State—fifteen credits' worth, which is how many credits more than you earned at Covenant?"

Whit pulled the phone away from his ear and sighed. "Fifteen."

"So tell me again which of us is the flunky?"

"You sound like mom. Just tell me why you quit."

"I got involved with this married Peruvian chick, and then her husband—oh wait. That was you."

"Really, Lib?"

"Fine." She took a deep breath. "Classes were boring. Professors were ridiculous. Dorm life sucks. Should I go on?"

He was trying to decide how to speak wisdom into his sister's circumstance when the door to the KFC opened and a pimple-faced shift manager stuck his head out into the frigid air. He tapped his wrist to let Whit know his break was over. Whit nodded, told him that he'd be right there, then turned back to Libby.

"I just think you need to have realistic expectations," he said.

"That's the same shit advice Byron gives me. How's Isaias?"

"Fine. Working a lot on his story project." He cracked the door open to make sure the manager—Austin, he thought the name was, or maybe Andy—was otherwise occupied. He could see him through the kitchen, standing at the register and trying to mollify a customer waving a receipt in his face. Whit figured he had maybe ten more minutes before he risked being fired. "Have you talked to Dad lately?"

Libby went silent, which is what she did just about every time he brought up their father. Even though she expressed nothing but contempt for the man, she'd nonetheless been the more favored child since Whit's disastrous exit from Covenant University had embarrassed Cole Allen in front of Brother Arneson and Dr. Crutcheson. On the rare days when he and his father did talk, Whit left the conversation feeling as though he'd spent the whole time pleading his case for existence to an unsympathetic judge.

"Listen, forget it," he said. "I didn't mean to put you in the middle."

"He's in Wyoming," Libby said. "I thought you knew."

"How on earth would I have known that?"

"Because you live up north."

"Minnesota is a long way—"

"—and because he's picking up Bonner Hanson."

Now it was Whit's turn to wait in silence. He'd always liked Bonner—even considered him a mentor, though perhaps a flawed one. But the time he'd spent working with abuse survivors at Operación Amor made him think differently about things he'd witnessed as a kid—where Bonner placed his hands when they prayed for a youth, things he said to Libby when their father was out of earshot. And of course, Tamara. If he'd known then what he knew now, Whit liked to think he would have turned Bonner in to the school or to the police or to the church, not that any of those was more likely than the other to dig into something they'd rather not know. He saw no use in dredging it up, though, not after all these years. He hoped Tamara hadn't been scarred too deeply, hoped that against hope. Wished that he could go back in time and warn her and everybody else that Bonner Hanson was not a sinner saved by grace. He was, not to put too fine a point on it, a shitbag.

"Bonner?" was all he could think to say.

"He's been in prison again—beat some guy up at a rodeo while you were in Peru. His parole was up last month, so he can move now. I don't know much more than that."

"But why is Dad—he's in Wyoming?"

"Probably on his way back to Alabama by now."

"Buy why—"

"Really? You're going to ask that again? All right. I don't fucking know why. I don't know why Cole Allen Whitman fucking does anything, except that he'll probably blame it on Jesus for telling him to. For fuck's sake, Whit."

He waited a moment. Listened to see if she was crying, but she wasn't. Rather, she was fuming, and he knew better than to throw another match on whatever gasoline pooled in her mind.

"I better get back to work," he said.

"You do that," she spat back.

"Lib, I'm sorry. Happy birthday."

"Yeah," she said. He waited for the beep of the line going dead, but could still hear his sister breathing on the other end. At last, and very quietly, she spoke. "You just won't let yourself know what you know, will you?"

"Yes. I do. I—what are we talking about here?"

More silence. Then finally, "Bye, bro. Love you."

She hung up without giving him time to answer. He folded the phone and dropped it into his jacket pocket and slipped back into the kitchen. Alex—that was the manager's name, he remembered now—was in the dining room, offering chocolate chip cookies to a couple of twin girls who must have been the daughters of the irate customer. Whit dropped his coat in the break room and took his place next to the deep fryer. He threw a few of the pieces into the basket. Lowered it into the hot oil.

"Sorry, bird," he muttered. "You get what you get and you don't have a fit."

The oil bubbled and fizzed around the chicken parts, spit a few fine particles back onto Whit's forearm. He didn't jump, though. By now, he was so used to the feeling of burning oil that he could viscerally imagine what it might feel like to be dropped into that fryer himself. But he chased it from his mind. Already in his young life, he'd thought too much about hell, and, he had to admit, the chicken smelled delicious.

CHAPTER 23

The sky was just beginning to brighten when he left for Northern Lakes the next morning for his 9:00 class. The sun, it seemed, just couldn't be bothered to shine, and certainly not to warm anything up. When it finally did peek over the trees, it shot lasers off the white snow, blinding drivers like they were the Apostle Paul on the Damascus Road. Whit navigated the last half mile mostly by feel. He was so tense by the time he parked that he feared a repeat of his first-day debacle. But he opened the door and let the cold air do its work and, when he arrived in class only five minutes late, thought he was doing okay.

He wasn't, though. The knot in his gut didn't get worse, but neither did it go away. Rather, it settled in, pressed hard on his insides. Between classes he tried to throw up, but that wasn't it. He went back, determined to will himself out of whatever virus had set up shop in his GI tract. As he lectured, he found that he kept pressing his tongue against the back of his one false tooth. It replaced an incisor knocked out by a patient named Lamont at the adult daycare in Minneapolis, and it was supposed to be anchored in place. But he could feel it wiggling over the screw implanted in his jaw. It kept his mind off of how icky he felt, but also off the details of his lesson. He stammered through the subjunctive mood of -ir verbs, but knew even as he did that he wasn't making much sense. Finally, a young woman named Jolene raised her hand.

"Mr. Whitman? Are you okay?"

"What? Yes. *Si. Por qué?*"

"Because you look like shit."

The class giggled, but everyone knew that Whit wouldn't call her out on profanity, even if no one knew why. Jolene had been one of the girls who'd stopped at his car the day he threw up, and he wasn't about to cross her lest she tell her story. The other students noticed how delicately he addressed her, he was sure, and probably thought they were sleeping together.

"*Estoy bién,*" he said. "*Y tú?*"

"I think you might want to lie down for a bit. Maybe you should let us out early."

"I said I'm fine." However advisable it was for him to keep his mouth shut, he was getting irritated now, and he didn't have the resources to stop the words. "Now can we please talk about *decir* and leave my appearance the hell out of it?"

He scanned the room, trying to look stern, which had usually worked with the kids at OA and occasionally made a difference in the NLCC classroom. But he pushed his tongue against that false tooth what must have been one too many times. He felt it give under the pressure, slide through his lips and onto the desk of a quiet freshman named Amber, who promptly left the room holding a hand over her mouth.

Whit looked down at the sliver of white on the laminate desktop. Even without picking it up, he could see that it had cracked vertically, leaving the interior threads spread apart too far to bite against the bolt embedded in his jaw.

Jolene fought back a laugh. "Class dismissed?" she asked.

Whit kept his lips sealed. Answered with a nod.

He gathered up the things Amber had left when she'd sprinted out. Set them outside the door so that she could retrieve them without coming inside. Then he sat down at her desk and examined the tooth. It didn't tell him anything he hadn't seen already, but it did give him reason to think about context. When he'd told his KFC coworkers about losing his front tooth in a fight, they viewed it as a badge of honor. But when the thing fell out in a college classroom, students were horrified. He wondered if these kids knew anything about the world. Then again, he didn't need to wonder. Not at all.

Before his mind found another theoretical rabbit to chase, Dr. Zevon entered the classroom, his face ashen.

"I'm fine," Whit said. He held up the tooth as if to explain.

"Right, well." Zevon cleared his throat.

"Really, sir. It's not a big deal."

"What? Oh that." he motioned toward Whit's mouth. "We've got an excellent dental plan, for an institution our size. There's something else, though."

Whit waited but didn't speak. He had the faint taste of iron in his mouth, but he couldn't figure out where it was coming from. He didn't want Zevon to see any blood between his teeth when he smiled.

"So your Spanish. It's from one of the Minneapolis schools."

"I learned most of it in Peru."

"But your degree. The credential. That's a bachelor's, right?"

"Associate's."

"Oh. So…two years?"

"More or less."

"Christ."

Zevon smoothed the rooster tail atop his head and stared for a long moment, looking for all the world like a chicken contemplating the fryer. But whatever he saw in his mind's eye was nothing he couldn't recover from. He cleared his throat. Pushed himself up on his tiptoes, then let his heels fall. "Well, HLC—the Higher Learning Commission—has their panties all twisted about the credentials of our teachers. An associate's won't do it, I'm afraid. We're going to have to figure something out."

Whit squirmed in his seat, thinking this must be what it felt like to be called on in his class. "What's that?" he asked.

Zevon turned to him and smiled. Motioned again toward Whit's mouth. "Well, that tooth for starters. And we'll go on from there. I hope."

Neither of the two dentists in Wilmer had quick access to a replacement tooth, which meant that he had to go a week with nothing but a metal nub where the incisor had been. He tried to hide it at first, but it was no use. Some of his students had taken to calling him *El Profesor Desdentado*—the toothless professor—and Isaias laughed uproariously at Whit's new appearance.

"Gangsta," he said, cackling.

And so Whit gave up trying to hide the fact of his lost tooth. The effort had made him uncomfortable to begin with. Besides, he had bigger chickens to fry—his work situation, of course, since Zevon's odd behavior had only worsened in recent days. But also the grenade Libby had dropped in his lap about Bonner. It made him angry at her—what did she expect him to do?—but also at himself for not seeing the signs. As an adolescent, Libby would have fit right in with the troubled kids at Operación Amor, and now it wasn't hard to draw a line as to why. He tried probably fifty times that week to call her, or tried to try, anyway. He pulled up her contact and let his thumb hover over the "call" key, but never pressed it. What good would it do? Even if he found some way to reintroduce the topic, Libby would laugh it off. She'd opened the door for him to know her secrets, and he'd backed away instead. Maybe, he thought, he was no better than his father.

More soluble was the problem with the tooth. Lauren Stringfellow, the daughter of one of the dentists, was fighting for a passing grade in his Spanish I class. She talked to her father, who called in a favor to one of his friends at a lab in Rochester. Dr. Stringfellow examined Whit's mouth and frowned.

"How long's it been since your last cleaning?"

"I don't know. A year?"

"Doesn't look like just a year. Who was your last dentist?"

"Maybe a little longer than a year," Whit said.

"Well, we need to clean them before we put that false tooth in. You've got—just trust me on this."

And so Dr. Stringfellow called in his hygienist supervisor and asked her to work around their morning caseload so that they could "jackhammer through the layers on this boy's teeth," as he put it. She emitted a heavy sigh and led Whit into a beige room with a flatscreen television mounted on the ceiling above the chair.

"Let's start with this," she said. She handed him a paper shot glass with a foul-smelling pink liquid inside. He swirled it around and sniffed. Made a face.

"What is it?"

"Mouthwash for sensitive teeth. It won't numb you, but it might help you take what's coming." She folded her hands in her lap and gave him a motherly look. "I suppose you know this will be unpleasant."

He set the cup back on the counter. "I'll be fine," he said.

The hygienist didn't even try to hide her eye roll. But she stepped on the control pad for the chair and lowered him onto his back.

"Okay," she said. "As long as you know it's coming."

He had to take a break an hour into the cleaning to call the college and ask them to cancel his classes until after lunch. Dr. Zevon's secretary didn't respond to his request right away, and he wondered if it was because he hadn't spoken clearly, what with the pain in his mouth. But he could hear mumbled voices, and then the squish of a hand covering the receiver. A few seconds later, it squished off again.

"Will you be at your 1:00 conversation and composition class then?"

"Yeth ma'am."

"Okay. We will see you then."

He thought about that during the rest of the cleaning, how the secretary had said, "*We* will see you." Did he have an appointment with Zevon, or maybe a faculty meeting he'd forgotten about? One more thing to worry over.

He didn't have to worry long. When he arrived back at his classroom, mouth throbbing but nonetheless cleaned and repaired, the desks were empty except for a rail-thin woman in a business suit. She was eighty-five, if she were a day, and when she stood she barely came to Whit's elbows. But the way she adjusted her glasses and stacked her papers and shook his hand told him that she was ready for battle, and that he had already lost.

"You saw this coming, right?" Isaias said that night at their apartment. "Even you had to see this coming."

"Should I have?"

Isaias raised his eyebrows and poured more tequila into the blender. After years of cautious experimentation with alcohol, Whit had discovered margaritas. Thus far, they were the only vehicle for the drug that he truly enjoyed, and tonight, Isaias said, was the perfect time to get blind stinking drunk.

"You think I'm naive," Whit said as he took his glass.

"Tell me, Mr. Big Man. How many of your colleagues at the Northern Lakes Community College have their associate's degrees hanging by their desks?"

"I haven't been in enough offices to know."

"I can tell you right now the answer is one, and that includes you." He vaulted over the back of the couch and landed next to Whit without spilling so much as a drop of his drink. "At least you weren't the one who falsified your records. Here's to Dr. Malcolm Zevon, God rest his academic soul."

They clinked glasses, and Whit sipped his drink as best he could with throbbing teeth. Dr. Roush, the woman who'd greeted him in the classroom, was a member of the NLCC board of directors, who had recently been alerted by HLC of some irregularities in their provost's administration of his duties. In particular, they were concerned that, in his haste to fill vacant teaching positions, Dr. Zevon had exaggerated the credentials of some of the professors—including Whit, who according to Zevon's records had a master's degree in linguistics. He'd done a similar thing with instructors in history, English comp, and computer programming, but those three had the good sense to know the score and so kept their actual diplomas hidden. Whit, on the other hand, had proudly displayed his in a frame above his desk. The sight of it triggered the suspicions of some astute observer—Whit couldn't be sure who, since he never locked his office—which led to a report, which led to an inquiry, which led to all sorts of unfortunate shit, as Isaias put it.

"At least you have KFC," Isaias said. "To the Colonel!"

"Glad you find this funny."

"I'm sorry," Isaias said once he'd composed himself. "It's the booze talking."

"I don't think..." Whit said, but the combination of two margaritas and intense tooth pain had caused the track between his brain and his mouth to malfunction. He tried again. "I don't...think?"

"I beg to disagree, my friend." Isaias' throat made a gulping sound as he stifled another laugh. "You never stop. That's what gets you in trouble."

"I can't help it though," Whit said. "The thinking."

Isaias gave him a pitying look. "I know."

They sat there in silence for a long time, letting their relative moods settle into alignment. At last, Isaias spoke softly. "You loved that teaching job, didn't you?"

"I did," Whit admitted.

"Right. Well, I am sorry." He took Whit's empty margarita glass and placed it on the table.

Whit drew in in a deep breath. He folded his big hands behind his head and looked up at the ceiling. His eyes moved to a dark spot at the edge of the fan. The stain—a blocky maroon splotch that looked vaguely geographical—preceded his and Isaias' residency in the apartment. He wondered again how it had gotten there and why no one had bothered to paint over it.

"I'm worried about Libby," he finally said.

"Lib?" Isaias pushed himself up so that he was seated at the back of the couch. He looked down at his friend. "What's wrong with Lib?"

"I just have a feeling, that's all."

"A feeling?"

"It's dumb."

"No!" Isaias wagged a finger down at him. "No, no, no. No, no. No! O, ye unhappy rationalist! Let intuition wake within!"

Whit felt tears gathering in the corners of his eyes. Alcohol always made him a bit weepy. "I think she needs me—maybe not right there in the same town, but closer to her at least. It's hard to explain."

"Yet as undeniable as that Kentucky-shaped stain on our ceiling."

Whit smiled. "It's more Oklahoma, really."

"Whatever. The point is that your heart tells you to go somewhere that isn't here. You have not been fired, my friend. You've been emancipated! We shall travel southward." He vaulted back over the couch and began assembling the next round of drinks. "So what's the plan? I can hear the Windy City calling!" He cupped his hands over his mouth and made a *whoosh*-ing sound.

Whit let the idea slosh around in his head. Chicago was Isaias' dream, but they both knew he wasn't cut out for big city life. "Too far from Libby."

"Maybe she would come live with us—get away from whatever mess she's in."

"I doubt it's that simple."

"Nothing ever is."

Whit ran his tongue over his teeth, which didn't hurt so much now. He wondered if Isaias had made him a double. He yawned and said, "I'm just trying to figure things out."

Isaias grinned. "That's 80% of the problem right there."

"Be serious."

"I am being serious, Mr. Big Man! You've got to stop trying to parse out every jot and tittle. How else are you ever going to fall in love?"

CHAPTER 24

Some years later, when Junius Whitman considered the greater story arcs of his life, he would decide that falling was the appropriate metaphor not just for how he came to love Novie, but for a good portion of what happened in this universe.

Exhibit A—an arbitrary designation, of course—Poplar Bluff, Missouri. In the grand scheme of things it was no more likely a landing spot for a tripped-up soul than Gillette, Wyoming, or Wilmer, Minnesota. But *likely* was beside the point. Whatever *might* happen, only certain things *did* happen. The trick was to respond to reality rather than to possibility. So while he *might* have made it to Paragould, Arkansas, where his mother and Libby were living, the reality was that he fell into a life 60 miles north, just across the state line, dumped there by God or fate or the universe, or—likely—by random chance.

"Sounds bleak," Novie said.

"No," Whit answered. "Just honest."

"Honest, as in bleak?"

"The truth doesn't have to be pleasant to be the truth."

"You poor man."

She rolled over and flicked on the light, illuminating their naked bodies, much to Whit's embarrassment. He was still lanky and pale as ever, but his mid-twenties had witnessed the arrival of a slight paunch in his midsection and a few patchy growths of hair on his chest and shoulders. He reached down for the covers even though it had to be at least eighty-five degrees in the upstairs bedroom of the townhouse he and Isaias shared. Novie kicked them down again. Wagged a finger at him without looking up from the sudoku puzzle she'd started working.

Whit rolled onto his side and laid a hand on her leg. Felt the taut muscles beneath her bronze skin.

November Burqvist was thirty-one years old and in better shape than almost every other woman Whit knew, thanks to a careful diet and daily yoga regimen. They'd struck up a conversation in the break room of Bootheel Technical Institute on Whit's first day as an auto mechanic instructor. Novie, the English professor and multicultural director at BTI, claimed she could still hear the Oklahoma in his accent. She'd been born in Tahlequah, she said, the daughter of a since-defrocked Catholic priest and a Cherokee teenager. If she knew anything about anything, it was how hard it was to get rid of Oklahoma.

He tapped the cover of the puzzle book playfully. "Need some help?"

She swatted him away with a grunt, and so he picked up the novel he'd been reading on these nights while he waited for her to decide to go home. They'd started going out in September, just after school started. By October, they'd finally admitted to one another that, while they enjoyed being together, they both thought the money and pretense spent on dating was stupid. They settled into a pattern of making dinner and going to bed two or three times a week. Still, he wasn't sure what to make of the relationship, if it could be called a relationship. The physical part wasn't all that different than he'd experienced with Mila, but the emotional landscape was as far as Poplar Bluff was from Peru. He had no doubt Novie genuinely cared for him. Once, after a particularly intense love-making session, she'd almost told him she loved him. He could hear the syllables forming in her mouth, but he appreciated her restraint. He could trust a woman like that.

Whit put down the book and draped an arm over her midsection. She pushed his hand away again.

"I'm not your emotional support animal," she said. "You want to cuddle, get a cat."

"I can't. Carlie has allergies."

"Mmhmm."

Carlie was Isaias' on-again, off-again girlfriend, and she was deathly allergic to pretty much any non-human mammal. Novie, a dog-lover with two pooches of her own, couldn't even leave her jacket on the couch for fear of depositing lethal amounts of pet dander onto the fabric. All in all, the situation was more high-maintenance than Whit would have liked.

"Do you think I'm high maintenance?" Novie asked absently.

Whit felt a thousand pinpricks dance over his scalp. He hadn't said that about Carlie aloud, had he? He was almost sure he hadn't. But, more often than could be explained by mere coincidence, Novie brought up out of the blue the very thing that was on his mind. He still believed in God, most days, and so couldn't completely discount supernatural phenomena such as mind-reading. But he couldn't square it logically. Thinking about it both thrilled and exhausted him.

"High maintenance?" Whit said. "No. Of course not. No."

"You know you can't keep a lie going. So if you feel about me the way you do about Carlie—."

"I've never been to bed with Carlie. Swear to God."

She smacked him with her puzzle book. "You know what I mean. Now do you think I'm a high maintenance person or not?"

"Not usually, no."

"All right."

And that was the end of it, from her perspective. Whit wanted to dig a little deeper, if for no other reason than to find out why she'd asked. But he reminded himself not to worry, that this moment was enough to hold for now. He wondered if she could hear him as he thought these things—hoped she might be able to. He wished she would stay, and he wished, more by the day, that he could find a way to convince her to do so.

The new semester at Bootheel Technical Institute began on a bitter January day, by southern Missouri standards. The temperature outside was 22 degrees at 4:00pm, and whatever good humor the students in Whit's basic mechanics class had possessed to start the day had turned icy in every conceivable way. As they opened the door on Bay #3 to let in the last vehicle on the schedule, a kid named Shawnson tossed water from his cup onto the concrete. It froze almost instantly, and when the bay door closed, it high centered on the new patch of ice. The north wind whistled through the half-inch gap that now showed all along the bottom of the door.

Whit wandered over to the bay. Shawnson's lab partners were chewing him out royally for the stunt, but they quieted down when they saw their instructor.

"Shawnson," Whit said. He motioned toward the patch of ice.

"It's too fucking cold to be working today," he grumbled. "My sister said SEMO cancelled their classes."

"You think your future boss is going to let good money stay home just because it's cold?" Whit replied.

"People won't even show up, weather like this. Shit."

"But people have shown up today." He checked his clipboard. "Fourteen oil changes, nine tire rotations, one tune-up, five brake pads. Busier than usual even, I'd say."

"I can't feel my fingers."

Whit reached into his back pocket and pulled out a pair of mechanic's gloves. He had a whole box of them in the office, but he gazed lovingly at them for effect before extending them toward Shawnson. "This is my best pair, but you can have them—on two conditions."

"What's that?"

"One, that you get a ball-peen hammer and break up that ice patch and close the bay door before your buddies freeze their nuts off. And two, that you do so without one more word from your dumbass mouth."

Whit turned to walk away, biting the inside of his lip hard enough to taste blood. Over his brief teaching tenure at NLCC and BTI, he'd learned that such moments of conflict or insubordination were no place for his natural, empathetic instincts. That was just asking for more trouble, whether in the form of aggression or misunderstanding. Instead, he had to imagine how Cole Allen Whitman would respond if he were in charge. The trick worked more often than not, and it made him laugh every time.

But when he looked up through the plate glass window to his office and saw Dr. Price, the Vice President for Institutional Advancement, his joy evaporated into the cold air. The VP sat in a chair opposite Whit's desk, looking over the top of his glasses at the screen of his smartphone. Whit took a deep breath and entered the room, just in time for his own cell phone—the same flip job he'd bought back in Minneapolis—to vibrate to life on his desk.

"You can take that if you need to," Price said without looking up.

Whit pressed a button to silence the phone. "What can I do for you?" he asked as the VP's thumbs continued to click across to tiny keys. Several seconds later, Price dropped the device into his shirt pocket and folded his hands in his lap. Whit fought the urge to pull his certified instructor paperwork unbidden from the file next to his computer.

"I probably don't say enough how happy we are to have you at BTI," Price said. "I truly mean that. A man so young and yet able to qualify as an instructor so quickly—well, that just goes to show. The Lord has brought you to such a time as this for his purposes."

Price's speech always sounded vaguely biblical, which wasn't all that uncommon for this part of the world. He was a Baptist, which meant he held to the same rigid standards of sexual purity by which Whit had been raised. He'd be less than thrilled to know that two of his employees flaunted the anti-fraternization rules the way Whit and Novie did. And he almost certainly knew.

Whit's phone buzzed again. Once again, he silenced it without checking the ID.

"You're a smart man," Price said. "So you might be able to guess why I'm here."

Whit almost smiled at that. He knew the game Price was playing here, employing the same trick Isaias used sometimes in his interviews to get people to out themselves. Whit wasn't about to take the bait. "Why don't you go ahead?"

"Lord bless you," Price said, smiling. "Well then. I'll get right to it. We've got a bit of a situation rearing its head. Mexicans, I mean."

"Mexicans?"

"You've seen them, I'm sure. They're moving into town like a swarm, and we've had more and more applying to BTI. Now, I'm not sure your opinion on Mexicans"—he looked up to try to gauge Whit's reaction—"but they represent an untapped market for the school. And President Yost and I believe that the time has come for us to reach out to them."

"Keep going."

"We have something of a language issue, of course. How then shall we proceed? Well, I have a colleague from Minnesota that I spoke with at the ATEA conference last month. He said you used to work for him up at Northern Lakes Community College."

"Dr. Zevon?"

"That's the one! He's a good man. It's a shame what they did to him up in Wilmer. Point is, he said you taught Spanish for him. So President Yost and I want you to help us develop a program in which the instructors learn a little Mexican and the Mexicans learn a little English. What do you say?"

"Well, Mexican isn't a language."

"No, no," Price said, laughing as he waved his mistake away. "Of course. Spanish and English. You teach both ways. How's that sound?"

Whit shook his head doubtfully. "I don't have the qualifications."

"I'm not talking about a for-credit class," Price said. "We're talking about something outside the curriculum. I can require the staff to take it, no problem. And if the Mexicans have to pass an English competency exam before we let them take classes, they'll be glad to pay for it."

"I don't know," Whit said, but he thought he knew perfectly well where this was going. If he took Price's offer, he'd be the jewel of Bootheel Tech for a couple of years, until people like Price realized that the Mexicans were smart enough to learn English somewhere that didn't charge them $500 per semester. The dollars wouldn't flow in quite like expected, and Whit would be out of a job once again. "I'd hate to leave my mechanics students," he said.

Price smiled. He tapped his forehead in salute. "I knew you'd be a tough negotiator. Zevon told me you were smarter than you looked—no offense, you understand. We can keep you in the garage for basic mechanics. Wylene Rader over in the business office has a cousin—Dillon, I think it is—who would be willing to teach the advanced classes in the afternoons. That would free you up for a few day classes in Spanish, and then maybe one or two night classes per week."

"I suppose—"

"Of course, there would be a small compensation increase. Not as much as we'd like to do, you understand. But it's a starting point, and if this takes off you'll have a chance to move pretty quickly up the salary scale. You know, if—"

Whit's phone buzzed to life again. This time he looked down, curious who might be bothering him this late on a Monday.

"You go ahead and take that," Dr. Price said. "I'll get you an official offer by Friday."

Whit thanked him again and rubbed his forehead. He'd ask Novie what she thought about the job offer later. Probably he'd take it, but there may be things that she saw that he didn't—almost certainly were things, given how long she'd been at BTI and how much she distrusted every last person in authority. But those questions could wait. As the buzzing of the phone died in his hand, he flipped it open to see five missed calls, all from the same number, and one voicemail. He pressed the *listen* key, but he could hear his sister's voice before he even got the phone to his ear.

"For God's sake, Whit. It's Lib. Dad's on his way to your place. Call me now."

CHAPTER 25

The "idiot light"—this was how Whit usually referred to the orange fuel indicator that came on when a vehicle was dangerously low on gas—had blinked on that morning before Whit was even out of his driveway. He'd made it twenty miles to work without addressing the issue, but he wasn't fool enough to think he'd be so lucky on the way home. He coasted into the Kum 'n Go station on fumes. Fumbled with his credit card in the bitter cold as he returned Libby's call.

For as agitated as she'd sounded in the voicemail, Libby gave him the rundown with her typical economy of words. Cole Allen had fallen out with Brother Arneson and the Montgomery Blessing, but opportunity had arisen again in Wyoming, where a newly deregulated coal industry was pumping fresh life into towns like Gillette. With little left for him in Alabama and souls to save at the mines, Cole Allen had packed up his earthly belongings and headed north to start a church.

"He showed up wanting a place to stay for the night," Libby explained.

"At mom's house?"

"Franklin and I got our own place. I told you."

"Oh, right," he said, although he could tell that he wasn't fooling her into thinking he had the slightest idea what she was talking about. But that would be another conversation for another day. "I guess you and Dad still aren't on good terms."

"It's not that. Not all that."

"Then what—"

"They're on their way to your apartment. Bonner is with him." She waited a moment for that to settle. "You better get going," she finally said.

As he raced home, Whit realized he was praying—something like praying, anyhow. He was thankful to whatever benevolent forces were at work in the universe for the gift—a coffee mug with a screw-on lid—that Isaias had given him on his first day at BTI. A small thing perhaps, but one that kept hot coffee off his crotch and brought warm feelings to his heart, both for his friend's kindness and for whatever spiritual forces may have inspired it.

But it was another prayer—one for help—that occupied the greater part of Whit's emotions. It was the kind of prayer people said in hospital rooms and sentencing hearings, what Isaias called "oh shit prayers." And in this context, Whit was certain, the profanity was at least appropriate and perhaps even essential to accurate communication.

He picked up his phone from the seat beside him and felt with his thumb until he'd pressed the sequence to speed-dial Novie for the third time since he'd left work. And for the third time, the call went to voicemail. Desperate as he was, this time he left a message.

"Hey it's me. I know we had plans for dinner at my place, and I'm really sorry. Something is up with my father."

He took a deep breath, wishing he'd thought more about what he would say prior to making the call. Before he could resume speaking, however, he noticed that the lights he'd been watching for the past half mile weren't from the flashing "Bridge Ices Before Road" sign he expected to see, but from a MO-DOT salt truck, straddling the center line and going 30 mph, tops. Whit dropped the phone into his lap and swerved to the right, certain that he was about to roll the car and doubtful that he'd walk away from such an accident. His passenger-side tires whisked through the grass while the tires beneath him roared against the rumble strip on the shoulder. The sound of the salt truck's horn seemed to come from a great distance away, even though Whit could have reached out and touched it from where he sat in the driver's seat. He expected to roll the vehicle at any minute. But an instant later he was, miraculously, back on the pavement in front of the truck. He lifted the phone again and picked up where he'd left off.

"Sorry. My dad is bringing one of his friends with him. He just called. They may already be at the apartment. We—."

A new set of lights behind him ended that thought. He didn't need a second look to know that they were not the benign flashers of the salt truck, but the insistent swirls of the highway patrol. The cop bore down on him and flipped the siren. Whit pressed the button for his hazard lights and eased over to the side of the road. He flipped his phone closed and dropped it into the floorboard beneath him, he hoped out of sight.

"Oh shit," he muttered.

When he arrived home, two vehicles were parked along the street opposite the duplex—Novie's Grand-Am, and in front of that an enormous blue moving van that presumably carried Cole Allen Whitman's earthly belongings on the way back to Gillette, WY. An oversized pickup was parked in Whit's usual space in the driveway, the contents of the bed strapped down beneath a thick blue tarp. Thankfully, Isaias was in Memphis shooting a documentary about abuses in the shipping industry, and so Whit squeezed his car into his roommate's spot. He left the $290 ticket the Hi-Po had presented him with for reckless driving in the center compartment of his car and trudged into his apartment, resigned to face whatever presented itself.

The reality was much like he expected, which was not at all like the scenarios he'd pleaded for in his desperate prayers. His father sat on the couch drinking an orange soda and watching Fox News. To his right, Bonner Hanson reamed beneath his fingernails with a bent paper clip. They both looked up at Whit, nodded their greeting, and went back to their business. He returned the gesture and walked into the kitchen, where Novie was pulling a tray of baked potatoes out of the oven.

"I tried to call," Whit said.

"Later," Novie hissed. "Go tell them dinner's ready."

They dutifully assembled into the four chairs around the kitchen table. Whit reached across for one of the canned biscuits she'd piled into a serving bowl. She brought her heel down hard on his toes. One look at the two men across from them and he understood.

"Bonner, would you bless our meal," Cole Allen said.

Bonner complied and then some, offering a meandering grace that blessed and beseeched for a solid three minutes. Whit cut his eyes toward Novie to see how she was handling what was, to the other men, the most familiar of offerings. She stared lasers toward the butter dish, but as soon as Bonner pronounced the amen, she smiled and moved her arm as though patting Whit's leg under the table. What no one could see but that Whit could surely feel were her long fingernails digging into his thigh.

As they ate, Whit tried to take in these two men, to see them as they were now rather than as they existed in his memory. Years of church work had softened his father's hard shoulders some, but he still had the powerful hands of a life-long mechanic. His conversational manner was different too, gentler than Whit remembered. Still, when he jabbed his fork at Novie to indicate to whom he was speaking, Whit felt his brain fritz and his body shrink back into its six-year-old form, and he was Little Whit once again, blind to what storm approached and afraid of it all the same.

"Are you a churchgoing woman?" Cole Allen asked.

"You might say that," she answered.

"Which one?"

"I grew up Catholic, but I attend the Episcopalian Church here."

Cole Allen exchanged a look with Bonner, who gave a single, somber, nod.

If Whit's father was an aged but recognizable version of his former self, Bonner Hanson seemed like a different person entirely. The expansive energy that had been his hallmark in Gillette was gone, or at least buried somewhere beneath his still muscular frame. His eyes still burned with intensity, but he spoke maybe five sentences the entire meal, and when it was over he retired to the living room to read his Bible. Novie stared him down as he left.

"I'll let y'all have dishes," she said, and stood up from the table and grabbed her coat as she passed the counter, not bothering to stop to put it on.

When she was gone, Cole Allen dropped his elbows on the table and folded his hands against his head to pray. Whit cleared the plates and ran water in the sink.

"You got anything you want to confess?" his father asked.

Whit squirted dish soap into the stream of hot water. He knew better than to turn around. "Nothing to tell."

"Hasn't been anything for a long time."

"Meaning what?"

"Meaning you've gone your own way. Throwing away the best education I could give you, living in sin with that Indian woman. When was the last time you went to church?"

"I don't know. A while ago."

His father shook his head. "All that I tried to instill in you, and you spit on every bit of it. You disappoint me, son."

Whit felt little boy tears sting his eyes. He was damned if he'd let a single one fall, though. He felt his mind go to that prayer-like place again, where a lack of good options opened the door to something like faith. He thought he heard Bonner enter the room behind him. Thought he felt something pass between the two older men before Bonner slipped away again. He didn't turn to confirm any of it, though. Just washed the dishes. Waited for it to pass.

"I guess you talked to your sister," Cole Allen finally said.

"She said you stopped by her place unannounced."

"Did she now?" His voice was growing more and more edgy, even dangerous. "I guess I didn't realize a father needed an invitation to see his own daughter."

"You surprised her. With Bonner, I mean."

Whit heard the chair kick back over the linoleum. He hunched his shoulders reflexively. Turned just enough to see his father step around beside him.

"You listen here," he said, poking a thick finger into Whit's skinny arm. "Your sister is a child. She makes up her mind about something, and it's so to her and there's no way to change it. I don't know what she told you, but you've seen Bonner. He's a different man now."

Whit turned to face his father. "I'm a different man too."

"I guess that's true," his father said, shaking his head in disgust. "That much, anyhow."

He turned away slowly, body still tense enough that Whit worried he might whirl and throw a fist against the side of his head, the way he'd done so many times when Whit was a boy. But three steps later he was across the kitchen and into the doorway that led to the living room. He looked in at Bonner and nodded. Flicked his fingers one time to indicate they were leaving.

"Thanks for dinner," he said. "We won't trouble you."

"You can stay," Whit said, his voice weak and dry to his own ears.

His father shook his head and moved toward the door. "Lord bless you," he said.

Once the door closed behind them, Whit turned out the living room lights and looked out the window. Cole Allen walked across the street, climbed into the moving truck and fired up the engine. Bonner cranked up the pickup, and the two pulled away—possibly to a hotel, but more likely to drive all night, buoyed against sleep by their own narrative of righteous suffering.

He didn't need to search to know where to find Novie, but he did anyway. He drove through the parking lots of several local watering holes, ostensibly looking for her car. But he was just buying time, hoping on one hand that driving would clear his head enough to know what he'd say to her, and on the other that he might find her somewhere other than the one place he knew she'd be. At last the adrenaline from the confrontation with his father wore off, however, and he became more aware of the cold and the dark and his need for sleep. Whatever small chance he had for smoothing things over tonight was not going to get any better as the evening grew later.

And so, when he rolled up next to Novie's Grand Am in the parking lot of the Thirsty Owl, Whit's mission was less about influence than discovery. Things would be what they would be. But he had to find out, and so made his way through the dim light to the far end of the bar, where Novie was drinking with two of her girlfriends. She whispered something to them as he approached, and they walked away, glowering at him.

"You've got balls at least," she said, raising her half empty glass. "I'll give you that."

"Hi." He drew in breath and held it, aware that it was his responsibility to say more, but suddenly blank on everything he'd rehearsed during the drive. It wasn't until he felt pressure building in his chest that he exhaled in a quick, violent burst of air. The bartender looked his way. Novie raised a finger to indicate that she had things under control.

"You better talk," she said. "If you're going to show up in my bar on my time, you better talk."

"I don't know where to start."

"Maybe with, 'I'm sorry'?"

"Right. Yes. I'm sorry."

She leaned forward, eyes blazing. "Too late."

Whit looked up, stunned. "But you just said—"

"To say 'I'm sorry.' Right. That was your play. But I reject any apology that doesn't get down to the specific ways that you treated me like your little lap doggie in front of your father. And that man with him—Bonner what's-his-name. That's the one, isn't he? The one you said abused Libby?"

"I don't know that for a fact."

"The hell you don't."

Whit dropped hard onto the stool next to Novie, afraid she might see the way his legs had started to shake.

"I tried to call," he said. "I didn't know they were coming until about the time I got off work. I would have warned you."

"About what? Your high-and-mighty father? Or Bonner, after all he did."

"Dad said he's a changed man."

"Changed? He barely says two words except to praise Jesus, then spends all night staring at my tits."

"I'm sorry—"

"You mentioned that. I guess you're sorry for expecting me to wait on them like a good little housewife, too? And sorry I didn't bake cookies and do the dishes and fuck you during the ten o'clock news?"

"I didn't mean any of that," he protested. "My father—things are a little tense there. You wouldn't understand."

"Of course I wouldn't. What does a poor little Indian girl—child of a defrocked priest, mind you—know about daddy issues?"

"Not fair," he said. Heat roiled beneath his skin all over his body. His scalp and fingers tingled. "I said I was sorry. What more do you want?"

"I want you to learn what it's like to be somebody else. I want you to get outside of your own goddamn head."

"Back off, okay?" Whit said. He could feel his temper starting to crack. Wasn't quite sure what would happen if it did. "You're not the victim here."

Now tears were welling up in Novie's eyes. "She was a child, Whit. A child! And you and your father just pretend nothing ever happened."

"That doesn't concern you."

"It does!" She threw back the rest of her drink and stared hard at him. "If we're going to love each other, it sure as hell does."

"Who said anything about love?"

She yanked her glass in close to her chest, cocked and ready to hurl the remaining ice cubes into his face. Whit squeezed his eyes shut, already regretting the words he'd said—words intended not for truth, but for injury. He hoped Novie wouldn't stop with the drink—hoped she would plant her hands on his chest and shove him back into the bar the way he deserved. It took longer than it should have for him to realize that impact wasn't coming. When he opened his eyes, the stool in front of him was empty.

Novie was gone.

CHAPTER 26

Whit awoke the next day to frigid temperatures inside and a frozen dystopia outside. The freezing rain that had been falling while he and Novie argued inside the Thirsty Owl had continued until it coated southern Missouri in nearly an inch of ice, stripping limbs from trees and knocking out power to God only knew how many people. He wasn't sure how long the electricity had been out, but the temperature had dropped to 42 degrees inside his apartment, according to the blinking digital readout on the thermostat. He stumbled through the rooms, collecting candles and setting faucets to trickle so that the pipes didn't freeze. Then he put on his heaviest coat and walked out onto the front step to survey the damage.

He didn't even make it to the edge of the steps before he started skidding across the sheet of ice that had blown in under the awning. He slipped and slid down the steps and onto the driveway and kept on going, since his only real choices were to fall down or follow his momentum. After a few feet he managed to get himself into the grass, which was still coated but offered more purchase than the concrete. He finally stopped with his hands on the hood of a pickup that had run aground on his lawn. The driver—an elderly man wearing only a flannel shirt and long johns—was slumped over the wheel in a posture that suggested the worst of all possible outcomes. Whit sidled over to the truck door, only to confirm that it was frozen shut. He tried to knock it free with the butt of his hand, and when that didn't work he banged on the windows in an effort to rouse the man, all to no avail. At last he went back inside and found his cell phone and, with the last micro-volt left in its battery, relayed the situation to the 911 dispatcher.

He returned to the pickup with a rubber mallet and some heavy screwdrivers, which he used in varying configurations for nearly half an hour before the door finally gave. He reached out and felt the man's neck for a pulse. By some miracle, he found one.

"Can you hear me, sir?" he asked several times. The old man groaned in response, but clearly was in no state for conversation. Whit hustled back inside and returned with two heavy blankets. That still didn't look like quite enough, though, and so Whit leaned him all the way back in the seat and climbed into the pickup over him. He shut the door and sat the man upright and, thinking that his own body heat might be necessary to keep the man alive, moved over so that their legs and torsos touched. When he wrapped the blanket around them, the displaced air rushed up into Whit's face and nearly made his eyes cross.

"A shower wouldn't hurt," he said. And when the old man once again failed to answer, Whit hunkered down to wait for help.

The quiet, though. That's what ultimately did Whit in. He supposed most people noticed the lack of electricity at night, when darkness reclaimed a usually well-lit neighborhood. But here in the morning sunshine, Whit became acutely aware of how quiet the world around him was, with vehicles unable to travel and HVAC units rendered mute. In such stillness, the old man's breathing sounded like a jet engine, the occasional pop of ice like gunfire. It worked on his nerves until he realized he was shaking, not from cold, but from tension. And so he started to talk.

"Dad and Bonner came by last night," he said. "Not sure how far they made it in this storm, though."

The driver didn't respond, of course, and so Whit kept on going with the story—how Cole Allen wouldn't take his call, and so he might as well wait to see if they got a next-of-kin visit from the highway police. How he wasn't sure when he would speak to his father again, or if Cole Allen's exit with Bonner had been the disowning that it felt like. He stopped short of explaining what happened with Novie, at least in part because he wasn't sure yet how to tell the tale, even to an unconscious stranger. Instead he switched to an explanation of his life in Trujillo at Operación Amor, followed by the roughest outline of the crazy plan he'd begun to formulate in his mind. Before he could work any of it through to clarity, he was interrupted by the roar of chains as a police cruiser approached.

"Here we go," Whit said.

He reached across and pushed open the door—anything to get this moving along. The Hi-Po officer greeted them formally and glanced around to assess if either of them was a threat. When he locked eyes on Whit, his eyebrows shot up.

"Oh," the trooper said. "You again."

"Wait, wait!" Isaias said between fits of laughter. "The cop who pulls you over the night before is the same one who comes to help with the old man?"

"Right."

Isaias busted out again. Leaned back into the couch and kicked his legs in the air as he cackled. "This is just too *good!* Tell it to me again."

Whit rolled his eyes, but he retraced his steps—most of them, anyway—for the sake of the story. He told about rushing home from work to meet his father, about the freezing rain and the power going out, and finding the old man slumped in his pickup. Mr. Ballantine, as it were, had gotten disoriented in the storm on his way back from a midnight run to Dale's Liquor and pulled off the main drag one street too early. He'd lost control a block from their apartment, sending his pickup careening from side to side down the length of the street, blasting mailboxes and overturning trash cans and taking out every gnome in an unfortunate fairy garden before crashing into the icy grass. He'd waited a couple of hours for signs of life before deciding that, since he wasn't going anywhere, he might as well start in on the bottle of Southern Comfort he'd intended to break out when he got home.

"So the guy wasn't dying," Isaias interrupted. "He was just snockered."

"That's how it sounds, yes."

The situation presented a conundrum for Officer Reeder, who had issued the reckless driving citation to Whit not even a 24 hours ago. On one hand, the driver was clearly intoxicated behind the wheel of a motor vehicle. On the other, he did not appear to have operated the pickup after he started drinking. It took several minutes to rouse the old man back from his stupor, and that long again for his speech to become intelligible. Once he realized the trouble he was in, however, the old man tried to argue that a horse would have made the whole thing legal. The trooper seemed to follow it clearly enough, although the logic confounded Whit. But the law was the law, and the pickup was not a horse, and Mr. Ballantine was still not entirely sober. Officer Reeder packed him up in the back of the cruiser and came back to talk to Whit.

"You've had an eventful couple of days," he said. "I hope you'll say that's unusual for you."

"Yes, sir," Whit answered.

"Right." He pulled out his notepad and scribbled something down. Tore off the pages and handed it to Whit. "When you go to court for that ticket you got last night, let me know. I'll put in a good word with the judge."

He thanked Whit and apologized about the pickup, which was just going to have to sit until it thawed enough either for Mr. Ballantine to come get it or the city to tow it. Then, seeing that his charge had walked around back of the cruiser to pee, he sighed and returned to his dutiful service.

"You saved that man's life," Isaias said.

"I don't know about that."

"Would he have frozen to death without you?"

"Eventually, if I hadn't called the cops. But I think he was still a ways from that when I got into the pickup."

"Hey, Mr. Big Man, in my mind, you are a hero." He raised his bottle. "Cape or no cape, a hero you are! But I got to ask."

"What's that?"

Laughter drained from Isaias' face, replaced by something between concern and sadness.

"Novie?"

Whit sighed. He had left out the part where she had cooked for his father—left out Bonner altogether, for that matter. From the look on Isaias' face, though, he knew the story already. "Libby called you, didn't she."

"You know I can never reveal my sources. Now come on. Let's hear it."

Busted as he was, Whit saw no harm in giving his friend the fuller version. And so he backed up and gave his account—every blessed detail of it—and waited for Isaias to respond.

"I'm confused," Isaias said. "Did you two break up? Or just have a fight?"

"It was a pretty big fight."

"That's not an answer."

"I'll probably find out more when school reopens."

"Still not an answer."

Whit thought about it some more, and finally came to the conclusion that the worst possibility was, at least in this case, also the most likely. "I think we broke up."

"Okay. Damn." Isaias said. He looked up, and Whit could see tears welling in his eyes. "That's going to make what I have to tell you even worse then."

Like so many events in Isaias' life, the project that would end his and Whit's time as roommates was the result of both dedication to his craft and stunningly odd fortune. He'd been editing video in a coffee bistro in Memphis when the espresso machine jammed. A well-dressed Latino man noticed what he was doing and struck up a conversation while he waited for his latte. So unexpected was the encounter that Isaias didn't even recognize him until, after a few minutes of banter, they exchanged names.

"Brax. Freaking. Lopez!" Isaias shouted when telling the story. He'd climbed up onto the arm of the couch and balanced there like some great bird. Even as he waved his arms in excitement, he looked perfectly in control. Whit wondered how he pulled it off.

"Wow."

"I know," Isaias said. He dropped back into his seat and folded his hands contritely into his lap. "I should be more sensitive to your grief."

"No, really, it's fine. I'm happy for you."

"You are?"

"I'm working on it."

That much, at least, was true. Isaias talked about Brax Lopez as the greatest American filmmaker alive today, known for his provocative independent films and cutting-edge documentaries. Whit had watched the entire Lopez canon with Isaias at least twice—enough to appreciate the art in his work, if not exactly enjoy it. The fact that Isaias had not only met his idol in person, but that the circumstances of such meeting resulted in an offer to join his team on his latest project seemed downright providential.

"The timing sucks, I know," Isaias said. "And if I'd known all that was going down between you and Novie beforehand, I might have—."

"No you wouldn't," Whit interrupted.

Isaias smiled. "You right. I'd have given my kidneys for this chance. Hell, I would have sold your kidneys."

"That's fantastic," Whit said.

"If I didn't know any better, I'd think you almost mean that."

"I almost do."

Isaias clapped his hands onto his thighs as though something had been decided. "Mr. Big Man, I see only one material with which to bridge the emotional gulf between our two present life situations."

"And what's that?"

"Alcohol."

Whit followed him into the kitchen and sat down at the bar with a pen and notepad. While Isaias made margaritas, Whit jotted down the logistics of the next few months. Isaias would leave his things in the apartment and keep up his half of the rent, which made Whit wonder if there wasn't more money in artistic pursuit than he'd been led to believe. But he'd be gone for the next six months, mostly in Puerto Rico except for a three-week shoot in Winnipeg. Whit tried to find a thematic link there, but Isaias fired up the blender before he could ask. By the time he got his drink, Whit had another question on his mind.

"What about Callie?" he asked. "Is she going with you?"

"We broke up two weeks ago."

Whit squeezed his eyes shut. He reached back for some memory of that conversation but found none. "I'm sorry," he said.

"For what?"

"I should have said something. I mean, I didn't know. But I feel like I should have known."

"It's all right," Isaias said. He was already prepping the mixer for round two. "I didn't say anything about it. We just decided we did not have compatible futures. It's not like—well, you know."

He did know. Some people seemed to be able to end relationships with grace of a descending bird. His pattern was more of a mushroom cloud.

"Want to watch a movie?" Isaias asked.

He started punching the remote without waiting for an answer, and Whit didn't need to ask to know what they were watching—*Requiem por un Asesino*, Brax Lopez' masterpiece of regeneration through violence. It opened with the graphic murder of a woman and her two children in Matamoros, which Whit didn't think he could stomach this evening. He offered to do dishes while Isaias began the movie. Once the shooting stopped, he threw back one last swig of tequila and moved to the couch.

"How you gonna survive until I come back?" Isaias said once they were settled in.

Whit smiled. He hadn't eaten much these past few days, and the alcohol was already causing his thoughts to slosh back and forth in his brain. "You're not coming back," he said. "Not here."

"Of course I am."

"I think the universe has bigger things in store for you. Besides." He tapped his temple with one long index finger. "I've got a plan."

"What's that?"

"Something I should have done a long time ago. Now are we going to watch this movie or not?"

On the screen in front of him, shots rang out and cars exploded and punches landed more or less in accordance with the accepted belief in a moral universe. The movie would take a darker turn halfway through, but Whit would be asleep by then. For now, he could pretend that things would work out—that the crazy idea he'd been toying with since it first popped into his head in Ballantine's pickup would somehow bear fruit. He would right a wrong that he'd tried to pass off as not his own for too long now. And with spring break coming up, he didn't even need to take vacation time. All he needed was a plane ticket back to Trujillo.

CHAPTER 27

One step onto the Cruz del Sur bus was enough for Whit to suspect that a past version of himself had lied.

A week ago, when he'd booked the plane ticket from Memphis to Lima, he'd sold himself on the notion that riding a bus for the last leg of his journey to Trujillo was the smart economic play. Improved though his finances were since his first sojourn in Peru six years ago, he still puckered at the price tag for a *norteamericano* who wanted to fly over rather than ride the three hundred or so miles between cities. Better to save the money. If things with Yesenia went as he hoped, he would need it.

But as he made his way back to his seat, he suspected that economics had little if anything to do with his decision to travel via bus. He'd wanted to feel himself back among the Peruvian people, to hear Spanish and Quechua spoken over stories of mundane affairs—workplace drama or family squabbles. He wanted to prove to himself that he could return to the same level of belonging he'd felt in the weeks before his unceremonious departure, to feel like he was still part of the country, since in his bones he felt the country was also a part of him.

If he'd been honest with himself about his motivations, Whit might have been able to talk himself out of that romanticized vision of Peruvian travel. The Sechura Desert was a vast stretch of sandy nothing—no towns, no people, no real variation in terrain—and ten additional hours of his long frame folded into a bucket seat caused pain to set up in every joint and vertebra. An hour into the trek, he already envied his tiny seatmate, a four-foot-four Quechua woman whose age likely exceeded her weight in pounds. Her feet didn't touch the floor, but neither did she look the least bit cramped. If the smell of the bathroom directly behind them bothered her, she didn't show it.

On top of it all—literally, as they were situated on the upper level of the double-decker bus—an American church youth group had made a similar calculation as Whit. Six adult leaders and thirty-odd teenagers, all wearing matching lime green t-shirts, ran back and forth above them, causing the bus to sway uncomfortably when their weight shifted too much to one side. Whit's seatmate bore it all—the heat and the confinement and the smell and the nauseating swaying—with perfect ease, as though all these things merely confirmed her suspicions of the world.

Fifty kilometers north of Huarmey, which is to say in the ever-loving middle of nowhere, the bus blew a tire. The drivers ushered everyone out and pulled out the spare, only to discover a busted check valve on the hydraulic jack. While they waited for a service truck to arrive, the youth group leader broke out his acoustic guitar and began leading the same old camp songs Whit used to play for his youth group back in Wyoming. The kids cheered and clapped sang at the tops of their lungs. Some of the boys gave a thumbs-up sign toward Whit, motioning with their other hands for him to come join them. He shook his head, but the old man next to him returned their gesture with a broad smile.

"Keep singing!" he called in Spanish. "That's why we're here, is to listen to you serenade the fucking desert!"

"*Buenos días!*" the kids shouted back.

The man clapped his hands to his heart. "Self-absorbed assholes," he said with the fakest of fake laughs.

"They're just kids," Whit answered, also in Spanish. "They might grow out of it."

The other man looked at him with raised eyebrows. "You speak?" he said in English. A second later, he broke into a hearty laugh and wandered off to light a cigarette.

By now, the team had broken into "Days of Elijah," a favorite among evangelical campers for its triumphal lyrics and snappy choreography. The kids lined up, arm-length apart so as not to smack each other on "Behold, he comes!" Whit felt a powerful urge to proclaim to all within earshot that, however much he might look like these fair-skinned American Christians, he no longer counted himself among their tribe. Before he could figure out exactly what to say, however, the little old Quechua woman stopped him short. She'd been drawn to the music from the start, standing at the edge of the circle and bending her knees in time with the songs. Now she picked up the hand motions as well, which caught the eye of two teenage girls. They pulled her into line with them and danced together, laughing and singing as though none of them were indefinitely stranded in the heat and the sand.

Whit doubted she understood a single word of the song. Doubted that it mattered.

They were up and going again by early afternoon, with a driver hellbent on getting his passengers the hell out of his bus as quickly as possible. He kept his foot on the floor, taking curves with all the daring of a Formula 1 racer. Every now and again, Whit could hear a teenager vomiting on the second deck, which of course set his already nervous stomach to churning. He focused on the desert, on the quiet humming of the little Quechua woman. On this fool's errand in which he was engaged.

He hadn't told anyone else about his plan to return to Peru, much less that he was going there to start the process for adopting a little girl. He thought he knew how Novie would take his suggestion and decided she'd be right to do so. But since they had almost certainly broken up that night at the Thirsty Owl, he was not obligated to let her be the voice of reason. The future he'd imagined with her had melted away with the ice from that winter storm, draining out toward some ocean of unrealized fantasies. Nothing to be done, though. It was time to welcome a new tomorrow, one not built on romance, but on doing the right thing for a kid.

The hostel he'd booked was a good 10km away from the bus station, but he decided to walk it to stretch out his aching body. He hoisted his backpack onto his shoulders and hiked through the streets of Trujillo, past the Sodemac Hardware and the big-box chains in the mall, along the smooth sidewalks lined with storefronts, through the familiar chaos of the Inca market. The whole thing—the haze of engine exhaust, the cacophony of traffic noises, the smell of frying from the food carts—both exhilarated and soothed him. Tall and white and emotionally clumsy as he was, he had belonged here once, hadn't he?

He dropped his pack off at the hostel and rented a bicycle and pedaled out to the Operación Amor facility, heart thumping as though he was fleeing a bear. He set the bike behind a row of succulents he'd planted when he was on staff, now grown almost tall enough to reach the handlebars. He took a deep breath and pressed the doorbell, the speakers behind the walls announcing his arrival with a synthesized version of "The Yellow Rose of Texas." The peephole door slid open, revealing a pair of dark eyes he didn't recognize. He squatted down so that his face would be visible.

"*Dios mío,*" a woman's voice said. She slid the door back in place, leaving Whit out on the concrete steps for what seemed like a long time. When he finally heard the tumbling of the locks, he couldn't help but smile. Like coming home, he thought.

That feeling lasted until the main door swung open far enough that he could see inside. What awaited him was not Tía Luz, open-armed and teary-eyed, nor Mila, still proud and angry even though she'd been the one who'd torpedoed their relationship. Rather, the lone figure in the doorway belonged to Tía Pilar, a bit stockier than he remembered, but no less formidable. Her left hand was balled into a fist, causing the knotty muscles in her forearm to pop up under her dark skin. In her right hand, she held the billy club she kept beside her desk in case of trouble. In his months at OA, Whit had never seen her use it. But he had no doubt that she could.

"What do you want?" she asked.

"I—I wanted to say hello, and—"

"Ah. Hello." She reached for the door to swing it shut in his face.

"Wait," he pleaded. "Things here didn't end for me the way I wanted them to. I wanted to make up for it."

"You can't. You should go."

"I sent an email, though—about two weeks ago? Did you—"

Before he could finish the question, he had his answer. She'd gotten the message all right, and something in it had pissed her off. She whipped the billy club around too fast for him to pull back his hand. It landed across the very ends of his fingers, sending spikes of pain all the way up into his shoulder. The next thing he knew, she was dragging him by the ear across the patio to her office. She flung him inside and closed the door behind her.

Whit blinked, waiting for his eyes to adjust to the dim light that filtered through the high windows. The bright yellow walls that he remembered from years ago had been painted an industrial beige and hung with various Christian totems—candle mounts, a large golden cross, a wooden box with "Prayer Requests" written across the lid in English. On the opposite wall was a mural of Jesus walking on water. The technique was more developed than the circus mural the Covenant team had painted while Whit was on staff, but the style was unquestionably similar—the bold colors, the disproportions among the various elements of the composition. In a dialogue bubble in the top right corner, someone had written "Dr. Charles Spurgeon Lawson Memorial Prayer Chapel" with a permanent marker.

"Memorial?" Whit said, but with more curiosity than sadness. He wondered how and when the poor professor had bought it. Secretly hoped a Moche priest had been there to collect his blood.

Pilar hooked her club around the leg of a stool, pulled it out a few feet from the wall and ordered Whit to have a seat. She hoisted herself up on the edge of her desk. Dropped the club onto the two-drawer file cabinet with a *clang!* He felt his mouth go dry. However the room might convert into a prayer chapel when the Americans visited, he had no illusions as to what it was used for under normal operating conditions. He flexed his throbbing fingers.

"Talk," Pilar said.

"Talk about what?"

"About that letter. You say you want to adopt? I say bullshit. Tell me what you intend to do with our Yesenia? Did you think she's old enough to marry? Or were you just going to use her like a whore?"

Whit felt his jaw drop open, as stunned as if Pilar had sucker punched him in the nose. And, in fact, it took him a few seconds to realize that he had not been physically beaten. He rubbed his face with both hands.

"I didn't think—she's just a kid."

"She's seventeeen, Whit! A woman now." She hopped down from her perch and squared her feet. Took up her club. "You think I don't know what men think about? You think I don't see what you do to these girls?" She was shouting now, pacing back and forth in front of her desk.

"I didn't mean that. Nothing at all like that."

"You didn't?"

"Swear to God!"

"To God?" She marched over to the mural behind Whit's chair. He turned, thinking it best to keep her in view. She tapped the misshapen Christ figure in the chest. "You mean this God?"

In the brief second that Whit thought about her question, he concluded that he really didn't know what God he meant, or why he needed to swear by him—or her. He didn't know what to make of any of that lately. The one thing he did know is that, in her current state, Pilar could lay a beating on him that would strike terror in the hearts of the Peruvian mob.

"Yes?" he said weakly.

"You mean Jesús then? You are sure?"

"I think so."

She propped her hands on her hips. Scowled at the painting. "I don't like this Jesús very much. Do you?"

"I'm not sure—"

"He's so smug. You can see it, right? Like he really can walk on water and get all these pitiful disciples to say *oh you're so amazing* and do whatever he says. You see this one here? You know who that is?"

She laid the end of the baton against the chin of a middle-aged man with one foot out of the boat—Peter, if he remembered the story right. But even in such poor caricature, he recognized the face. Whit moved in closer, squinted at the pasty figure's sparse beard and rounded glasses.

"Dr. Lawson?"

"He looks so happy, so devoted to his God! So much that he came to Peru every year to teach the poor children that everything will be fine if they love Jesus and accept him in their hearts. But then he dies, and your friends come and make my office into a prayer chapel. They paint these pictures and pray and cry, and they leave Jesús there on the wall. Do you know what was responsible for the professor's death?"

"No."

"Throat cancer. They said it was so painful and the treatments so terrible that he lost his mind. You think the God you swear to cares?"

"Maybe. I hope so."

Pilar's lips spread into a thin smirk. "Then I hope things work out better for you than they do for Jesús' other friends." She walked around her desk and dropped into her chair. "Why did you come here, Whit?"

"For Yesenia."

She shook her head. "No. It was not that."

"I wanted to give—," he began, but he was reeling, stumbling through his thoughts as though someone had rearranged all the furniture in his mind and then cut the lights. He threw out the first thing that felt solid. "I didn't leave the way I wanted to last time."

"So you want—how do you say it—closure?"

"I want to make things right."

"And you think you could use Yesenia to do that?"

Whit threw up his hands. They landed on top of his head, the tips of his middle fingers meeting over a patch of thinning hair he had only noticed a few days ago. He stood.

"I should never have come," he said.

"No," Pilar answered softly. "Probably you should not."

Whit nodded slowly, unsure if he should apologize. Not that it mattered. His circuits were so overloaded by the encounter that he had a hard time fishing a single coherent sentence out of the jumble. It took him several seconds to say, "Can I see Yesenia, at least? Just to say goodbye?"

Pilar looked hard into his face, working her jaw the way she did when deciding on a punishment for one of the children. "She's gone."

"Gone?"

"Yes. She isn't here. And don't ask! It is all private, these things. All I can say is that she was adopted by another family—Germans. I have not spoken to her since she left. It is best."

He nodded slowly, felt tears leaking from the corners of his eyes. A moment later, the dam burst. He sat down in the chair and folded his hands over his face and wept, hoping as he did that someone—Father Guillermo, Tía Luz, even Mila or Yesenia—would find her way to him and put a hand on his back and tell him it was all right. No one did, though. He tumbled through those dark thoughts, alone and spinning, crashing into one regret after another.

When he finally looked up, he was alone in the room, and he knew what was expected of him.

He slipped out of the office and then out the front door, making sure it latched tightly behind him. His bicycle was not where he'd left it. Stolen, he presumed, and nothing to be done about it now. He turned his face away from the sun and started walking.

Figure 9: Sechura Desert

CHAPTER 28

He spent two full days in bed, rising only to get an occasional drink of water and answer nature's call. He tried to counsel himself using the same steps he took with his students—first compassion, then reason, and finally ultimatum. But the technique worked no better on his own psyche than it did with the kids in his mechanics or Spanish classrooms. He half decided to spend his last two days in Peru in a similarly slug-like state, but even the act of half-deciding felt like more than he'd done since he arrived back at the hostel with blistered feet and another broken heart. He thought it best to seize what little momentum making a half-decision offered, if he wanted to do something besides die alone in a dingy room in a building that smelled like piss.

And so on the third day he got up from his bed and bathed in the sink, the way he used to do at the Paredes house, and bandaged up his blistered feet and walked out into the sun. By now he was used to having the Peruvians—among the world's shortest people on average—gawk at his tall white frame. But he could tell that, despite his half-hearted efforts at grooming, he looked like death warmed over. Old women gasped and crossed themselves when he passed. He kept his head down and walked on until he finally reached the Catedral.

He hadn't been inside long when Father Liu, the Chinese priest who had taken over as rector, came to find him—alerted by staff no doubt. The priest moved with a kind of haunting stillness, his robes barely even swishing as he walked. His skin was almost as light as Whit's, making his jet-black hair look even darker. Whit wondered when the last time was this guy had been outside, but decided to set that question aside and inquire about his friend.

"Guillermo, yes," the rector said in Spanish. "Such a talented priest! We worked together for only two months before he renounced his orders. A pity for the Church. A bigger pity for him."

"I see. So is he still in Trujillo?"

"Yes. He manages a seaside nightclub called *El Gallito*." He held up his palms. "I have never been to that establishment. Guillermo does come to visit occasionally, though. I have seen him at mass a few times. Tell me, my son, when was your last confession?"

Whit let that slide without comment. "*El Gallito*," he said. "Thanks."

The priest frowned. "I must advise you, for the sake of your body and your soul, not to go there. Carnal relationships between two men are sanctioned neither by God nor by His Church."

"Oh. All right. Thanks."

The priest sighed and brushed something off his hands. He turned and glided back to the shadows of his sanctuary.

Whit hailed a cab and gave the name of where he wanted to go. The driver raised his eyebrows skeptically. "It'll be closed," he said. "I don't think they open until maybe 16:00."

"It's okay," Whit answered. "I'm meeting a friend."

The cabbie shrugged. "Your funeral."

As the cab zipped in and out of traffic on the way to Huan Chaco Beach, Whit wondered if the driver's words had been a prophecy rather than a mere convention of language. In a city full of aggressive cabbies, this one proved even more daring than most. Once, he even whipped up onto the sidewalk for half a block to get around a snarl at an intersection, only pulling back into traffic when he got near enough to reach out the window and bang on the hood of a yellow Volkswagen. When, against all odds, they arrived at *El Gallito* unscathed, Whit was so thankful to be alive that he thrust several bills in the man's hand and told him to keep the change. He was already twenty feet from the car when the driver called out to point him toward an entrance in back of the building.

"Say you're buying eggs for your grandmother," he said, and drove away.

Whit puzzled over the cabbie's words until he saw the two enormous bouncers sitting on folding chairs, one on either side of the door. They stiffened when he approached and stared dumbfounded at one another when he delivered the password. Finally, though, they let him pass with a warning to keep his skinny white dick in his pants.

If Whit had learned anything from all those forays into subculture with Isaias, it was to be slow to judge. He reminded himself of that lesson as he waited for his eyes to adjust to the dim light inside *El Gallito*, wondering if the slowly receding dark would reveal druggies or strippers or even more seedy things he could not bring himself to name. No matter, though. People were people, from Poplar Bluff to Peru, and most of them were doing the best they could with what life handed them. The appropriate posture with which to address the unknown was compassion, and it would probably work if he didn't get himself killed first.

"I've never been with a white man before," a deep voice mused to the apparent delight of the other patrons. The man stepped forward, chest so thick Whit doubted he could fully cross his arms. Whit's heart pounded against his breastbone. The mass of humanity before him looked familiar, but not familiar, like some generic brand version of a man he'd known once upon a time.

"I'm looking for Father Guillermo," Whit said.

A buzz rippled through the dark room. Now that his pupils had expanded some, he could see about twenty people split between the high tables near him and the stools along the bar.

"Friend, I don't think this is your kind of place," the muscled man said. "Perhaps you should come back in a few hours."

That was enough to confirm Whit's suspicions, which made him feel smart if not quite safe. He'd been to any number of gay bars while helping his roommate Isaias film his documentaries, and he knew his way around such establishments. But any comfort he might have taken in that fact was immediately overridden by a realization of who the broad-chested man reminded him of. If this wasn't Diego—Mila's husband, the gangster—then he was clone enough to scare the bejeezus out of Whit. Whatever compassion he'd been nurturing drained from him in an instant, replaced by more primal instincts of self-preservation. He ran his tongue over his false tooth. Reminded himself to not step back.

A door opened behind the bar to his right, casting harsh fluorescent light into the room. Whit thought it best not to look, though. If the shadow that emerged from that office carried a gun, he was already as good as dead. Better to maintain eye contact with the muscled man, to try to bluff him off. In a straight up fight, Whit figured his chances were only marginally better with this guy than with a bullet, but better nonetheless.

The other man—the one from the office—emerged as a shape at the edge of Whit's vision. He was dressed entirely in black, which Whit later supposed was to be expected. He came up alongside the Diego look-alike and placed a hand on the man's giant pectoral as he spoke softly.

"This guy is okay. Probably lost or something. Let me take care of it."

The muscled man didn't reply, but his jaw relaxed. The man in black patted him on the chest again. He held the other hand out, palm down, to signal the others to go back to their drinking or flirting or grieving. Then he turned and smiled and, except for the gray hair that now framed his face, was the same Guillermo Whit had known those years ago. His eyes were not quite settled, though, and Whit had to remind himself of the abrupt nature of their parting. If the former priest showed no signs of animosity, neither did he offer much warmth.

"Let us find out where you should be," Guillermo said, and motioned for Whit to follow him around the bar and into the office. He explained the situation to a woman at one of the two desks in the room and told her he'd be back once he got the *gringo* taken care of. A moment later, they exited into the alley from a door on the side of the building.

"I'm sorry," Whit said before Guillermo could speak.

"Sorry?"

"For the way I left. Before."

Guillermo's eyebrows danced in puzzlement for a few seconds, as though the file for that particular story took a while to retrieve. When comprehension finally dawned, it brought with it the same amused look that was the very picture of Whit's memory of the man.

"Why hold on to something so far past?" Guillermo said. He spread his arms and gathered Whit into a genuine embrace. "It is so good to see you, my friend!"

"I didn't mean for things to happen the way they did," Whit said. "Mila—"

Guillermo pulled back at the mention of her name. Held up a finger to silence Whit.

"Not here," he said. "Come."

As he led Whit through the alleyways, Guillermo explained his arrangement with *El Gallito*. Although not forbidden by law, same-sex relationships were blessed neither by the Church nor the Peruvian government, and gay bars were just asking to be vandalized. Crusaders were making headway for gay rights in Lima, but Trujillo was a don't-ask, don't-tell city, and Guillermo's years in the Church had trained him for that space. He had worked out an arrangement to rent the bar for a few hours every afternoon before it opened up for the tourists who came to surf Huan Chaco. One of the local business conglomerates had agreed to offer security services for a reasonable rate, so long as he kept things out of sight.

"Business conglomerate?" Whit asked, but got no answer.

Guillermo bought coffee from a shop just off Avenida La Rivera. He handed a paper cup to Whit and sat down at a metal table in the back corner near the restrooms.

"I make a place for people who have no place," he said. "It's not much, but it is my calling for now. We just have to keep it on the D-L, as the kids say."

"I see."

"Do you? Because you seem to be confused. Your face, I'm talking about."

"I guess I just never expected you to quit the Church."

Guillermo looked down at the table sadly. "Perhaps there is some question as to who quit who, in that regard." He wrinkled his nose. "Whom?"

"I guess things must have gotten weird," Whit said. "After what happened with Father Yairo, I mean."

"That, and more than that. It's complicated."

"Did they kick you out of the priesthood?"

Guillermo shrugged. "It is enough to say that my calling no longer lay with the Church."

"So your calling is in a bar now?"

"The work is not so different as you might think."

Whit nodded as though he understood, and in the silence he had once been so accustomed to with Guillermo, he worked out what his friend meant. The religion Whit remembered from Covenant University—what had become his father's religion—was all about spectacle and adherence, about brand loyalty. But it hadn't always been so, even for Whit. In Claremore and at Light of Azusa, he had been held in the arms of a loving—if theologically incoherent—community. Even though Mrs. Koontz had hated fat

Mr. Stuckey for his part in her husband's firing from the chicken plant—Whit had found all of this out from his father when he was a teenager—she had still prayed over him at the mercy seat and mourned over his body when she discovered he'd been called home. He'd seen similar levels of care in many of the bars he and Isaias visited, and even in his classrooms at Northern Lakes and Bootheel Tech. People gathered to care for one another in a variety of settings—even in the Catedral. Even in *El Gallito*.

"Leave your guilt behind, my friend," Guillermo said. He was staring into Whit's face now. "*El Chancho* would have killed you if you'd stayed."

"*El Chancho*? 'The Pig'?"

"Cliche, I know," Guillermo said. "You get a big enough promotion with the mob, and you get a stupid nickname to go with it. But your friend is *El Chancho* now, although I would not call him that to his face and expect to still have a face."

Whit held up a hand. He thought he knew where this was going, but he half hoped he might still stave it off. "My friend?"

"Diego. Mila's husband. His brother Andre greeted you back at my bar."

Whit felt his face flush red. He sat up straight. Looked around for anyone who might want to hurt him.

"Relax," Guillermo said. "Andre doesn't have a clue about who you are. Anyway he was too busy trying to impress Miguel—but that is another story." He leaned forward on his elbows. Smiled. "Please, before we go any further, tell me you are not here to see Mila."

"No."

"*Gracias a Dios.*"

"But." Whit shifted in his chair, his knees scraping against the bottom of the table. "Do you remember me talking about Yesenia?"

"From Operación Amor," Guillermo said. Something in his expression flickered involuntarily, as if he'd just grabbed the nodes on a car battery. "She was, ah, a little girl when you were here, if I remember."

"Yes. I used to teach her guitar. She was waiting for me the day I had to leave. I thought—it's crazy, I know—but I asked about adopting her."

"Adopting."

"I sent Tía Pilar an email about it, but she never responded. So I just showed up. I know it's crazy. But things weren't going so well back home, so adopting her seemed like a way to, I don't know...."

"Give yourself a purpose in life?"

"Something like that."

"Because you feel as though your life lacks purpose now."

"No. Maybe. Anyhow, it all worked out for the best."

Guillermo fidgeted with his watch, twirled the band around his wrist. "How do you mean, 'for the best?'"

"Pilar said Yesenia got adopted by a German family. She couldn't give me details."

"German."

"Yes."

"Well then. Pilar is kind."

Whit nodded, although with that billy club still swinging in his memory, "kind" wasn't exactly the word he would have used to describe her. He placed his hands on the table, ready to push himself up. But the look on his friend's face stopped him cold. It was the same panicked expression he'd worn that day on the Plaza de Armas, when Father Yairo had stepped out in front of that cab. Every drop of moisture evaporated from inside Whit's mouth. He looked around to see if Diego or his goons had spotted him and, seeing no one, dumped the last few drops of coffee into his tongue.

"What is it?" he asked. "Am I in trouble?"

Guillermo looked at him for a long time before he finally blinked away whatever thought had paralyzed him. "We should leave it there," he said. "Yes. We should do that."

"Leave what where?"

"Don't let it trouble you."

"Trouble me?"

Guillermo squeezed his eyes shut and held up a palm, more in defense than in blessing. Whit stopped talking. Waited for his friend to wrestle down whatever thought gripped him. At last he relaxed.

"You carry too much from the past," he told Whit. "This is not good for your soul."

He tapped his watch and stood up from the table. Whit wasn't sure if he'd said all he had to say or if he'd just given up. In either case, it was clear that they were out of time.

"Can I see you tomorrow?" Whit asked. "My bus doesn't leave until evening."

Guillermo looked up into his face with an expression mournful enough to snap Whit's heart. "I would like nothing better," he said. "But it is not wise. You cannot hide from *El Chancho* long in this place. The closer you come to people he may know, the greater the danger for you—and for those of us who love you."

Something in Whit's chest broke free at the word "love." He lurched forward. Tried to pass it off as a cough. "I just wanted to make things right."

Guillermo reached across and gripped his arms just above the elbow. "These things you carry are unchangeable," he said. "They cannot be repaired—only forgiven." The former priest's fingers contracted hard enough that Whit winced. He released his grip and stepped back. "I forgive you," he said. "Whatever hurt you have caused me—and it is less than you fear—I forgive you."

"Yesenia, though."

Tears dripped from Whit's eyes. Guillermo reached up to wipe them away with his thumbs. "Let us trust that God is merciful."

And so Whit returned to his hostel and bolted the lock and moved the dresser against the door. He lay the mattress down on the floor, in case *El Chancho's* henchmen had figured out who he was and where he was and decided to shoot the place up without bothering to enter the room. After that conversation with Guillermo, all sorts of terrible things seemed plausible. Maybe even inevitable.

He picked up the bottle of pisco he'd bought at Roger's, preparing to drink himself into oblivion. But after only three shots from this convenience-store version of the liquor, he couldn't stand the thought of putting more of it into his mouth. He lay on the mattress on the floor and stared at the ceiling.

The more he examined it, the more he could see what a ridiculous tale Pilar had tried to sell him in regard to Yesenia. Aside from the team from Covenant University, he'd only known of one other international group that regularly visited—a hard-partying crew from the Netherlands who, according to Mila, presented a different but equally vexing challenge as the American holy rollers. But Germans? Whit had never heard of such connection. The longer he studied it, the more convinced he became of what Tia Pilar had been trying to tell him without telling him. Yesenia hadn't been adopted at all. She'd run away, perhaps, or returned to her birth family. She'd been kicked out of the shelter for bad behavior or rejected the continued help OA offered when kids got too old to be residents. Maybe she'd flirted with Diego when he visited Mila and become his mistress.

Or worse. There were worse things. Oh God.

Whit turned onto his stomach. Propped himself up on his elbows and leaned his forehead down on his knuckles. Started to pray but couldn't even get past the salutation.

"Dear Lord," he said.

But there it stopped. If there was a Lord—Jesus or Muhammed or whoever the hell it might be—they didn't seem to give a shit that humans suffered in body and in spirit, wracked with pain from their own depravity on one hand and their very consciousness on the other. To think about the way life turned out for most people—the hurt and disappointment and isolation—was to argue against goodness itself. And if there was an afterlife? A heaven for Yesenia and a hell for *El Chancho*? Then why weren't there more glimpses of justice on earth?

He stayed there, prostrate on that thin mattress, for hours, wishing he had the structure of his father's faith or the courage of his sister's practical atheism. Wishing his mother was there to comfort him, not that she'd ever done that much. Wishing Isaias would appear to pour the rest of that bottle of pisco down his throat. Wishing for Novie—her scent, her body, her comfort in having a body.

When he looked up, orange light from the streetlamps spilled through the window. He didn't know what hour it was, but it didn't matter so much. Nothing to do but wait for daylight. No one was coming for him tonight.

No one at all.

CHAPTER 29

The pathway to customs was lousy with signs printed in English and Spanish, instructing passengers what items needed to be declared using which forms at which sets of kiosks. Whit stopped to read each one in both languages, each time creating a little disturbance around which foot traffic had to flow. He didn't mind the curses lobbed his way, preoccupied as he was with the irony his reading implied—the fatalism to which it bore witness. More clearly stated, when you had no choice but to go one way and do one thing, what was the point of reading the instructions?

Not surprisingly, Whit's pensiveness landed him at the very back of the crowd, behind even the most patient of the Peruvians who had flown along with him from Lima. He was the last one to exit the hallway proper, and thus the last to enter into the rope maze that compressed the line into its zig-zagging form. A bored man in a uniform called out which entrance was for Americans and which one for foreigners—he even used that word, *foreigners*—and reminded those about to enter or re-enter the United States that it would be worth their time to check their bags over the 64-gallon trash bins provided against the walls. Whit ignored him, still engrossed in the inexorable nature of this journey. When he reached for his backpack once it passed through the X-ray scanner, however, another officer stopped him.

"Do you have anything to declare?" he asked. The way he said it—as in, *Ah do decla-ah!*—reminded Whit of a cartoon rooster he used to watch as a kid. This was clearly not some transplant lured to Atlanta by an airport job. This man was a native, and he wore his accent like a badge of honor. "Sir?" he said. *Suh!*

"Huh? Um, no. Nothing to declare. I don't think so. No."

The officer narrowed his eyes at Whit. Motioned for his passport and held it open between them. Printed beside Whit's full name—Junius Onesimus Whitman—was a glossy square photograph of a certain version of Whit, a ruddy and clear-eyed nineteen-year-old, jawline framed by the hood of a Covenant University sweatshirt. A nice kid, the way he remembered himself. Unburdened by the moral complexities of the modern world. Innocent of what it cost to live in it.

"You don't *think* you have anything to declare?"

"No, sir. I don't."

"There's something in your carry-on bag, though. A liquid. Do you mind removing the bottle, please?"

Whit unzipped the compartment, truly perplexed at the request and stunned by what he found inside. There, among the hodgepodge of clothes and toiletries he'd taken to Peru, was the half bottle of pisco he'd been unable to polish off his last night in Trujillo.

"You know you can't take this on an American flight," the officer said. He let fall a heavy sigh and punched something into a laptop that rested on a folding table beside him. "What was your purpose?"

Yoh puh-poss.

"Purpose?"

"Purpose. As in, was this trip for business or pleasure?"

"I was hoping to adopt," Whit said.

"You were—adopt? Is that what you said?"

"Yes, sir."

The officer punched more keys on this computer. He was an older guy, at least two decades beyond Whit's father. Whit doubted that there was much he hadn't seen in his job, what with the world in the state it was in. But he kept his eyes scrunched up as he worked, not trying to hide an expression that told Whit he couldn't quite square any of this. "So did you?' he asked. "Bring back a baby?"

"She isn't a baby. She's—." He saw the officer check his birthday. Decided he didn't want to explain why a 25-year-old man would want to adopt a 17-year-old girl. "It's complicated."

"I'd say so." He pointed at the bottle. "I can't let you take that on an American plane."

"Understood."

"You have anything else in there I need to know about?"

Whit shook his head, but without conviction. He had no memory of packing the bottle of pisco in his backpack. For all he knew, he might have stuffed a live rabbit in there along with it. The officer sighed again. Raised his hand toward a woman in uniform who had been surveying the customs desks with her hands behind her back. She was younger, probably halfway between the officer's age and Whit's, but she looked about as humorless as dishwater. He handed Whit's passport back to him. "Welcome home, son."

That welcome included another two hours of questioning. The root of the problem, he knew, was his inability to translate what he was thinking into comprehensible speech. Things came out wrong, or had double meanings. The business with the signs, for instance. He tried to bring it up as a way of making conversation while another officer went through his bag with gloved hands. But even to Whit's ears, his commentary sounded like something out of Brother Arneson's apocalyptic sermons. At last the officer began shoving things back to his bag, leaving a pile of suspect items for last and suggesting he dispose of them before he tried to board his flight to Memphis.

As he reached for the bag, the customs officer leaned down so that he could see her face.

"Would you like me to call someone for you?" she asked. "You don't look so good."

Whit thought for a moment. He'd been in South America for four days and back on U.S. soil for three hours. Yet his phone had not buzzed a single time since his arrival. If anyone had missed him in his absence, it wasn't enough to warrant even a text message. He was even more alone now than he'd been in the Minneapolis airport the last time he returned from Peru.

"I don't really have anybody to call," he said.

"Nobody? A coworker, or a girlfriend?"

Whit shook his head.

"What about your parents?"

"It's complicated."

"A sibling then. How about that?"

Whit didn't answer. He'd already thought about Libby, four and a half years his junior but the most stable influence in his life nonetheless. If it came to it—if he got himself arrested—she'd get the call. She would bail him out or pick him up or otherwise do what needed to be done.

Still. The self-pity that he'd been nursing in the days since his failed attempt to adopt Yesenia was too powerful to give up just yet. He wanted to feel alone and forgotten—to have no one or no thing he could count on. If he couldn't save Yesenia from whatever fate had befallen her, he could at least live in parallel desperation.

And so, when the beleaguered officers finally waved him on through the doors to the concourses, he stopped at the first trash can he could find to deposit the toiletries the customs officer had marked as suspect. Before they'd even hit the bottom of the liner, he tossed in one last, unsolicited item.

That damned cell phone, and all the rejection it represented.

He walked through the concourse until it ended in a hub filled with more signage—a veritable Babel of neon advertising newsstands and souvenir shops and eateries. These were signs of a different sort, not so much portents of the future as bait. He stood in the middle of the wide hallway, a chain coffee shop on one side and an airport bar on the other, and pondered the two distinctly different outcomes available to him. In one, he was jolted awake enough to make it back to Poplar Bluff to resume his life. In the other, he passed out at the bar, only to be awakened by airport security and brought to some holding room. Probably get a visit from the chaplain.

He elected to go the coffee route, if for no better reason than there seemed to be fewer people in there than in the bar. The barista delivered his cup with his name misspelled—"WIT," in all capital letters.

"Did I get it wrong?" she asked. She was about his age, with straight blonde hair and blocky glasses and a face full of concern.

"It's okay."

"No, now it's not, neither. Everybody deserves for me to get their name right." She reached for the cup. "So how do I right this wrong?"

Her kindness annoyed Whit, who was tired of answering questions and at any rate just wanted his coffee. But he spelled it out for her. Waited while she drew a carat between the *W* and the *I* and wrote a lowercase *h* above it.

"Have a blessed day," she said as she handed the cup back to him.

"I don't know about that," he said. "But thanks."

He trudged down the concourse, knowing he had plenty of time to catch the flight back home but not caring all that much. He took a seat in the empty waiting area across from his gate and sat down to watch. Some walked and some ran, a few with children or spouses in tow. No one looked particularly happy. What was it about people, anyway?

He was maybe sixteen ounces into the oversized cup when something began to gnaw at him—some undefined omission that pressed on his mind, like he'd left the iron on or forgotten to roll up his car windows. He checked to make sure he had his wallet and passport and car keys. He half considered going back to the coffee kiosk to ask the friendly barista if she'd found anything he'd left behind. But the airline worker was calling for pre-boarding to begin, and so he stood up and waited until his group was called. Shuffled to his seat in the rear of the plane and closed his eyes.

CHAPTER 30

The skies opened up just past Marked Tree, Arkansas. The storm was one of those early spring bangers that he'd see on the news tomorrow morning, when the light was finally right for the helicopters to get a clear shot of the devastation. The rain and hail came down so fast that his wipers couldn't keep up. All around him, he could see cars pulling off Highway 63 to wait it out on the shoulders or, if they were lucky, under the scant few overpasses on this stretch of road.

It reminded him of the move to Wyoming, twenty years ago now. He'd been too preoccupied with his baby sister and his mourning over the box of forgotten things to really gauge the storm's progress until it was upon them. It hit like a rodeo bull just out of the gate, snarling and bucking and blowing their box truck all over the road. Cole Allen didn't stop, though. He sang hymns over the clatter of hail on the hood, incanted in his quasi-English prayer language for Jesus to calm the storm. The upside was that all the noise gave cover for the Whitman children to cut loose. Libby had screamed her tiny self hoarse. Whit had wailed without fear of reprimand, at least for a time. Somehow, they'd made it to the other side, although it was a stretch to say they had done so together.

Tonight, however, Whit was alone on his journey home from the airport. He had one close call, nearly hydroplaning off the four-lane into a field just west of Bay, but he righted the ship and kept on going, even when a second wave of storms bore down on him. If there was a tornado out there that had him marked for annihilation, he might as well meet it head on.

At last, however, the wind and hail eased, and he was left with a steady driving rain through which to make his way north. He was almost to the Missouri border before he saw the lights from a police SUV blocking his way along Highway 135. The state trooper explained that an EF-3 tornado had uncorked on the little town of Whiskey Spigot, leveling a courthouse that had stood since the Great Depression. The highway was impassable, and the alternate routes were under water. He turned Whit around with the suggestion that he find somewhere to stay in town, meaning thirty miles south in Paragould.

And so, just after midnight, Whit pulled into the driveway of the house Libby and Franklin rented. He reached for his phone first, thinking that, since Franklin was known to be both a hot head and an avid gun collector, it might be better to call before he knocked. But his pocket was empty, and he remembered that he'd thrown that device away at the airport, although with the benefit of hindsight that decision seemed suspect. Nothing to be done about it now, though. He pulled the flashlight from his glove box and turned it upon himself, hoping that whoever came to the door in whatever condition would at least see his face before they fired. He pulled open the storm door and raised his hand to knock, but it opened without him ever making contact. Libby raised a finger to her lips and pointed to Franklin, passed out on the couch. She motioned for him to follow her into the kitchen. Clicked on the dim light above the stove and sat down at the table, pulling her long black nightshirt down over her knees.

"Sorry to wake you," Whit said.

She waved him off. "I been up. Storms get you?"

"They knocked out the road north of here," Whit said.

"Let me guess—Whiskey Spigot? I swear, that town gets leveled by something every six months."

Whit forced a laugh, but something in Libby's voice wasn't right. She wasn't nervous, exactly, but she was wound tight. Before he could ask, he heard a shuffling behind him, feet too small to be Franklin. A second later, little Zeb—their half-brother by their mother and Byron—ran past him and jumped hard into Libby's lap. Her arms clamped down on him.

"Zeb, *shit!*" she cried. She quickly repositioned him onto the other leg.

The boy eyed Whit doubtfully. He stayed locked in that stare, even when Libby had recovered from the jolt and begun to sooth him.

"This is our brother Junius, remember? We call him Whit?"

The boy smiled and offered a tiny wave. He tucked his head up against Libby's neck. "Can I have a drink?"

"Of course."

Zeb hopped down and stepped over to the sink. He pulled a cup from the dish drainer and filled it with water, held it with both hands as he gulped it down. When he'd finished, he set it back in the sink and reached back into the cabinet. He filled two more cups with water and set them on the table for the adults.

"Thanks, sweetie," Libby said. "You heading back to bed?"

"Yeah."

The boy yawned and waved simultaneously, then turned to go. As he passed through the doorway, he reached back behind the fridge and flipped on the switch for the fluorescent light overhead. Libby twisted in her seat and snapped at him to turn that back off. She was too late, though. The glaring light was on just long enough for Whit to see the bruises on her left thigh, dark and swollen and unmistakable as a thunderhead.

"Lib?" Whit said, but she clamped her fingers down in a way that told him most clearly to shut the hell up. She waited until they heard Zeb's footsteps leave the stairs and walk across the bedroom above them. Then she got up and went into the laundry room. Came out wearing black leggings.

"You know Mom and Byron split, right?" she asked.

"No. When?"

"Couple months ago. Things had been getting bad for a while before that. Zeb's been spending a lot of time over here. It's more stable."

"Stable?" Whit asked. His brain was processing slower than usual, he knew, and he couldn't quite square what he expected to hear with what his sister was actually saying. "I thought things were good with Mom. She seemed pretty good at Christmas. I mean, Byron's kind of an asshole, but everything else was—I don't know. Good."

Libby glared at him for a long moment. "Are you shitting me?"

"No. I thought she looked happy."

"We didn't get together for Christmas this year, remember? Mom and I had to work. You and Novie went to visit Isaias on that shoot in Jackson. Ring a bell?"

Whit felt little beads of sweat rising up on his scalp. "Oh. Right. So those things with Mom, that was—"

"Two Christmases ago." She spread her index finger and thumb across her forehead. "For the love of God, Whit." She went to the fridge and pulled out two cans of beer. She winced as she sat back down, but launched into a family update before he could ask her about it.

Bethany Whitman Farris had gone off the deep end, so to speak, sometime around Labor Day of the previous year. She claimed to be racked with grief at the death of a great aunt in Kentucky, although Libby suspected at the time—and since had confirmed—that all was not well with her and Byron, either. She started drinking again, possibly abusing pills, although that seemed to be more Byron's vice than hers. The one thing Libby could say with certainty is that Bethany's employment at the hospital had been terminated for stealing drugs, and whether they were for her or her no-account husband didn't matter shit.

The last straw came, as is often the case with these things, on a holiday. A post-Thanksgiving dinner party devolved into a fight over dishes, and Byron said something that went a step too far. Bethany clocked him with a stainless-steel ladle, still crusted with bits of turkey gravy. Byron landed a blow of his own with a cutting board. Thankfully, one of the neighbors heard the commotion and called the cops before anyone resorted to carving knives, but it was still all past the point of no return for Bethany. She left to stay with one of her friends in Jonesboro later that night. Ever since then, Zebadiah had been shuttled back and forth between worthless parents, and in the intervening times dumped on Libby.

"Not dumped," she said, shaking her head even as she polished off her beer. "I didn't mean that."

"How, though?" Whit asked. "How did I not know about any of this?" Libby sat there and let him work through that answer for a few seconds. He remembered the youth group in the airport, grating against the nerves of their Peruvian flight mates. "Because I'm a self-absorbed asshole?"

Libby shrugged.

"Sorry," he said.

"It's okay. You get caught inside your own head sometimes."

"Wait a minute," Whit said. "What happened to your leg?"

"Nothing."

"Seemed like more than nothing to me."

"I hit the corner of the coffee table."

He shook his head doubtfully. "Looked more like someone took a hammer to it."

"I have it handled."

"I don't know—"

She bent forward in her chair until her face was maybe eight inches from his. "You don't know shit from shit. Understand?"

He leaned back slowly. "If you need a place—"

"I have it handled." She stared hard at him, daring him to say another word. When he didn't, she leaned back. Rubbed her forehead. "How's Novie?"

"Couldn't say."

"You're such an idiot." She stared wearily at Whit. "She's been trying to get hold of you for a week now. Told me you weren't replying. That's a jerk move, bro."

Whit paused, but it didn't take as long for him to work through the implications of what she was saying. His sister and girlfriend had hit it off from the start. He should have known that they would have stayed in touch.

"We broke up two months ago," he explained.

"You sure?"

"Yes. I think so. Probably."

He rubbed his eyes. When BTI had finally reopened after the ice-pocalypse, as people were referring to the winter storm a few weeks' back, he and Novie had mostly stayed away from one another. Any school the size of Bootheel Tech was a fishbowl, of course, and so they had to be cordial whenever they crossed paths. Still, she made a point not to visit his office, and he didn't go by hers. He'd assumed from their intentional lack of contact that they'd broken up.

"When did she try to call?" he asked.

"Off and on the last week. I just got another text from her today." She narrowed her eyes at Whit. "I don't think you ever told me what you're doing here."

"Yes I did. Coming back from Memphis."

"Buy why were you in Memphis?" She waved that question off with a finger. "Wait. That's the second question. First is why are you ignoring Novie?"

"I'm not. I never got a message or anything. I threw my phone away."

"Come again?"

"I threw it away. In the trash."

She nodded somberly, but the frown gave way to laughter. Her giggles soon crescendoed into a full, snort-producing cackle. It was a harsh sound—she'd inherited their mother's shrill vocalizations—but one he'd have taken above any in the world at that moment. He wanted to do something—to laugh with her, maybe, or reach across and take her hand and tell her things would be okay—but he was afraid to break the moment. And so he just sat and waited, even when she started to cry. Even when she lowered her head onto the table and fell asleep.

Figure 10: Help for Victims of Domestic Violence

CHAPTER 31

Highway 135 was still only open in one lane through Whiskey Spigot the next day, leaving Whit and two pickups to wait at the south end of the closure until the pilot car had cleared out the vehicles coming from the north. When it was their turn, Whit and his comrades inched through at barely 20 mph, if for no better reason than to take in the spectacle of destruction. The courthouse was blown apart, as reported, but daylight revealed a smorgasbord of carnage. The remains of one steel building had been twisted around the enormous pole of a billboard advertising cotton seed. Uprooted trees lay over demolished roofs. Deck boards were splintered at the base of high line poles, some of the shards sticking out like darts from the wooden posts.

It had been a day of ruins so far, he thought. He'd passed out in the laundry room not long after Libby had dropped onto the table, only to awaken four hours later to a kitchen full of beer cans and no sign of his sister or her car. Franklin was still sacked out on the couch and from the smell of things may have peed himself in the night. Only Zeb was up-and-at-'em at this early hour, standing on a chair and frying eggs. Whit offered to help, but the boy declined. He had the situation handled, he said, and even fixed two over easy for Whit. A study in resilience, that little man.

Just past the billboard with the twisted steel, the souped-up Dodge pickup in front of him slowed to a crawl. Whit drummed his fingers on the steering wheel. Any Oklahoma kid had seen this kind of destruction a dozen times or better. Not so for the couple in the pickup, apparently. More than once, the driver came to a dead stop so that the man in the passenger seat could lean out and snap photographs with a fancy camera. Whit could hear his wife or girlfriend or whatever she was chew him out through the open windows.

"Just shoot the damn picture," she ordered.

"Hang on."

"You'll be lucky if that guy behind us doesn't come out of his car and kick your butt. I swear you don't even think, do you? My daddy tried to warn me."

Whit considered the poor man's fate as they putted along behind the pilot car, which was struggling not to pull off and leave them. Such nagging might have been his own future, if by some miracle he and Mila had stayed together. He could imagine her here now, chiding him for not honking his horn, insisting that he tap the rear of the pickup with his bumper, raging in Spanish about the timidity of American drivers. She would never have been happy with him, and he would have gotten fed up with her—already was, just thinking about it.

Novie, though—that would have been different. Might still be different. After what Libby said last night, he could feel the slightest of hopes stirring behind his throbbing temples—the same sense of possibility he'd felt when he was waiting at the door of Operación Amor only—what was it now? Four days ago? And here he was, Fool #1, setting himself up to be crushed yet again.

He was still trying to quash that silly trace of optimism when the pickup pulled through a break in the orange cones to the right. Whit followed it obediently. When he glanced down the road, however, he saw the pilot car at the end of the hazard zone, already pulling around to lead the southbound convoy. Too late, Whit understood that he had not followed the pilot to the end of its route, but the pickup into the gravel parking lot of the Living Waters Church of Christ. The pickup behind him pulled in as well, leaving him nowhere to go but forward, nothing to do but wait.

He parked facing the road and watched the southbound line of traffic roll past—mostly pickups, but also two sedans, one of which veered into the church lot on two wheels. Whit checked the time—11:02am, late enough to cause any born-again to question his salvation. A quarter mile back came a tractor-trailer rig, inching through the tiny space between the cones. Whit almost turned out behind him to go north, even without the pilot car. But a state trooper had set up on the shoulder, just waiting for somebody to make his day.

"Brother?" a voice said. "Sir?"

Whit looked into his driver's side mirror and saw a fat man in his late thirties, belt cinched up beneath his giant belly so tight that Whit wondered if everything below it wasn't tingling or numb. Then again, maybe that was the point.

"Brother, can we help you?" The man was sweating, even though it couldn't be more than 70 degrees, now that the front had passed to the east. The bulge of a pistol showed beneath the suit coat on the left side. "Service started only a minute ago. It ain't too late."

"I'm just passing through," Whit answered.

"Well Brother," he said with a chuckle. "We're all just passing through till the Lord calls us home, ain't we?"

Whit let that slide, knowing from long experience how persistent evangelists could be. He decided to deflect attention, and he knew the subject that would do it. "Big crowd this week, huh?"

"Not gonna lie. I wish it was like this every Sunday. But that storm—praise Jesus, you can see already what the Lord is doing through it. Everything happens for a reason. Amen."

Whit nodded. He'd been in such conversations a thousand times when he was younger—enough to know that what he was about to say breached evangelical etiquette on multiple levels.

"Does it, though?" he asked.

"Does what?"

"Does everything happen for a reason. You just said it did."

The fat man leveled a gaze at Whit that was equal parts irritation and pity. "It does, Brother. This storm was no random event. It serves the Lord's purpose."

"Well," Whit said, and knew he shouldn't try to take it any further. But his mouth was dry and his eyes hurt, and that pilot car was still puttering southward. "What purpose, though? Destroying a town like this?"

"Oh you'll see the good if you look. We've been here before. The spirit of these people—."

Whit held up a hand to stop him. "I'm not doubting their spirit. I'm questioning the premise. Your town gets leveled, and people bounce back, and that's because it had to happen that way? Because it's God's plan?"

"I believe so, Brother. If you would come inside the church, you might see."

"Hold on," Whit said. "Let me set up another scenario for you. Let's say you have a girl—a Latina girl, maybe, from Peru—and let's say her parents dump her when she's a kid. So she ends up in this residential center, along the coast maybe, and stays there while she finishes school."

"Brother—"

"And then let's say she doesn't get into college, not that she could have afforded it anyway, and decides she's going to make her own way without the help of the same people who have cared for her all her life. Maybe she gets involved with a guy, and he's no good, and he gets high one night and beats the shit out of her on the beach. The tide comes in while she's unconscious, and—wouldn't you know it—she drowns. Now, tell me, what reason could there be in a thing like that?"

"It would be a tragedy, brother. I'm sure the Lord would weep, as he did over Lazarus' grave."

"But did he *cause* it? Is that girl's death God's will?"

"It has to be."

"Because that's the way it turned out. And things turn out the way they're supposed to. Right?"

"We don't always understand the ways of God."

"That's not an answer."

The man shook his head. "Brother, I can tell you are carrying a heavy load. I'm here to tell you, though, that the Lord doesn't give us more than we can handle. The Book of Romans teaches us that things work to the good of those who love the Lord."

"I see," Whit answered. He turned in his car seat. Wondered if he could reach through the window quickly enough to grab the fat man's tie and punch him in the face before he got to his gun. "Those that don't love the Lord, though. Do things work for their good?"

"The rain falls on the just and the unjust, brother."

"Another non-answer."

The fat man held up a fat palm. He looked at Whit with somber, earnest eyes. "All I can tell you is that tornado could have killed us all, and it didn't, and we're going to praise the Lord."

"Because you're safe."

"Yes, sir."

"But the girl—the one in my story?"

He let the question to hang there. He could see in the man's face that he'd touched something there, that some pang of empathy was at war with his assumptions about the world. His internal wrestling proved barely a flicker, though. When he looked back at Whit, he was once again the unwavering servant of the literal King James Word of God. Whit expected him to walk away, righteous and vindicated, back into his church. Instead the fat man stepped back and planted his feet, giving himself a firm base from which to shoot. Whit ducked instinctively.

What he heard was not gunfire, however. It was a crystal-clear tenor voice, singing out an old hymn. *"Come home! Come home! Ye who are weary, come home!"*

Whit wished he could just stay hidden in his car, knowing even as he wished it that he was too tall to disappear entirely. He slowly raised his head and glanced over, not wanting to meet the singer's eye. But the fat man had turned to face the ruins of his town, as though he were singing to the rubble, calling it to rest.

"Oh, sinner, come home!"

He finished that verse and turned back toward his church. Raised two fat fingers in a wave toward Whit. He sang the next verse on his way to the door.

The headlights of the pilot car appeared again, this time on the northbound leg of its ping-pong route. Whit moved the gear selector to reverse and backed out of the spot. A moment later, he was tucked in behind an old brown and yellow El Camino, inching along as though it had all the time in the world. He left the windows down and focused on the rusted tailgate, on keeping his tires on the pavement. To the east, he could still see the thin outline of dark clouds, the western edge of the system that had passed through last night. The radio news said it had killed two people in Tennessee. Maybe they didn't see it coming. Maybe it just didn't matter.

When classes resumed at Bootheel Tech the next morning, Whit found himself newly sympathetic to the plight of American technical school students. All of them were on their way to somewhere else—jobs at Great Clips, maybe, or an auto shop, or maybe servicing the giant windmills that had been sprouting up all over the region. What came next mattered a hell of a lot more to them than school did—black, white, Mexican, whatever. None of them cared anything about sounding like Marquez or Shakespeare. They were there because someone had told them they had to be educated in order to increase their paycheck. They wanted a better insulated house and a more reliable pickup and more money for beer. His classes were at worst a roadblock and at best a bridge. Whatever the case, no one wanted to be there any longer than absolutely necessary. Life was too short and death too near.

"Mr. Whitman?"

Earlier that morning, he had made it through his Auto-Mechanics 101 class despite all his thoughts about chance and death and the futility of human existence. The very nature of teaching how to change brake pads required him to stay busy in the physical world, where logic and spatial reasoning could usually fix whatever had gone wrong. It kept him out of his own head, for which he was grateful.

That song, though. It started playing in his brain as soon as he gathered his books to walk to his Spanish class. "Softly and Tenderly Jesus Is Calling." He still remembered all the words from his childhood in church, and the fat man in Whiskey Spigot had somehow wedged them anew into his brain. *Come home! Ye who are weary, come home!*

"Mr. Whitman?"

He wasn't sure how long the young woman in the front row had been holding up her hand. She sounded like she'd been trying to get his attention for some time already.

"Kindra," he said.

Softly and tenderly, Kindra is calling. That song again. Jesus.

"Yes," she said.

"Okay. Right. You have a question?"

She looked around the classroom. Most of the other students were either asleep or on their phones. "I was—I think all of us were wondering if we were going to do anything in class today."

Whit lifted his eyes to the clock on the back wall. It read quarter after the hour, and he was fairly certain he hadn't uttered a meaningful sentence since he greeted them with a perfunctory

"Good morning." The lesson he'd prepared—one that had been sitting on his desk since before he'd left for break, eight days and a lifetime ago—was on the imperfect tense. Action begun in the past, but as yet not completed. He looked up at the blank white board. *O sinner, come home.*

"Mr. Whitman?"

"Yes. Okay. *Los verbos.*"

It wasn't going anywhere, though, which was as clear to the rest of the class as it was to him. One young man muttered something that included the word *bullshit* and stormed out. Kindra watched her professor with concern until movement in the hallway caught her eye through the glass window in the door. She left her things on the desk and stepped away, presumably to flag down someone with the authority to address the situation. Whit couldn't see who it might be, but he could feel the potential for disaster growing by the minute.

"I think that's enough for today," he said. "I'll see you all tomorrow."

"Tomorrow is Tuesday," someone piped up.

"Right. I'll see you the next time we have class."

This last bit was lost, however, drowned out by the squeak of chair legs against the tile floor, of the insertion of books into backpacks, of hushed speculations about the shrooms their teacher must have eaten over spring break and whether his condition might be permanent. He didn't bother addressing any of it. Instead, he hurriedly gathered his things together and tried to file out among the dozen or so students, hoping Kindra and whoever she was talking to wouldn't see him. Before he'd even made it to the door, however, Novie had hold of his elbow, dragging him back toward the teacher's desk. She dismissed Kindra and sat down next to him on the desk and waited.

"That lesson could have gone better," he finally said.

"Jesus." She kicked her feet out in front of her as though she'd been shocked. On the downswing, her heels clanged against the metal facing of the desk loud enough to make his teeth hurt. "That's how you start this conversation?" she said.

"I threw my phone away."

"You what?"

"At the airport. I threw my phone away." He searched her face for comprehension, but he could tell none of this was connecting and his window for reconciliation was closing. "I had turned it off when I left for Peru, and I forgot to turn it back home when we landed. Because it wasn't turned on, I didn't get any messages. Because I didn't get any messages, I assumed no one cared. Does that make sense?"

"Good lord."

"Did we break up?"

She was staring at a spot somewhere on his neck now, and he was pretty sure this could go a few different ways. Best case scenario was that she'd lean over and kiss him and tell him it was all right. He licked his lips just in case, but her low tone quashed his hopes. "You said some pretty shitty things."

"I know."

"You know." She reached back on the desk and spread out her palms. Leaned back and tossed her hair as though she were on a picnic in the sun. As though he mattered no more than a few stray ants on the blanket.

"I know. I'm sorry."

She whirled on him then, sliding down from the desk and squaring her shoulders to him. "Sorry for what?"

"A lot," he said, but knew that didn't cover the half of it. He had a pile of regrets heavy enough to sink a barge, and that just from the last week. "I'm sorry for a lot of things."

"Ain't we all," she said. She turned her head to look at the clock. The hands were swinging upward now. The more dedicated students would be arriving in this room in a few minutes. Classes in other rooms would be expecting Whit and Novie to show up to teach, or at least to get them one step closer to being rid of school forever.

"Maybe we could get together later," Whit said.

Novie shook her head. "I told you before. I'm not your therapy pet."

"That's not what I meant."

A heavy door clicked down the hall—Dr. Price's door, swinging shut behind him. The echo soon gave way to the sound of urgent footsteps approaching the classroom.

"You got bigger worries than me," Novie said. She gave his arm a squeeze, kind but not particularly intimate, and then stood beside the desk and smoothed out her pants and waited.

Figure 11: Softly and Tenderly

CHAPTER 32

Dr. Jerome Price, Vice President of Institutional Advancement at BTI, checked his watch and smiled across his cherrywood desk at Whit.

"President Yost will be along directly," he said. "Don't worry."

Whit nodded politely but made a mental note to add "Don't worry" to his notebook. Ever since that night in the Thirsty Owl when he'd hurt Novie's feelings so badly, he'd been keeping a diary of stupid things people said—things like "it just goes to show" or "God needed another angel in his choir." So far, the two most represented speakers in his little book were, respectively, Junius Whitman and Dr. Jerome Price.

The VP propped his feet up on the desk. Tented his fingers together as if in prayer. Taken together, the man and his furniture reminded Whit of Dr. Crutcheson's office at Covenant University—the high-back leather chair, the posh area rug, the mahogany desk and matching file cabinet. Such appurtenances were, so it seemed, part and parcel with academians marking their territory. Taken in context, however, the scene looked out of sorts, like someone wearing a tuxedo to a church potluck. The industrial beige walls and tile floors and bad fluorescent lighting provided contrast between the man's aspirations and his situation. The whole scene gave lie to the incontrovertible fact that Price was compensating for something.

"In times like these, I find comfort in the old, old stories," Price said. "*I desire mercy, not sacrifice.* That's a thing worth thinking about. Am I right?"

"Yeah," Whit said. "I hope so." He wished he'd brought the notebook with him.

"And I hope you know the same is true here. This meeting isn't about punishment. It's about redemption." He lowered his feet to the floor. Leaned forward until his elbows were across his desk calendar. "As long as we're waiting, maybe we should figure out your story about what happened on Monday. How you're going to tell it."

"I thought maybe I'd just explain what happened."

"Of course, of course. But the truth can be told in different ways. I think it might be best if you told your story in the most favorable light possible. Best for both of us, if you get my meaning."

Whit fought off the urge to sigh. He'd already told Price his story, or at least told the nearest approximation he could come up with. The facts hadn't changed since Monday, and neither had his understanding of them. But this was a disciplinary meeting, after all, and he didn't have a lot of room for objections, even if that meant going over the same humiliating event multiple times for his bosses.

"I'd had an eventful spring break," Whit began. Price cut him off.

"The trip to Peru, you mean—visiting old friends. But some of those friends weren't so excited to see you as you'd hoped. And then the tornado on the way home, getting stuck in Paragould. That's all background. You need to spend as little time with background as possible. President Yost doesn't care much for context. Are you tracking with me?"

"I think so."

"Good. Let's get background out of the way quickly. The day really starts with your mechanics class. And you didn't have any trouble in there, right?"

"No. That kind of work keeps you occupied a little better than teaching languages. You don't have as much room to think about other things."

"Good! That's good. So then you go to your Spanish class, and...?"

"A lot of things just hit me at once."

"Such as?"

"It may not make a whole lot of sense to you. Not without some context."

Price winced. Shook his head. "Do the best you can."

"Okay, well. On the walk to class, I was caught up in the unfairness of life, for example. Why things work out for some people and not for others."

"You're talking about luck."

"Not really. Circumstance." He spread out his hands in front of him. "This kid I knew in Trujillo—."

The VP held up his hand to stop Whit. "You've got to make it simple. How about we say you weren't feeling well?"

"I feel fine, though."

"But Monday you didn't." He raised his palm as though it were an antenna, preparing to receive a missive from the Lord. "You felt fine physically, but your mental health was off that day. Family issues that you'd rather not talk about. You're seeking treatment. How does that grab you?"

Whit found a mole on the right side of Price's neck and stared at it, the way Novie had stared at him the day of his meltdown. He sucked a thin piece of his cheek between his eye teeth and bit down until it hurt.

"You with me?" Price said.

"Not entirely. No."

Price rubbed his temples with his delicate fingers. Whit wondered if they'd ever done anything more taxing than punch letters on a keyboard. Price didn't seem to realize he was being judged. Instead he nodded as though another answer had just come to him. He glanced at the door. "It may not be my place," he said softly. "But when's the last time you went to church?"

Whit felt his face go hot. In spite of himself, he searched his memory for the answer. The last time he attended Sunday meetings with any regularity was just after he landed in Minneapolis from

Peru, when he was still trying to put his life back together and Isaias had not yet joined him in the Cities. Last December he'd gone to Christmas Eve service at the Episcopal church with Novie, and he recalled going at some point to the Poplar Bluff Missionary Baptist Church for the funeral of an old janitor from BTI. That was about it, though, assuming he didn't count the conversation with the fat man in the parking lot in Whisky Spigot. "It's been a while," he said.

"Let me be frank with you," Price answered. "Your life is just one long answer to questions about eternity. If you don't tend to your soul, every little thing can throw you off the path. And if you leave the path—well, I don't have to tell you what your eternal fate would be. But it's never too late to turn things around. The Good Book tells us, seek ye first the kingdom and ye shall find what ye desire."

Whit shook his head. "I don't think that's quite how it goes," he said.

"A different translation, maybe. But you see my point. We humans are spiritual beings, Mr. Whitman. You have a soul in need of care. I would be happy to introduce you to Reverend Morrison at First Baptist. I think you'd find it helpful to have a spiritual guide as you're sorting things out. Someone to feed your hungry soul."

Whit stared at the mole, hoping some appropriate answer might appear miraculously sprout forth to get him out of this conversation. Among the spiritual leaders he'd known, from Brother Reinbeck to Brother Arneson to Bonner Hanson to Cole Allen Whitman, he wouldn't trust a single one to feed his goldfish, much less his soul. The people who cared for him best—Isaias, Libby, Novie, Guillermo—were all religious expatriates. But how did you explain that to someone like Price, for whom the old-time religion was still as natural as breath?

"Let's just get through this meeting first," he finally said.

"Okay, Mr. Whitman. Okay." He dropped his hands on his desk. "Try to remember what we talked about, at least. Although I suppose you're just going to tell the truth your way."

"What is truth?"

Price smiled, apparently recognizing it as a Biblical statement, but clearly not able to place the speaker—Pontius Pilate—or the setting—the trial that would send Jesus to crucifixion. "See? The Word is still in you, my friend. Buried though it may be, still it has the power—."

He dropped the thought mid-sentence and sat up straight. A half second later, the door to Dr. Price's office opened with a whir. President Yost strode in, heels clicking against the tile, sharp as the drum roll before a hanging. She shook hands with Whit and Dr. Price, ignoring the chair he'd set out for her, and started in.

"Junius," she said. "Please explain yourself."

PART IV

Figure 12: Part III Recap

CHAPTER 33

"You grab those boards," Zeb said, pointing to a pile of graying two-by-fours by the small outbuilding. "I'll bring the hammer and saw."

Whit did as he was told and followed the boy back around to the front yard. Zeb motioned for him to be quiet and showed him where to drop the wood at the base of a large oak tree. The boy then crept up onto the porch and peeked in the window to see if Franklin, Libby's boyfriend, was paying any attention. Whit had only spoken with Franklin a handful of times, but he thought he understood the boy's hesitation. Franklin was the kind of man Cole Allen might have been, had he not discovered religion. As things stood, though, Franklin was already high when Whit arrived at 10:00 in the morning to watch his brother while Libby picked up an extra shift. Zeb didn't comment on Franklin's state, but whatever he saw through the window was enough to satisfy him that it was safe to get to work. He ran back to the tree and showed Whit which branches he wanted to use to make the tree fort he'd been imagining.

"What do you think?" he asked.

"I think we're going to need more wood."

The boy smiled. "Leave that to me. But you have to do the fractions."

Zeb sprinted around back without waiting for a response. The boy was up to something—that was easy enough to see. But Whit stayed put so he could have his fun. He'd learned at Operación Amor in Trujillo not to go chasing trouble, especially if the trouble involved was harmless mischief. A few minutes later, Zeb returned with another armload of boards, albeit of lower quality than the others. Whit eyed them doubtfully.

"I'm not sure these are going to hold much weight," he said.

"We'll just use the good parts."

And he was off again for more.

So they proceeded through the rest of the morning, with Whit measuring and cutting and offering occasional engineering suggestions while Zeb performed most of the physical labor. Whit was amazed by the boy's strength and dexterity, as Libby had predicted he would be. He wondered if anyone else—their mother, or the boy's father Byron, or maybe even Franklin—had ever taken notice of what a little marvel the child was. By noon, they had a credible platform built. Whit suggested they get something to eat before they start on the rails, but Zeb insisted they keep going, lest Franklin wake up and put a stop to the whole thing before they finished.

"We have to eat sometime," Whit protested. "Besides, Libby should get off work before long."

"We can do a little more," Zeb said. "Please."

Whit shrugged, which was all the cue his little brother needed. And why not, Whit thought? This was the last day of the week's worth of paid leave Dr. Yost had given him in the disciplinary hearing. She'd put only one condition on the time off—that he pull his head out of his skinny ass—and Whit thought he'd been fairly successful in fulfilling that requirement. He'd bought a mountain bike and started riding trails. When a bad landing banana'ed his front wheel, he'd set that aside and offered to spend some time with Zeb. After a couple of days roaming through the woods in the vacant lot north of Libby's rental house, Whit thought he and Zeb understood each other, as much as any two humans could claim such a thing.

He was still in the midst of these thoughts when the front door opened and Franklin emerged, wearing a zip-up hoodie and jeans that draped over the tops of his bare feet. He squinted against the light, scanning the yard until his eyes rested on Zeb—or at least, on the place where Zeb had stood a few seconds before. The boy had disappeared, Whit realized, leaving him holding the hammer.

"What the hell," Franklin said, and then saw the tree fort. His eyes narrowed. Even from this distance, Whit could see the veins in his temples pulsing. He gripped the porch rail and bellowed after Zeb. "Where are you, you little shit?"

When no answer came, he stood straight and pointed a finger at Whit. Then he whirled and disappeared into the house. Whit scanned the yard again for Zeb and this time found the boy—or part of the boy, anyhow. When he'd heard Franklin coming, Zeb had sprinted off to the left side of the driveway and jumped into the bed of Franklin's pickup. One ratty shoe had fallen off, however, and lay on the gravel below the bumper. Whit wasn't sure exactly how the child had managed to crawl in there without being seen, much less how he'd managed to close the tailgate from the inside. But Whit knew better than to out the boy's position—not after seeing Franklin's handiwork across his sister's thigh that night he'd returned from his failed Peru expedition. He gripped the hammer tightly. Wondered how hard he could swing it, if it came to that.

A few moments later, Franklin wandered back out, down the steps and into the yard, this time wearing a Carhart hoodie and his heavy work boots. He carried a bottle of beer for himself and another for Whit.

"That little shit's got you doing his dirty work," Franklin said as he handed over the bottle. "You best watch him."

Whit reached up and draped his wrist over one of the branches supporting the tree fort. He was disappointed how much wobble was still in the platform, but he could see no quick remedy to it. "I think he just wanted a project. We used that pile of scrap wood in back."

Franklin turned up his bottle and downed half of its contents before pausing for air. "I think there's something you need to see, Professor." He motioned for Whit to follow. They walked past the pickup where the boy was still hiding, around the side of the house and into the back yard. Franklin paused at the edge of the gray deck. Motioned with his bottle for Whit to have a look.

As a collection of wood, the deck was in worse shape than the scraps with which they'd begun construction on the fort. The rails were bowed so badly as to pull free some of the nails that once fastened them to the vertical posts. The boards were the color of ashes, with thousands of cracks running along their surface. Judging by the remains of one that had splintered beneath the grill, they were beyond even turning over to use with the other side facing up.

Sorry condition of the wood aside, it was clear what had gotten Franklin so worked up. The southeast corner of the deck had been ripped apart—rails, flooring, even the header joist. Whit did a quick mental inventory of the missing pieces, but any fool could see what had happened. As spongy as the lumber was, it hadn't occurred to Whit that Zeb's forays for more supplies might have included his disassembling the back deck.

"I—ah, didn't—," he said. "Well."

"Them joists are all twisted now," Franklin said. "I don't see how that's going to go back together with what we got. May have to tear this thing out and start over."

"We'll see what we can do."

"You and Zeb? Nah. He knows better than this. Me and him are going to have a talk, once he shows his sorry ass again." He turned and squared his shoulder to Whit. "You, on the other hand."

Whit flexed his fingers around the hammer, knowing he should have left it at the tree fort. He would never use it on Franklin, but if he lost his grip on it the reverse might not be true. "I think we can fix it," he said again.

"I think you better tackle this one on your own. Tell that boy to stay inside and play video games. It's about the only damn thing he's good for." He side armed his empty bottle through the gap between posts of the deck. It landed with a hiss in the dry weeds beneath. "I got to run to town."

He turned and marched back around the house. Whit followed a few paces back, ready to sprint to the pickup to rescue Zeb as soon as Franklin went inside. But Franklin kept marching, belching and spitting as he tromped across the gravel and climbed into the truck, where his keys were waiting in the ignition. As he backed up, the rear tire ground Zeb's vacated shoe into the mud. Panic seized Whit. He raised his arms to try to flag the pickup down, but Franklin didn't see him. Instead he gunned the engine, sending the tires spinning the rear of the truck fishtailing down the driveway. Whit drew his cell phone—a new flip model, only slightly more advanced than the one he'd discarded at the airport—and tried to get his shaky fingers in place to dial Libby.

At the edge of the drive, however, Franklin had to slow up so that he could make the sharp turn left onto the county road. The tailgate dropped and Zeb rolled out, his exit perfectly timed so as to land him behind the honeysuckle-covered mailbox. He crouched there until the pickup was a quarter mile down the road, then took off his other shoe. He waved at Whit, beaming. And then he took off running toward the house, little feet churning over the stones. If the rocks hurt at all, he didn't show it.

It took less than thirty minutes to get the tree fort down and the wood returned to the back yard. The longer they worked, the more relieved Whit felt that Zeb and his friends would never get a chance to play on that platform. Even mostly completed, the thing was no sturdier than that rotten back deck, and probably less so. It would have collapsed sooner rather than later, Whit decided. At least they dismantled it before anyone got hurt, and so maybe things had worked out for the best.

Reconstructing the deck, on the other hand, was an exercise in frustration. It took half an hour to convince Zeb to actually wear shoes—the ground was littered with old nails—and twice that long to figure out which pieces went where. Further complicating matters were the cuts they'd made to suit the purposes of their tree fort, which left several of the boards too short to span neatly across the joists. They kept hammering away at the project, though, and eventually began to enjoy the puzzle it presented, even though the end product was no more stable than anything else in little Zeb's world.

They finished the deck and made sandwiches from the smoked sausage and cheese in a Christmas basket Libby had never opened. They sat on the couch and told each other stories. When Whit told him about his tooth falling out while he was teaching at Northern Lakes, the boy laughed so hard that flecks of white bread spewed out from between his lips. Whit dodged the soggy missiles, but the yellow rings on the boy's teeth along his gums caused him more concern.

"When was the last time Mom took you to the dentist?" he asked.

Zeb shrugged. Stuffed the remaining half of the sandwich into his little mouth and gulped it down like some exotic lizard. "Want to play catch?"

Just like that, Zeb was off again, out to the porch without bothering to close the front door. He dug through a pile of toys in a plastic bin until he located two baseball gloves, the bigger of which he laid on the porch rail for Whit. He windmilled his arm in an unmistakable gesture of *come on! let's go!* Whit stood up, but not quite all the way up. Something in his back caught, just a little, and his sore hamstrings balked at the notion of full extension. He waddled a couple of steps to the recliner so that he could steady himself using the back of the chair. A few seconds later he was fully vertical and no worse for the wear, but he knew—and his reflection in the black screen of the television confirmed it—how much he looked like his father did after a day at Grey Butte's mechanic shop.

The glove Zeb selected for him was ratty black Wilson model with a clean slice across two of the fingers, presumably from the blades of the county mower that had thrown it from the ditch into the road. Whit's own childhood baseball gloves had been obtained in similar fashion, and like this one, they never fit either. In fact, Whit couldn't even get his fingers inside the mitt. He tossed it onto the grass and held up his bare hands.

"You sure?" Zeb called. "It might hurt to catch like that."

"It's okay," Whit said. "I don't think you can hurt me."

The way he meant it—that an adult should be able to handle what a child throws at him—was innocent enough. But he could tell instantly that Zebadiah Whitman Farris took it as a challenge to his little manhood. He reared back, ball cocked behind his ear, and pushed off with his back leg. Whit did not know much about the mechanics of pitching, but he discerned two clear truths in that instant. First, his little brother could throw a ball harder than most kids his age. And second, Whit's bare hands were in trouble. He thought about lunging for the glove, thinking maybe he could swat the ball down before it made contact. But he could tell as soon as Zeb released it that he wasn't going to be fast enough. He could hear the *whoosh!* of the seams cutting through the air as the ball approached. However, as was so often the case in his adult life, the knowledge of the impending crash did not suggest a way to avoid it. Too late, he decided to duck.

The baseball's impact against his nose made no sound, that Whit could discern—no audible *pop!* that might indicate to the boy the level of pain that instantly shot through his sinuses and around to the back of his skull. He doubled over, hands on his knees, and waited while the first thick round of snot and blood stretched toward the grass. He unzipped his sweatshirt, already ruined from working with that mildewed decking, and held a relatively clean patch up against his face. When he looked up, he could see Libby's car making the turn onto the driveway, and Zeb getting ready to sprint for cover.

"Hang on," Whit said through the blood and the cloth. "It's fine. You just explain to Libby while I take care of this."

He went inside and cleaned himself up and found some old rags in a basket beneath the sink. He held one over his face to keep blood from dripping everywhere and stuffed another with ice and lay down on the tile. The hard surface pressed up against the bones in his shoulders and hips, but the throbbing in his head subsided enough that he became aware once again of his surroundings. He could hear voices out front—the calm, insistent tones his sister adopted when things got tense, and the loud slurs of a belligerent drunk. He was about to raise himself up to check out the situation when he heard Zeb's quiet footsteps come through the back door.

"Are you okay?" the boy asked.

"Yeah," Whit said. "Nice throw."

"You need a bigger mitt."

"I'll work on that for next time." He pushed himself up on one elbow. Tested his nose to make sure the bleeding had stopped. "I should probably go—"

"Hey," Zeb interrupted. "Can I ask you a question?"

"Sure."

"You're my brother, right?"

"Yes."

"Because we have the same mom but not the same dad."

"Right." He checked the boy's face to make sure he'd accepted the answer. "Why do you ask?"

"This kid in my class—Blake—he says I can't have a brother as old as you. He says you must be my uncle or something. But we're brothers?"

"Yeah. Mom was really young when she had me and Libby, and she was a lot older when she had you."

Zeb nodded as though it all made sense now. "That's my dad out there, yelling at Libby. His name's Byron. Who's your dad?"

"His name is Cole Allen. He—he doesn't live around here anymore."

"Oh."

Whit was still waiting for the next question—clearly the boy wasn't finished—when the front door opened. Zeb was off like a bullet. Before the back door closed behind him, Whit could see him take two long strides across the old deck before launching himself over the steps and into the grass on his way to God knew which hiding spot.

"What the hell are you doing on the floor?" Libby asked. "God, you're bleeding."

He looked down at his chest. Sure enough, blood was once again dripping from his nose onto the linoleum. "It's nothing," he said.

"Can you drive?"

"Yeah." But he could feel the trickle restarting. He held the ice rag up to his nose again. "Maybe later."

Libby pressed her fingers against her forehead. "Zeb's dad is here to get him. He's drunk, though. I talked him into letting me drive them home in his truck, but I need you to pick me up."

He turned over on his back and stared up at the ceiling. "Give me just a sec."

Libby stood over him, hands on hips. She shook her head. "Franklin will be back any minute. I've got to get Byron out of here before then. It's the brick house across from the Church of Christ over on Kingshighway. Promise you'll come get me as soon as you can?"

He told her he would, but he wasn't sure she heard him. Before he'd finished the sentence, she was out the back door, calling Zeb's name.

Whit lay there, listening, wondering how long it would take her to locate the boy. But she either knew his hiding spot, or he knew the score well enough that he came when called. However that part of it played out, the two of them must have sprinted to Byron's pickup, because it seemed like mere seconds between the slam of the back door and the crank of the engine. He heard the crunch of tires on gravel and the honk of horns, which was enough to tell him that they'd met another vehicle in the driveway. Sure enough, Franklin came stomping through the house a minute later, cursing Libby's name for driving away with another man. He went straight to the kitchen for a beer, but it wasn't until the refrigerator door banged against Whit's shoe that he noticed he wasn't alone.

"The fuck, man!" he yelled.

"Sorry," Whit said. "Zeb hit me with a baseball."

Franklin closed the refrigerator and reached instead for a bottle on top of it. He unscrewed the cap and took a drink. "Then I hope you beat the shit out of him" he said. Before Whit could push himself up again, Franklin stepped across, the heels of his boots digging into Whit's waist just above his belt line. "Why is Libby driving off in that son of a bitch's truck?"

Whit lay on his back and forced himself to consider his situation. His was a vulnerable position, to be sure, but raising up on his elbows would put him eye-level with the other man's crotch. He decided to stay put.

"She went to take Zeb home," Whit said. "Byron showed up drunk."

"That ain't my problem." He took another drink and looked down at Whit. "I think maybe you're my problem. You and that boy."

"It was just a misunderstanding. With the deck. It's all put back together now."

"That ain't it, either."

"Then what is?"

Franklin stared for a moment. Took another drink. He hadn't expected the question and so had no ready answer, either. He just stood there in the shabby kitchen, glowering down like men Whit had known all his life, from the miners at Gray Butte to the student security officers at Covenant to the guards at *El Gallito*—frightened men, blind to themselves. Men who only knew how to hurt. He squatted down over Whit and draped his elbows over his knees, tipped the bottle so that a shot of whiskey fell onto Whit's bloody shirt.

"You tell your sister that I don't want to see that little shit in my house. Not one more time."

"I think maybe that's a conversation the two of you should have."

Franklin grunted. Leaned further in, to the point that Whit feared he might fall right on top of him. "I don't want to see you around here either," he said.

He let out an unpleasant laugh and moved away, making sure to rake the toe of his boot across Whit's chest as he did so. Whit waited until he heard the television come on before he sat up and checked his nose, crusty and sore, but no longer bleeding. He stayed like that for a long time, indulging in revenge scenarios involving various acts of violence toward Franklin's body or his pickup—some of which he thought he had the power to carry out. What stopped him in the end wasn't fear or even conscience, but pragmatism. He had to pick up his sister, and so he wiped the floor and went out the back onto the deck, careful to step where he could see the heads of the nails, knowing that's where the real support was.

CHAPTER 34

He missed the Church of Christ on his first pass down Kingshighway and so had to make a U-turn at the rural fire station to go back and look for Byron's house. On the second pass, he saw Libby already standing in front of the mailbox, fingers tucked up into her armpits, bouncing at the knees to stay warm. She didn't even let him stop the pickup before she flung open the door and dove into the passenger seat. He steeled himself to receive whatever she hurled his way, but she paused and sniffed the air.

"Smells like a distillery in here," she said. She narrowed her eyes at him. "Have you been drinking?"

"Franklin spilled some on me," he explained. "Poured, is more like it."

She stared straight ahead, worked her jaw back and forth for a moment. "Drive," she said. "Shit."

And so he drove, back down Kingshighway and over to Highway 141, winding over and around the low hills of Crowley's Ridge. Pangs of guilt gnawed at him when he thought of the boy, fending for himself while his father slept off whatever pills he'd taken. Whit wondered where, exactly, their mother was. But while there may not ever be a good time to ask Libby that question, he could see clearly enough that this was an exceptionally poor time. He drove on, guilt-ridden and miserable, until Libby broke the silence and drove the knife in further.

"Why were you at my house?" she asked. "That night of the tornado."

"I was coming back—"

"—from Memphis, yeah. That's a bullshit answer. Where had you been? Back to see that Peruvian girl, maybe."

"Something like that."

"No, Whit. For real."

The house was in sight now. The hood to Franklin's pickup was up, but Whit couldn't tell if the man himself was out and about. Just to be safe, he eased off onto the shoulder near the entrance to a dirt road. While she picked at the fraying upholstery in her seat, he told her the whole story, or at least the most coherent version he had available. He explained about Yesenia and why he wanted to adopt her and what probably happened to her—not Pilar's version with the imaginary Germans, but the more likely scenario of her becoming an addict or sex worker or similarly awful statistic. He told her about Guillermo and his bar, about his sorry emotional state upon his return to Memphis. When he finished, he looked across to gauge her reaction. He thought she would be crying, but she was as calm and dry-eyed as if he'd been delivering a weather forecast.

"The world is truly and utterly fucked up," she said at last, and wiped her palms on the faded thighs of her jeans. "What made you go back for her? To try, anyway."

"Oh. That." He squirmed in his seat, as much as any man his size could be said to squirm in a motor vehicle. "The night Dad passed through town, when he and Bonner stopped at my apartment. I realized that maybe I'd not done all I could."

"For Yesenia?"

"For you."

Libby straightened suddenly so tense that he could see the muscles in her jaw. "Don't," she said through clenched teeth. "You don't know shit."

"I can guess."

"Don't." She balled up her fists. Pressed them into her leg. "Don't guess. Don't ask. Don't mention his goddamn name. You know all you need to know, if you'll just let yourself know it."

Whit waited nearly a full minute. When it was clear she had no more to say, he reached down and started the car again.

"We shouldn't have left Zeb there," she said.

"I don't think it would have worked to bring him back here," he answered. "Franklin is pretty set against it."

"Franklin is an asshole. I can handle him."

"He hits you, though. He'll hit Zeb too."

"The day he does I'll cut off his balls and feed them to him. I shit you not."

He tried to smile. Raised his hands. "If you see where this is heading...?"

"You can start driving or I can start walking."

He pulled back onto the road and drove the last quarter mile to the driveway. The hood of the pickup was still up, but Franklin was nowhere to be seen. Libby jumped out of the car. When Whit killed the engine and got out, however, she stopped in her tracks. Turned to glare.

"Mind if I use your bathroom?"

"Christ, Whit! I'm a grown woman."

"I just need to use your bathroom."

"Fuck's sake." She folded her arms. Shook her head. "Go piss in the back. And then get your ass back home and out of my business."

She whirled and marched toward the house, but Whit could see her slow up just a little as she reached for the door.

He listened for the sounds of fighting—verbal or otherwise—as he walked around the house and into the back yard. After a few minutes searching in the dim evening light, he found the hammer he'd been using most of the day. He hooked the claw end through a hole in his jeans and eased the back door open. Libby was sitting on the floor with her back against the cabinet, a bottle of cleaner and a rag between her feet. Whit could still see the shine of the liquid on the linoleum where she'd mopped up the residual mess from his bloody nose. She didn't seem surprised to see him. Didn't even look up. He dropped onto the floor beside her. The hammer fell out of his jeans with a thud. He peered around the table through the kitchen door.

"Passed out beside the coffee table," she said. She held her left hand out in front of her. Traced the veins on the back with her other fingers. "They're starting to look like Mom's hands." She flattened out one of the veins, then released it again. "She's back with Byron. I saw her coat laying on the couch when Zeb and I carried his drunk ass into the house."

"Maybe—"

"Don't. You know better." She brought her hands up to her face. Pressed the tips of her fingers into the skin over her cheekbones. "I'm turning into her. And you're turning into Dad."

"I hope not."

"It's probably going to happen. Probably no way around it."

"Probability isn't destiny."

"God. Is that the kind of shit you teach in your class?"

Whit shrugged. "Maybe I just think too much."

"Always have."

"Zeb, though."

"Yeah. Zeb." Tears welled up in her eyes. "I can't keep bringing him here. It's only a matter of time before Franklin—you're right, okay? That's where this is heading."

"It doesn't have to."

"Well."

Whit let the silence settle between them for a long time. He could hear Franklin's breathing in the next room—a surprisingly gentle sound, for such a violent man. He knew what he wanted to say. He just had to make sure it was true first. But after all, he'd been ready to adopt an adolescent Peruvian girl, hadn't he? Why would he not apply that same level of sacrifice for his little brother?

No reason he couldn't. No reason at all.

"I know what you're thinking," Libby said. "Don't you say it unless you mean it."

He placed his big hands on his thighs and rubbed them on his jeans the way his sister had done in the car. If he was going to trust himself to follow through, he had to speak it to the universe. "I can take Zeb."

She whipped her head around. Stared hard at him. "For how long?"

"As long as it takes."

"Bullshit."

"I'm serious, Lib."

She kept her eyes locked on him. He could feel her scanning for any sign of weakness or falsehood. His heart pounded as he awaited her assessment. At last she simply nodded and turned to stare at the bottle of cleaner.

"Okay?" he asked.

"Yeah." She sat up straight. Took in several deep breaths. Looked around the dingy kitchen. "If you're taking Zeb, then fuck this."

She stood and dusted herself off and started upstairs. Her footfalls quickening as she crossed into their bedroom. Whit could hear drawers being yanked open, hangers sliding across the metal bar in the closet, the muffled creak of the bed as she stuffed clothes into a suitcase. He stood up, but by the time he reached the bottom of the stairs, she was already barreling down toward her exit. She pushed by him, through the front door and out to her car. He thought she might drive away then and there, but she came back into the house, panting from exertion and excitement.

"Ready?" he asked. "Lib?"

But her eyes had locked in on Franklin's slumped figure, stretched out on the carpet. She squatted beside him and fished out his wallet. Took out the cash and stuffed it into her pocket. Next she removed all the cards and licenses, and then used the hunting knife he wore on his belt to slit them in half, one by one. She picked up the empty whiskey bottle from his chest and stood over him.

"I think we'd better go," Whit said softly. "Before you do something—"

"Shut the f—." She gulped in air, unable to finish the sentence. Her shoulders heaved up and down. It wasn't until she brought her hands together around the bottle in front of her chest that he knew what she was about to do.

"Lib, don't."

She paid no attention. Instead she stepped back, bottle hanging from her right hand, and windmilled her arm up and around like the pitcher she'd been on the high school softball team. She released it low, so fast that Whit couldn't even see the bottle as it traveled from her hand to Franklin's crotch. She hit her mark though. The bottle stuck in place for a long, ball-crushing moment before finally clinking to the floor between his thighs. Franklin moaned but did not wake. Libby grinned down at him.

"You'll feel that in the morning, you son of a bitch." She turned back to Whit, eyes wild with victory. "Just one more thing."

He didn't even try to stop her this time, so lasered was her focus. And, he had to admit, that crotch shot was one of the most gratifying things he'd ever witnessed—far better than if any of his own revenge strategies had come true. But when she emerged from the kitchen with a five-pound bag of sugar, he shook his head.

"I think maybe enough's enough."

She paused as she walked by him. Placed a hand on his chest over his heart and gave him two pats. "That newspaper ad on the table will do."

She walked outside, unhurried. Unscrewed the gas cap on Franklin's pickup and waited. Whit twisted the sales circular into a funnel as he walked out to join her. He stuck the small end through the opening and held it while she poured the sugar slowly, making sure every last granule slid down into the gas tank. Whit nearly pitied Franklin for the way he'd wake up, balls swollen and engine blown. But if the hammer of justice was to smash him in the man parts, Libby Whitman might as well be the one to wield it.

Whit watched his sister's face as she poured, his heart proud and terrified and hoping—praying, even—that this might set her free.

CHAPTER 35

Whit parked in Byron's driveway next to a small black car that hadn't been there when he'd picked up Libby that afternoon. At first he thought it was her old Cavalier, that she'd driven out ahead of him and gone inside to give Byron the same treatment she'd given Franklin. A second glance, however, told him something worse was probably true. When he looked past the smashed front fender and spiderwebbed rear windshield, he recognized the Toyota he'd helped his mother pick out when she was working at the hospital in Memphis. He was still inspecting the damage when the front door opened and Zeb walked out in bare feet.

"She hit one of those concrete stick things at Wal-Mart," the boy explained. He raised his hands and made an exploding noise to illustrate the event.

"What about the rear windshield?" Whit asked.

The boy shrugged. Said nothing.

"Did you eat supper?"

"Yeah. I made eggs."

"Just eggs?"

"I would have made toast, too, but the bread was moldy. Mom says Dad doesn't pay attention to shit." He shuffled his feet. "Am I going with you back to Libby's?"

"Not tonight. Franklin and Libby had a fight, and—well, she probably isn't going to live there anymore. You understand that?"

Zeb nodded as though that was to be expected.

"Maybe you could come to my place for a while," Whit said. "If you want."

"For how long?"

"It's hard to say. I'd have to talk that over with Mom and your dad."

"They're asleep."

"Oh. Maybe I should come back tomorrow."

"Libby usually just leaves a note."

"Well. Okay."

"I'll get my stuff," Zeb said, and just like that he was off, back into the house, little feet pounding up the stairs.

Whit followed him inside. Byron was passed out in his recliner and breathing unevenly through his mouth. Bethany sat cross-legged on the floor.

"Mom?"

She turned to look at him, but her eyes couldn't quite focus. If her face registered anything, it was contempt.

"I thought you was at church," she said. "Praying the devil out of that boy."

He glanced over to the stairs, where Zeb had ascended a moment before. But he knew that wasn't the boy she meant. Whatever she had swallowed made her see him, not as her grown-up son, but as her ex-husband—Cole Allen Whitman, the holy roller, and worthless besides.

"Son of a bitch," she said, and nestled her head back against the sofa cushions to sleep.

Whit found an unopened bill from the electric company and scribbled on the back. *Zeb is with me.* He printed his name below, along with the number for his new cell phone. The boy came back downstairs just as he finished writing, lugging a green and gold duffel bag with the Greene County Eagles logo printed on it. He hoisted it up on his hip as he passed by, not looking, and walked out through the night and into the truck. He carried himself like a pro. Like someone who had done this too many times to be scared.

It took more than the usual hour to make it back home to his apartment, owing to the stop at the gas station for bananas and chocolate milk. Zeb had fallen asleep once he'd eaten, his little head wedged between the window and the doorframe. Whit drove slower than normal, trying not to jostle the boy through the curves, and munched on sunflower seeds to keep himself awake.

The front light to his apartment was on when he pulled up, and someone sat wrapped in a sleeping bag on his front steps. For a moment, he thought it was Denise, who lived in the adjacent townhouse and locked herself out at least once a month. But when she stood and dropped the blanket, Whit saw not the frumpy, body-by-McDonald's frame of the neighbor, but the sleek, yoga-devotee figure of Novie Burqvist. She walked over to the passenger side door of Whit's car and, without a word, lifted Zeb out onto her hip. Whit reached into the backseat for his bag and hustled up to get the door. But Novie had already unlocked it with the key he'd given her months ago. She slipped inside ahead of him and carried Zeb upstairs to the bedroom. She'd already plugged a night light into the outlet by Whit's dresser and set out a pallet of blankets on the floor beneath it. She laid Zeb down and pulled the covers up over him and tip-toed back downstairs.

Whit set down the bag and waited for a moment, listening for the sound of the front door. He didn't hear Novie leave, but when he finally went back downstairs, he was nonetheless surprised to find her seated at the kitchen table, drinking tea she'd brought with her.

"Did Libby call you?" Whit asked.

"Does it matter?"

He went to the stove and made his own cup of tea, just to give himself something to occupy his hands while he decided what to do next. At last he sat down across from her, folding his long legs back underneath him so that he wouldn't accidentally brush up against her. She stared at the steam rising from his mug.

"You hate tea," she said. "You say it tastes like grass."

"Or furniture polish."

"That's the lemon kind."

She smiled at him then, and he smiled back, and for the moment things were less uncomfortable than they'd been since that night at the Thirsty Owl.

"Libby thinks you're in over your head," Novie said. "I'm talking about Zeb here."

"She's probably right. But the way things are—Mom, you know."

"Your mother has a disease, Whit."

He nodded. Swirled the tea. Shrugged. "A boy Zeb's age, though. He can't—he'll get damaged. Might be already."

"I get it. You did the right thing."

"I just wish I knew what to do next."

"Lot of that going around."

They sat a long time while Novie sipped her tea. When she was done, she reached across and gently peeled Whit's fingers off his mug. She gave him her empty one and took his to drink.

"I can't decide if we're good for each other or not," she said. "We get our hands on something decent and hopeful, then throw it away before we can fear losing it. I suppose that's our raising."

Whit ran his finger around the lip of the mug. "Is that a confession or an apology?"

"I don't know. But it's your turn—and don't you say, 'for what?' or I will kick your lanky ass right here in your own kitchen."

If she was kidding, she didn't show it, and he knew better than to ask. He folded his hands and rested them on the top of his head. He could feel the beads of sweat through his thinning hair.

"I'm sorry—especially for that night when my father and Bonner showed up.'

"Wrong answer," she said. "Try again."

"All right. Then I'm sorry—"

"You can't undo anything," she said. "And you don't have to. Just tell me what you want."

"I want to do the right thing."

"Do you know what that is?"

He picked at the string of the spent tea bag in the mug he was holding. "For tonight? Yeah, I know. I can't see much beyond that."

"Okay then." She took the two mugs and discarded the tea bags and washed them in the sink. She turned back to the counter and reached for the tea and honey. Instead of putting them back in her bag, however, she opened the cabinet door and set both inside and closed it again. "Let's get some sleep."

PART V

Figure 13: Part IV Recap

CHAPTER 36

The heat index was 94 degrees at 9:00am on Labor Day weekend, and at least 20 degrees more than that on the roof, by Whit's estimation. If he could stop sweating long enough, he thought, he might get this little patch job done so that he could take a cold shower. He knelt on the shingles and tried to focus.

The lease he'd negotiated for the house on Hunter Drive included a 20% reduction in his first six months' rent in exchange for performing some needed repairs on the house. He had already turned over all the deck boards—a task he convinced their landlord to add to the list, based on a personal experience he'd had last spring. He'd repaired a rotted joist beneath one corner of the house and rerouted water from the yard to keep it from pooling there again. Now, he needed to reseal around the ventilation pipes before the rain forecasted for next week moved through.

With Novie's discretion in mind, Whit decided it would be best to do the roof work without inviting the boy to tag along. Eager to please as he was, Zeb struggled to focus on anything for more than twenty-five seconds, which of course led to more than one behavioral concern. After only a couple weeks of having him in her first-grade classroom, Mrs. Woods had called Whit in to tell him little Zebadiah had been caught poking the single-serve milk cartons with a thumbtack so that milk leaked out below the spout every time a child turned the carton up to drink. Harmless though it may seem, she considered it a sign of larger, possibly undiagnosed issues.

"Maybe I should have his eyes checked," Whit said.

"His eyes?" Mrs. Woods asked.

"Kids who can't see do some weird things."

"No, I don't think that's it." She cocked her head to one side and folded her hands in front of her—a pitying pose. "His circumstances are unusual, even in this day and age. Perhaps it would be good for him to see a therapist—maybe someone who could test him for ADHD and prescribe an appropriate treatment."

"I'm not a fan of pills," Whit said.

"Oh me neither." Mrs. Woods put her hand over her heart. She might as well have said aloud, *perish the thought.*

"I'll talk to Novie about it and see what she says," he told her.

"Try to keep an open mind."

"Sure. Of course."

But he'd forgotten to tell Novie about the conversation, which had happened last Tuesday, and wondered if it was too late to bring it up now. He was arguing with himself about that answer when he heard the branches of the oak tree beside the house bend down and brush the shingles. He looked over to see Zeb, shimmying across from the tree fort they'd built the same week they'd moved in. Whit had seen him do this before—climb into the branches above the fort and slide out on them until they bent enough for him to drop onto the roof. He hadn't told Novie about that, or about the dismounts he'd seen Zeb do, jumping off the low roof over the master bedroom into a pile of soft dirt left over from the drainage engineering project.

This was different, though. Novie knew Whit was up there. If she saw Zeb with him, a six-year-old with raging ADHD running side to side across the pitched roof, she would have both of their hides.

But as long as the boy was already here, Whit supposed it wouldn't hurt to give him a lesson in applying roof sealant. He showed him how to load the caulk gun and slice off the end based on the size of the bead required for the job. He didn't expect Zeb's hands to be big or strong enough to actually squeeze the trigger, but they were. The boy stuck his tongue out the left side of his mouth, the way he did when he was really concentrating, and walked around the plumbing vent pipe with the sealant. He nipped one wayward strand of sealant with his finger and wiped the glob on the side of his tennis shoes.

"Zebadiah Farris!"

Whit froze. He didn't need to look down at Novie to know the pose she was striking, hands over hips, feet spread to shoulder width, face stern and terrifying. Neither did she need to say any more. Her mere presence was enough to shine a light on several aspects of the situation that would have both Whit and Zeb in trouble. The new shoes they'd bought him for school, for example, now irreversibly marked with a finger-width swath of black rubber sealant. Zeb must have had the same thought. He stared down at his shoes, wide-eyed, and then finally back up at Whit as if to ask where in the world he was and how in the world he had gotten there. Whit had seen that look plenty over the last six months, in both the boy's face and his own—enough to decide that the expression must be something passed down on their mother's side.

Novie called Zeb's name again and told him to look at her. He did, but only for an instant. That glance was enough to unmoor his feet and set off the most reliable defense mechanism he'd discovered in his six years on this planet. He sprinted in the opposite direction, up the roof and over its apex, despite Novie's screams for him to stop right there. Whit stood just in time to see him launch off the edge. He stayed suspended in air, limbs poised for impact, for what seemed like a long time, until at last he landed so softly that he made no sound at all. Whit wanted to applaud.

Instead, he turned around and spoke to Novie.

"He's fine," Whit said. "He uses that pile of dirt in back for a landing spot. I think he's been practicing."

"You think?"

"It's really not as dangerous as it looks."

She sucked in her lips. Nodded slowly. He knew well enough that he was about to pay for his lack of oversight. Sure enough, Novie walked up to the ladder and grasped it firmly with both hands. He nearly warned her to be careful, since she wasn't heavy enough to stabilize the ladder with her own weight. But he didn't have to say anything. Instead of climbing, she pulled back on the ladder, swung it to the side and laid it gently in the grass.

"He was just being curious," Whit protested.

"So am I."

"Novie, come on. I've got a lot to do today."

"Then you better jump on down like Zeb did. It's not as dangerous as it looks." She dusted off her hands and walked back into the house.

Whit yelled at her to come back, but he didn't waste too much breath on it. Novie rarely gave orders, but neither did she obey them. He'd have to adjust to the situation as it stood. And so he lowered himself back to his knees and finished the sealing. Then he walked to the edge where Zeb had jumped and gently tossed down the caulk gun. It landed with a less than reassuring *clang!* onto the pile of dirt below.

While he considered his options—swinging from the flimsy gutters, jumping onto the dirt, climbing the thin outer branches of the oak tree until he reached the tree fort—Whit returned to a question he'd been thinking about since the fall semester at BTI began two weeks ago. By one reckoning, this was his and Novie's anniversary. One year ago today they'd gone on their first date—a picnic dinner at the lake, until the mosquitos finally chased them off at dusk. He still wasn't sure what to make of their weeks-long hiatus that winter, whether that counted toward the 12-month time period or not. He'd never asked Novie about it, not so much because he feared the answer as that they'd had so much to do since patching things up. Work, moving into their own house, learning how to care for a child—and one as high-strung as Zeb, no less—all left them with little time for searching their feelings about the past. Besides, what was a year, really? An eternity to a bee. No time at all to the sun.

Whit looked up toward the sky. The rays were coming down at harsher angles now, baking his skin and radiating off the asphalt shingles, reminding him how easily heat could undo him.

To hell with it.

He stood and dusted himself off. Stepped to the edge of the roof where Zeb had made his leap. Before he could talk himself out of it, he jumped, knowing even before he landed that he had chosen poorly.

On the way home from the ER, Whit marveled anew at Novie's ability to maintain silence. Not long after they'd all moved in together, the two adults agreed that they would not raise their voices at each other in front of Zeb. Resilient though he was, he'd seen more than enough shouting and dysfunction to last a lifetime. They would not be the ones to pile on, Novie decreed, and her steely self-discipline assured that it would be so. He wondered if she was aware how powerfully unnerving her silence could be. Thought she probably was.

She passed the pharmacy without slowing down, which was just as well. He had mixed feelings about pain pills, knowing what they'd done to Byron and now to his mother and, by extension, Zeb. He repositioned his left leg. He could feel the ankle swelling inside the boot. The sooner he could get home to ice it, the better. He didn't say this to Novie, of course, because he wasn't saying anything to her. If she wanted to give him the silent treatment, he'd respond in kind.

And so he couldn't really blame her for stopping at Walmart on the way back to the house. Pain from his badly sprained ankle aside, he knew she wasn't out to torture him. She only needed to pick up whatever it was she needed to pick up—which, of course, he could only guess at, and that in silence. Once she'd exited the car, Zeb turned around so that he could look at Whit's ankle, laid across the back seat.

"Does it hurt?" he asked.

"It does."

"My dad said his back hurt. That's why he took so many pills."

Whit made a face like this was news worth considering. In truth he never knew how to respond when Zeb brought up his parents. They hadn't tried to regain custody—seemed relieved, in fact, to no longer bear responsibility for the boy. On the rare occasion they came to visit, their mother brought gifts and wept when it was time to leave. Byron would roll his eyes and say, "Come on. You don't mean it no how," which only set Bethany off further. The first time it happened, Whit expected Zeb to run away like he'd done from Franklin. But the boy watched the whole show, albeit from far enough away not to be hugged and snotted on. Once his parents left, he would climb to the roof and jump, over and over again.

Novie reemerged from the store a few minutes later with lettuce and avocados and a bag of cat food. She stepped into the car, but Zeb was on them before she could even crank the engine.

"You two need to call a truce." He looked back and forth between them, but didn't find whatever it was he sought. He threw up his hands. "Do y'all even know what a truce is? It's when two armies are fighting, and they just decide to stop. Like the Christmas truce during World War I. The soldiers decided they wouldn't fight on Christmas, and so they didn't. That's a truce."

"Where did you learn that?" Novie asked.

"From a book. I can show you when we get home."

"Okay."

She backed out of her parking space and pulled onto the highway, but Whit could tell she was thinking. She rocked her neck to one side and then the other. Rolled her shoulders.

"Truce?" Whit offered.

Novie lifted one hand off the wheel, then brought it back down as though the matter had been decided. "Truce," she said.

An hour after supper, Whit was in the bedroom with his foot propped up, and Zeb was back on the roof. Whit could hear him when he dropped from the tree onto the shingles, then ran down the slope above his head and launched. He thought it best not to tell Novie, but she'd come in to check on him just as the landing *thud* sounded above them. She put a hand on her hip and glared upward at the ceiling.

"Tell him to stop if you want," Whit said, trying to keep his voice neutral.

"You don't think that's dangerous?"

"Probably it is."

She shook her head. Stepped over to the bed and dropped a book onto Whit's lap. "I got this out of Zeb's backpack. It's that one about the Christmas Truce," she said, and handed it to him. "You ever heard of it?"

"No."

"Zeb pretty much had it right—World War I and everything."

"Mrs. Woods said he was a good reader."

"It's more than that." She snapped the book shut and held it up to him like Exhibit A. "This is not some first-grade, see-spot-run picture book. This has to be eighth grade reading, maybe more. I guarantee you a third of the kids at BTI couldn't get through the first paragraph. Libby must have worked with him."

"Or Mom."

Novie grunted, but he let it go, and she did too. They both knew how she felt about his mother, and anyway they were still in a truce. She put a hand on his thigh. "Hurt much?"

"I've had worse."

"So have I." The boy's steps pounded again on the roof above them. "How long you think he'll keep that up?"

"Til it gets dark or we make him stop." He reached down for his crutches. "I can tell him to quit, if you want."

"He's fine," she said, and stood up from the bed. He opened his mouth to thank her, but she swung the door closed and turned around and slipped her shirt off over her head. "Unless your ankle hurts too bad." Whit shook his head no, the mere suggestion of her body enough to refocus sensation out of his injured limb. She smiled.

"I'll take top."

CHAPTER 37

The first Tuesday in January, on what would have been Elvis Presley's 72nd birthday, Whit inexplicably dropped virtually everything he tried to hold. The spoon for his cereal, the electric toothbrush while he was using it. His water bottle, which mercifully had the lid on, and his coffee mug, which regrettably did not. Each of these created minor messes in the kitchen and the car and the office. He flexed his hands and checked the internet, just long enough to rule out a stroke, but the pattern continued. In the garage where he had just begun a new semester teaching basic mechanics for Bootheel Technical, he let an impact wrench somehow slip out of his big hands and smash against the concrete floor.

"Jesus!" a kid named Bradson cried as he danced out of the way. "You all right, Mr. Whitman?"

Whit told him he was fine and thanked the kid for asking. His half-brother Shawnson had been a student the previous spring until he commented on a female instructor's ass within earshot of Novie Burqvist. Novie had a Title IX complaint filed by noon, and Shawnson was now in basic training, preparing for Afghanistan. Bradson wasn't any more academically gifted than his brother, but he was at least polite and conscientious.

"I'm fine," Whit said. He reached down and pulled the impact wrench up by the air hose attached to it. "Didn't mean to put your toes in danger."

Bradson said that was okay and went about his business as though the incident had never occurred. As they were cleaning up, however, Whit lost his grip on a jack stand and sent it crashing into the toolbox of Bradson's station mate. The kid, a greasy blond-headed transfer student from somewhere in Arkansas, speculated in the most colorful terms that their professor must have caught his wife in bed with another man. Whit gave the kid one of his best looks, a Cole-Allen-deluxe stare that he could count on to wither any recipient not named Novie or Zeb. The kid merely saluted and chewed his gum, too tough or too dumb to respond appropriately. Whit squared up to him.

"It's been my experience," he began, then let that hang for a moment. "That men who talk about another man's wife or mom or girlfriend are usually compensating."

"Compensating?" the kid said.

"It means you're using one thing to make up for something else," Bradson explained.

"I know what it means, dickweed," the kid said.

Collin. His name was Collin. Remembering that bolstered Whit's confidence. "Very good, Bradson," he said. "So a guy like you, Collin, is compensating for something else—low self-esteem, maybe, brought on by having a dick skinnier than a Phillips screwdriver."

That struck a nerve, as Whit knew it would. Nothing cut to the heart of a blue-collar American male quite like questioning the size and functionality of his genitalia. Collin lurched at him, but Whit could tell immediately he was no threat. Rather than step straight at his instructor, the kid came in at an angle, making sure his shoulder caught against Bradson as though he was being held back.

"Slow down," Bradson said between clenched teeth. "You want to end up in the desert with my brother?"

Whit waited for the obligatory second lurch, the you-better-be-glad-he's-stopping-me one. Once it came, he ordered the class to finish cleaning up and went into his office. He focused on his right hand as he gathered up materials for his Spanish class next hour, virtually daring it to fail with him watching. Sure enough, though, just when he let his guard down, the folder with his class notes in it slipped from his fingers. His efforts to catch it just added a horizontal dimension to the downward momentum of the folder. A half second later, papers were scattered all over his floor in no particular sequence—a situation made worse by the air that rushed in when someone opened his office door.

"Sorry," Bradson said. He squatted down and started gathering the pages. "I'm sorry about Collin. He can be a real jerk."

"I've had students like that before. But thanks."

"It's just that I know his timing is bad."

Whit unzipped his work hoodie and draped it over the chair. Bent down to help Bradson. "Timing?"

Bradson sighed as though about to deliver an unwelcome diagnosis. "You and Miss Novie. There's a lot of talk that she quit because you and her, you know, split."

"She just took another job, over at the middle school."

"Right. But she's been out of town since Christmas." He handed over the jumbled pages with an apologetic look. "It's a small school in a small town," he said. "People notice things like that."

Whit gave a laugh so unconvincing that he didn't even bother following up with an explanation. Well-meaning though he was, Bradson had laid bare the fear he'd been tamping down since New Year's, when Novie had left to visit some family in Oklahoma. She'd gotten permission from her new principal at Jackson Middle School to be gone to start the semester, but she'd insisted that Whit stay behind and keep Zeb on routine. That hurt Whit's feelings just a little, but he could see the logic in it. He had to make a conscious decision not to dwell on the possibility that she's changed her mind about the whole instant family thing. They'd talked before about how strange it all was, the way parenting and partnering worked. The same day that started with a major fight and an emergency room visit could end up with spectacular make-up sex, and laughter over breakfast could descend into verbal fisticuffs by lunch. This sort of relational living wasn't for the faint of heart.

"She just went back to Oklahoma for a visit," Whit finally said. "She had a cousin die, I think."

"You think?"

"Someone died. A cousin, maybe." Or was it an uncle?

"That seems like something you should know, Mr. Whitman—if you don't mind me saying."

"I'm sure it will be fine," he said. "Thank you for your concern, though."

The boy told him he was welcome and left, closing the door quietly behind him. Such a patient kid, as night and day from Shawnson as any two siblings could be. He wondered if people thought that about him and his sister. When Novie broke the news that she was going to visit family, Libby had volunteered to stay at their place and help with Zeb until her new semester started at A-State. Whit never would have thought to make such an offer. When it came down to it, he supposed everyone knew she was the conscientious one and he the asshole. He resolved anew to work on being a better person. Then he stuffed his book and notes into a backpack and flung it over his left shoulder, knowing better than to trust his grip.

He stopped at a grocery store on the way home and picked up a $20 bouquet of flowers—the most expensive on the shelf—as a thank-you gesture to Libby. It was the first time he'd ever gotten a woman flowers, though, and it made him anxious. He wasn't sure if she even liked flowers, or if such a gesture was appropriate between siblings. In the end, he unwrapped the cellophane sheath around their stems and tossed them out the window, one handful at a time. Maybe he'd just cook dinner instead.

When he arrived at the house, however, Libby was sitting alone on the porch swing, eyes fixed in a thousand-yard stare. He greeted her but got no response. And so he went inside and found Zeb, who sat cross-legged on the floor playing video games.

"What's up with Libby?" he asked the boy.

"Huh?"

"Libby. Our sister. She's sitting out in the cold and won't talk."

Zeb jerked his whole body to one side along with the controller, as though he might be able to physically dodge the virtual alien on the screen. "That's weird," he said.

"You don't know why she's out there?"

He shook his head. Whit had a sudden, powerful urge to reach across and turn the TV off mid-game. He didn't, though, what with his renewed effort to not be an asshole. And so he turned away and put his coat back on and even grabbed a blanket from the couch. He draped it over his sister's shoulders and sat down beside her on the swing.

"You realize what today is?" she finally asked.

He'd heard the bit about Elvis' birthday on a morning talk show, but he thought it best not to offer that as an answer. "Probably not," he said.

"A year to the day since the last time we saw Dad."

Whit flipped through his memory. He couldn't have put a date to it, but he knew it had been around this time that Cole Allen and Bonner had cruised through town, staying just long enough to pass judgment and drive a wedge between him and Novie that, were it not for her virtues, would have proven fatal to their relationship. That thought—how she'd stuck with him, even when he wasn't aware of it—gave him new comfort now in her absence. But even as he tried to use the anniversary to ease his mind, something in Libby's reminder gnawed at him.

"Since *we* saw Dad?" he asked. "I didn't think you let him stop by your place."

"He showed up," she explained. "But he hadn't told me he was with him when he called."

"You mean Bonner."

"Fuck sake, Whit!" She dropped her hands into her lap and whirled her head toward him. "Does it make you feel better to say his name? Yes, Bonner fucking Hanson."

"Sorry," he said, angry at himself for failing once again at his be-good pledge. "Really, I am."

"And then I end up living with Franklin, who is just as big a shit as any of those other guys Dad used to bring home. And what did I tell myself? 'Oh, well. At least he's not Bonner.' That's some fucked up logic."

"I guess."

"You guess."

"It is. You're right. I just don't know what to say." He stared at his hands, big and strong and useless. "I should have done something."

"That time has passed."

"I know."

She let him sit like that for a long time, twisting inside. "I started talking to one of the counselors at A-State. It's free to students, so what the hell, right? I thought I'd better get my shit together, if I was going to be a big sister."

"That's good," Whit said. He felt the tears sting his eyes again.

"It's not your fault," Libby said. "We were kids. Besides, none of it can be undone." She turned her body to face him. Put her hands on her knees. And leaned forward. "Mom's dead."

"What?"

"You heard me. This time I know you did."

CHAPTER 38

The first sentence of Bethany Whitman Farris' obituary recorded her age alongside the date and place of death. But those figures, of course, buried the lead. The chronological coordinates presented only the outcome of her life, not the story of it. Even the requisite paragraphs that followed about origin and employment and surviving family provided scant context for who she was or tried to be. These were facts about her, nothing more. Truth was stickier, even contradictory.

"Was it drugs, though?" one of her Kentucky relatives asked once Garland Funeral Home had opened the door for visitation. He might have been a cousin or an uncle. It was hard to tell with that crowd, and Whit didn't have enough history with them to figure it out.

"We think it was her heart," he answered.

"Not an overdose, at least. That's what happened to Gerald, you know. And Susie."

The relative—whatever he was—glanced over Whit's shoulder to where at least twenty relatives from his mother's birth family clustered around a black leather sofa set near the entrance to the visitation room. He gave a barely perceptible shake of his head, although it was impossible to tell whether he meant "the answer is no" or "this guy has no clue."

Early on in the evening, the visitation crowd settled into two distinct groups. The Kentucky family staked their turf and intended to hold onto it, even when a Garland employee named Beatty had to ask them to please put away the whiskey bottle they'd been passing around. Whit, Libby, and Zeb stood on the opposite side of the room by the casket, ignoring the folding chairs set out for them, and greeting the occasional former coworker or family friend. A few of Bethany's patients from when she worked at the hospital even stopped by to tell the children what a wonderful caregiver their mother had been when they were at their most vulnerable. As they passed to look at the casket spray, Libby would turn to Whit and make a gagging gesture.

"Maybe we should call it," Whit suggested during a lull in the visitors. "I think most everyone who would want to pay their respects has already been through."

"Not until Novie gets here," Libby said. She paused, doubt clouding her face. "You did call her, didn't you?"

"We missed connection. I'll try again after this is over."

"God, you're a dumbass."

She was about to lay into him when Beatty appeared in the doorway, ushering in more guests. Whit didn't recognize the woman who entered first, but there was no mistaking the man who followed, grasping her hand. Bonner Hanson turned sideways, as though his broad shoulders needed room to get past the doorframe before he could square up. He nodded a greeting in Whit and Libby's direction. Cole Allen Whitman followed on his heels, just ahead of another young woman Whit didn't recognize.

"Jesus Christ," Libby said.

Whit had not told his sister, but he'd had a sneaking suspicion that their father would show up for the funeral, possibly even with Bonner. It was not hard to imagine Cole Allen making an appearance as the dutiful husband, faithful to the last despite his ex-wife's waywardness. It would be a sign of his Christian devotion and duty, and Bonner would be his witness. Never in a million years, however, did Whit dream of them bringing dates.

"Did you fucking call him?" Libby whispered.

"No."

"Then how—?"

But she didn't need to finish the question. Three steps into the room, Cole Allen peeled off toward the sofas to greet the Kentucky family, who embraced him like a lost son rather than an ex-in-law. He shook hands and gave hugs and introduced his companions.

With the shock of his father's arrival, Whit was slow to realize that the woman who'd entered after him had not belonged with him. Instead she turned toward the casket and began making her way toward Libby and Whit. She wore a gray suit and a black shirt, but what stood out was the tiny white clerical collar at the base of her neck. She might have been five feet tall in her heels, and she was not more than thirty years old, but she carried herself with the authority of St. Paul himself.

"That's your priest?" Whit whispered.

Libby nodded, but her eyes were threatening tears and she didn't try to speak aloud. It had nearly floored Whit when she told him she wanted her priest—Reverend March—to officiate their mother's funeral. He'd never imagined his sister going to church in the first place, much less having a priest she could call by name. In a thousand lifetimes he never would have conjured this woman as the mental picture of Reverend March. She touched his forearm in greeting, but it was clear she was aiming for Libby. She stepped in front of her slowly, as though Libby might tear off like a startled cat.

"So that's the guy." Reverend March said.

"Yeah."

"Want me to kick his ass? In the name of Jesus, of course."

Libby shook her head and wiped away a tear and breathed out a genuine, if tiny, laugh. She blinked, and the tears were gone. She squeezed the reverend's hands and stood up straight.

"You must be Whit," the woman said. She extended a hand. "Emma March. I'm the rector at St. Luke's Episcopal."

"Oh, ah, thank you," Whit stammered. "Sorry. When Libby said 'priest,' I had—"

"Something different in mind? Most people do. Call me Emma." She looked around the casket. "Where's Zeb?"

Whit glanced down at where their brother had been sitting, working a logic puzzle. Two metal circles, now separated, lay next to one another on the chair.

"I'll go find him," Whit offered.

But Libby grabbed his wrist in a way that told him to stay put. When he turned again toward the room, he saw their father and his party walking toward the casket. Cole Allen reached out to shake Whit's hand, then gave Libby a quick hug. He introduced Maddelynne, Bonner's fiancé, who didn't look a day over twenty.

"Been a week or two since we saw you," Cole Allen said to his son. "I would have thought you'd call—especially at a time like this."

"I wasn't sure what to say."

"Don't suppose you ever are."

They waited there for a long moment. Cole Allen tried to wither his son with a stare, but Whit had been wise to the technique for a while now. He kept his face calm and watched a place on his father's chin where a patch of gray stubble had broken through the skin. He did not see what passed between Libby and Bonner, but when the group finally moved past she was as dry-eyed and triumphant as Queen Esther herself. She reached across and patted Emma's hand, then lifted a middle finger toward her father and Bonner. The priest looked away, biting her lip to keep from laughing.

"You did beautifully," Emma whispered to Libby.

Whit glanced toward them, but he could see instantly that she hadn't meant for him to overhear. She kept one hand on Libby's back and reached the other up to squeeze her shoulder. In that gesture was everything Whit had never expected from his sister, along with an ache that gripped his chest and told him that she was right in her earlier assessment. He was undeniably a dumbass, and here he was alone, trying to hoist an impossible weight all by himself.

He was about to excuse himself when he saw Zebadiah sprint in through the back door. Whit brought the edge of his right hand down onto his left palm—the sign for stop, which seemed to work better with the boy than verbal commands. But Zeb wouldn't be denied his excitement this time. He ran up to his big brother and grabbed his sleeve and pulled.

"Come on," he said. "Novie wants you in the chapel."

CHAPTER 39

Zeb led him down the hall to Garland Funeral Chapel. At the entrance, he stopped. Turned to face Whit.

"Those people back there," the boy said. "Are we related to them?"

"A lot of them, yes."

"Because of Mom."

"Yes."

He processed this for a moment, giving Whit time to once again dread the questions he expected to come about their mother. Questions about her absence and her death, about the wounds and vices—inseparable things, really—that kept her from really showing love to her children. But the boy didn't pursue any of those at this moment. The worry he expressed was not for the woman who gave him birth, but for Novie.

"I've already talked to her some," he said. "You better go in. She looks sad."

Whit entered the dark chapel and eased the door shut behind him. Track lighting in the ceiling shown down on the chancel area, illuminating a wide pulpit and a heavy, altar table, bare except for two oil candles. The collateral glow fell into the aisle and first pew, where Novie was staring up into the rafters. The weight of the moment settled down into Whit's feet, it seemed, and he had a hard time lifting them. It took him a very long time to get into the aisle proper, much less all the way down it. When he finally did, he looked back, half expecting to see the tracks in the carpet, evidence that he'd been dragged here against his will.

"Retractable Jesus," Novie said.

"Huh?"

She pointed to the place where the four panels above the nave came to a point in the rafters. Pressed against the ceiling on the near side, so as to be invisible to those in the pews, was a massive crucifix, held fast by quarter-inch cables. The Lord's face was pressed into the boards of the ceiling, but his ivory-skinned limbs hung over and around the thick cross that had been bolted into his back. Whit ascended the chancel steps and put his hands on his hips as his eyes traced the cables and pulleys attached to the crucifix. Apparently this Jesus hung over the altar for Christian funerals, but was hoisted up into storage for everyone else. Whit saw a switch built into the inside of the pulpit, beside which lay a brick with an eye bolt driven into it.

"What in the world?" he said. Novie shrugged.

He pressed the switch and held it, activating a winch somewhere above the Christ figure. The crucifix bounced along with the unwinding until gravity pulled it plumb and the cable went slack. Whit walked over to the foot of the cross and unhooked the silver carabiner fastened to an eye bolt in the sole of Jesus' foot. He attached it to the brick, the weight of it needed to keep the line taught so that the cable would spool properly and reversed the switch.

"And lo, he shall ascend," Whit said, and smiled at the woman across the aisle from him. But she was staring up at the crucifix.

"That's convenient," she answered, and turned her gaze upon Whit. "I'm sorry about your mother. She was not a bad woman, when I think about it. Just hurt. I wish I'd seen that sooner."

"It's okay. I'm sorry too." He drew himself up, ready to launch into a mea culpa worthy of the Lord's suffering. But she cut him off.

"It was my brother—the reason I went back to Oklahoma. He got arrested New Year's Eve for DUI. This is number five, so it could mean serious jail time. I was working with the courts, trying to get him into rehab instead. The rest of my family—well, it had to be me." She nodded toward the crucifix. "Nothing grieves poor white Jesus more than a drunk Indian."

"I would imagine he's got bigger problems than that." Whit caught himself. Raised a hand. "Not to say your brother—."

"Kenny. His name is Kenny."

"All right," Whit answered. "Kenny."

She clapped her hands onto her thighs. "I'm trying to let you in, okay? The least you could do is not be so goddamn smug." She lifted an apologetic hand toward the crucifix. "Sorry, Lord."

Whit stepped down from the chancel and walked to the end of the pew where Novie sat. She kept her hands on her legs, drummed her fingers along with some thought Whit couldn't intercept. Maybe she was picturing the two of them, standing at some other chancel on their wedding day. Or maybe she was already planning her exit. Or—and this seemed most likely, when he thought about it—she was still just trying to figure out if she could trust anybody for long enough to make a habit of it.

He looked up at the statue of Jesus, graphic in its depiction of suffering. All that about loving your enemies and doing to others as you'd have them do for you—that's where the trouble started for him. A person that puts himself out there like that should have expected bad things to happen. Probably he did expect that, and still couldn't stop himself.

"I'm trying too," Whit finally said. "I'm glad you're here."

Novie let out a quiet sound, like a hiccup. It was as much of a sob as she could allow herself. "You should go back in," she said. "I'll be there in a minute."

Whit leaned forward as if he were about to get up, but he didn't follow through. His eyes were locked on that hand, lying there on her leg without any seeming expectation. He looked for it to turn, or give even a little twitch—anything to signal that she wanted him to take it into his own. He saw no sign whatsoever.

"Go on," Novie said.

And even though it wasn't what she meant, he reached out and let his hand hover above hers, holding his breath while he waited to see how she'd respond.

Together they walked out of the chapel and down the hallway to the visitation rooms, fingers interlocked so tightly that Whit worried he might be crushing Novie's small hands. But she pressed back with at least equal force, and the joy he derived from the squeeze of entwined metacarpals was enough to make him feel guilty for being this happy in such a gloomy circumstance. He had to make sure his face was appropriately somber before they rounded the corner that led to the viewing room.

True to form, however, Whit was too focused on his interior world to pay appropriate attention to what was going on around him. The Kentucky clan had spilled out into the hallway for an impromptu family conference. Despite Beatty's pleas for them not to drink in the funeral home, Bethany's kin had managed to consume enough liquor to get half the group fully snockered. The ringleader, a hulking cousin everyone called Danny Joe, was speaking loudly enough to be heard above the throng.

"I'm just saying it's not what Bethany would have wanted, that's all."

Novie gave his hand one last squeeze and untangled her fingers. His hand felt suddenly cold, but he understood. She stepped over to a long table against the wall, beneath which Zeb sat cross-legged, watching the drama unfold. She squatted down and said something to him. He shook his head. Whit almost smiled again, so familiar had the scene become in the months they'd lived as a family. Novie would get her way, he knew—would pry the boy away from the action and into safer territory back in the chapel. But he wouldn't go without a fight.

Danny Joe cleared his throat. Whit turned again to the crowd, which was looked straight at him in awkward silence.

"Is there a problem?" Whit asked.

Danny Joe looked around, gauging the onlookers for support. "We don't want to cause no trouble," he said. "But that preacher you got for Beth's funeral. Well, we just don't know about her."

"And why is that?"

"Well, we're just not sure she's qualified."

Whit glanced through the open door into the viewing room. He could see Reverend March—Emma—standing back a few paces and staring ahead toward where the casket lay. She rocked slightly, heel to toe, jaw muscles working as she swayed.

"And why's that?"

Now it was Danny Joe's turn to look into the visitation room. Judging by his hesitation, he'd come to the same conclusion that Whit had—namely, that Emma could hear every blessed word they were saying. But he hadn't settled on a clear strategy of either belligerence or calm, and the hesitation cost him some momentum. He turned to Whit and lowered his voice.

"I don't believe your mother approved of women being preachers, is all. Now I know the reverend can't help it, but the Bible says what it says."

"And where does it say that?" Whit asked.

"Where does it say what?"

"That women can't be preachers."

"Right there in the gospels, I think." He looked around for support and got a few head nods, but he looked disappointed, as though he'd expected someone else to come to his defense. At last he turned back to Whit. "I believe that's right anyhow."

Whit pretended to consider this, but he could see that Danny Joe didn't possess the biblical chops for such an argument. The idea had probably been planted by Cole Allen Whitman, who had stayed on the couch in the viewing room with Bonner and Maddelynne, all three with heads bowed in prayer. Left to fend for himself, Danny

Joe was no match for Whit, who despite his apostasy in later years could still pull chapter and verse from his memory as easily as if were a 3/8 socket to tighten an oil drain plug. But he could also tell that Danny Joe was not a man to be reasoned with, especially with an indeterminable volume of whiskey now swirling through his veins. As he'd done so often in his classroom, Whit asked himself what his father would do. And so he drew up his shoulders and crossed his long arms.

"Mom didn't care shit about church. But this is the pastor her daughter wants, and this is who we have. I'd appreciate your cooperation."

The Kentuckians exchanged looks with one another until, finally, a stooped old woman—Danny Joe's mother, judging by their shared features—spoke up. "Just because we let you do it don't make it right."

"Thank you," Whit answered. "See you tomorrow."

Reluctantly, his hillbilly relatives filed out the door and into the parking lot. Whit didn't know if there were enough sober among them to drive the rest back to their hotels, but those were not his monkeys and that not his circus.

As they cleared out, he noticed his father, rising up from the couch. He whispered something to Bonner and Maddelynne, nodded an acknowledgement toward Rev. March, and walked alone into the hallway. He sat down on the table where a moment ago Zeb had been hiding. He folded his big arms across his chest, set his face in the same incomprehensible expression with which he'd always looked at his son.

"I guess I should say thanks for coming," Whit said.

Cole Allen shook his head. "I've never been much for niceties."

"Well. Okay."

They waited in silence.

"That was some display, a minute ago," Cole Allen finally said. "Talking down like that to Danny Joe and your family."

"I was just trying to do the right thing for Libby."

"Libby. Right. You always did think she's all that matters."

"You don't think she matters at all."

Cole Allen smiled at this. Shook his head. "I tried my best to teach you. Sometimes I wonder if you learned anything at all."

"Sometimes so do I."

They stared at each other for a long moment, stubborn and uncomprehending, neither one with the courage—Whit could see this now, plain as day—to enter the other's world. Maybe that's how it went with fathers and sons.

"Lord bless you," Cole Allen said.

He lifted two fingers toward Whit and turned and was gone.

CHAPTER 40

The baby blue hearse—a signature of Garland Funeral Home—failed to complete its delivery of Bethany Whitman Farris to the graveside. Rather, it sat marooned at the entrance to the cemetery, high-centered on one of the concrete retaining walls that bracketed the tiny bridge over the ditch. The driver had misjudged the angle necessary to get such a long car off the highway and onto the narrow lane of asphalt that led to the grave, but rather than back up and try again, he'd gunned the engine to try to force his way through. Now the hearse balanced almost entirely on its frame, only one tire left in contact with the ground, its rear compartment swinging in the air over the culvert.

The driver clicked on his hazards and eased his way out of the vehicle. He squatted down, as though the disaster might look different from another level, and shook his head. He was a baby-faced man, maybe twenty—a part-time employee from Arkansas State, perhaps. Whit could hear the hung-over Kentuckians making cracks about college boys.

A second later, the pastor emerged from the white SUV that had been leading the processional. She jogged past the hearse to the next car and pointed to the second cemetery entrance a little further down. She motioned to the other cars to follow. Once the mourners were again en route, this time around the back of the cemetery, she gathered Whit, Libby, and Novie into a huddle. Not to be left out, Zeb sprinted over and squeezed his way in.

"So can we pull the hearse out?" Emma asked. She glanced back at the salt-of-the-earth gathering. "Surely someone in this crowd has a tow chain."

Libby shook her head. Answered in a patient tone Whit was not expecting. "It's sitting at too much of an angle. You'd take off the whole undercarriage. It's not moving until the tow truck gets here."

They all turned to look at the hearse, see-sawing precariously in the light breeze. A quick run through the physics of the situation left only one option, really. Whit looked over the faces in his immediate circle, then back toward the people in front of the tent. He could see they'd all come to more or less the same conclusion. Danny Joe was already forming a posse of the sturdiest people—four men and two women, ready to do what had to be done. After a brief conversation with Whit and Libby, they whistled for one last helper. A fat man in overalls—four hundred pounds if he was an ounce—waddled to join the group, which was already moving toward the hearse.

"Say what you want about them," Novie whispered. "They get shit done."

No sooner had he seen them coming than the driver began shaking his head. "Just wait," he said. "Beatty is sending a tow truck."

"We ain't towing Beth to her own funeral," Danny Joe said.

He began deploying people around the tailgate, preparing to rescue the departed. Whit walked over to the kid and spoke softly to him.

"Don't worry," he said. "We're not going to blame you if anything goes wrong."

"It's already gone wrong," the kid answered. "Jesus."

"It's okay. Besides, we're going to need your help."

The kid wavered, but Whit could see he'd prevailed. In times of grief, most people just wanted something to do. The kid followed Whit to the front of the car. Together they pushed the front bumper downward while those in the rear lifted up. As soon as the front was low enough, the fat man sat down on the edge of the hood, pinning the hearse beneath his bulk.

"Now you sit here too," Whit told the kid. "This should only take a minute."

He walked around back and took his place next to Danny Joe. As the tallest, the two of them were positioned in the lowest part of the ditch. The others had lined up according to height, so that Libby and Zeb were nearest the tailgate. They undid the safety latches on the underside of the casket and slid it backward, passing it along until it had cleared the rear bumper. In minutes, it was sitting in the grass alongside the road. While the rescuers climbed out of the ditch, Whit moved again to the front of the hearse.

"Ready?" the fat man said. He scooted forward.

"Go easy," Whit answered.

He placed his hands on the hood, then had the hearse driver slide down to help him. At last, the fat man lowered himself back to the ground. The hearse teetered for only a second before stabilizing again, this time with the front two wheels touching the pavement.

"Leverage," Whit said to the kid. "It's one of those key life lessons."

When he returned to his mother's latest stop on her way to her final resting place, a makeshift band of pall bearers were lining up on either side. At the back end of the casket, Danny Joe saw him coming and stepped out of the way so that Whit could take his place. Whit thanked him, but fear instantly gripped him across the chest. He'd been dropping things again this week—oil filters, ink pens, his flip phone, which was thankfully as near to indestructible as any piece of modern technology. But this thing had to be done, he told himself. And so he wrapped his long fingers around the handle and pinned them with his thumb.

When he looked up to give the *ready* signal, however, it was clear something more had gone wrong. The pallbearers had fixed their eyes on a scene beneath a young oak, where Cole Allen and Libby were locked in a tense exchange. They spoke for several seconds in low tones he couldn't quite make out, until finally Libby squared up to him and folded her arms over her chest.

"Then I'll do it myself. Coward."

Their father reached for her elbow, but she shook him off and marched toward the casket—or, more specifically, right toward where Bonner Hanson stood, ready to help carry it up the hill. Whit unwound his fingers. He didn't think he could bluff a man like Bonner, and he hadn't thrown a punch since he was a fifth grader at G.A. Custer, but he readied himself now. Took one step away from the casket.

"*Don't!*"

The command was delivered in a whisper, but it reached his ears like an explosion. Ten feet to his right, Novie was glaring at him with the intensity of a thousand suns, searing a single unmistakable message into his brain.

Don't you dare take this from her.

Libby walked to within arm's reach of Bonner. Planted her feet shoulder width apart and stood up straight. "You're in my spot."

"She's a lot to carry," Bonner said. "I'll just get her up the hill for you."

"You think I can't?"

"I'm just trying to help," he said. "Your mama had a hard life."

"And I'll be walking her home."

He held up his hands. Libby pushed her way in behind him and grabbed the long handle. Bonner turned to face her. His expression feigned amusement, but his eyes blazed with indignation. He smiled as though humoring a child. "You're the boss."

Libby's voice quivered, but she delivered her message with the conviction of God's own judgment. "Get out of my way."

He stood there a moment longer, baiting her to try to push him back. Likely she would have, had Danny Joe not chimed in.

"That's her mama," he called.

And even though he said no more, it was enough to tell Bonner that he'd misjudged his crowd. The Kentucky relatives seemed to bow up as one, as ready to defend their kin as any Scotsman of old.

From the looks on their faces, both Cole Allen and Bonner could see that they were as good as hanged.

"If this is how you want it," Cole Allen said. He puffed out his chest. "We came in respect. I never gave up on you or your mother."

"Don't matter," Libby said. "You gave up on me."

Cole Allen glared at her, but she didn't wither. This time he looked to Whit for support and, finding none to be had in his son, scowled in contempt. He spat on the ground and walked away in tandem with Bonner. The little fiancé was the only one of them who looked back, casting what she must have thought was a menacing glance. A few of the Kentucky relatives actually laughed at her before turning their attention, like everyone else, onto Libby. She ignored them. Waved instead at Novie to collect Zeb, who had occupied himself throwing acorns at headstones.

"On my count," Libby said. "Ready?"

The pallbearers shifted to make room for Zeb and then took hold of the rails. When Libby said the word, they raised Bethany up and began to walk.

Whit wasn't sure how much time it had taken to rescue his mother's casket from the high-centered hearse, but it had been long enough to cause the sparse crowd of remaining mourners to take their comfort into their own hands. Dr. Price and the two BTI representatives had apparently returned to campus. Mrs. Woods, who had taken the morning off from school to come support Zeb, sat alone on a headstone, soaking up what warmth the stingy winter sun offered. The rest of the mourners—obligatory and otherwise—had pulled the folding chairs from beneath the blue tent and set them in circles. Were it not for the casket rail locked in their fingers, Whit and his fellow pall bearers might have been walking up the hill to join a picnic.

The pastor lifted her arms as they approached, and the ragged congregation stood. They waited reverently as Emma led the processional into the tent and the pallbearers settled the casket onto the nylon straps. Emma took her place by the head and pulled a thin leather book from inside her jacket pocket and motioned for the pallbearers to join the congregation.

Whit pulled off his glasses and rubbed his eyes, which were slow to adjust from the bright sunshine to the dark of the tent. When they did, he found himself adrift once again. The front row of cushioned chairs, usually reserved for the closest family members, had been the first to be appropriated by those wanting to sit down while the mess with the hearse got sorted out. Only one remained near the casket, a ridiculous little mercy seat with no one to sit in it, no one to pray over it.

No one, that is to say, except the dark figure behind it, clad in a tight black suit. Isaias gripped the back of the seat with one hand and, flourishing the other, motioned for Whit to sit down.

Whit shook his head. "I'm fine," he said. "You take it."

"Not on this day, Brother Big Man."

Before Whit could protest any further, the fat man waddled back into the tent with two chairs folded under each arm. The Kentucky relatives helped set them up, and before long Whit, Novie, Libby, and Zeb were all seated in a kind of semi-circle before the casket. Libby patted the empty seat next to her and spoke to Isaias.

"We saved you one."

"No, really—."

"Isaias," she said, and smiled. "Sit your skinny ass down so we can bury our mama."

Emma leaned in so that Libby and the others could see her. "We good?" she asked.

"I think we are," Whit said.

And so Emma turned and began her liturgy, her voice booming out of that small body with the assurance of the Almighty's chosen. She read the scripture and the prayers—read them word for word, for all he knew. He wondered how much of it his mother had believed, but in the end decided it didn't matter. Emma believed it enough for all of them, judging by the way she delivered God's pronouncements of love and peace, here at the end of a life. Danny Joe and some of the Kentucky relatives grunted their assent. Libby fixed her eyes on a spot of grass in front of her, but even she nodded along with the blessings. At one point, Isaias even uttered a "Yes, Lord!" that seemed to unnerve some in the congregation.

Whit, for his part, lost track of the words partway through the Psalm. *Walking her home*—Libby had used that phrase. He and his sister were lost souls, according to the definition used by every preacher of his childhood. And yet it seemed right, to be burying one of the great mysteries of their lives alongside one another, wrapped in love. Warmth rose in Whit, beginning at his feet and continuing up to his scalp—the feeling of assurance. Of solid ground.

A tug on his shirt pulled him back into the moment at hand. He looked down to see Zeb motioning for him to lean over so he could say something.

"This lady who's reading," he said. "She thinks Mom is in heaven."

"I think she does, yes."

"Do you think so?"

The question was one Whit had been avoiding, even when his own thoughts had strayed toward it. Nothing he or his father or anyone else could do would change God if God was real, and no amount of preaching or praying or speaking in tongues could conjure up such a deity if God was not. He hated the lack of clarity, the inability of any living being to answer the most vital question of all. Every human on the planet would give up their bodies eventually, and the earth would take them. In the meantime their souls—or whatever part of them felt like souls—grasped at any hint that this human endeavor was, in fact, going somewhere. Maybe it was. Maybe God was there already, waiting for everyone to catch up.

When he looked around at the scene, though, an even stranger thought overtook Whit. His mother had lived most of her life in the grip of one pain or another. He and Libby might just as easily have been collateral damage, torn apart by their parents' injuries and failures—probably would have been, if they'd been left alone. But maybe there was a collateral grace as well, one that glued together people who might have splintered otherwise. He and Novie and Isaias and Libby and Zeb—what would they do without one another?

That wasn't Zeb's question, though. The question was heaven, and maybe that answer lay in what they did *with* one another. Maybe heaven was more than what came next. Maybe heaven was now, whenever love outweighed life's devastation.

"Yes," Whit answered. "I think she's in heaven. I hope we all will be."

Zeb turned back to the casket. Whit let his own words ring in his head, turned them over and examined them. Decided that they were true enough for now.

END

AFTERWORD

Whit's near orbit includes...

Cole Allen Whitman—Whit's father; proudly uneducated religious fundamentalist

Bethany Whitman (Farris)—Whit's mother; Kentucky girl who can't quite numb the pain of her abusive upbringing

Libby Whitman—Whit's sister; almost five years his junior, but more aware of how the world works than her brother

Bonner Hansen—ex-con turned fundamentalist with an eye for very young women

Isaias Granderson—Whit's roommate and lifelong friend; talented, flamboyant, adventurous; the first Black man to befriend Whit, and the one who counters his prejudiced upbringing

• • • •

IN PERU:

Mila—his first love; pouty and manipulative, but wondrously sexy

Farther Guillermo—young priest who introduces Whit to Catholic understandings of God

Yesenia—12-year-old at Operación Amor who reminds Whit of his sister

Tía Luz—Mila's mother, who loves Whit like a son

Tía Pilar—fierce defender of the children at Operación Amor, where Whit works

Trey—jock who vies with Whit for Mila's attentions

Dr. Lawson—Covenant University professor and fundamentalist; mission trip leader

• • • •

IN MISSOURI:

Zebadiah Farris—Whit and Libby's baby brother, born to their mother and Byron Farris

Byron Farris—Bethany's no account second husband and Zeb's father

Dr. Zevon—Whit's provost at Northern Lakes; hired him without proper credentials

Novie Burqvist—Whit's true love; coworker at Bootheel Tech

Dr. Price—Bible thumping provost at Bootheel Tech

Franklin—Libby's alcoholic and abusive boyfriend; gets his man parts crushed by a whiskey bottle

And a host of other folks whose stories branch off from this one.

Also by Eric Van Meter

Earth: A Novel
Home from Away

Watch for more at https://www.ericvanmeterauthor.com.

About the Author

Eric Van Meter writes stories that reflect the quirky, rhythmic, hilarious ways that people try to cope with being human. In between doomed efforts to master various musical instruments, Eric directs a camp in Central Kentucky. His previous novel, *Earth*, is available through his website and on most author platforms.

Read more at https://www.ericvanmeterauthor.com.

Milton Keynes UK
Ingram Content Group UK Ltd.
UKHW040816051024
449151UK00004B/247